THE HORSES REJOICE

The Horses Know Book 2

LYNN MANN

Coxstone Press

Dedicated to the memory of my mum,
Ann Carolyn Palmer (3/10/40 - 9/10/16),
to whom I owe so much.

Now I know that she is me,
The truth is easy to find.
For we are both Infinity,
One love, one heart, one mind.

Amarilla Nixon

Prologue

4th May 2842, The Gathering

Dear Mum, Dad, Robbie, Con and Katonia,

I hope you are all well, I think of you so often. I'm sorry it's been ages since I was last able to write, I know it will be summer before this reaches you. I'll be picturing you all working long days and then sitting down to eat dinner together in the garden, chatting as the sun goes down.

So much has happened here and I have so much to tell you, I hardly know where to start – but here goes. Brace yourselves!

The Woeful need our help. A group of them attacked our horses a few months ago out of sheer desperation, because they and their families were starving at the end of the awful winter we all had. They were terrifying, with their fangs, talons and sheer size, but they were so human at the same time, and so hungry, so sad and frightened. I'm ashamed that the Woeful have been feared and shunned for so long, and I'm sorry that they had to be driven to such extreme measures before we could see that we should be reaching out to them and trying to help. Anyway, at least we've realised now that there is a wrong that needs righting.

You're not going to like this, but I have to tell you that two of my friends were killed when the Woeful attacked. Please believe me, their deaths were totally accidental, the Woeful never meant to hurt them. Both men had help from their horses to move on to a better place and they are absolutely fine where they are now. A horse was also killed and a few others, including Infinity, were injured. Infinity was very badly hurt, but I managed to heal her using both bone-singing and tissue-singing – I did, I promise you! It was such a horrible thing to happen but at least some good came of it, as I managed to unintentionally demonstrate that multiskilling is possible with no training, just by knowing I could do it.

Unfortunately, some of the Horse-Bonded were so frightened after the attack that they stopped listening to their horses. They were adamant that the Woeful should be hunted down and killed, and a group of us and our horses had to stop them leaving to go on their hunt. Once we managed to calm them down, they were able to hear their horses' wisdom again, and then there was no way they could think of hurting anyone, thank goodness.

Changing the subject, I have good news... I know I told you all that I was trying really hard to improve my riding so that I could help Infinity to balance better, well guess what, I did it! I'll try to explain. When I ride Infinity, I sit just behind her shoulders. To begin with, that meant that my weight was pushing her down onto her front legs. She couldn't move very easily and her chest was being compressed, so she was shutting down (she couldn't think straight or communicate very clearly and her emotions were dampened down). I had to work on helping her to lift up her front end and sit her weight back onto her hind legs, so that her chest could open and she could express herself fully. When I finally managed it, her chest area opened right up and released emotions and memories that her soul had been holding on to for many lifetimes. It was heart-wrenching for her to relive all of the memories but she released every single negative feeling and emotion that had been trapped within her body, until she was clear of it all. She was so happy about it!

In helping Infinity to improve her balance, my own improved to a point where something amazing happened... I found myself in perfect balance with Infinity – our bodies were aligned so perfectly within themselves and with one another that they were in complete harmony. There were no barriers between us at all, or between us and anything else! I felt totally at one with everything and I still do – it's amazing, to feel my connection to everything, to be Aware (with a capital 'A'!) of everyone, of what they are thinking and feeling.

It's helped me to not miss you all quite so much, as I can be Aware of you any time I want to – I know when you're tired, when you're happy and when you're sad. Don't worry though, I don't pry any deeper than that. I've been trying so hard to nudge at your minds in case you can feel me there, but I don't think you have so far. I normally try before I go to sleep, so please, please, if you sense anything around sleep time, anything at all that reminds you of me, notice it and try to open to it, and maybe I'll find a way to communicate with you in the same way Infinity and the other horses do with me – oh and how Justin does too, I need to tell you about him.

You already know that he's a really good friend of mine here, well he and his horse have achieved perfect balance in the same way that Infinity and I did, with the same result. So now that he and I both feel at one with everything, we're Aware of each other's thoughts and feelings. It's not easy at times, as I'll be talking to someone and he'll come crashing into my mind to tell me something (he's not subtle like Infinity is) and throw me off completely from whatever I was saying or doing. We're both working on getting more used to what we can now sense from everyone and everything around us, so hopefully it will get easier soon.

You should have had a visit by now from one of the Horse-Bonded who are spreading the word that anyone can do any of the Skills they want to, just as I did when I healed Infinity. I know you'll all find it hard to believe, as we've thought for so long that we have to show aptitude for a Skill during testing to be able to learn it, but please believe Salom when she gives you this letter (she is a Herald after all!) and whoever of the Horse-Bonded comes to Rockwood to tell you about it, because it's true. There are Tree-Singers here who are now singing the weather to help the growth of their trees, there are Glass-Singers who are singing metal so that they can make lids for their bottles and jars, Mason (my friend, who is the Saddler here) is singing metal into bits for the horses' mouths and making all of his own stirrups and buckles, and nearly all of the Healers here are doing all three Healing Skills, whether they showed aptitude for them all during testing or not. All of us have been able to do these extra Skills as soon as we knew we could do them.

Another thing to tell you is that my friends and I now teach the other Horse-Bonded to help their horses to balance better, in the hope that they'll achieve perfect balance. As soon as one of them does, they'll be able to take my place teaching and I'll be able to come home to see you all. I can't wait, there's so much more to tell you than I can fit into a letter.

Anyway, I'd better go, Infinity is waiting for me to go for a ride with her, Rowena and Oak and then we have three lots of students each to teach, and that's all before lunch! Remember to try to sense me when I reach for you before you go to sleep.

I love you all,

Amarilla xxxxxxxx

PS. Enclosed is a letter for Katonia's eyes only – it's sister stuff!

4th May 2842, The Gathering

Dear Kat,

I know that Mum will have either fainted or had one of her rants after reading my letter to you all and I'm sorry for you and Dad, as I know it will be down to you both to cope with her. I knew that she'd hear about the Woeful attack from Salom anyway and I wanted you all to know that Infinity and I are absolutely fine, so please Sis, reassure Mum and Dad that everything is okay.

There are a few things that I don't want them to know, and since Salom doesn't know the exact details, they won't find out, but I want to tell you.

Adam, my friend and Master of Herbalism here, sadly died. Sadly for me, anyway – he's ecstatic! He reached the same stage as Justin and me and once he knew of his oneness with everything, he stayed just long enough to help us turn back the group who were leaving for the Woeful hunt, before taking himself off to where his original Bond-Partner, Peace, was buried and then leaving his body to join him. I felt him go and I have been Aware of both him and Peace since then. They are so happy! I didn't mention it in my main letter, because I didn't want Mum and Dad worrying that having reached the same stage as Adam, I would leave my body too. I did have an experience where I could have made that choice though - when I achieved perfect balance, I did what Infinity did and released a load of emotion that was tied to an experience I had in a previous life. I kind of fainted as it was all a bit too much for me, and then I left my body. Infinity was with me and we had the choice of returning to our bodies and continuing our lives here, or leaving and moving on. I was deciding what to do when Justin and Gas arrived with us! Apparently, Justin had been so worried when I collapsed and he couldn't bring me round, that he and Gas worked flat out until they achieved perfect balance. As soon as Justin felt his oneness with everything, he was Aware of what had happened to me and where I was, and he left his body voluntarily to join me.

Anyway, obviously, we all chose to come back and much as I love you all, it wasn't because of what I would have been leaving behind. I know I can tell you this and you'll try to understand when no one else in the family will – I came back because I need to help the Woeful. I need to find them, befriend them and then try to integrate them into human society. It's exciting being here, seeing how hard everyone is working with their horses and how much their balance is improving, but it's frustrating having to stay when I'm desperate to be off on my mission to find the Woeful. I don't need to ask you not to tell anyone any of this as you know how they'll react. I'm sorry to give you a secret to keep, but as always Kat, there are no secrets between you and me.

I miss you so much and will come to see you as soon as I possibly can. In the meantime, please write back with all of your news. Remember to see if you can sense me at sleep time – if anyone can, it will be you.

Lots and lots of love,

Am xxxxxxxxx

14th June 2842, Nixonhouse, Rockwood

Our Darling Amarilla,

I am writing this letter while your mother has a lie-down. She was coming back from the village hall with your Aunt Jasmine when Salom arrived in the village, so she heard about all that has happened at The Gathering before she could read your letter. You can imagine her response to hearing everything that befell you all – she was hysterical and it took Jasmine and two others to get her back here. Salom came here as soon as she could with your letters and stayed for a while to reassure us that you're okay.

I can hardly believe everything that has happened, yet from the sound of things you're doing fantastically well, despite it all. It's hard, knowing that your beloved Infinity was so badly injured and that you endured all that you did, while we were safe here and none the wiser. As your father, I feel I've let you and Infinity down by not being there to protect you and this is something with which I will need to come to terms, but I am also tremendously proud. To think that my little girl is not only Horse-Bonded, but has now worked out how to perform Skills for which she has no training (Salom confirms your assurance that we are all capable of this, but I am finding it very hard to believe) and is also helping her fellow Horse-Bonded with their riding.

I am not going to pretend that I agree with you about helping the Woeful, or that I understand exactly what it is that you have achieved when you speak of having achieved perfect balance. There is so much I would like to know about your experiences, your life now and of course your fabulous Infinity, please come and visit us as soon as you possibly can. It's been all I can do to restrain your mother from packing her bags and coming to visit you there, even though she doesn't know where "there" is! She's all but threatened Salom with physical harm in the past for refusing to take her along on one of her trips to The Gathering, even though we all know that the Horse-Bonded must be allowed their space if they are to learn what their horses have to teach.

And we missed you on your birthday, love. From the sound of it, you would have been too busy trying to keep Infinity alive at the time to even remember it was your birthday, but we celebrated it here and hoped that somehow, you would know we were thinking of you. Sweet seventeen and changing the world, it doesn't seem possible!

You seem very upbeat in your letter and Salom assures us that this is indeed the case, but I would still like to offer my condolences for the loss of your friends and the horses who died, as their deaths must have hit you all very hard.

Salom tells us that she will only be here for a day or two (she has a long trip planned, spreading news of multiskilling and all that you and Infinity have achieved), but I'm sure that Katonia at least will get a letter written to you in that time. Your mother will probably take a while to calm down but don't worry, we'll get her through it as we always do.

All that remains is for me to say, once again, how proud I am of you Amarilla, and that I will be sure to try to stay open to the thought of you nudging my mind before I sleep. It would please me no end to be able to hear you there.

Stay safe and give Infinity a pat from me.

With all my love,

Dad xx

~

15th June 2842, Nixonhouse, Rockwood

Dear Am,

I'm so shocked, I hardly know what to write to you! I'm starting to worry I might be taking after Mum, as it's taken me a whole day to calm down after reading your letters.

On one hand, I'm thrilled for you, as you sound so happy and excited. On the other hand, selfishly, I feel sad and lonely as I feel as if my little sister is pulling away from me. You've experienced things that I can barely understand: previous lifetimes, leaving your body and then returning to it (??!!), being what you call "Aware" – it's being aware of things on a whole new level to how the rest of us are, I think? I'm trying to understand, I really am, but this is all so mind-blowing, so removed from how I thought things were.

One thing I do know about, however, is boys and in that respect, I can still pull rank on you so Am, you need to tell me everything and I mean EVERYTHING about Justin. None of this "very good friend" nonsense that you feed Mum and Dad, a guy doesn't leave his body (LEAVE HIS BODY for goodness' sake – how is that even possible?!!!) to go after just anyone. And isn't he a lot older than you? I'll be expecting your next letter to include ALL DETAILS about him – as you said, no secrets.

The news here is that Greg and I have split up and Mum is devastated. Greg's a lovely guy, but he and I want different things. I always thought that a family of my own was what I wanted, but now I'm not sure it is – I keep feeling this restlessness somewhere deep within myself, as if there's somewhere else I need to be or something else I need to be doing.

Dad is still very much in demand for his rock-singing and so am I by association (although how much longer that will be the case if more people begin to multiskill, I don't know). We often work together, as he says my strength is a match for his. Between us, we can get whole buildings up in no time. It's usually the Glass-Singers who slow us down, as they refuse to believe we can work at the speed we do until they see us do it and by then, they can't get the windows made on time!

Robbie and Con get a surprising amount of earth-singing done considering how much time they spend chatting up girls. Mum is beginning to despair of either of them ever settling down, which puts even more pressure on me as I'm fast becoming her only hope for grandchildren (unless you fancy becoming the first Horse-Bonded to have a baby? You've turned everything else on its head, so why not that?!).

Mum is okay and the same as ever; proud of Robbie and Con for being such talented Earth-Singers one minute, despairing of them and their "wild ways" the next; proud of me for my strength as a Rock-Singer one day, wringing her hands the day after because I haven't found the right man to settle down with yet; proud of you for being Horse-Bonded and a major subject of news whenever Salom comes to the village, terrified at the same time that she's never going to see you again. We ride the storms with her as best we can.

Nerys always asks after you when I see her, she's waiting for the news that you're the youngest ever qualified Herbalist! Talking of which, what will you do now that Adam has passed away? Is there someone else there who can take on your apprenticeship until you qualify? Or don't you need to qualify now that you can multiskill? There's so much to get my head around, I can't think straight.

I will do my best to sense you at sleep time, I hope I can, as we have so much to talk about.

Love you as always,

Kat xxxxxxxx

~

2nd December 2842, The Gathering

Dear All,

Thanks for your letters, I hope you're all well, and ready for whatever winter decides to throw at us this year. I'm so sorry not to have written back before, but Salom went on such a long trip after her last visit to Rockwood that she's only just made it back here and I've been avoiding all the other Heralds because they're driving me nuts! We've been besieged by them all wanting to hear first hand all of the details of the Woeful attack, how multiskilling was discovered, and details of rumours they have heard about Justin and me being Aware. Anyone would think we have nothing better to do than be grilled by them for hours on end.

Anyway, the big news is that my lovely friend Quinta has achieved perfect balance! We're all so excited as she's been close for ages, she just had to let go of a tiny little bit of grief for her previous horse, Noble, that was stopping her from feeling exactly what Spider's body needed from hers. She's finding adjusting to being Aware every bit as difficult as Justin and I have done, but she's so happy.

Soooooooo, the good news is that as soon as winter has passed, I can come home for a visit! I'm so excited, I've checked in with each of you every single night and tried to get you to feel me there, so far with no success, but at least I know that after only a few more months, I'll be seeing you in person. I'll be with friends as we'll be going on one of the trips around the villages that all Horse-Bonded have to make, so I won't be able to stay too long, but I promise it will be long enough to catch up on everything.

I can't wait until then to say to you, Dad, that it's bonkers for you to think that you let me and Infinity down when the Woeful attacked. I've been here at The Gathering because it's where I've needed to be and you accepted that, despite the fact that I left you all in the way I did – so, far from letting me down, you've been amazing.

I am enclosing another letter for Katonia (more sister stuff!)

I love you all and I can't wait to see you.

Amarilla xxxxx

2nd December 2842, The Gathering

Dear Kat,

I'm sorry to hear about you and Greg. I was surprised at first, as from your letters he sounded perfect for you, but I think you're right to listen to your restlessness. I know what it's like to feel like that – it's how I felt from the time I first dreamt of Infinity to when she finally tugged me.

I haven't lied in my other letter about why my friends and I will be visiting Rockwood, but I haven't told the whole truth either – now that Quinta can take my place teaching, Infinity and I are free to go and find the Woeful. We'll give the impression of just being on a trip visiting villages to offer the horses' advice and to help people to open up to multiskilling, but I wanted you to know what we'll really be up to.

Rowena and Oak will be coming (she warned me against even trying to leave without them), as are Marvel and Broad (Marvel would follow Rowena to the moon and back) and then there will be Jack with Candour and Vickery with Verve (Jack and Vickery were members of the group we stopped from going off to hunt the Woeful, funnily enough. Neither is comfortable staying at The Gathering for long anymore, so they both asked if they could come) and I think two from my teaching groups will be coming – Sonja with Bright and Aleks with Nexus. Sonja's a joy to teach, but Aleks is difficult. I could do without him coming, to be honest, but I can feel how hard Nexus is working to try to keep him moving in the right direction, so I need to give them the help they ask for.

You'll be disappointed to know that Justin won't be coming. It would be too much for Quinta to be the only one with perfect balance left teaching at The Gathering, especially when she's only just found it, so Justin is needed there. He's not happy about it but he knows that I've waited as long as I can and I need to be on my way. As for telling you everything about him, well you already know what he looks like as I've told you about all of my friends and their horses. You know he's bonded to Gas and you know that he and I are very good friends – and that's all there is to tell. We both know how we feel about one another (and about everything else, come to that, seeing as we're both Aware!) but Justin has this ridiculous, outdated idea of chivalry that he won't be talked out of. He's ten years older than I am, and apparently there are lines that aren't going to be crossed until I'm older. Exasperating doesn't even cover it! Rowena thinks it's hilarious.

You asked what being Aware is like... well when someone sits down beside you for dinner Kat, you're just aware that they are there. I'm Aware of the day they've had, how they're feeling, their plans for the evening and all of the other thoughts that are uppermost in their mind. I can know a whole lot more if I delve deeper, but I'd never do that unless I was asked – in fact I try to block out as much as I can from people so I don't discover things they wouldn't want me to know. When a fly lands on me, I'm Aware of everything it's landed on recently, what it's looking for, what it senses. Oh, and I can be Aware of anyone who has passed on from this world if I think of them. So yes, you're absolutely right when you say that being Aware is being aware on a whole new level!

When you see Nerys, please tell her that Adam pronounced me a qualified Herbalist before he died – I should have said, but that news seemed insignificant in the light of everything else.

I can't wait to see you Sis, we have so much to talk about. I nudge your mind every night in case you can sense me, but I hold myself back from your thoughts and feelings, as they're private. You'll have loads to tell me, particularly about whether you know what your restlessness is about yet.

With all my love as always,

Am xxxxxxxxxxx

28th February 2843, Nixonhouse, Rockwood

HAPPY 18TH BIRTHDAY AMARILLA, FROM US ALL!!!!

We're so excited that you're coming to visit in spring! We don't know exactly when you'll be coming, so we thought we'd write you an 18th birthday wish on your birthday. We'll either give it to Salom to take to you if she passes through soon, or hopefully, we'll be able to give it to you in person when you visit.

We love you and we can't wait to see you and Infinity very soon!

Dad, Mum, Kat, Robbie and Con xxxxx

ONE

Mission
___

S he's muttering to herself again,' I heard Aleks say. 'How do we know that she's really Aware, and not just mental?'

'Well, what do you think, Aleks? I mean, really think? Deep down?' Jack said sharply.

There was a pause and I realised I was holding my breath.

Aleks sighed. 'I trust her,' he muttered. 'And even if I didn't, Nexus does. It's just hard, blindly following a young girl on a crackpot mission to befriend monsters who will likely kill us all as soon as look at us, especially when all that said girl seems to do is mutter to herself.'

'You volunteered to come with us, Aleks, and you and Nexus can leave any time you like – but I would remind you that Amarilla also spends a decent amount of time teaching you to ride Nexus better and you are both continuing to improve in balance whilst on this "crackpot mission" as a result. So either stay and offer support and strength to the group, or leave,' said Jack.

He Who Is Candour was a wise choice of travelling companion, noted Infinity.

I sighed and nodded. *I can't blame Aleks for doubting my sanity though, I question it myself sometimes.*

You have yet to master your new Awareness and you have removed yourself from the company of those with whom you share it, I was informed.

Justin and Quinta had to stay behind to teach our students, I protested.

There was no hurry for you to leave.

I thought of the impatience I had been feeling during the year since achieving perfect balance and the knowledge of my oneness with All That Is that came along with it. I could be Aware of any of the other parts of All That Is whenever I chose, be it human, cloud, snowflake, pollen grain, horse, Woeful... The Woeful. The source of my impatience.

I hung on as long as I could, Fin, you know that, I told her.

But longer would have been better, and you know that! Justin's thoughts crashed into my mind.

I smiled. *I know nothing of the sort,* I thought back to him, unable to stop my lips from muttering the words as I did so.

Well, I miss you. Quinta's a good instructor and becoming even better now, but it's not the same here without you and Fin.

As soon as the next person achieves perfect balance, they can take your place teaching alongside Quinta and you can come on after us.

Give us a chance, you've only been gone a week! And Gas isn't helping at all – every time I ask him to help me demonstrate something, he demonstrates what he happens to want to do that day, whether it's helpful to my students or not. He denies it but I know how much he loves it when everyone gasps at what he can do.

I laughed out loud and then stopped abruptly when I realised that all conversation between the riders behind me had quietened.

I miss you and Gas too, Jus, you know that, but you also know how much I need to do this.

I felt his acceptance that what I said was true.

Take care, Am. A wave of love accompanied his words and I returned a wave of my own. I felt his spirits lift as I turned my attention back to Infinity.

You told me that I would be the first human capable of fully expressing my soul through my personality, well this is me doing exactly that, I told her. *My soul speaks to me of the one thing that drew me back*

to my body when I could have left it – my concern for the Woeful. I'm
going to find them and help them.

I felt Infinity scrutinizing my mind with interest.

What? I asked her.

I expected to find interesting the consequences of a human who has
found the necessary Awareness to allow her soul to be expressed through
her personality. It is so. To begin with you had a tendency to deny your
humanity. You ignored or counselled yourself out of experiencing human
thoughts and feelings. Now that you have progressed to allowing yourself
to live as a human you are developing a tendency to attribute every
thought and feeling you have as originating from your soul.

Fin, are you trying to say that I am mistaken in thinking that my
mission to help the Woeful is in line with my soul's wishes?

Do you attempt to convince me that you do not already know?

'DAMMIT!' I shouted and then looked to my fellow travellers.

Aleks sighed loudly and raked a hand through his dark curly hair as
he always did when he was annoyed, as his grey mare, Nexus, came to a
halt beneath him. Blond-haired Jack glared across at Aleks from dapple-
grey Candour's back, his piercing blue eyes saying more than any words
could have. Rowena's eyebrows were raised in question above her dark
eyes. She tucked a stray wisp of her long, black hair behind her ear as she
turned to watch tall, handsome Marvel rein Broad, his tall, solid bay, in
alongside Oak, her black stallion. Behind them, red-haired, freckled
Sonja brought her dark bay, Bright, to a halt beside blond, stocky
Vickery's white stallion, Verve.

'Infinity and I need a little time on our own, very sorry, we'll be back
soon,' I told them all and tried to ignore their rolled eyes and looks of
confusion as Infinity spun and took off into the trees at a canter.

Infinity's black and white ears flicked back and forth, ever alert to her
surroundings as we weaved effortlessly between the trees. When we
reached a small, sunlit glade, Infinity slowed to a graceful halt and I
jumped from her back and began to pace back and forth while she
nibbled at the vibrantly green spring grass.

As Infinity had just reminded me, I hadn't exactly blossomed as a
result of achieving perfect balance. I had become so entranced and

distracted with everything of which I had realised I was Aware – the infinite peace and wisdom of the horses, the exact origins of the myriad of scents on a given breeze, the energy currents that drew animals to follow the behaviours of their species, the intermittent interest in the physical from those who had passed into the realms of the non-physical, the thoughts and feelings of those around me – that I had struggled to care about anything beyond that. I had absented myself from thinking or feeling anything human. Infinity had let me be that way for a while and my friends had only commented in passing that I seemed a little distant, with the exception of Justin, who I knew was experiencing as much wonder and confusion as I was.

As time went on, Infinity had nudged my mind when she felt me distancing myself from my humanity, and my friends had been a bit more pointed in their remarks, Rowena in particular. It was when she told me that she couldn't blame some of my students for asking to change to a different instructor due to my distracted, lackadaisical air, that I began to pull myself back into my life as a human being.

I threw myself into my teaching with a passion. My Awareness of those I taught meant that I knew what held them back from being able to give everything of themselves to their riding – whether it be a mental block, a physical lack of strength or coordination, or an emotional hindrance, such as fear of failure, physical harm or of embarrassing themselves in front of their friends – and I did all I could to try to help them to push past their blocks, so that they and their horses edged ever closer to achieving perfect balance. I knew that when someone reached that point, I could leave and do what my soul was calling for me to do – to help the Woeful. And now that I was doing it, Infinity was telling me that that wasn't what my soul wanted at all?

When we left our bodies, when we were just thought, you told me that if I returned to my body and used it to change the way the Woeful are perceived and treated, there would be enormous evolutionary potential for humans. I can feel that the one thing that ties my soul to continue inhabiting a human body relates to my concern for the Woeful. I am acting on what you told me and on how I feel, and yet somehow this is wrong? I challenged Infinity.

We are always just thought. You know this, she replied.

I don't even know my own name sometimes. When we left our bodies and floated in All That Is, I remember thinking that everything was so easy, so uncomplicated. I couldn't think why anything here should have bothered me the way it did, why anything should have mattered to me. I remember that experience and I remember how I felt, so why can't I just be like that now I'm back in my body? Why is everything so hard? When you said I'd be able to express my soul through my personality, I thought I'd be able to live my life as you do, always knowing everything I would need to know, but I'm still getting it all wrong.

I did not say it would be easy.

No, you didn't, you left that part out.

Would it have changed your decision had you realised?

What, that being Aware would mean being on permanent sensory overload while still trying to live life as a normal, socially acceptable human being? I sighed. *No, it wouldn't have changed my decision. I need help though, Fin. I don't understand what it is that you're saying I'm doing wrong.*

How old were you when you first sensed me?

Twelve. I sensed you once you were born.

And when you had a more definite idea of my existence?

I was fourteen. You told me that I was able to sense you more definitely when you began to consider your purpose here – when you began to consider me.

I knew you were the one. I knew that we would find each other. I knew that we would achieve our goal. How long passed until I reached for you?

You left it another two years.

Infinity stilled within my mind. I thought of my concerns about how the Woeful had been so badly treated in the past and how vulnerable their existence must be for them to have been desperate enough to brave a river crossing and attack a settlement, as they had when they attacked The Gathering. Their plight was something that needed to be addressed, of that much I was still certain. I thought back to when I had been out of my body and considering why helping the Woeful was important and I remembered how I had felt – a calm knowing that it was the right thing to do. I hadn't felt restless, worried or impatient. I understood.

The plight of the Woeful is something that needs addressing. That is my soul's desire. The impatience to get on with it, the worry I feel, that is coming from my personality. It isn't necessary and it isn't helpful, I told myself as much as I did Infinity. *If I'd allowed myself to know that the issue will be addressed and dealt with in good time, I could have saved myself and my friends a whole load of hassle. I could have waited until Justin could come with me, but I've gone storming off ahead and made things more difficult than they needed to be for all of us. Oh, Fin, I'm making a mess of it all aren't I?*

That will depend on how you proceed henceforth.

???????

You know that denying your personality and being Aware only of All That Is defeats the object of returning to your body. You also know now that expressing your personality so forcefully that you fail to notice your soul's message in its entirety is pointless. There is a balance between the two extremes. A state of being where the soul and personality complement rather than hinder one another. You must find it. When you lose it you must find it once more. You must find it over and over until that balance is and remains perfect. You speak of perfect balance. You have already found your perfect balance physically, mentally and emotionally. Your challenge now is to find your perfect spiritual balance. Your centre.

As you have.

As all horses have. To us it is a natural state of being and to humans it will be so eventually. You and your friends will prepare the way for other humans to find it so. The Sorrowful will help.

The Woeful? They can help with this? But the horses can help us. Why do we need help from the Woeful?

My kind can help some of you. The Sorrowful will be able to help all of you.

I sat down next to where my beautiful black and white mare grazed, the sunlight warming her even as her dazzling white fur reflected its beams so that dust particles sparkled as they danced around her. I pondered on what I had just learnt. Then I quietened my thoughts and found the stillness that allowed me to be Aware. Immediately, I was flooded with a feeling of happy and fulfilled busyness from the birds that plucked flies from the air to feed to their young. I was the blossom buds as they burst open and the insects as they rushed to gather nectar. I was the fox who lay in wait by a game trail for the rabbit he could scent approaching. I was the irritation and impatience of my travelling companions. I snapped back to myself. I felt anxious to get back to them before their irritation with me grew further.

I jumped to my feet and took a step towards Infinity... and then stopped. I was doing it again; jumping from being entirely focused on my Awareness, to being ruled by my personality and its fears. I stilled myself once more and allowed my Awareness to occupy a place in my mind... but only a place. I decided, calmly, that Infinity and I needed to return to where my fellow travellers waited, and continue on our journey to Rockwood. We would do that now.

The observed has become both the observed and the observer, noted Infinity. *Now you will learn more quickly.*

TWO

Encounter

*A*s we continued onward towards Rockwood, it was agreed that I would take over from Rowena – the only one of us to have made the journey between Rockwood and The Gathering before – in directing the way, in an effort to follow Infinity's advice and practise finding my centre. I followed my Awareness of my family whilst attempting to maintain full consciousness of my physical environment, and it wasn't easy. In reaching through All That Is to my family, I was also Aware of a myriad of other beings, from whom I had to try to zone out so as to be able to concentrate on those I needed to find, at the same time as being mindful of my surroundings, including holding conversations with my travelling companions and taking care of my physical needs. When we stopped to make camp each night, I was exhausted and still had my teaching to do for any of the bonded pairs that requested it, but at least as I worked with each partnership, I could focus solely on what I felt from them and them alone. There were times when I felt that my sanity depended on it, although Infinity informed me that I was being melodramatic.

'Not too far now, everyone,' I yelled over my shoulder one morning.

Marvel, who rode next to me, made a show of cowering away from my shout and I heard Rowena's chuckle from just behind him. 'Well, at least they'll be ready for us, you have no idea how far your voice carries, Am,' she said.

'My voice...?' I stammered. 'Mine? It's my voice that prevents birds from settling anywhere near us when we set up camp?!'

'Can I help it if Marvel will insist on building fires without taking the wind direction into account, or if Aleks starts moaning AGAIN about being hungry, or if I need you to come and help me with Oak and you're nowhere in sight? There are times when I need to raise my voice with very good reason, but at no time does it carry the way yours does, Am,' Rowena said.

'You're going to need to decide whether to say the words you're thinking of, or whether to just close your mouth, Am,' Marvel said with a grin. 'I'd opt for keeping quiet if I were you, it's by far the easiest option.'

'My mind's trying to do so many things at once at the moment that I can't actually think of the words I want to say and I'm not sure I...' My voice faded as I became Aware of a familiar pattern of energy. Just as I was about to turn my attention away from it and return to focusing on my destination and on the conversation in which I was engaged, I realised what kind of being it was. I felt the Woeful's attention settle on me and Infinity, and I registered her curiosity. And her hunger.

We revisit an old situation. Infinity's thought was very carefully calm. I could feel the panic that her equine personality tried to inflict on her, but that she was successfully holding at bay.

Infinity stopped beneath me and I turned to Marvel and Rowena. 'There's a Woeful nearby,' I told them with a slight shake in my voice. 'She's making her way towards us now.'

Marvel whistled though his teeth and Rowena took a long, deep breath. I felt them both overcome the fear that tried to build within them, and then they each emitted light. My light joined theirs and we projected it in all directions, cocooning the horses and the rest of our friends as they caught up with us, their faces questioning.

'Am can feel a Woeful approaching,' Rowena said, 'and that means that we'll all feel her too, as soon as she's close enough to stare at us. Everyone stay close together, keep calm and remember the procedure –

we all surround ourselves and the horses with light so that we stay calm and the Woeful can see we mean no harm, while Amarilla uses her Awareness of the Woeful to work out how to befriend her.'

At that moment, we all felt the Woeful's stare from up in the trees ahead of us. Marvel, Rowena and I strengthened our light flows as our friends' panic erupted all around us.

'She's hungry, which the horses all know,' I said, urgently. 'They'll find it hard not to bolt, unless we give them something calm and reassuring to hold on to.'

Rowena said, 'Remember what we've practised. Think of everyone you love in your life, your horse, your friends and family. Find the light within you. Find it and hold on to it. Now expand it. Sonja, you're doing fantastically. Aleks, it will be alright, just focus on what I'm saying. Focus on your love for your horse. That's it, now push all of your light, all of your love and positivity, outside of yourself. Jack and Vickery, you both look terrified. Don't fight your fear, just concentrate on the light within you, on every positive feeling you have. That's it, now radiate your light. Keep making it stronger. That's it, the horses are calming down.'

'She's curious as well as hungry,' I told my friends. 'I'm going to send light to her. I think I might be able to get her to understand that we want to be friends.'

Rowena nodded. 'I'll send my light to Aleks to help him maintain his own. Jack, Vic and Marvel, can you use your light to surround us all and keep the horses calm? Sonja, your light is strong, can you give Am any help she needs with the Woeful?'

Marvel, Jack and Vickery all nodded to Rowena as she sat astride Oak, staring at Aleks, within whom I could feel huge conflict. He and his horse were both terrified and wanted to flee but Aleks was trying hard to follow the drill we had practised over and over. Rowena's light battered at his fear and every now and then, when her love reached through to him, Aleks found his own light within himself and pushed it out to surround himself and his horse. Then a fresh wave of fear would extinguish his light and fuel Nexus's instinct to bolt and he had to battle to hold on to her. Rowena kept her light stream towards him bright and steady.

Sonja sat calmly astride Bright, her light radiating strongly about them both. She smiled at me and I felt her keen anticipation for the task ahead.

I returned her smile a little nervously and then asked Infinity, *Ready, Fin?*

Infinity didn't need to answer. Her calm, assured love already steadied the way to where the Woeful crouched on a branch, regarding us all.

My pride in Infinity increased the intensity of the light that streamed out of me into a flow that was so brilliantly white, it was almost blinding. I directed it towards the Woeful, allowing it to settle gently around her. In the instant that she was my sole focus, I knew her. I felt her hunger – it was several days since she had last eaten. She was young and daunted by the prospect of having to survive by herself. She was frustrated at her lack of hunting prowess and worried that she would fail in the task she had been set, but she would die rather than return home before she was due, and risk disappointing her family. She had an enormous capacity to love, to share and to connect with all around her. There was something about our horses that would normally have made them unacceptable to her as prey, yet her hunger had driven her to identify Nexus as the one most likely to separate herself from our group and make herself the easiest target.

She felt my love infuse her and was reminded of times when her mother had comforted her. She was used to being loved unconditionally by her family and by her community. She basked in my love for her and I felt her fears about her current situation begin to wane. Confusion tried to rise within her but my love dispersed it. I loved her and she had nothing to fear from me or my friends. We would help her. I was Aware of her registering my intention and I felt her surprise. Her disbelief. And then I felt something else. For a second, her attention went somewhere else. Somewhere far distant. Then she was back and she was more, somehow, as if someone were with her. Someone WAS with her! Not physically, yet

I could feel both her and an older female. Both Woeful were observing Infinity and me with a combination of interest and disbelief.

With a jolt, I recognised this older Woeful and she recognised me. She was neither of the Woeful I had encountered before, yet she was someone whose essence I knew very well. My shock caused my flow of light to waver. Instantly, Sonja's flow wove its way through mine so that the light reaching the Woeful remained constant. Infinity immediately reminded me of myself and as my light flow steadied and regained full strength, Sonja gently withdrew her own.

Am, are you alright? Justin crashed into my mind with his concern.

I'm fine, Justin, stay with me but be small in my mind.

Justin did as I asked and my focus returned to the Woeful who was now two. The young Woeful was worrying that by contacting one of her Elders, she had failed in the task she had been set, but she had taken the risk as she thought her community would want to know about something this extraordinary. I sensed the scrutiny of the older Woeful and I kept my light flowing strongly towards them both, along with my intentions. The Woeful had nothing to fear from us. We wanted to help them and we wanted to work towards them and humans being friends. I kept my thoughts to them very simple, very clear. We would be leaving food on the ground for the young Woeful and we would then continue our journey.

I felt the Woeful Elder's distaste at the word we used to describe their kind and was instantly sorry as I saw how it would cause them offence. She communicated briefly to the young Woeful that she must do as she saw fit, and then she was gone. Realisation seeped through me. The Elder had been sitting within the young Woeful's mind, just as Justin now sat within mine.

I felt the Woeful's indecision and hunger and focused on sending my light to her at full strength, reiterating my earlier message. *We mean you no harm. We have food and we will leave you some. In time, we would like to be friends.*

The Woeful decided that she would wait to see if we left food for her as promised. Immediately, I felt Nexus relax as she felt the Woeful's interest in her wane.

'The immediate danger is over,' I said to my friends. 'I'm going to dismount and leave some food for the Woe... I mean, our friend in the tree, and then, Ro, if you could lead the way onwards to Rockwood, Infinity and I will bring up the rear. Our friend has decided to trust us for now, so it's really important that we all keep doing exactly what we're doing and keep calm as we leave.'

I dismounted slowly, maintaining my light flow towards my friend in the tree. She registered the change in the way I thought of her and I felt her brief surprise and then... did a little warmth come in my direction from her? It disappeared as quickly as it had arrived, but I was sure that was what it had been.

Marvel held out two brace of rabbits that he'd brought back from his dawn hunt. I rubbed Broad's neck as I took the rabbits and then went back to Infinity, who continued to steady the atmosphere with her warm, nurturing energy even as she stood transfixed by my friend in the tree. I rummaged in my saddlebags and found one of my tightly wrapped loaves of traveller's bread, and then another. I took them both and the rabbits and laid them a short distance from our group, so that my new friend could easily see them. I felt her hunger become the whole of her.

'We need to leave right now,' I said quietly as I sprang up onto Infinity's back.

Rowena and Oak moved away slowly towards Rockwood, and Marvel indicated for Aleks – who was sweating profusely but managing to radiate a weak, pulsing beam of light around himself and Nexus – to go next, before he followed them. Vickery and Verve went after, followed by Jack and Candour. Sonja and Bright remained where they were, with Infinity and me.

'Thanks for helping me the way you did, Sonn, you and Bright go too though, we won't be far behind you,' I said to Sonja.

She shook her head. 'You're very strong, but if she does something to shake your concentration again, you'll need my light until yours is steady again.'

'Thanks, but I'll be fine. Justin's with me now, he can help if need be,' I said, hoping it was true and then instantly knowing that it was.

Sonja's eyebrows shot up in surprise and then she flushed as red as her hair. Her green eyes flashed with the jealousy I could feel from her and I thought for a second that she would argue, but then she nodded slowly. 'Okay, follow along soon then,' she said and Bright obliged her by moving slowly off to follow the others.

I turned my attention back to my new friend, who was slowly descending her tree. I could feel her hunger raging within her, yet she had made a conscious decision to move slowly and calmly, as she could feel my companions and me doing. My light flow to her continued, along with my firm intention of friendship. She reached the bottom of her tree and stood in the hunched posture of a Woe... of a... who?

Kindred. We are the Kindred. Her thoughts settled so gently into my mind that it felt natural for them to be there.

I am Amarilla of the Horse-Bonded, and this is Infinity, I thought back to her. *We know how hungry you are, so we'll leave you to your meal.*

As Infinity turned to follow our friends, I couldn't help but feel a thrill. I felt the young Kindred register my emotion and stop in her tracks. Why was I happy? Had I trapped her? Poisoned her?

Immediately Infinity and I sent her all the love we could muster in a powerful burst. *We are Infinity. We are happy to have met you. We are happy to have left you food. We are happy that you have trusted us with the name of your kind. We are happy. That is all.*

We felt her fears melt away as her fangs tore into the first loaf of bread.

We found our friends waiting for us just at the edge of the forest.

'She's eating,' I told them. 'Jack? Vic? Are you alright?'

'If only we'd kn... known,' sobbed Vickery.

'If we'd had any idea, any idea at all what they're really like, we'd never have... we'd never...' Jack shook his head as tears streamed down his face.

I felt their agonising remorse for the way they had behaved after the Woeful – after the Kindred, I corrected myself – attacked The Gathering the previous year. 'You'd never have organised a hunt to try to kill them,' I finished for Jack. 'We all know that. Guilt is pointless though, Infinity taught me that. You did what you did back then out of fear, and just now you overcame your fear to be part of something that hopefully will be a new beginning, so it's all good. What did you feel from her?' I asked them.

Jack and Vickery had felt the Kindred's uppermost thoughts – her hunger, her curiosity and her concerns – and so, it transpired, had everyone else. Interesting, I thought to myself; just as I had during my first two encounters with Kindred, before I was Aware, my friends had all picked up information from our new friend. It was as if the Kindred couldn't help but broadcast aspects of themselves, as if they had a way of connecting with humans that we ourselves lacked.

'They're just like us, aren't they?' said Rowena. 'They have worries and challenges in life just as we do, they have families they love.'

'They're like us and more than us at the same time,' I said. I told them all about the Kindred Elder who had joined our acquaintance briefly and then about what had happened when our friends had left Infinity and me alone with the young Kindred. 'She placed her thoughts so carefully, so gently, in my mind,' I said. 'The Kindred are used to communicating that way. And she knew of me as soon as I was Aware of her – that was what drew her to us. She easily felt my emotions and my intention towards her. The Kindred are Aware.'

'Aware? Like you, Justin and Quinta? Like the horses? And you say you recognised the Kindred Elder? Is she the one who hunted you and Infinity on your way to The Gathering? Or one who was there when they attacked it last year?' asked Sonja.

'She wasn't either of the Kindred I've come across so far. I'm not sure how I knew her, I didn't really have a chance to look into that at the time, all I know was that I recognised her and she recognised me,' I said, reliving the experience in my mind, reliving my connection to her... and then I knew exactly who she was. I felt Infinity's knowing and Justin's understanding a split second later.

Well, of everything that's just happened, that's the most unexpected! Justin informed me.

Unlike your tendency to state the obvious, I grinned, unable to stop myself from muttering the words out loud.

I felt his humour, followed by his frustration at not being with me in person while I digested my realisation. Infinity's nurturing energy permeated my being and I felt Justin relax. *I love it when Infinity does that for you,* he told me. *You'll be okay. Will you tell the others?*

Not all of it. Not yet, I need to process it myself, I muttered as I thought.

'Anything you want to share, Amarilla?' Aleks said haughtily.

Rowena and Jack both glared at him and then looked at me, expectantly.

'Um, well, there's something I've just realised,' I said. 'The Kindred Elder I sensed? She's the one we need to find.'

'Because you somehow already know her?' said Rowena.

'Partly. But mainly because she's the key.'

'The key to befriending the Woeful... sorry, the Kindred?' Rowena asked.

'Yes. She's the key to everything,' I said thoughtfully.

THREE

Homecoming

I was feeling nervous. The enormous rock at whose base Rockwood nestled, was in sight. I was so close to those I'd missed so much and to whom I'd caused so much heartache and worry, and I couldn't begin to think of how I was going make it up to them.

You are yet choosing to express your personality's desire for high emotion and melodrama, observed Infinity with interest.

And that's what? Good? Bad? I challenged her.

We both know that good and bad do not exist.

I paused to consider. *Agreed. So, if I must find a balance between awareness of my soul and expression of my personality, then presumably it's up to me to choose which aspects of my personality I express?*

It is.

Then your point?

You are also choosing to pretend that you do not already know the answers to your questions.

I sighed. Infinity wasn't going to let up. I recognised that my tendency towards melodrama was unhelpful at times, as was my habit of asking Infinity questions to which I now had the answers as readily as did she. I sensed her satisfaction with my admissions and I smiled. I realised, however, that having access to answers was only useful if I were pushed to ask the questions; Infinity's role as my teacher was different now, but still very necessary. I relaxed and managed a deep breath.

'Everything alright, Am?' Rowena said.

'Yes thanks, I'm excited but a bit nervous. It's been so long since I saw my family and it's not as if I left in the best of circumstances.'

'It's true that most people do let their family know if they're going to be leaving and possibly not coming back, rather than just disappearing without a word and leaving their belongings in a heap on the ground, but it's also true that you had an understandable reason for doing so. Your family know that – I made sure of it the last time I was here. I would be worrying far more about the fact that the Nixons' little girl is now a young woman who has changed so much since they last saw her that they'll struggle to recognise her, and if they do, they'll be so shocked that your mother won't be the only one to faint!'

'Thanks, Ro, with friends like you...'

'...you know you'll always be fine. Haven't Oak and I looked after you ever since your insane dash from Rockwood to find Infinity?' Rowena's dark eyes glinted mischievously.

I grinned. 'You have.'

'Do you want me to lead the way into the village, or do you think you can manage it?' Rowena said and we both laughed.

Cantering hooves sounded behind us. 'Wha've I missed?' said Marvel breathlessly, as he and Broad drew level with Rowena, Oak, Infinity and me.

'Rowena's just being the good friend that she is,' I said.

'Oh, I was wondering if you'd thought up a humorous explanation for why there are seven Horse-Bonded descending on Rockwood, when they'll be used to seeing one or two travelling together at a time, at the most?' Marvel said, his hazel eyes sparkling.

I stopped laughing abruptly. 'Curse the clouds, I never thought of that. I warned my sister we'd be coming and that we wouldn't be mentioning our true purpose, but it never occurred to me that the rest of the villagers will think it odd for so many of us to be travelling together.'

'It's a good job that I have it figured out then, isn't it?' said Rowena. 'We'll tell the truth, just not all of it. You are here as a living historical figure, to meet your adoring public. Sonja and Aleks are two of your top students who can't possibly have their tuition interrupted just because you need to be out and about meeting said public, so they have tagged along. Jack is adept at opening up those who want to multiskill, and is along with you to help those who are inspired to ask for his help by your very presence, and Vickery is with him to watch and learn. Marvel and I are here as your bodyguards because I for one can't have the worry of not knowing what scrapes you're getting into at any given moment, and Justin will never speak to Marvel again if you come to any harm, which by your track record is bound to happen at some point. Got all that?'

I was laughing again. 'Can't we just say that so much is changing and we're all busy learning from one another, so we've decided to travel as a group so we can learn as we go?'

'I think that sounds like the simplest explanation, and far easier to remember than Ro's convoluted concoction,' said Marvel and then turned around in his saddle. 'Hear that, everyone? We're travelling in such a large group because so much has been changing and we're learning from one another as we travel.'

Everyone except Aleks nodded. 'I can't for one minute think what any of you can be learning from me,' he said.

'Oh, I can think of a great deal,' said Rowena. 'Patience is the first thing that springs to mind.'

Aleks scowled as laughter erupted around him.

Sonja leant over and prodded him in the ribs. 'Come on, Aleks, she's only teasing you.'

Aleks raked his fingers through his hair and then rubbed his unshaven face. His pale blue eyes had shadows beneath them. 'I'm glad you all think it's funny,' he said. 'I'm finding this hard, you know. I don't like camping every night, I don't like the constant threat of danger to Nexus when we're in woodland, I hate having to eat the same travelling rations every day and I've no idea how long I'm going to be living like this. I'm sorry, everyone, I know you're wishing I hadn't come along. I've thought about going back to The Gathering lots of times, but I can't. I'm where I need to be. I don't like it, but I know it's true even if Nexus weren't constantly reminding me. But I'm... finding... it... hard.' His voice wavered.

I saw Jack and Vickery roll their eyes from behind Aleks. Infinity felt my need and slowed until she was beside Nexus. I subdued a smile as Infinity wrinkled her nostrils at Nexus and flattened her ears momentarily, warning her not to come too close and definitely not to pass in front.

I spoke quietly. 'Aleks, we're not wishing you hadn't come along. You and Nexus are improving your balance every day, and part of the reason for that is because you're so willing to push yourself. You're out of your comfort zone in pretty much every way possible at the moment, yet you're still here, refusing to give in to your need for comfort, because you're sensing that it's what your soul wants you to do. If it's any help, I've learnt that the more you push yourself out of your comfort zone, the bigger your comfort zone gets. I was every bit as uncomfortable as you are now while I was learning that, and way more unpopular, so give yourself a break, okay? And Rowena is only teasing, I think she considers it one of her gifts to the group.'

Aleks gave a small grin and I could see a measure of relief in his eyes. 'Thanks, Amarilla. I do appreciate all the help you're giving me and Nexus, even if I don't always seem to be able to show it.'

'I know. I also know that there'll be a time when there'll be things I'll need to learn from you, so you'd better be as happy to teach as you are to learn,' I warned him.

'From me? I highly doubt it... what have you seen in me?' Aleks said.

'No more or less than you've seen in you,' I replied.

'So, it's not enough that Nexus answers me in riddles, now you're doing it too?' Aleks laughed and as I laughed with him, I remembered with a pang that I'd once accused Adam of the very same thing.

I missed Adam acutely all of a sudden. Then I was Aware of him. He and Peace were drawn to my thoughts as surely as a floating twig follows a river current and I felt Adam's delight that they could be in contact with me in this way. I felt his pride in our group and his joy for what we were attempting on our mission; he was thrilled with the way our first encounter with the Kindred had gone. And then the two of them – who were really one – melted away from my immediate Awareness, leaving a trace that would always allow me to find them easily if I needed them.

'Am? Are you okay?' Aleks asked.

I smiled up at him. 'Yes, sorry. I'm still learning how to keep up with what's happening around me physically when things come up in my Awareness and take my attention. When it's Justin who drops in for a conversation, I can't seem to help muttering while I'm communicating with him. I don't know why as I've never done it when having conversations with Infinity. When it's other things that take my attention, I glaze over or just drop out of conversations. Sorry.'

'So, the weird stuff you do, it's because you're not really with us? But you're trying to be?' Aleks asked.

'Yep, and Infinity is hard on my case at the moment for me to do better,' I replied.

'And there's me thinking that you're all so sorted and it's just me who is struggling. Sorry, Amarilla, I had no idea,' Aleks said.

I chuckled. 'I think you and I are going to have to agree to stop apologising to one another. We're both learning stuff, we're both going to be a pain in the arse at times and we're both going to just have to accept that's how it is for now. Okay?'

'Got it. Thanks again, Am. You know, for everything.'

'No problem. I'm going to get back up in front before we reach Rockwood, otherwise Rowena is going to start telling everyone her version of why we're here and that can't happen, so if you'll excuse me...'

Infinity obliged me by cantering back up to the front of the group.

'I love that you think you're learning patience,' Marvel was saying to Rowena. 'I think it's a little fanciful, but it never hurts to see yourself in a good light.' He swooped to avoid being swatted by Rowena's outflung arm.

'Rockwood, here we come,' I said as Infinity's hoof struck the first cobblestone of Rockwood's main street.

It wasn't long before heads began to poke out of windows of the stone cottages that lined the street, at the clatter of our horses' hooves on the cobblestones. Those villagers who were out and about their business in the street stopped and turned to stare. Mouths dropped open at the number of horses and riders and then eyes widened as one by one, the villagers recognised me.

'By the breeze of spring, it's Amarilla Nixon,' I heard a voice say as its owner rushed into a stone cottage and returned seconds later with her two children. It was Lacey, a friend of my parents. She and her children waved to me, the children looking slightly unsure of what it was they were seeing. Lacey called out, 'Amarilla, it's so good to see you, and your horse, wow, look at her!'

Infinity, whose mane and tail shone silvery-white in the spring sunshine and whose eyes would, I knew, be shining their intense blue at anyone she deigned to notice, pranced down the street, sitting her weight and mine on her powerful hindquarters so that her front legs were free to flick elegantly out in front of her. She revelled in the stunned admiration she was receiving from everyone watching her. I in turn revelled in feeling her power, her grace and my oneness with her. I smiled and waved back to Lacey and her children, while Rowena chortled behind me.

More voices called out to us as people leant out of cottage windows or stopped to watch as we passed them on the street, and I looked behind me to see all of my companions smiling and waving back to the villagers who were clearly so delighted to see us all. I caught Rowena's eye and winked. 'Just waving to your public?' I said and laughed as she stuck her tongue out at me.

'Amarilla? Our Amarilla? By the wind of autumn, Amarilla, is that really you? Oh, my goodness, I can hardly believe it, but it is! Jod, go and fetch Mailen. Actually, on second thoughts, no, don't, we'll all go to her.' My Aunt Jasmine stood with my Uncle Jodral at the side of the street. Aunt Jasmine had her hand over her mouth and Uncle Jodral smiled as he waved at me. Both seemed unsure whether to approach Infinity.

Infinity halted gracefully, allowing me to jump from her back and then rush to embrace my aunt and uncle. 'Of course it's me, it's so good to see you both,' I said excitedly. 'Come and meet Infinity. Hold the back of your hand out for her to sniff, like this.'

Aunt Jasmine tentatively held out her hand as I'd shown her and Infinity immediately reached to sniff it. I felt her inspecting Aunt Jasmine's connection to me, all that she and I were to one another and all that we had shared. She liked my aunt's gentleness.

Aunt Jasmine looked worriedly at me as Infinity continued to sniff her hand. 'Am I doing it right?' she whispered.

I laughed. 'You're doing fine, she likes you. She's never met any of my family before, well not in the flesh anyway, and she's curious.'

My aunt and uncle looked at me as if they'd never seen me before, and I realised that Rowena's warning to me about how much I'd changed might not all have been in jest.

Infinity finally turned slightly from Aunt Jasmine and looked expectantly at Uncle Jodral, who smiled in wonder and then held out the back of his hand for her to sniff. He looked repeatedly from me to Infinity as she sniffed his hand, short sniffs interspersed with longer ones. I felt her inspecting his relationship to me in the same way she had done with Aunt Jasmine.

'I can't believe this,' Uncle Jodral whispered. 'I've never introduced myself to a horse before, never had reason to really, or the desire, but Infinity, she's... well she's...'

I laughed. 'She's Infinity. And there are six more horses here if you'd like to meet more of them? I doubt the others will feel the need to inspect you quite so closely as Infinity just has. That's Oak and Rowena is his Bond-Partner, Broad and Marvel are just behind them...' I pointed out each of the horses and their Bond-Partners, all of whom nodded and smiled.

My aunt and uncle moved to each horse in turn and introduced themselves, before engaging in enthusiastic conversation with my friends. I turned back to Infinity to see that she had a crowd of people admiring her from a respectful distance. She was delighting each admirer with a glance of her blue eyes and a bat of her eyelashes before moving on to the next.

'Hi, everyone, Infinity will be pleased to meet you if you come one at a time,' I said and beckoned for the first person to approach Infinity. Her inspections of the people who filed past her were brief, until I noticed her pause over a large, tanned, male hand. I looked up to see the face of its owner and felt a rush of emotion.

'Robbie!' I said, throwing myself at my brother.

He laughed as he returned my hug. 'Steady on, Am, anyone would think you'd missed me.' He released me, took hold of my arms and held me away from him. His laughing, brown eyes had a measure of seriousness in them, something I'd never seen there before. 'Look at you, Am, just look at you. My little sister left, you've come back in her place and I can hardly believe that you and she are the same person.'

My eyes filled with tears and I hugged my brother again fiercely. When he began to laugh, I released him and saw that Infinity was nuzzling his ear.

'No teeth, Infinity, his skin's even weaker than mine,' I said.

I laughed as Robbie said in a slightly higher-pitched voice than normal, 'Teeth? No, definitely no teeth please, Infinity, I depend on my rugged good looks, of which my ears play a large part.'

Infinity settled for a final wiggle of her upper lip on his shoulder, before leaving him be.

'Not scared, were you, Rob?' I said.

'Who me?' he said, his voice returning to normal. 'Well maybe just a tiny bit, I mean she's a big girl, isn't she?'

'Big? Um no, not really, if you'd like to meet some big horses, come and meet Oak and Broad,' I said and beckoned to Rowena and Marvel.

'Ah yes, Oak, I remember him from when Rowena came to explain your disappearance,' Robbie said and lifted a hand in greeting to Rowena. 'I love your style by the way, a much less stressful way to leave than enduring Mum's histrionics. Now this is Broad?' He held his hand out for Broad to sniff and I introduced him to Marvel, with whom he struck up an instant rapport.

Rowena glanced from the two men to me and grinned. 'Everything alright?' she mouthed to me.

I smiled back and nodded as Aunt Jasmine and Uncle Jodral reappeared.

'I think we'd better get you home before your mother hears that you're here and practically the whole village has seen you and Infinity before she has,' said Aunt Jasmine. 'Your Dad, Con and Katonia should be there by now, for lunch. Robbie meets his girlfriend most lunchtimes,' she told me with a wink. 'I think he may actually be close to settling down this time.'

'Mum can dream he might be, anyway,' I said and she laughed.

I yelled out to my friends that Infinity and I were going on to my family's house, and those that had dismounted to chat to people immediately remounted. Robbie lifted his hand and called out that he'd see me at dinner that evening, then shook hands with Marvel before continuing on his way. I stayed on foot and walked between Infinity and my aunt, my hand resting on Infinity's withers. People waved and called out greetings to all of us as we passed and I was glad that they were making my friends as welcome as they were me. But we were all Horse-Bonded, I realised. After being immersed in life at The Gathering, I'd almost forgotten that not everyone had a bond with a horse and that as Horse-Bonded, we were awarded a level of prestige. How silly that seemed now. We were all just people, all dealing with our own challenges, some of us with horses to help us and some of us without, but no one more or less important than the next.

You see the truth. Your fellow humans yet do not. You will need to relate to them in terms of their reality in order to be of help, Infinity advised.

As you and the other horses have been doing for us, all this time.

Not for much longer.

If we can do what needs to be done, then not for much longer, I agreed.

We arrived at my family's stone cottage. My mother had been busy in the garden, judging by the mass of flowers that waved in the breeze, the freshly stained picket fence and the newly weeded cobble path. The upstairs windows were all ajar and their curtains danced as the spring breeze buffeted past them. The front door stood open and beyond it I could see the red rug that warmed the flagstones within. I drank in every detail of the family home about which I had dreamt so often and within which, when I had been missing them all most keenly, I had pictured my family chatting and laughing as they shared meals and went about their daily routines.

Aunt Jasmine touched my arm. 'Wait here and I'll fetch them all out,' she said.

As she disappeared into Nixonhouse, I turned around to see that my companions all waited at a respectful distance and a crowd of people stood peering around from behind them. Marvel winked at me and Rowena gave me a reassuring smile and nod. I put an arm under Infinity's neck and leant into her warmth as I hugged her. She sent a burst of love through my being by way of a reply.

There was the sound of running feet and then Katonia appeared in the doorway. Her eyes widened and both of her hands went to her mouth as she took in the sight of me, Infinity and all of our companions. I just had time to move away from Infinity before my sister hurled herself at me, nearly knocking me off my feet. She was crying and laughing as she hugged me, then held me away from herself while she looked at me, before pulling me close and hugging me again.

Another pair of arms enfolded us both as Con's voice said shakily in my ear, 'Welcome home, Am, welcome home.' I reached an arm around him and hung on to my brother and sister for all I was worth. Eventually, they released their hold and moved to either side of me so that I could see my mother and father standing in the doorway. My father was smiling as tears ran unashamedly down his cheeks. He had his arm around my mother, supporting her as she clung to him, sobbing.

I was Aware of it all. I felt their pain when my belongings were discovered in the woods with no sign of me. I felt their anguish as the days went by with no word of my fate or whereabouts. I felt their utter relief on eventually hearing from Rowena where I was, what had happened to me and that I was safe. I felt my father's pride and my mother's sense of loss as they came to terms with whom I had become. I felt their constant hope that they would hear news of me and my horse – how we were, what we doing, when we might visit. I felt their spikes of joy when news, however brief, arrived, followed by their helplessness at being so far away from me, both physically and in terms of how my life now differed from theirs. I felt their wonder at the sight of Infinity standing at their gate, radiating beauty and power along with a gentleness they struggled to reconcile. I felt their amazement at the sight of the young woman in front of them who bore all the hallmarks of the daughter they had lost, but whose bearing almost removed the possibility that she could be that person. I felt my father's love and pride at the sight of me and I felt the conflict within my mother; she wanted to give in to the overwhelming emotions with which she battled constantly, and have one of her characteristic meltdowns, but she also wanted to find the strength to overcome them so that she could welcome the daughter whom she had missed so much that at times, she'd wanted to pack a bag and run somewhere – anywhere – in the hope of finding her. I felt it all.

Their challenges are not yours. Do not adopt them as such. Infinity's mind nudged mine firmly. *You know how best to help them.*

Help them. I could help them. Instantly, I felt my love for them. For all of my family. Light burst out of me and settled in a haze around my parents. Katonia and Con shifted beside me, looking from me to my parents.

'Am, what's happening? Mum and Dad look hazy but brighter at the same time... and so do you. Is it you doing that? What are you doing to them?' Katonia said.

'Loving them,' I said simply, and then cocooned my brother and sister in light as they stood alongside me. 'Loving you all.'

I felt the intensity of my parents' suffering subside. My father was looking from my mother to me and my brother and sister in confusion. My mother was smiling. She let go of my father and wiped the tears from her face with the back of her hand. I ran to her and threw my arms around her neck. She embraced me warmly but softly. Gone was the desperation to keep her little girl close that had given her hugs a firmness in the past. I felt her pure joy at seeing me and her wonder at how she seemed to be able to feel her emotions one at a time now, instead of all at once. My father's arms enveloped us both and cheering erupted from my friends and the crowd out on the street.

～

Rowena sat down beside me on the sofa with a bump. 'Everything alright?' she asked.

I nodded as I watched Katonia and Robbie flicking soap suds at one another as they washed the last of the dishes. My homecoming party had been wonderful – friends and family had pulled together to whip up a buffet, the lounge furniture had been cleared to the edges and there had been music and dancing on the flagstones. I had been hugged and kissed so much that I'd almost forgotten what it felt like to be just me, in my own skin, by myself.

'I'm fine thanks, just tired. I'm getting better at holding other people's feelings and thoughts away from me when they get overwhelming, but with as many people in one place as there were this evening, it's a bit of a struggle, lovely as it's been to see everyone.' I drew closer to her and whispered, 'In many ways, it feels as if I never left, but you were right about how much I've changed, I can see it in how everyone is reacting to me.'

'And you don't think enveloping your parents in light on their own doorstep had anything to do with it?' she grinned. 'I get why you did it, I do, but it was enough of a shock when we all saw you do it to Feryl that first time at The Gathering, and we had our horses to help us understand what we were witnessing. I'd have been surprised if everyone wasn't acting differently towards you after seeing your parents and then Kat and Con go all ethereal like that, and you seemingly the cause of it. You just have to remember that it's all good. Everything that has happened, all the changes that you and Fin have set in motion, it's all good. Okay?' She put an arm around my shoulders and hugged me. 'If it'll help, I'll tell Marvel and the others to spread a bit of light around as well and then people will be looking at all of us as if we've just landed from the sky and not just you.'

I laughed. 'Thanks, Ro. Is everyone happy with where they're staying?'

'We're all fine. Your aunt and uncle's cottage is lovely. Marvel, Sonja, Aleks and I will be very comfortable there and our horses are more than happy with their paddock out at the back, there's plenty of grass for them and your Aunt Jasmine's donkeys. Jack and Vic are staying at Holly's. Her mum was expecting her to arrive any day so when we showed up, she thought Holly would be with us. She was so disappointed when she wasn't that she insisted some of us stay with her instead, and I don't think she's going to let Jack and Vic go until Holly turns up. She's put the word around that Jack and Vickery are here to help people to multiskill, and they've been inundated, which is why they didn't make it to the party – but don't worry, he and Vic will be fine.'

I nodded and yawned.

'I know you need time with your family over the next few days, but if you need to talk about anything, come and find me, okay?' Rowena said quietly.

I nodded and smiled as she got up and went over to say goodnight to my family before leaving with Marvel. I checked in with Infinity, to find that she was grazing contentedly alongside my family's two donkeys.

I can hardly believe that I'm home. I'm finally home, I told her.

You attempt to convince yourself.

Well, physically, I'm home. It doesn't feel like it used to though, I admitted.

You have changed much. You realise who you now are through the eyes of your loved ones. A useful experience. Infinity turned her attention back to her grazing.

FOUR

Rockwood

I stirred as the first few voices of the dawn chorus began to chirp questioningly. As other birds began to twitter in response, I felt confused as to why their voices seemed so far away, why I was so warm and comfortable, and why I couldn't smell smoke from the campfire or hear Marvel snoring. I was in a bed. I was at home. I was at my family's home, I corrected myself and then felt a pang. Of what? Not sadness and definitely not regret. No, of recognising that I was in a home that I had loved, but that no longer felt like my home. I checked in with Infinity and then remembered with a smile that home wasn't anywhere physical.

My bedroom door creaked open and soft footsteps padded in. 'Am? Are you awake?' Katonia whispered.

'Yep, come on in,' I said and sat up, yawning.

My sister took a running jump and landed on my bed, the way she used to do when we were children. We hugged one another, giggling.

'I can't tell you how good it is to have you home,' she said. 'How long are you staying?'

'A week or so I should think. It's good to be here. Good and...'

'...weird?' Katonia finished for me.

'Yes. Good and weird. But now we're on our own, tell me how everything is with you? Are you still feeling restless?'

As soon as I asked the question, I was Aware of the answer. My sister radiated her restlessness, along with her frustration at not knowing the cause of it and her desire to find something, anything, that would ease it. Conflict raged within her; a part of her still wanted what she'd always wanted – a home and family of her own – but her restlessness pushed that to one side and confused her.

As she opened her mouth to tell me of her feelings, I said, 'Never mind, I know.'

'And do you also know why I'm this way? Why it started all of a sudden? What it is that I need to do to make it stop?'

Infinity increased her presence in my mind, interested, but content just to observe.

'With a bit of effort, I can know. But if I go looking, nothing you think or feel will be private from me. Are you okay with that? Do you want some time to think about it?'

She shook her head, frantically. 'No. Do it now. Please.'

I allowed Kat's restlessness to take up more space in my mind and immediately, I knew when it started, why it started and what it was that her soul felt was so important that it prodded her consciousness so relentlessly.

You will need to proceed with caution, Infinity warned me.

How much do I tell her? Flaming lanterns, Fin, how do I know which bits to tell her and which bits not to? If I tell her too much, she's going to be overwhelmed and frightened. If I don't tell her enough, her restlessness will get worse and I'll have been no help whatsoever.

Trust yourself.

Trust myself. I took a deep breath and made my sister and my physical surroundings my focus once more.

'Is it something awful?' Katonia peered into my eyes.

My brain sifted frantically through all the information I had gleaned. Trust myself. 'No, not at all,' I said. 'It's something amazing, actually, and it's my fault.'

'Your fault?' Katonia said.

'Yes, in the same way that it was Infinity's fault that I spent the better part of my childhood feeling as you do now. I felt that way because of an agreement I made with Infinity in another lifetime. When circumstances in this lifetime caused me to remember her, my soul spoke to me of the agreement we had made in the only way I could hear it.'

Katonia's blue eyes flicked back and forth between my own. I looked back at her and waited.

Finally, she said, 'You're saying that I'm feeling restless because my soul is speaking to me about an agreement I made? With you? In another lifetime? How is that even possible?'

'It's hard for us humans to understand,' I told her. 'I found it hard to begin with, even though Infinity showed me the life we lived together before. Our souls never die, Kat. They live over and over in different bodies, in different lifetimes. They remember all of the experiences they've had in all of the lives they've lived and when something affects them deeply enough, they carry it with them from one lifetime into the next. My agreement with Infinity was an example of that, my agreement with you is another.'

Katonia stared at me. 'As much as my brain is saying that what you're telling me is impossible, something deep down is telling me that it's true.' She cleared her throat and then breathed deeply and slowly. 'What agreement did we make?'

Trust myself. I rubbed my face with my hands. 'Do you trust me?' I asked my sister.

'Of course I do.'

'Then will you accept what I'm about to say, knowing that I'm not going to tell you everything, but trusting me that when the time is right, you'll know the rest for yourself?'

'Will you tell me enough for this restlessness to stop?'

'I doubt it'll stop completely, but what I'll tell you should help you to live with it more easily.'

'Then I'll accept what you tell me,' Katonia said.

I took a deep breath. 'There's no need to feel torn between wanting a family and doing what your restlessness, your soul, is nudging you to do. In fact, it's unlikely that one will happen without the other. Find the partner you've always dreamt of, Kat, but as you've already learnt from your relationship with Greg, the person you're looking for isn't someone who wants a quiet, predictable life. The man you're looking for will need to be open to new possibilities, to change. He'll need to be your equal in terms of the roles you'll both play in the future of humanity. Because that's what you agreed to help me with, Kat. Just as I made an agreement with Infinity to help horses and humans to evolve further when the time was right, you agreed to help me.

'I awoke your soul to the memory of our agreement by nudging your mind, night after night, whilst my plans to find and help the Woeful – sorry, the Kindred, as we call them now – were at the forefront of my mind. There will come a time in the future when I'll need your help. Only you will be able to do what is necessary, with the support of the man you will find.'

Katonia frowned as she stared at me. Her cheeks were flushed pink and her breathing was rapid as she digested what I'd told her.

Your trust in yourself was well placed, Infinity told me.

That wasn't easy. And you've done it time after time for me, Fin, telling me just enough to keep me on the right track but not so much as to be more than I could handle – horses have been doing it for us for centuries.

It is more difficult for you than for us since you are attached to the outcome.

You don't fear that you'll get it wrong. You just know you'll say as much as is needed and if humans don't do as you had hoped with the information you give them, you just wait and try again, I observed. *The human fear of failure has a lot to answer for.*

Only if you allow it a voice.

I grinned. I loved receiving counsel from Infinity now that I tended to know what it meant.

I saw Katonia's mouth twitch with the beginnings of a smile. 'There is a man out there for me? I can have a family? And my restlessness is to do with an agreement I have made to help you?'

I nodded and then was flung flat on my back amongst my pillows as my sister threw herself at me, hugging me for all she was worth. 'Then everything's okay. I don't really understand all of what you've told me, but the bits I get, I'm soooooo happy about.' She sat up suddenly. 'Mum can't know about this. She'll home in on the fact that I'm looking for a man again and I'll never hear the end of it. Promise me, Amarilla, you won't breathe a word of this to her? To anyone?'

I laughed as I promised her, knowing that it was a secret I wasn't going to have to keep for long.

I spent most of that day on my family's sofa. I'd been informed at breakfast that with the exception of a couple of breaks to go and see Infinity, I was going nowhere until each and every one of my family's questions had been answered as to what I'd been up to in the eighteen months since I had disappeared.

I was awarded frequent and emotional hugs from each of my family as I recounted my tale. I neglected to mention my out-of-body experience and the decision I had made to continue inhabiting my current body in order to go on a mission to find the Kindred, and I was grateful when Katonia asked a question relating to something completely different as soon as I reached that time in my story, allowing me to rejoin it at a later, safer – as far as my parents were concerned – stage.

'So you are now a qualified Herbalist, you can multiskill, you are perfectly balanced at all times and you're what you call "Aware" as a result, and you teach other Horse-Bonded how to ride as well as you can?' my mother said with tears in her eyes. 'And now you're travelling around to the villages, spreading word of your experiences, opening people up to be able to multiskill, and helping your fellow Horse-Bonded as you go.'

'Well, um I wouldn't put it quite like that, I mean the other Horse-Bonded are helping me too, in fact I wouldn't have been able to do what I have without them. And it's Jack who's helping most of the people who ask for help to be able to multiskill – he's the best at helping them to open up to knowing they can do it, although Vic and I help him out if there are too many people for him to be able to see them all...'

'But none of it would be happening without you, would it? Without you and Infinity?' my mother persisted.

'Mum, give her a break, she's trying to be modest and you're ruining it for her,' said Con, winking at me, 'and for Dad, he's trying very hard not to look pleased that she inherited at least one attribute from him.'

I threw a cushion at Con. 'And what exactly do you mean by that, brother of mine?' I said. 'Which attributes have I inherited from Mum?'

Robbie chuckled. 'You walked right into that one, mate,' he said to Con.

Con was unfazed. 'Now, let's see. You're determined and you won't be moved once you have an idea in your head. You have a tendency to be melodramatic...'

'I do not!'

'A pile of belongings left on a cloak with no sign of what happened to their owner would tend to disagree with you there, Am, and lastly, you appear to have inherited her overwhelming desire to love everyone.'

My mother said, 'Oh, Con,' and hugged him, her tears wetting the shoulder of his shirt.

'Oh, Con? Is that all you can say, Mum? What about our apparent tendency for stubbornness and melodrama?' I said, laughing.

'Well, he's not wrong, is he, dear,' said my mother, winking before turning to pick up the tea tray.

My family collapsed into laughter at my stunned face. I was Aware that my mother felt calmer than normal, despite the emotion of my homecoming; the light that I had sent to infuse her the previous day was still providing comfort and allowing her to merely feel her emotions instead of being overwhelmed by them. As I joined in with the laughter, I made a mental note that opening people to multiskill wasn't the only thing we should be offering to help people to do.

Aunt Jasmine assured me at dinner that evening that my friends were all well fed and rested, and had spent the day enjoying exploring Rockwood and meeting its inhabitants. They had been called on by many villagers to ask their horses for advice about differing matters, and all of those who had asked had apparently been very happy with the counsel they had received. Apparently, Jack had been in much demand for his ability to open people up to being able to multiskill and there had been a steady stream of people visiting Holly's house to see him.

'Do any of you want to be able to do any of the Skills other than those you trained for?' I asked my family.

'I dunno, Am, I had enough trouble training to be an Earth-Singer. It all sounds like a lot of work to me,' said Robbie.

'But it would be worth the effort to be able to weather-sing,' said Con. 'Just think about it, Rob, being able to keep the rain away until we've finished earth-singing for the day, that would be useful, and it would be pretty amazing to be able to do the Healing Skills, but I never showed any aptitude for those at testing.'

'Con, it doesn't matter.' I was unable to keep exasperation out of my voice. 'You showed aptitude for the Skills that you thought you would show aptitude for when you were tested, but the Skills are all the same. All you need to do is to know that you can do any of them that you want to, and you'll be able to do them, with no training, just the absolute knowledge you can do it. Apart from herbalism – obviously with that, you need to learn which plants are which, where to find them, how to store them, all of that, but apart from that, no training is needed.'

'But how come in practice, people aren't finding that what you're saying is the case, Amarilla? Everyone who has tried to believe that they can do any of the Skills has found that they can still only do the ones for which they showed aptitude and for which they were trained,' said my father.

'And there's the problem. They've tried to believe that they can do other Skills. They have to KNOW they can do them and there is a world of difference between believing and knowing. I know how hard it is to make the jump between the two, because I found it difficult even with Infinity's coaching. That's why we're offering to help people to open up to KNOWING that the ability to perform any of the Skills is inherent in all of us. After all, the first Rock-Singers, Earth-Singers, Tree-Singers and Glass-Singers had no training, they merely remembered knowledge that was buried in the human psyche. That remembering was stimulated by precise wording that Jonus, the first Horse-Bonded, told them, words given to him by his horse, Mettle. You all know that as well as I do.'

My father nodded thoughtfully. 'And that is what Jack is doing? Telling people words given to him by his horse – Candour, isn't he called? – so that they remember they can do it? So that they know they can do it?'

'That's exactly it. Jack is particularly good at helping people to remember what they know because he's very articulate and very honest. He delivers the words that people need to hear, gently but with no concern over how they will be received, and he leaves people with no doubt that what he says is the truth. They take his words deeply within themselves and in no time, they know that they can do any of the Skills they want – and they can.'

'And you can help people in this way too?' my mother said.

'In many cases, yes, but not all. Those where I fail are usually because the person is struggling to trust me because of how young and inexperienced I am.'

'WHAT? AFTER ALL YOU'VE DONE?' shouted my mother. 'AND YOU'RE HORSE-BONDED! THEY SHOULD LISTEN TO WHATEVER YOU HAVE TO SAY.'

'I am young and inexperienced in most ways though,' I said. 'For someone to open up to knowing something that their life experience tells them is impossible, they have to completely trust the person who is helping them. I'm telling you from personal experience; I only knew that I could sing my broken arm back to health because I had absolute, total trust in Infinity when she told me I could. I don't always inspire enough trust from people to be able to help them, but Jack does. Vickery's learning quickly from him and I'm learning from them both.'

'I trust you completely, Am,' said Katonia, 'and I'd like you, please, to help me to open up to know I can multiskill.'

'And me,' said Con.

'Me too,' said my father. 'I'm curious.'

One by one, each of my family asked for help to be able to multiskill, even my mother, who had shown no aptitude for any of the Skills at testing and so had trained as a Baker.

'I'm going to need to enlist Jack's help to deal with all of you,' I said and grinned inwardly.

'It will be good to meet the young man,' said my mother. 'He and Vickery were whisked off so soon after your homecoming, I barely even got a look at him. And talking of young men, Amarilla, it hasn't escaped my notice that you mentioned a good number of them in your letters. Is there anyone in particular we should be aware of?'

Instantly, I felt heat rising in my cheeks. 'Ummm, no, not really.'

'I think we can take that as a yes,' said Robbie. 'Come on, Am, spill, who is he? And where is he? Oh, is he here? No, Marvel's too old, Jack's too intense and Aleks is too... now what is Aleks? Too unsure of himself, I would say?'

My brother's perceptiveness surprised me even as my embarrassment prickled its way right down to my toes.

Am? Justin's concern changed to amusement as he became Aware of what had caused my discomfort.

I'm glad you think it's funny, what do I tell them? I thought to him.

'Don't mutter, Amarilla, tell us who he is out loud so we can hear you,' said my mother.

I hadn't thought it possible for my face to go any redder, but it turned out that it was.

Tell them that there's nothing to tell. We're just friends who can share minds because of what we've achieved with our horses, came Justin's reply. He knew I felt the untruth of his words, but he was adamant that was how our relationship would remain, at least for now.

'Bloody man,' I said to myself.

Katonia, sitting next to me, came to my rescue. 'Amarilla is close friends with Justin, which is only natural seeing as they're both Aware and can share minds in the same way that the Horse-Bonded do with their horses – remember, she told us about that in one of her letters? Justin is at The Gathering, where he and Quinta are needed to teach,' she said, and squeezed my hand under the table.

'Close friends, eh? That explains totally why Amarilla has a face like a beetroot,' said Robbie.

I sighed. 'Yes, close friends.'

'If you can share minds with him like you do with Infinity, can you speak to him right now? Even though he's at The Gathering?' Con asked.

I nodded. All of my family, except for Katonia, were staring at me and I felt their surprise, curiosity and discomfort.

My mother frowned. 'Can Justin know everything you're thinking, whenever he wants to?'

'Yes, he can, but...'

'Who is this Justin, exactly, and how old is he?' There was an edge of hysteria to my mother's voice and I could feel her emotions bubbling up, threatening to break through the layer of peace that she had enjoyed since the previous day.

'Justin is someone who has looked out for me since the first day I met him,' I said. 'Yes, he can know anything he wants to about me and I can know the same about him, but the fact is, as soon as we became Aware, we both knew, as the horses have always known, that we are one with All That Is. We're one with each other. He knew me before I was me, just as Infinity did, just as all of you did, actually. There's nothing hidden between us and there's nothing that needs to be. And in answer to your question, Mum, Justin is twenty-eight.'

All of my family, with the exception of Katonia, were looking at me as if they'd never seen me before and I felt their fear as strongly as I felt Katonia's acceptance.

Do not attempt to alleviate their emotions. They will need to experience their full range in order to be ready for what is to come. Infinity's counsel was as comforting as it was welcome.

Katonia got to her feet. 'Come on, Am, let's clear away and get pudding so everyone can talk about you,' she said, winking at me.

I gathered plates and cutlery and followed her to the sink. 'Well, that went well,' I said.

'At least you understand now why Justin has insisted that you and he stay friends for now? Can you imagine what would have happened if you'd told them that your first boyfriend is ten years older than you and can share your mind?' my sister said.

As understanding dawned on my face, Katonia laughed. 'Honestly, Am, you can be so dense sometimes. You and Justin may have reached a deeper understanding of reality than the rest of us, but you're still people, living among people, and Justin clearly understands that better than you do. The more I hear about him, the more I like him.'

Tell your sister I said thanks, and not just for the compliment.

I'd forgotten you were still there, Jus. Had you been more help, I'd likely have remembered, I told him.

I could almost hear Justin chuckling.

'Remembered what? They're all talking now so you can speak up,' Katonia said.

'Sorry, I was answering Justin. I always mutter when I talk to him, my brain can't seem to get the hang of the fact that I don't need to say the words out loud.'

'He's with you now?'

'Yep, has been since I flushed like a tomato at the table. He wanted to know what was wrong, I asked him what I should say and he was no help whatsoever, in fact he thinks it's funny. He said to say thanks to you, and not just for the compliment.' I laughed at my sister's shock.

'Tell him he's welcome. Oh wait, can he... hear me somehow?'

'He knows what you've said when I process your words as thoughts, but only if his whole attention is with me at the time. Don't worry, if you want to speak to me in private, it will be private.'

Katonia was thoughtful. 'But he can know everything you know. Does he know what you know about me? About our agreement?'

'If Justin wanted to sift through everything I know about everyone, then he could know everything about you. But he wouldn't do that, Kat, even if he had the time, which he doesn't. He's living his own life and that takes up most of his attention. We might share minds for a while if we need to talk something over, and if I feel an emotion strongly enough, it might be enough to draw his attention to me, but we both respect the need that most people have – that we used to have – for privacy. There may be a time when I'll need to tell him, though. Will that be okay? Some of it will be common knowledge soon, anyway.'

'What? Which bit? Amarilla, tell me.'

'Believe me when I tell you that you wouldn't thank me for stopping you finding out for yourself, and also believe me that after having been bonded to Infinity for nearly two years, I know exactly how annoying you'll be finding me right now,' I said.

'Change annoying to insufferable and you're nearly there,' Katonia retorted. 'We'd best get the rest of the plates cleared and see if anyone's remembered that they haven't eaten pudding yet. You always did know how to make family dinners memorable.'

I thought back to the dinner when I'd announced that I was going to become one of the Horse-Bonded, and grinned.

FIVE

Serendipity

*R*owena laughed so hard that she had to lean on the pommel of Oak's saddle to steady herself. I looked across at Marvel to see that he also found my tale amusing.

'I can just picture their faces,' Rowena gasped. 'Blimey, Am, "he knew me before I was me," "he and I are one", could you not have thought of any way to maybe tone it down a bit? Honestly, when I first met you, and also, incidentally, the last time your family saw you, you were a mild, innocent people-pleaser with a bit of a stubborn streak. Now, you say it like it is, even when no one really understands what "it" is, and then you wonder why people look at you as if you just told them that their pants are on fire.'

'What else could I say? Justin was no help whatsoever, Infinity couldn't care less about stuff like this and Mum was building up steam for a meltdown.'

'Oh, I don't know, maybe something like, "we've shared a lot of the same experiences and have become good friends as a result, there's a chance I may have a bit of a crush on him" – enough truth to be believable, but none of the flaky stuff that freaks people out?' Rowena said, wiping her eyes.

'I guess that would have been easier,' I admitted, allowing myself to giggle.

'You guess? Seriously?' Rowena said, her giggles echoing mine.

When I had a hold over myself, I asked, 'What are the others up to this morning?'

'We told Jack and Vic yesterday that we three were going for a ride this morning and they seemed to think that they'd be too busy helping everyone who wants to multiskill, to come with us,' said Marvel.

'What about Aleks and Sonja, didn't they want to come?' I said.

'They weren't invited,' said Rowena. 'I needed a break from Aleks, so Sonja insisted that he and Nexus ride out early with her and Bright.'

'What's going on?' I said.

'Oh, just Aleks being Aleks. His latest moan is that in the two days we've been in Rockwood, he hasn't seen hide nor hair of you and he's worried that his progress with Nexus is suffering as a result of interruptions to their training. Sonja knows what you were working on with him and I think she was going to try to help him a bit while they're out,' Rowena replied.

'Anyone fancy a bit of a blast? Broad's got a bit of energy to burn,' said Marvel.

Infinity immediately launched into a powerful, ground-covering canter. 'You can take that as a yes. See you back at Rockwood,' I shouted over my shoulder.

'No way, we're right behind you,' shouted Rowena and I heard Oak's and Broad's big hooves thundering up behind Infinity across the open pastureland.

Infinity's decision was made as soon as the stallions increased their pace. I felt the strength in her hindquarters as she pushed herself up to a gallop, and I whooped for the joy we shared as we tore for home.

The warm spring breeze felt like a buffeting wind as we ripped our way through it and my eyes watered so much that Rockwood was a blur as it loomed up in front of us. Infinity slowed to a canter and then to an elegant trot as her hooves touched cobblestones, her white neck arched like that of a swan, her powerful hindquarters fully engaged underneath herself, carrying her weight and mine effortlessly, and her silvery-white tail held out behind her. She flicked a black and white ear backward as Oak whinnied from some distance behind. I grinned.

Deny it as much as you like, Fin, but you do love to win a race, I told her.

I merely demonstrated the difference between the power my body can express and the power to which Broad and Oak have access whilst their bodies are organised in the way that they are.

Oh, I see, so you were providing a demonstration to Marvel and Rowena of what their horses will be able to do once they've helped them to balance as well as you can – an incentive, if you will?

It was unlikely that Infinity would have deigned to answer even if we'd been on our own, but with so many people gasping at her adoringly as she passed by, there was no chance whatsoever. I waved at some of them as we slowed and turned to watch our friends catch up with us.

'Isn't that Serene, standing outside Holly's house?' said Marvel as Broad slowed to a halt next to us.

I turned back to see a small crowd of people taking it in turns to offer their hands for a slim, grey horse to sniff. As we neared them, I could see that it was indeed Serene. Holly, Serene's tall, slender Bond-Partner, was standing on the step of her family's cottage, embracing her mother.

'Holly,' called Marvel, waving.

Holly's long blond hair swirled around her as she turned and waved back. 'Fancy seeing you lot here,' she called out to us as we rode towards her. 'I gather I've got nowhere to stay, as Jack has taken root in my room and Vic has the spare room. Charming, isn't it? I get here a few days later than planned, and my family just finds replacements!' She put an arm back around her mother and hugged her.

We all laughed. 'There's room at our house for one of you. Holly, you can come home with me?' I said with a wink.

'She'll do no such thing,' said Holly's mother. 'She's going to show Serene to her paddock and then she's coming straight in for a bath and a good meal, she looks like she hasn't eaten properly for weeks.'

'I've been travelling, Mum, and I've been well fed wherever I've stayed, honestly.' Holly rolled her eyes.

'Well, shall I take Jack with me then? He can see anyone who wants his help at ours – Mum will love having everyone there, you know she will,' I said.

'I don't want him to think I'm throwing him out,' Holly's mother said with a guilty glance behind her.

'He doesn't think anything of the sort and he's very grateful to you for putting up with people traipsing in and out of your house to see him for the past two days.' Jack's voice carried from inside the cottage. He appeared in the doorway and planted a kiss on Holly's mother's cheek. 'Thanks, Sylvie, you've been brilliant, but it's time for me to take my mayhem elsewhere. Do you hear that, folks? I'm going to Amarilla's house, so you can find me there later today, or Vic is here if you want to see her now. Wait for me a few minutes, Amarilla? I'll grab my stuff and bring Candour round from the back.'

I nodded and jumped down from Infinity as Holly approached. 'Any plans after you've visited your family?' I whispered to her as she hugged me.

'I was going back to The Gathering. Why?' Holly whispered back.

'Rowena, Marvel, Jack and Vic aren't the only ones here with me. Sonja and Aleks are here too,' I said quietly as I released her.

'That's some group,' Holly said and then her eyes widened. 'You're going to...'

I interrupted her with a sharp nod. 'You'd be welcome if you wanted to come. Think about it, we'll be here for a few more days.'

She nodded, thoughtfully. 'I will. I'll see you soon, Am.'

As Jack and I saw Infinity and Candour to the paddock behind my family's house, we chuckled at the donkeys' disdain at having another strange horse sharing their quarters. Infinity wrinkled her nose at them before settling into a grooming session with Candour, who appeared not to have noticed that the donkeys even existed.

Jack heaved his saddlebags onto his shoulder. 'Are you sure your family won't mind me being here, Am?' he said. 'They've only had you back a few days, won't they want you to themselves for a bit longer?'

'No, they'll be fine. They'll love having another Horse-Bonded to
grill and you'll be doing me a favour by taking the heat off me. I was
going to ask you to come round and see them all, anyway. They want
help to be able to multiskill and you'll get through to them far better than
I'll be able to; they're always going to see me as the baby of the family,
no matter what I do, and I think that'll stop them trusting me enough to
know that they can do what I'm saying they can. And my Mum really
will love having everyone coming to her house to see you, she's always
in her element when she has lots of people around her.'

'Well, if you're sure, then thanks.'

'No problem. We're just in time for lunch, come on, this way.'

I opened the back door to the sound of my mother berating Con for
"traipsing mud all the way through the house when I've just mopped all
of the floors". Jack hastily took his boots off and left them outside,
before following me in to the kitchen. Everyone except Robbie was
there.

'Everyone, this is Jack,' I said.

Instantly, my mother was in front of us, shaking Jack's hand. 'This is
a lovely surprise, you must be the Jack that we've heard so much about,
welcome to our home. And you appear to have your belongings with you.
Surely Sylvie hasn't thrown you out? Oh, you poor lamb, leave them
there and come and sit down and tell us all about it. Obviously, you must
stay here. You can have Con's room and he'll go in with Robbie. Jack,
dear, are you alright?'

Jack appeared to be unaware that his hand was still clasping my
mother's, in fact he appeared unaware of anything except for my sister, at
whom he was staring unashamedly. I grinned as I felt the thread that
linked him to Katonia – the thread that I'd seen when I'd looked into the
source of her restlessness – strengthening now that the two of them
occupied the same physical space. As it almost seemed to solidify, I was
Aware of an agreement between two souls, made long ago, settling into
place.

Katonia was as mesmerised by Jack as he was by her. I felt her shock
and confusion. She frowned slightly and began to shake her head, as if
trying to release herself from whatever it was that held her. Then her gaze

flickered to me very briefly and her face relaxed into a broad smile of understanding. Jack smiled back.

'Jack, this is my sister, Katonia,' I said.

Jack came back to himself. He looked down at his hand, still holding my mother's, and flushed red. 'Oh, um, sorry,' he said, 'how rude of me, I'm Jack.'

'Yes, I know, dear.' My mother beamed, looking from him to my sister. 'Come and sit down next to Katonia. Shove up, Con, you can sit around the other side.' She picked up Con's plate of food and moved it across the table.

'Oi!' said Con through a mouthful of vegetables.

Jack moved to where my sister sat, and held out a trembling hand. 'Hello, Katonia,' he said, quietly.

Katonia's cheeks were a pretty pink as she stood up and shook his hand. 'Hi, Jack, it's um, well it's very good to meet you.'

'Kat, why don't you and Jack go and sit in the garden and I'll bring your lunch out to you?' I said.

Katonia flashed me a grateful smile and nodded. 'Er, this way then,' she said to Jack and he followed her out the way he and I had just come in.

'But...' said my mother.

'Mum, believe me when I tell you that if you ever want grandchildren, you need to leave them alone,' I said.

My mother looked at me in consternation. Then her expression changed to wonder and her eyes filled with tears. 'He's the one? Finally? Do you really think so? I mean it was obvious that something just happened, but are you sure?'

'Yes, I'm sure. You'll have all the time in the world to get to know Jack, but for now, you need to leave him and Katonia alone. Okay?'

My mother nodded.

Con had retrieved his lunch and was looking from me to my mother in confusion. My father, who was sitting at his normal place at the far end of the table, said, 'Would anyone like to tell me what just happened?'

My mother threw her arms around me and hugged me, rocking from side to side in her glee. 'Frank, you just saw your future son-in-law, but we mustn't interfere,' she said, giggling.

'Okay, well firstly, you always say we mustn't interfere and then you interfere,' my father said. 'Secondly, if that young man is who I think he is, then he's Horse-Bonded, and we all know that the Bonded rarely marry and never to non-bonded folk. And thirdly, you've seen your future son-in-law in just about every male that Katonia's ever spoken to, so how can you possibly be sure this time?'

I caught my father's eye, raised my eyebrow and nodded.

'Oh,' he said.

I was just finishing my breakfast when there was a frantic banging on the front door. My father got up to go to see who was there and shortly afterwards, a breathless Vickery burst into the kitchen. 'Amarilla, your Dad tells me that Jack's not here. Do you know where he is? I can't do another day like yesterday, there are just too many people who want help. Poor Verve is stuck in that paddock with Serene, who just squeals and kicks out at him whenever he looks in her direction, and I've had no time to ride him out to give him a break,' she said, breathlessly. 'And I've had some of the people who've come to see me tell me that they've already been here to ask for Jack's help, but he wasn't here. I thought he was going to carry on helping people once he'd settled in here, not disappear off the face of the earth and leave it all to me.'

'Do you want a cup of tea?' I said, already pouring one for her.

'No, I haven't got time, I need to get back before people start queueing outside Holly's house. Hello, everyone, by the way,' she said with a wave of her hand to Robbie, Con and my mother, 'and sorry to interrupt your breakfast. Am, if you can just tell me where you think Jack might be, I'll go and find him and leave you all in peace.'

'I don't know where he is, I haven't seen him since he arrived here,' I said.

'But that was the day before yesterday. I don't understand,' said Vickery.

I handed her the cup of tea I had poured for her and poured another for myself. 'Come on, we'll go in the other room,' I said.

Vickery listened intently as I told her of Jack and Katonia's meeting.

'But nothing will come of it, Jack's Horse-Bonded and your sister isn't,' said Vickery. 'Or do you think she will be at some point?'

I shook my head. 'I don't think so. But it doesn't matter. Everything else is changing, why not this? It used to be that the Horse-Bonded set themselves apart because they needed time and space to learn from their horses, but we need to integrate with the villagers more now that we've learnt so much and have so much that we need to pass on to them. Maybe Jack will be the first of many.'

Vickery slumped in her chair. 'Hmm, maybe,' she said. 'And you say you haven't seen Jack or Katonia since the afternoon they met?'

'Nope, I took their lunch and then their dinner out to them in the garden and they were still out there talking when I went to bed. When I got up yesterday, they and Candour had already gone somewhere and by the time I got back from dinner at my aunt's, everyone was in bed. This morning they were already up and gone again. I can't say I blame them, they have a lot to talk about and they'll get no privacy here, no matter how hard my mum tries to contain herself. I'm sorry you were so inundated yesterday, I helped some of the people who came here to see Jack, but there were some I knew wouldn't be able to accept help from me, so I sent them on to see you.'

Vickery said, 'Don't worry, I got through them all eventually, but I really do need to get Verve out for a ride today, he's going stir crazy at Holly's.'

'If you fancy some company, Infinity and I could come with you both?'

'We'll only be here another day or so though, what about all the people who want help?' Vickery said.

'We'll only be here for a few more days, but I have a feeling that Jack may well be here a good while longer. I think there'll be plenty of time for everyone to get the help they want.'

'You think he'll stay longer and catch us up? That won't be easy, I mean we don't exactly move slowly, do we? Oh, hang on. You think he's going to stay here? With Katonia?'

I nodded. 'I don't see another choice for them. Katonia can't come with us, she'd never keep up on foot and it's not her... I mean it wouldn't be the right thing for her anyway. You can help as many people to multiskill as you can as we pass through the villages, and we'll spread the word that Jack is in Rockwood and will help anyone who travels to see him there. He could also do trips out to the surrounding villages.'

Vickery nodded slowly. 'I guess that would work.'

'Are you okay? About Jack staying here, I mean?'

'I'll miss him like fury, I'm not going to pretend otherwise, and going to find the Kindred will feel a whole lot scarier without him and Candour there. No, I'm not even remotely okay about it, but don't breathe a word of that to him,' Vickery said, and sighed. 'I think I'll just go on that ride with Verve, he's what I need right now. You and Infinity are welcome to come along, but I can't promise I'll be much company.'

'That's okay, you'll be looking at Fin's tail in the distance most of the time, anyway,' I said with a wink.

A glint appeared in Vickery's eye. 'Fighting talk, eh, we'll see about that. Infinity may be able to summon an impossible amount of power in that hind end of hers, but Verve's improving all the time, in fact he got very excited about the amount of lift and connection he achieved just before we arrived in Rockwood – it may not be too long before Infinity's breathing his dust.'

That is unlikely, Infinity noted.

I laughed. 'Not if she's got anything to do with it!'

I woke up suddenly and sat bolt upright in my bed, my heart racing. I felt for Infinity and found her grazing contentedly in the moonlight. Instantly, I calmed.

You had a dream that was not a dream, Infinity informed me.

Yes, it was like the one I had when I first dreamt about you, and the ones after that when I could see where you were and I knew what you were doing. Only this one was about the Kindred Elder.

You are in her thoughts. She is curious about you.

I thought through what I had just dreamt. *And about you. When the young Kindred found us, the other horses were all terrified, yet you chose not to feel fear and you helped me to convince her that we wanted to be friends. The Elder witnessed it as she rode within the young Kindred's mind. She knows what she felt from us and from the others, but she can't believe it, she won't let herself believe that we're sincere. And then she remembers who I was to her and she wants to hope. I could have known all of that any time I wanted to if I'd given any time to being Aware of her, I've just had so much to think about since we arrived in Rockwood.*

This she knows.

She's Aware, I agreed. *She reached me while I was asleep because she knew I have too much on my mind at the moment while I'm awake.*

I felt a warmth towards the Kindred Elder as I realised that she could have come crashing into my mind at any time of her choosing, yet had chosen to nudge my mind in the gentlest of ways, letting me know of her interest in me, her curiosity and her concerns in the least intrusive way that she could. She was more used to being Aware than I, I realised, and then remembered how the young Kindred had also placed her thoughts so gently into my mind, with such ease.

What do I do, Fin? Shall I try to communicate with her?

She will need time. Our mind will be open to her touch at any time and in any manner of her choosing. We will not recoil from her as she probes for the information she needs. But we will not attempt to return her contact unless she asks.

I relaxed as I felt my horse's wisdom permeate my being. *Agreed. It will be difficult not to reach for her, knowing who she is, but it's the only way she might learn to trust us.*

Who she was to you has relevance only with regard to the agreement you made. Do not be distracted by who she was and who you were.

Easier said than done, Fin.

It is something to which you will need to become accustomed. Now that you are Aware you will see connections between yourself and others that would previously have been invisible to you. They were invisible by your choice when you incarnated into a human body since your mind would not have been capable of comprehending so much information on so many levels. Now that you are Aware of these connections you must not allow them to become a distraction. View them merely as a point of interest and then revert your attention to the task before us.

And what about the connections I see between others? Like the one I saw between Katonia and Jack? Should I not have helped that to come to fruition?

Your interference was irrelevant.

I saw it immediately. *They would have met whether I brought Jack home or not. And I was so distracted by the connection I saw between them that my mind was too busy to register the Kindred Elder's interest. Okay, I understand. I'll try to focus on what's relevant to our mission.*

Do not try at all. Position yourself between being Aware and being present and then merely observe. The way forward will be obvious.

It's about finding my centre again – finding it and staying in it.

Whilst you are incarnate it always will be.

SIX

Celebration

*K*atonia and Jack were married before we left Rockwood. My mother was as hysterical about organising a wedding at such short notice as she was joyful at her daughter's engagement, but since Katonia insisted that she wouldn't get married without me as her bridesmaid, my mother calmed down and chose focused determination instead. The result was beautiful.

Everyone who could tree-sing, including many new to the Skill thanks to Jack's help, took shifts sitting in our paddock and singing two newly-planted rows of pink-blossomed cherry tree saplings to grow up and arch towards one another, forming a tunnel for Katonia and me to walk through to meet her husband-to-be.

The Earth-Singers, led by my brothers, moved earth in from surrounding fields to form a large horseshoe-shaped mound around the end of the pink-blossomed archway. Robbie and Con trusted no one but themselves to then lift sections of turf and sing them into place until they covered the mound, providing an enormous seating area upon which family and friends could position themselves to watch the ceremony.

The Metal-Singers provided ornate, twisted metal posts which were placed at intervals along the top of the mound and linked by ribbon, from which the Glass-Singers hung opaque baubles that they had sung in pastel colours, each one featuring the intertwined letters K, J and C – my sister had insisted that Candour's initial was included. Having had experience of Infinity's complete refusal to be involved in the personal affairs of humans, I wasn't sure whether Candour would necessarily appreciate the gesture, but I guessed that it would mean a lot to Jack. The Glass-Singers also provided open-fronted glass lanterns which were attached to each post. Scented candles, provided by the village Chandler, were placed in each lantern, to be lit once the wedding ceremony was complete; the flaming lanterns would symbolise the warmth and love of the new marriage.

The Carpenters laid down boarding for a dance floor within the grassy horseshoe and they erected a raised platform off to one side where the fiddlers could sit, safe from the frivolity of the dance floor.

The Tailors worked around the clock to make a beautiful white wedding gown, whose bodice was embroidered with Katonia's favourite flowers. They made a waistcoat for Jack in the same white cloth and a plain but beautifully cut and stitched gown for me in mauve – Katonia's favourite colour.

The village Baker provided the food for the wedding banquet with the help of many of our friends in order to get it all done in time, but my mother insisted that she and Aunt Jasmine would make the wedding cake – for which we were all grateful since once their work began, everyone else was left alone to do their own jobs in peace.

On the morning of the wedding, the Weather-Singers were up at dawn, singing up a forceful wind to blow away the clouds that threatened rain, until the weak rays of the morning sun shone down uninterrupted. Then, a gentle breeze was encouraged from the south, providing a warmth that complemented that provided by the sunshine.

Finally, everything was ready, although in the case of the wedding cake, only a few minutes before the wedding guests arrived. It was rushed outside by my father and brothers, and then there were excited shrieks as my mother and Aunt Jasmine hastened to wash icing from their hands and get changed, before racing out of the back door towards the paddock where everybody would be waiting for Katonia and me.

Katonia looked at me and blew out a slow, deep breath. She looked beautiful. Her brown hair was drawn back into an elegant pleat with a few tendrils hanging loose. She wore little makeup, just enough to accentuate the blue of her eyes and the red of her lips. Her gown followed the gentle curves of her slim body and the flowers with which it was embroidered matched those woven into a delicate circlet upon her head. A lump formed in my throat.

'Don't you dare,' whispered Katonia, drawing me into a hug. 'If you cry, I'll cry and then we'll both have Mum to answer to when I have eyeliner running down my face.'

I took a deep breath as I hugged her back. 'Come on then, our steeds await and we don't want to keep them or your groom waiting, although how we are both supposed to get on board in these dresses with no outside help is beyond me.'

We giggled as we linked arms and went out to the front of the cottage, where Infinity and Candour waited patiently. My breath caught in my throat at the sight of them. Candour wore a garland of white flowers to match Katonia's dress. His dapple-grey coat shone from the grooming Jack had given him and his mane and tail gleamed a bright white. His ears were pricked and his brown eyes sparkled with interest in Katonia as she approached him.

The sun's rays made the black patches of Infinity's coat glisten even as they bounced merrily off the white that was her main colouring. She wore a garland that matched the mauve of my dress and I couldn't suppress a grin at the slight wrinkling of her nose at fulfilling her agreement to wear flowers, some of which, to her, would have made for interesting browsing. I'd added insult to injury by plaiting the top of her tail and then inserting more mauve flowers into the plait. She looked beautiful though and my heart melted as her blue eyes watched my approach.

'Right, Kat, we'll get you on first. You're going to have to stand on the fence next to Candour and then throw your leg over his back as Jack showed you yesterday, while I hold your dress out of the way as best I can. Ready?'

At Katonia's nod, I gathered as much of her dress up as I could and threw it over my shoulder as I stood behind her, ready to give her a push up on to Candour's back if needed. My sister climbed on to the fence and mounted easily. She leant forward and stroked Candour's neck with obvious fondness. 'Thank you, Candour,' she said.

I arranged the long, full skirt of Katonia's dress over Candour's rump as my sister settled herself on his back. 'Thanks, Am,' she said, quietly.

I squeezed her leg and grinned up at her. 'You both look stunning. This is going to be the best entrance made by a bride in the whole of Rockwood's history.'

Katonia smiled. 'It is, isn't it, thanks to Candour and Infinity.'

'That's if I can get on her bareback by myself, in a dress,' I said, 'and I haven't ridden her without a saddle since the first time I ever sat on her, and that didn't exactly end well. Right, Fin, bear with me, apologies in advance if I make a mess of this.'

Infinity helpfully positioned herself alongside the garden fence while I climbed on top of it. I pulled the back of my skirt forward between my legs and then threw my leg over Infinity's back and sat astride her. Katonia roared with laughter as I almost slipped off of the other side.

'Okay, so maybe grooming her to the point of gleaming and then sitting on her in a slippery material wasn't the best idea,' I admitted, laughing as I repositioned myself. Infinity's ears flicked back and forth with slight uncertainty over the feel of my seatbones on her back, then she gathered herself together and moved alongside Candour. 'Ready?' I said.

Katonia nodded and Candour moved off to take Katonia along the route that Jack had shown him the previous day, with Infinity to his side and slightly behind.

'How wonderful is this, having the most beautiful horse take me to my wedding? Candour, thank you so much,' Katonia said, leaning forward to rub Candour's neck as the horses walked to the end of our row of cottages and then turned down a pathway to the gardens and paddocks behind. She sat very naturally upon his back and I noted that she would probably have taken to riding far more quickly than I did, had she had cause.

It felt very strange to be riding saddleless and bridleless, but I was pleased to find that although Infinity definitely preferred the feel of a saddle on her back to that of my bony backside, we didn't miss the bridle at all; she no longer needed it as the fail-safe it had once been for her. If it weren't for the fact that I was trying not to slide off her back due to the slippery material of my dress, I would have thoroughly enjoyed the ride through our neighbours' paddocks until we reached those of Nixonhouse.

There was a collective gasp as the wedding guests turned to watch our arrival. Candour and Infinity took us to the far end of the blossomed archway, and then walked slowly, majestically, through it until we reached Jack where he stood, beaming, with my parents and brothers. Jack rubbed Candour's face and then helped Katonia down from his horse's back, while I slid as gracefully as I could manage down from Infinity and then attempted to smooth my dress into some semblance of decorum.

Never again, Fin, that's the last time I EVER wear a dress, I told her.

And the last time you hang herbs around my neck, she replied.

Agreed.

Before we knew it, my family and I had all embraced Jack to welcome him into our family, Jack and Katonia had spoken their vows and exchanged the wedding bracelets that they had designed for one another, and my mother had wept into and soaked through three handkerchiefs. At a raised hand from my father, the lanterns were lit and the celebrations began.

Infinity and Candour, who had stood patiently through the ceremony, cantered away from the party and jumped the fence into a neighbouring paddock, where they proceeded to buck and leap around joyfully. I saw Infinity's garland fly off into the air and I laughed as I saw her circle back to it and proceed to munch on some of its content before joining Candour in galloping another circuit of the paddock.

I sighed. My friends and I would miss Candour and Jack immensely and I knew that they would miss us. They were needed here though, with my sister and all of those who needed Jack's help to multiskill, not to mention his and Candour's counsel during this time of change.

'Enough of those solemn thoughts you're thinking,' said Marvel in my ear, 'it's time to dance.' He held his hand out to me as the fiddlers launched into a frantic tune. I grinned as I took it and followed him to the dance floor where Rowena was already wheeling around delightedly with my father, and my mother was being sedately and respectfully manoeuvred around by Aleks.

Before I knew it, I was being whirled around like a grain of sand in a sandstorm, with no idea where on the dance floor I was, or how it was that I didn't crash into anyone else. When Marvel finally released me, gasping, I was so dizzy that I staggered into Katonia, became entangled in her dress and then fell to the ground, pulling her down with me.

The laughter that broke out around us nearly drowned out my mother's shrieks of horror, but not quite. I was lifted to my feet by a very apologetic Marvel, and Jack was there in a flash to help my sister regain her footing and brush the dirt from her dress.

'Elegance isn't really your thing, is it, Am?' said Rowena from nearby, tears of laughter rolling down her cheeks. 'It's hard to fathom that you and your sister are even distantly related.'

'Well, Marvel was just saying that you're next on his list, so let's see what you can do,' I retorted, chuckling. Under my breath, I said to Marvel, 'Go on, give her your best and if she's still standing by the end of it, there'll be no beer for you.'

The celebrations carried on well into the night. The dancing was interrupted only briefly by Jack and Katonia cutting their wedding cake and then each making a brief speech. Katonia began by thanking everyone for all of their efforts in helping to make the wedding possible at such short notice, and then thanked everyone for attending. She went on to speak of how one of the saddest moments of her life – when I went missing after Infinity tugged me – had resulted in one of the happiest; meeting Jack when I brought him to our family home. Jack glanced over at me and winked and I grinned back at him with affection. His talent for delivering truth in an easily receivable way, combined with his sensitivity, made him a formidable force for the good of everyone. He was the perfect match for my sister.

When it was Jack's turn to speak, he put an arm around Katonia and gently pulled her close as he thanked my family for giving him such a warm welcome. His own family members had either passed on or scattered to various villages and he had never expected to belong to another family aside from that offered by the companionship of the Horse-Bonded at The Gathering, where he confessed to now feeling uncomfortable for any length of time due to his past mistakes. My brothers shouted out that he had no idea what he was letting himself in for in becoming part of our family, until my mother swatted them both and told them, with a smile, to be quiet.

Jack then spoke of his and Katonia's plans to settle in Rockwood and provide a permanent place of help for anyone wanting help to multiskill or receive Candour's counsel. He echoed my own observation that the world of humans was changing quickly and that he and Candour would help in any way they could, with Katonia's assistance. He spoke of the ease with which his new wife had opened to her knowledge of being able to multiskill and nobody could miss the pride in his voice as he assured everyone that it wouldn't be long before she would be his partner in his work as well as in his life.

When the speeches were over to loud cheering and applause, and the dancing had resumed, I climbed the grassy horseshoe and sat down to lean upon one of the lantern posts, enjoying the scent of lavender from the candle flaming above my head as I watched the celebrations going on below. I could see Katonia and Jack dancing cheek to cheek, her brown hair contrasting against the bright blond of his and I missed Justin acutely, all of a sudden.

I'm right here, Justin spoke in my mind.

Sorry, I didn't mean to disturb you, I replied.

From what? Lying awake, picturing all the dancing and hilarity going on there without me?

I thought you'd have been asleep ages ago, it's late.

It's hard to sleep when you're not where you want to be. How's it all gone?

It was beautiful. Jack and Katonia are so happy they could burst, that's if Mum doesn't burst first, and the party's still going with a swing, literally in Marvel's case – he's had me, Katonia and Rowena on the ground so far with his exuberance and by the look of things, my aunt might be next.

I could feel Justin's amusement. *And you're off tomorrow?* he asked.

If it's past midnight now, then yes. We'll recover today, get a good night's sleep and then leave tomorrow at dawn.

Have you had any further contact with the Kindred Elder? Justin was immediately Aware of the answer to his question. *Hmmm, she's checking in with you from time to time and observing, but still making no attempt to communicate. Interesting.*

She knows I'm Aware of her whenever her mind touches mine but I'm following Fin's advice and allowing the contact without reciprocating, I explained.

I felt Justin's understanding and approval just as Katonia's voice said beside me, 'From all the muttering, I take it that you're talking to Justin?'

'Well hi there, sister of mine, wife of Jack's, mother of Mum's future grandchildren, how're you doing?' I grinned up at my sister.

Katonia plopped down on the ground beside me and put her arm around my shoulders. 'I'm doing just fine. Say hello to that man of yours and tell him we wish he was here.'

'He knows.'

'And does he have any suggestions as to how you can get me to hear you when you're trying to reach me through my mind?' Katonia said.

It must be the same as when horses tug their Bond-Partners, Justin suggested.

I nodded, thoughtfully.

'Is that a yes? Oh, please say it is, I can't bear the thought of you going off to find the Kindred and me not knowing what's happening to you,' said Katonia.

Infinity, can you help? How do horses reach their humans for the first time when they tug them? I asked.

In the same way that we communicate now. It can take many attempts, she informed me.

But Katonia's sensitive, surely it should be as easy for me to reach her as it was for you to reach me?

You had already carved a pathway between our minds by your reachings for me when you could sense me and by your imaginings when you could not.

My imaginings? They helped you to reach me more easily?

Imagination is thought. It is of interest that humans think imagination to be removed from reality when indeed reality is a dream and therefore of the imagination.

I could almost see Justin sitting up in bed, nodding in amused wonder at Infinity's musings, and I giggled.

At my sister's raised eyebrows, I said, 'Kat, try to use your imagination. Imagine I'm there in your mind with you, imagine that you can hear me in your mind as easily as you hear your own thoughts. Imagine that I'm there and know that you can hear me, and that might stop you blocking me.'

Katonia was nodding and smiling, thoughtfully. 'Okay, I'll try it.'

'Don't try it, do it. That's what Infinity's always said to me and she's always been right. Do it. Okay?'

Katonia hugged me. 'I'll do it. And in the meantime, I want you to look into my mind at any time you want to know what's going on here, you have my permission, okay?'

'I'm not sure that's something that's really...' I began.

'Please, Am, I'll do everything you say to make sure I can hear you as soon as possible, but in the meantime, I want to know that you can at least draw comfort from knowing what we're all up to here. Jack's told me everything about the Woeful attack on The Gathering and all that happened afterwards, so I know that when you told us about it, you glossed over just how terrible it was for you. Jack's also been honest, as only he can, about exactly what is in front of you. He feels awful that he's not coming with you to help and I feel dreadful that I'm the cause of him staying here, so please, let me give you the little comfort that I can?'

I nodded. 'Okay, thanks. But honestly, neither of you should feel bad that Jack's staying here, in fact I'm glad he is, because Candour will know what we're up to and can tell Jack, so you'll know we're alright. Be warned though, you'll only be told what Candour decides is relevant and that will usually be a good deal less than you'll want to know. But as Infinity used to have to constantly remind me, everything happens as it should.'

I'll remind you of that when Aleks is driving you all mad without Jack to keep him in line, Justin teased.

Go to sleep. You have students to teach today, I reminded him.

I do. Tell everyone I said hi. And rest easy until you leave, Am, because then it all begins.

Yes, I replied. *Then it all begins.*

'Then it all begins,' repeated Katonia, squeezing my hand tightly.

SEVEN

Attraction

*A*ll of my family insisted on seeing my friends and me off on our journey, despite the fact that the sun was only just beginning to rise over the woodland to the east. Jack ensured that my departure was as painless as possible by radiating a gentle light that settled amongst my family, calming the building emotion.

I hugged my brothers goodbye, and then my father, who whispered, 'You'll always be my little girl, no matter where you are or what you do. Take care and come back to us soon. I love you.'

'I love you too, Dad,' I said as I released him.

As I reached my mother, Jack strengthened his light flow towards her. Tears streamed down her face, but she was calm as she held her arms out to me. 'I wish you could all have stayed longer,' she said as she held me close, 'but I know you have to go. Thank you for bringing Jack to us. Come back soon and in the meantime, stay safe, promise me?'

'I'm always safe, Mum, don't worry about me. And I'll be back before you know it.'

My mother released me and I gave her a kiss on her cheek before moving on to hug my new brother-in-law. 'We'll miss you and Candour loads,' I told him.

'We'll both miss you all too.' He lowered his voice. 'I'm sorry, Am, you're going into danger and Candour and I won't be there to help. You and Infinity are a force to be reckoned with though, and you've got this motley crew behind you,' Jack gestured towards our friends and Vickery stuck her tongue out at him, 'so you'll be fine. And don't worry, I'll look after everything here.' His eyes flicked to my mother.

I squeezed his arm in thanks and moved on to where my sister waited for me. She flung her arms around me and whispered, 'I'll imagine you're in my mind every chance I get, so you make sure you try to reach me every single night, do you hear me?'

'Loud and clear,' I said, 'and get Jack to teach you how to radiate your light, and then teach everyone else to do it, okay? It'll help you all to help Mum, and each other.'

'Will do. Now you promise you'll take care of yourself? And you'll search my mind whenever you want to know what's happening here?'

'Yes, to both. Go back to bed, you and Dad have got your and Jack's new cottage to start building in a few hours and you'll need all of your strength.'

I mounted Infinity, whose bridle was now stored in one of my saddlebags, and then my friends and I waved our final farewells to my family.

Holly and Serene appeared next to Infinity and me. 'Are you alright, Am?' Holly said, keeping her place easily as Serene shied in response to Infinity's protest that she was too close.

'I'm great, thanks, I'm happy we're on our way. I'm glad you decided to come with us, was your mum okay about it?'

'She'd have preferred me to have stayed longer, she always does, but she's used to me coming and going now. As far as she knows, this is just another ordinary trip around the villages,' Holly replied. 'Talking of which, where are we actually going?'

'Vic told you about the Kindred we met on the way here?'

'Yes, and about the Elder who was with her in her mind, if I understood correctly?'

'You did. Well the Kindred Elder is Aware of me and Infinity as a result of that meeting, and she's curious. She reaches out and observes our mind, and in doing so, she's left a thread back to her that I can easily follow. I have a sense of where she is and that's the direction we'll travel in, stopping off for a day or two to help in any villages we come across, until we find her.'

'Because you think she'll accept you?'

'Because there's a chance she might, if I live up to being the person I agreed to be.'

Holly frowned. 'This is one of those things that I'm not going to understand until it unfolds in front of me, isn't it?'

I let out a sigh of relief and grinned. 'It's good to be back amongst you guys.'

Holly chuckled. 'This was your first trip back to the realms of non-bonded people since you bonded with Infinity, wasn't it?'

I nodded.

'You'll find it's the same every time. At first, all you feel is happiness at being back with your family. Then you notice them looking at you strangely and you realise how much you've changed since your last visit home – in your case, that would have been far more than most, Am. Then you feel as if you don't belong in your family anymore and you watch what you say so that you don't have to explain everything you say, and then just as you're getting used to that, you leave and you're back with other Horse-Bonded or just on your own with your horse again, and all you can feel is relief that things are suddenly a whole lot easier. Ring any bells?'

'That's it exactly. Flaming lanterns, how's Jack going to manage, now he's there for good?'

'By being Jack. He'll say it like it is and by the time we get back to Rockwood, we'll find a village of multiskilling, light-emitting non-bonded who'll be so used to not knowing what's coming next that they'll just accept our weirdness as part of the norm.'

We both laughed.

～

Infinity and I settled back into leading our group over the days that followed, as I once again practised being Aware whilst remaining present in my physical surroundings. I rarely lost the sense of the Kindred Elder that I was following, even whilst holding conversations with my friends, coaching them as they rode their horses, and performing all of the daily tasks necessary while travelling. Sifting through all of the other things of which I was Aware whilst maintaining focus in the physical was harder, however, as the constant distraction of assessing whether they were worthy of more attention was tiring, but I was improving.

One morning, I found that I could hold a conversation with Justin without muttering, though my lips still moved to the words that my mind thought to him.

'Branching out into silent muttering now, Am? Aleks will be pleased,' Rowena said with a grin as she dried the last breakfast plate and handed it to me to pack into my saddlebag.

'Don't knock progress when you see it, you've no idea how much effort it's taking,' I retorted.

Well, I know, and I'm almost sweating in sympathy, Justin teased. *Hello, is that who I think it is?*

I paused from doing the buckles up on my saddlebag as I too became Aware of a familiar essence. Several of the horses whickered nervously. Justin made himself small in my mind.

'Our friend in the tree is nearby,' I said.

'I don't sense her,' Rowena replied.

'She's not close enough to stare at you but I'm Aware of her and so are the horses.' I raised my voice. 'Everyone, listen up, send light to your horses because our friend in the tree is nearby. She isn't hunting the horses, but they know she's there so we need to help them to stay calm like before.'

Rowena immediately sent a flow of light to where Aleks sat open-mouthed in horror by the campfire, and then extended the flow past him to settle around Nexus. 'I'll sort Aleks and Nexus again, and I'll keep an eye on Holly and Serene, as they weren't with us last time,' she said.

Sonja appeared from the other side of Bright with a hair-covered brush in her hand. 'Do you want my light supporting yours again, Am?'

'No thanks, I think Infinity and I'll be alright this time. Please could you add your light to Rowena's, to help Aleks and Nexus, and Holly and Serene if they need it?'

Sonja's light immediately joined Rowena's by way of reply.

I felt Infinity's nurturing warmth spreading out from her towards our friend in the tree and I sent a gentle flow of light along with it. As it touched our friend, I felt her anxiety fade away to be replaced by relief and a small measure of hope. She'd had little success hunting in the past few days and she was hungry again. She was feeling despondent at her lack of hunting prowess, something she had known may be her downfall when she undertook the challenge to survive by herself, yet still she had made the decision not to hunt our horses, easy prey as they would have been in the dense forestry in which we had camped for the night.

I sent gentle thoughts to our friend. *We are Infinity. We would not see you go hungry, we have food we are happy to share with you. We are just packing up to leave and we will leave food and our campfire behind us when we go.*

I felt our friend's gratitude. Then, knowing that her immediate problem had a solution, she turned her attention towards Infinity. Try as she might, she couldn't understand how my horse was choosing to completely disregard the instinctive fear of her species and send love and reassurance to a potential predator. She admired Infinity's courage and strength. As her attention shifted back to me, I continued to send a gentle light flow in her direction and invited her to touch my mind with her own, to begin to know more of me.

Then I was Aware of the Kindred Elder joining us, but not via our friend in the tree – this time she observed the proceedings through her connection with me. I felt our friend recoil in shock as she became Aware of her Elder observing us in this way, and I increased my flow of light towards her.

The young Kindred calmed. She was tempted to ask the Elder whether or not to accept my invitation, but something powerful held her from doing so; she knew she must decide for herself. I felt her considering. Then, she touched my mind with the intention of taking up my invitation. She and I both felt the Elder's approval and then the Elder was gone.

Our friend was pleased with herself but then I felt her slight discomfort at Infinity's and my involvement in, and observation of, her Elder's scrutiny.

'Everyone, our friend needs some space from us, so we need to be gone,' I called out urgently and my friends responded by increasing the pace with which they had already begun clearing our camp and getting their horses ready to leave.

Minutes later, we were all mounted and making our way through the forest, having left a pile of food by our campfire. My friends all cocooned us in light, including Holly, whose flow was strong, and Aleks, who was managing to contribute a steady stream, albeit not as strong as the rest. As a result of everyone having been able to combine their flows with the same intention, the horses were all calm and coping much better with the Kindred's proximity than during our previous encounter.

I was Aware that our friend waited until we were some distance away before approaching the campsite and falling on the food we had left for her, so that she wouldn't cause our horses any undue distress. I was grateful for her consideration and felt the beginnings of a mutual trust and understanding forming between us.

It is fragile but it is a beginning, agreed Infinity.

And her Elder is observing the proceedings, so hopefully she's beginning to trust us too.

We are not the only ones under her scrutiny, observed Infinity.

No, our friend in the tree seems to be of more interest to her as well now, I agreed.

It's a bit of a web you seem to be tangling yourselves in, isn't it, observed Justin. *It feels right though. Take care, Am.* And he was gone.

'Did you pick up any of what just happened?' I asked my companions.

It became apparent that our friend in the tree hadn't been close enough for my friends to have picked up any information from her, so I told them all that had transpired.

'Fitt,' said Aleks.

'Huh?' I said.

'Fitt. Friend. In. The. Tree. If she hasn't told you her name, we should call her Fitt, for now. I think it's obvious that we'll be seeing more of her now she knows we'll feed her.'

'We're not feeding her, Aleks, we're leaving food for her and there's a world of difference between the two,' said Rowena.

'Which is?' Aleks said.

'It would probably help you if you took the time to figure it out for yourself,' said Marvel.

'I second that,' said Vickery. 'What do you think is going on between our friend and her Elder, Am?'

'Our friend is a young Kindred, trying to fulfil a challenge to survive on her own. It seems to be important to her to make her own decisions and the Elder was observing her resolve to do that. And there's more to it; the Elder is particularly interested in decisions that our friend in the tree – sorry, Aleks, that Fitt – makes with regard to us,' I replied.

Marvel whistled. 'It hasn't taken us long, has it? I thought we'd be travelling for months before things began to happen that might point us in some sort of direction, but we only left The Gathering a matter of weeks ago and we already know who we need to find and where we need to go, and now we seem to be finding ourselves in the thick of relationships between the Kindred, whose name is rolling off my tongue as if it's what we've always called them.'

'Have you really not got hold of the fact that this is what happens when you spend any time around Amarilla and Infinity, Marvel?' Rowena said. 'In case anyone else has missed it as well, this is the reality of being part of Am and Fin's mission to change life as we know it. It's like being in a vortex and if you're not strong enough to stay in the centre of it with the two of them, you'll be spat out as Feryl was, and as Justin and I almost were. Is anyone else just realising what they've let themselves in for? Because if so, and if you think you mightn't be strong enough to hang in there with us through what's coming, then you'd be better off speaking up and leaving now, because the vortex is gathering strength and staying within it isn't going to be easy. Trust me, I know.'

There was silence as my friends looked at each other, and then finally, at me.

'I've never thought about it like that before, but I guess Rowena does have a point,' I said. 'Does anyone want to leave? Your horses will easily find the way back to Rockwood.'

Marvel, Sonja, Vickery and Holly all shook their heads immediately and Rowena rolled her eyes at me for even looking to her for an answer. I was Aware of the battle going on within Aleks, but finally he shook his head.

'Onwards we go then,' said Marvel. 'Am, lead the way. Ro, nice speech, very stirring. We were just about due for one of your classics and I for one wasn't disapp...' He ducked as Rowena tried to flick his ear and we all dissolved into laughter.

'Helloooooooooo, earth calling Amarilla,' Vickery said loudly and not without a little impatience.

My attention was wrenched away from the essence I had sensed for the fourth time in only a few days, and back to the conversation I'd been having before I was distracted. 'Curse the clouds, sorry, Vic, and I've been doing so well recently, too.'

'Is Fitt back with us again?' Vickery asked.

'No, it's someone else, someone I've been Aware of before. It's weird though, each time I feel her, she immediately withdraws from me and I know she doesn't want my attention, but then after a while, I'm Aware of her again.'

'Is it another of the Kindred?' Vickery asked.

I shook my head. 'From the little I've been able to grasp, I think it's a horse, but not one like ours. And there's something wrong with her.'

'Should we go and find her?'

I shook my head again. 'I think she'll find us. Anyway, what were we talking about?'

'I was suggesting that we stop off at Jonustown, as we seem to be heading in that direction. I have family there and we could top up our supplies. You were agreeing with me but considering whether to suggest to Sonja and Aleks that you camp near the town with them to put more time into their training, while the rest of us do what we need to do in town. For what it's worth, I wouldn't want to be stuck camping with Aleks when he knows he could be sleeping in a soft bed.'

'Good point, but if it's his choice, then either way, he can't really moan,' I said.

'Want to bet?' she replied.

We were nearly at Jonustown when I was Aware of the same essence checking in with me again, this time with no effort made to hold me away from her, and with every intention that I would know of her proximity.

We will need to be careful. She is very frightened and her pain is great, Infinity observed as I gasped, almost overwhelmed by waves of terror and agony.

Immediately, I radiated light around myself, pushing the fear and pain away so that my mind could function. I held my hand up to warn my friends behind us as Infinity halted. I turned to my right, towards the source of the pain and emotion that had threatened to swamp me. In the distance, from behind some sparsely leaved bushes, peered a horse. She was the deep orange of the most beautiful sunset, with a white blaze on her delicate, pretty face and white socks on each of her extremely long legs. She rested her right hind awkwardly and as I tuned in to her body to see why, I was horrified at the wrongness that assaulted my mind.

Instantly, I saw her grazing peacefully with the rest of her herd in a patch of rich pastureland, surrounded on all sides by trees. I felt their collective fear as they sensed the presence of a Kindred and then they were off, nostrils flaring and muscles firing urgently as they galloped away from the predator. The Kindred swung easily through the trees and just as the chestnut mare reached the woodland at the far end of the pasture, the Kindred launched himself through the air and landed with his upper torso on her rump. Her scream only added to the terror of the herd, all of whom continued their flight. Just before she hit the ground, the mare kicked out behind her with both hind legs. The Kindred grunted and his hold on her rump loosened. She kicked out again once she was on the ground and the Kindred's talons retreated.

Her relief from the searing agony of the Kindred's talons in her flesh was short-lived; as she launched herself to her feet, they sank back into her, this time embedding themselves in her right hind leg. She screamed again and tried to run but the Kindred held on fast. Her leg was wrenched out behind and to the side of her, terribly, agonisingly. In an attempt that she knew would be her last to free herself, she lashed out with her left hind leg, managing to land back on it before her hind end went down again. There was a grunt and a total release from the talons that had been embedded in her leg, and she felt the Kindred's soul release its hold on his body as blood pumped from his head onto the ground. Fleetingly, she was aware of her soul feeling its oneness with the soul of the Kindred before her physical instincts took over and she tried to flee the site of her ordeal. But her right hind leg wouldn't do what it should. It didn't feel as if it was in the same place as it had been – nothing in her hind end did – and agony ripped through her every time she tried and failed to make it take a forward step. My mouth opened as my own scream welled up inside of me.

Infinity wrapped herself around my mind and brought me back to the present. I gasped as she let me go and I came back to myself. *More practise is needed at remaining centred*, I was informed.

Sorry, Fin. Her ordeal was so like yours that I couldn't help getting lost in what happened to her.

You are in no position to help anyone if you allow your Awareness of them to affect you. You are either centred with your Awareness in balance with your physicality or you are not. At present you are not.

Justin's presence came crashing into my mind. He quickly grasped what was happening and to my relief, quietened his presence so as to give me space to think.

I took a deep breath and turned to my friends, all of whom were watching me in consternation. 'Sorry about that. If you look slightly to your right, you'll see a horse trying to hide behind those bushes. She's injured and in terrible pain and I'm trying to get a hold of myself so I can think straight without being distracted by everything I can feel from her.'

'I see her. Take your time, Am, and let us know if we can help,' said Holly.

I nodded. *She's come as close to us as she dares, but I could do with getting closer to her so I can see the condition of her external injuries. Will it be better if you come with me or if I go alone?* I asked Infinity.

She has been drawn to you by the light that you sent to the Kindred youngling. She wants to trust you but your similarity to the Kindred holds her back.

If I go to her alone, walking on two legs will reinforce my similarity to the Kindred. We'll go together, I decided.

I turned back to my friends. 'Fin and I are going to try to approach her,' I told them and then Infinity obliged me by walking forward and gently turning to the right on an arc, so as to approach the mare politely, from the side.

I saw the mare stiffen as she watched us. *She's very brave,* I observed. *She felt me sending light to Fitt, who is kin to the one who came close to killing her, and yet she's still dragged herself to find me, wanting to trust that I can help her.*

Love trusts love, observed Infinity.

Infinity exuded the assured, ageless love of the horses as she walked slowly towards the mare, who watched our approach with her ears flickering anxiously and her nostrils flaring. Oak, Broad, Nexus, Serene, Verve and Bright added their love to Infinity's and their gentle energy infused the chestnut mare, slowly and tenderly. I felt her relax a little as she continued to watch Infinity's and my approach. I felt her relief at the prospect of no longer being alone.

I radiated my own light and sent a very fine flow towards the mare. I was Aware that her desire to trust me and to have my help warred with her instinct to flee a being so like the one who had attacked her. I wasn't surprised when I felt my light being deflected by the barrier of fear that she held between herself and anything that wasn't horse. I felt uncertain. I could increase my light flow to full strength and bombard her with it until it penetrated her fear barrier, but she might find my contact overwhelming and try to flee.

If she is to accept your healing then she must first accept your love, Infinity counselled.

I increased my flow of light towards the mare and as she stiffened, I felt the horses begin to gently swirl their energy, moving it in currents as it wove its way into her being. She allowed herself to be lulled by the rhythm of their reassurance and so I increased my light flow even more. I felt her fear barrier begin to waver and immediately she panicked and reinforced it with memories of her ordeal and of the pain she had suffered. As Infinity and I reached the bush behind which she stood, I strengthened my light flow to full strength. It surged at her fear barrier, pushing at it and probing for areas of weakness through which it could reach her. All of a sudden, the barrier gave way. She was held fast by the love and support of Infinity and the other horses as she felt my light infuse her. As her body began to let go of the tension caused by the fear to which it had clung, she looked exhausted and for a moment I feared that she would collapse. I loved her with all of my being. I knew, I absolutely knew, that she would be alright now that she was with Infinity and me. And I felt the tiniest glimmer of hope from her as she allowed herself to begin to believe that might indeed be the case.

All of a sudden, I recognised the danger. As my light continued to permeate the mare and she gradually allowed herself to relax, everything that had driven her – her fear of being attacked again, her need to find food and water every day as she struggled on in the vain hope of finding her herd, and then her hope of finding me, of getting help once she'd sensed that I was near enough for our paths to converge – was being released and all that was left was a broken, pain-racked body that would soon be too much for her to bear. She needed healing, right now. She began to tremble. Her eyelids began to droop and she lowered her head.

I leapt from Infinity's back and called to my friends, 'I need your help.'

I rushed around the bush and got my first uninterrupted view of the mare's body. I had to breathe deeply and focus on maintaining my light flow to her until the shock that wanted to gain prominence in my mind subsided. The mare was desperately thin and her injuries were terrible. She had four inflamed, oozing gashes on each side of her rump, where her attacker's talons had sliced through flesh as he had tried to hold on to her. There were gashes on her right hind where he had grasped it, and the leg was twisted out from her at a sickening angle. Her whole hind end seemed odd in its positioning and as I began to tune into her body, I could feel that her pelvis had been cracked and then parts of it cruelly twisted when her attacker had pulled her leg out and away from her with such force. None of the muscles in her body were healthy, having been strained beyond measure in moving such a heavy, badly-damaged body. Dried blood was matted into her fur along with dirt and pus.

My friends' horses thundered to a halt nearby and suddenly all of my friends were at my side.

'Oh, no,' breathed Holly, as she took in the sight of the mare.

'Flaming lanterns, how is she even alive,' said Vickery.

'The poor, poor love,' said Sonja.

'Her legs are trembling and if they give way, she'll hurt herself even more,' said Marvel. 'We need to support her while we heal her enough for her to lie down safely. Aleks and Sonja, come and lean against her left side with me, the rest of you lean against her other side.'

We all moved quickly to obey Marvel's instructions and as Rowena took up her place leaning against the mare's right side behind me, I was Aware of her remembering how we had supported Infinity in the same way. 'Just like old times,' she muttered.

Marvel said, 'Okay, all of us except Aleks can multiskill, so, Aleks, can you watch her closely and let us know if you see anything that worries you, while we focus on the healing? Good man. Am, I think the mare will probably be most comfortable if you lead the healing, while the rest of us lend you our strength.'

I nodded. 'Okay, I'll start with her pelvis, are you all ready?'

Everyone murmured their assent, so I plunged in. I soon found the guttural, unpleasant tone that resonated with the discord of the broken pelvis and my friends quickly joined their voices with mine. I sent my intention along the pathway created by our voices to the fragments of bone, willing them to free themselves from the flesh in which they were embedded and reattach themselves to one another. I was glad of the strength of intention that my friends added to my own, since the shards of bone had been out of place for long enough that tissue had tried to heal over many of them, encasing them in place, and they weren't easily freed. I tried not to wince as one by one, the broken fragments burst free from the tissue in which they were implanted, and came together in their proper places.

Gradually, we changed our singing to a smoother, lighter tone in order to continue resonating with the pelvis as it healed. As soon as it was whole, I swapped from bone-singing to tissue-singing. My friends were only a split second behind me and soon our voices had paved the way for our healing intentions to reach the surrounding tissue and encourage it back to health. I noted briefly that the mare's pain had lessened a fraction, before I tuned in to the wounds on her rump. They were badly infected and would need poulticing, but I could feel healthy tissue deep down that we could encourage to knit together, to prevent the infection from spreading. When that was dealt with, I moved my attention to the flesh wounds on her leg, which were dealt with in the same manner as those on her rump. I made a note in my mind of the herbs I would need both to poultice all of her flesh wounds and to encourage their healing once they were clean.

I tuned into the internal mechanisms of her right hind leg next, and leaned into her further to steady myself from the shock. I heard someone vomiting behind me and felt the horses include us in the supportive energy that they were still giving to the mare.

'Sorry about that,' whispered Holly, spitting to clear her mouth. 'It's almost too much to bear.'

Vickery whistled between her teeth. 'How, by the wind of autumn, has she borne it for so long?'

'What is it?' asked Aleks.

'No time, we'll explain later,' Sonja told him.

'Is everyone alright, or do you need more time to steady yourselves?' I asked.

Everyone assured me that they were okay, so I turned my attention back to the hind leg. When the Kindred had grabbed hold of it and hung on with all of his might, he had wrenched a limb with limited lateral movement out to the side, with considerable force. Somehow, the hip was still in its socket but from there down to the cannon bone, the leg was a mess. There were few bones that weren't fractured or broken completely, many of which had begun to heal badly. The damage to the muscles, tendons and ligaments was too extensive to list. But it wasn't the extent of the damage that had unhinged us all – it was the pain that the mare was suffering as a result. I knew I wasn't the only one wondering at her strength and courage in bearing it for so long. I worried that she wouldn't be strong enough to cope with all of the healing that her body required.

Marvel and Holly were far more experienced Bone-Singers than I was. 'How much do you think we should do?' I asked them. 'She's so weak already, we could leave her without any strength to live if we try to heal all of it now.'

'I would heal all of the bones for now, and leave the muscles, ligaments and tendons. At least then we can help her to lie down without the bones splintering further, and once she's down and has rested, we can go to work on the tissues,' said Holly.

'I agree,' said Marvel. 'We have enough painkillers with us to help relieve her discomfort for a day or so, and with your and Vic's herbal knowledge, Am, you can both make more and teach the rest of us how in the process. Then, when she's had a break from all of the pain, we can work on the tissues, including those in the rest of her body. Her back muscles are strained, torn in places, and her pelvis won't be straight until we can encourage the tissues attached to it to pull it back into its proper alignment...'

Aleks whistled. 'How has she survived? How has she dragged herself around on three legs for weeks on end? And how, by the wind of autumn, has she endured the pain?'

As his questions settled in my mind, I knew their answers. 'She has something that she needs to do. She's fought to stay alive because there's something that's important enough to her to do, that dying without doing it would be worse to her than enduring all that she has.'

'Then we need to do everything we can to make sure she gets to do whatever it is,' said Rowena, fiercely.

'We do. We'll start at the top of the leg and work down, shall we? We're going to have to re-break the bones that have begun to heal – I hope she's strong enough. Aleks, please keep a close eye on her,' I said.

'Will do. At the moment, she looks as if she's unaware that any of us are even here, let alone what you're all doing to her.'

'That's what worries me, but we have no choice, we have to do this now,' I replied.

By the time we'd healed all of the mare's bones to our satisfaction, it was hard to say who was more exhausted. As time had gone on, the mare's trembling had increased, punctuated only by sharp jerks every time we managed to re-break the bones that had been healing wrongly. It was a strange thing for us, as Healers, to do – to use our voices to create a sound that resonated with bones that were healing, and then use the pathway created by the sound to send our intention to them to fracture, gradually adjusting our voices to sing in tones that were less pleasant in order to resonate with bones that were now broken. It was all back to front. It was necessary, though, and the discomfort we all felt at having to do it was quickly replaced with relief as we then sang the broken pieces of bone back to solid, healthy ones. At one point, Aleks had requested that we all lean in to the mare's trembling body with more force in order to keep her upright, and by the time we had finished bone-singing, all of our legs trembled as much as hers.

'Right, we're going to need to lower her to the ground on her left side,' said Marvel. 'That means that Aleks, Sonja and I will push less against her for a few seconds and you guys over the other side need to push a little more, so she begins to topple our way. When she does, you guys get round this side as fast as you can and help us take her weight, and we'll try to lower her to the ground with as little impact as possible. I know we're all exhausted, but she's managed to endure all that she has until she found us, so I think we can manage to follow her example and dig a bit deeper too. Any questions?'

'Yes,' panted Rowena. 'Can you do all the motivational speeches from now on?'

We all managed a breathless chuckle and then Marvel said, 'Now.'

Rowena, Holly, Vickery and I all pushed harder into the mare's side. My tired leg and back muscles screamed with the effort. As soon as we felt her begin to fall away from us, we rushed around to her left side, filling in the gaps between our friends who were straining against her, trying to brace her collapse. I found myself by her head just as her brown eyes snapped open with shock. I took her head in my arms and her right eye locked onto mine desperately.

I flooded her with light. *We've got you, you don't need to struggle alone anymore,* I told her. Some of the terror disappeared from her eye, but as we lowered her to the ground, she held my gaze searchingly. *You're safe, we'll look after you. Sleep now,* I told her.

Once her head rested on the ground, I knelt down by her chin and gently stroked the side of her face. There was movement behind me and Infinity's white legs appeared by my side. Oak, Broad and Verve moved to the mare's other side and all four horses lowered their heads as if to sleep. I felt their loving energy wend its way around and through the chestnut mare and knew that they would support her body as it healed. The mare slowly closed her eyes.

EIGHT

Flame

$\mathcal{V}$ickery and Aleks went on to Jonustown to see Vickery's relatives and to gather supplies. We estimated that we would need to camp where we were for at least a few weeks, so we would need more food for us, hay to supplement the horses' grazing, more blankets to replace those with which we had covered the injured mare, and herbal supplies; I'd used all of the poultice I had with me on the mare's wounds, and most of the painkillers, and although I could find many of the herbs I needed to make more, some of them could only be found in habitats other than the bushy scrub in which we found ourselves camping. At least there was a stream nearby, so clean water was plentiful.

The rest of us busied ourselves making a semi-permanent campsite near to where the chestnut mare slept. Sonja, Holly and I cleared the scrub from a large circle around our campfire and then we strung waterproof sheets up between bushes, under which we could store our gear and sleep. Marvel and Rowena gathered firewood from woodland a mile or so away, and Broad and Oak dragged it back to camp in bundles. They returned from one such foray dragging logs instead of firewood, which we arranged around the fire to sit upon.

Aleks and Nexus returned later that day, each dragging a litter loaded with supplies. They had left Vickery and Verve behind so that Vickery could help anyone wanting to multiskill. Aleks moaned that he'd thought he might get at least one night in a bed, but apparently Vickery had made him return to us immediately with the supplies. I had a feeling that it wasn't solely because she thought we had urgent need of them.

Our horses took turns supporting the injured mare and we took turns sitting with her. She stirred at times and rose up onto her elbows to drink small amounts of painkiller-laced water that we offered her from a bucket that Aleks had brought. Apart from that, she slept. I remembered that Infinity had been the same after she had been injured and then undergone a similar amount of healing. She had been healthy to begin with though, and this mare had been weak, thin and exhausted. Whenever I found myself worrying that the mare wouldn't be strong enough to survive, I focused on being Aware of her and feeling her strength of will, her resolution to do what she had chosen to do, and I remembered the counsel that Infinity had given me so often – *everything happens as it should.* And I knew, again, that she was right.

On the fourth day after her healing, the mare woke, drank water when I offered it to her and then let me know of her hunger. Immediately, I grabbed some hay from a pile nearby and put it on the ground by her front legs. She began to eat, a few wisps of hay at a time. Her eyes were dull, as was her coat, and her ribs protruded even more markedly than before. She was so tired of being afraid and in pain. I bathed her in light and felt her warm to me a little.

As soon as you're a bit stronger, we'll finish healing you and then you won't be in pain anymore. You'll feel a whole lot better, I told her but she made no attempt to reply to me.

She has no need, Infinity told me.

Immediately, I realised what she meant. *She knows that I'm Aware. She let me know she was hungry by...* How had she done it? I wondered, suddenly. She hadn't placed thoughts in my mind, yet I had suddenly known what she wanted me to know.

Enough humanity remains in you that you yet believe that everything that occurs is for your benefit, I was informed by Infinity.

So, she wasn't letting me know? She was letting all of us know? Me, you, the other horses, all of us who are Aware?

There is no all of us.

No, there's only one of us. We're all one. My mind was spinning as it hadn't for a while. I sighed. Just when I was beginning to believe that I was getting closer to understanding everything of which I was Aware, I was floundering.

Then do not flounder. You have surrendered to melodrama as a result of your fear that you must again question your current understandings and perceptions. Centre yourself. Much understanding can be gained as a result of this new question.

I calmed myself and began to sort things through in my mind. I was used to either direct communication from Infinity and the other bonded horses, or to just knowing how they felt by being Aware of them. The chestnut mare, however, appeared to have communicated her hunger to me using a combination of the two; she hadn't waited for me to notice her hunger in my Awareness, she had let me know of it, yet she hadn't communicated directly with me. Oneness. That was what it all came back to. Understanding flooded through me. The horses know of their oneness and therefore anything felt by one of them is felt by all of them, something of which I was now a part. Anything they want to highlight – as the chestnut mare had done when she needed her hunger to be addressed – is focused upon more strongly. All will know of it but only those who need to will recognise it as something to which they need to respond.

Bonded horses had all found a way to concentrate their thoughts in the way of humans, so as to reach the individuals to whom they would bond. It could take a long time, both for the horses to learn how to refine their thoughts enough from their natural state of oneness to those that their chosen human could recognise, and for the humans concerned to register that another mind touched theirs.

My musings led me onto the Kindred as I realised that Fitt, though like the horses was Aware and knew that I was too, communicated directly with me very easily. But hold on, the Kindred did more than that, didn't they? They also broadcast information about themselves to humans in their vicinity, whether they were Aware or not... The Kindred were different. They were animal enough to know of their oneness with all of life, with all of reality, but human enough that they formed focused thoughts as easily as we did. The combination of the two meant that the Kindred could reach us easily, and not just those of us whom the horses had managed to reach – they could reach all of us. As I made sense of everything I had felt from the Kindred in my Awareness, understanding began to form in my mind. The Kindred could help humanity to know of their oneness. To be Aware. And once that happened, there could never be a return to the ways of The Old.

My ponderings drew the attention of the Kindred Elder. I felt her gentle browsing of my thoughts and realisations. I felt the small bud of hope that she had carried within her since she had become Aware of me, burst open and begin to blossom. Then a flash of fear shot through her, followed by disbelief at her stupidity at allowing her hope to grow when her kind had hoped fruitlessly for so long. I almost reached out to her. Infinity was with me instantly, enfolding me in her warm, loving energy, distracting me momentarily, long enough to realise that my instinct to reassure the Elder was unwise. The Elder's attention was with me for a few moments longer and then was gone.

JUSTIN!! I crashed into his mind excitedly.

Flaming lanterns, Am, I may as well just have come with you for all the time I'm getting to concentrate on teaching at the moment. I've only just got over everything that happened with the Kindred and the chestnut mare – how is she, by the way? Is that what you're excited about?

See for yourself.

Justin's question drew my experience into his Awareness and he witnessed it all for himself. *Well, that's just flaming well awesome,* he told me. *I'm so glad we put ourselves through finding perfect balance in order to know of our oneness and be Aware, when we could have just asked a Kindred to sort it for us.*

I grinned. *I don't think it's going to be that simple though. The fact that we both became Aware as a result of finding perfect balance meant that it was easy for us to accept that the truth of reality isn't what we thought it was – we became one with our horses and so it wasn't a shock to then feel at one with everything else. For people becoming Aware as a result of help from the Kindred, it will be a huge shock to suddenly feel their oneness with everything and have their idea of reality turned upside down. They'll probably block themselves from knowing what it is they can feel, and that's all assuming they will accept assistance from the Kindred to do it in the first place – which in turn is assuming we can even persuade the Kindred to provide that assistance. Our horses helped us to be in a position to accept the truth and the Kindred can help the rest of humanity, but it will take time. Our job for now is to create a situation where it's all possible – you and Quinta by teaching more of the Bonded until they achieve perfect balance and become Aware, and me by reaching out to the Kindred. The more of the Horse-Bonded who are Aware and can back up whatever assistance the Kindred can give, if I can ever persuade them to give it, the better.*

I could almost hear Justin's sigh as he replied, *I almost thought I had a case for joining you then, almost, I was so close...*

You'd never catch us up.

Honestly? You really believe that, knowing what Gas is like when he has an idea in his head? And unlike you guys, we wouldn't be diverting via Rockwood. In terms of the speed and determination Gas can muster, you're really not that far in front of us, Am.

You've given this some thought, I observed.

Yes, oddly, since I don't get much time for my own thoughts these days with all of your adventures invading my mind, he retorted.

Sorry, Jus, I know how hard it is for you, being stuck there.

You'll get to make it up to me some day, now leave me be, I'm getting odd looks from my students again.

I grinned as I transferred more hay from the large store pile to the area by the chestnut mare's legs, pleased to see that, slowly but surely, she was eating her way through a respectable amount. I couldn't keep thinking of her as the chestnut mare, I decided, but I didn't know how to choose a name for her, or whether she would even want one. She wouldn't communicate with me in the way that Infinity did but I supposed I could choose a name for her that matched what I felt from her. What should I call her? She had a massive inner strength and she was resolute about fulfilling her goal, but the overriding feeling I got from her was that of warmth; she was a mare with a huge heart. A word came into my mind and as I focused on it, I felt the mare's warmth more strongly. Flame. That was what I would call her, for her warmth and her colouring. She may have no need for a name for herself, but I knew it was the right word for me to use for her. She pricked her ears and turned her dull eyes towards me and I thought I saw a flicker of something there.

Flame ate and drank more and more over the following days, with the result that my friends and I were needed to support her periodically as she heaved herself painfully, heart-wrenchingly, to her feet in order to urinate and clear her bowels. We leant into her, three on each side, as soon as she was up and once she had relieved herself, we walked next to her, still leaning into her, until she found a clean patch in which to lie back down.

Hard as it was to see her struggle so much, we all noticed the increase in her strength as the days passed and finally, ten days after we had performed the initial healing, we felt that she had the reserves to cope with having her tissues healed.

I was Aware of her keenness for us to perform the healing as soon as possible, but I also felt her concern that she may never return to the fit, strong, sound horse she had been; her injuries had worn away her confidence in her body. She had five strong Healers who would be joining their strength and their intention for her body's tissues to return to full health, and she had built up strength in her body to fuel the healing, but I, of all people, knew that healing wasn't just a physical process. We would do everything we could for Flame, but some of her healing, very possibly a large part, would be down to her.

'It's good to see that she's free from infection now,' Sonja said, crouching down by Flame's rump, having just cleaned the last of the poultice away. 'She's ready for your healing unguent now, Amarilla, and then these wounds will heal over in no time. Thanks,' she added as I handed her the pot. The green paste was smeared into all of Flame's wounds as she lay, dully, waiting for us to begin healing her internal tissues.

'You lead the healing again, Am,' said Holly. 'And, Aleks, she isn't in as much danger as last time, but it would still be a help if you could watch her closely and let us know if you see anything that worries you at any time.'

'It'd be even more help if he'd knuckle down and let someone help him to multiskill so he could give us his strength,' muttered Rowena and then glared at Marvel for nudging her to be quiet.

Our horses stood side by side along the length of Flame's back, lending their subtle assurance and strength to us all.

'Everyone ready?' I asked. At my friends' nods, I said, 'Okay then, we'll start at the muscles in her neck and work towards her tail.'

After a few hours, we had healed all of the damaged tissues as far as Flame's pelvis. I was Aware that Flame had fear attached to the injuries in her rear end due to them being the direct and immediate results of her attack, and it was very possible that they wouldn't be easy to heal. We were tired, and I thought that food and rest were needed before we attempted to heal the tissues that held the pelvis in place and then encourage them to tension correctly, so as to pull the pelvis into its proper alignment.

'Shall we stop for lunch?' I suggested.

Everyone nodded wearily, and all of the horses but Oak and Infinity drifted off to graze nearby. Flame closed her eyes and went to sleep. I could feel her drifting off into an easier sleep than of late and I was glad that we had managed to lessen her pain so much already.

Will the other horses come back to give you and Oak a break, Fin? I asked her.

They will or they will not.

I put a pile of hay next to Infinity, Oak and Flame and placed the water bucket within easy reach of all of them. Then I went to join the others for lunch around the campfire.

None of us who had taken part in the healing spoke much. We just wanted to eat, rest our minds and recharge. Aleks, on the other hand, couldn't seem to stop talking. He wondered out loud how Vickery was getting on, asking if we thought he should go to check on her and pick up more supplies at the same time, and making a case for him and Nexus being able to stay there for a night or two this time. He went on and on until Rowena threw one of Oak's brushes at him. He glared at her and then, blessedly, was quiet.

When Flame woke and heaved herself up to rest on her elbows, and the grazing horses took up their places around her once more, we knew that it was time to resume healing. Aleks took up his place at Flame's head and the rest of us sat in a semi-circle around her long, white-socked legs.

'Has anyone had experience of trying to heal wounds that hold emotion within them?' I asked.

Everyone shook their heads.

'Me neither, but as some of you know, I carried one such wound around for quite a while,' I said.

'You did?' said Sonja.

'Yes. The details don't really need going into but from personal experience, I can tell you that in these cases, the wound, whatever it is and however it was caused, won't heal until the emotion associated with it has been cleared. The only one who can do that is the one who owns it – Flame in this instance. No amount of strength or purity of intention on our part will make something heal that isn't ready to, so if we feel resistance to our healing, we'll need to respect that what is resisting us isn't ours to heal, and move on. Okay?'

Sonja looked at Rowena, who was nodding knowingly, and then back to me, her green eyes flashing. I was Aware of Sonja's jealousy flaring as it tended to whenever she felt that someone was closer to me than she. Everyone else looked thoughtful as they nodded their agreement.

'Sonja, are you okay?' I said.

Sonja flushed and I felt her get a hold of herself. She breathed in and out deeply and then nodded. I felt Flame prepare herself and when she was ready, I tuned into the first damaged muscle.

We healed all of the tissues in the pelvic area with no problems at all and I felt wisps of fear being released as we did so. I began to hope that my concerns had been ill-founded and that Flame was determined enough to get better that she was allowing the fear associated with her injured tissues to dissipate as we healed them. But then, when we tried to adjust their alignment and tensioning so that the pelvis would be pulled back into position, none of them would budge. We felt our way around all of the muscles, blood vessels and connective tissue in the pelvic area in case we had missed something, but all of them were now completely healthy. There was no reason for the tissues not to adjust according to the intention we were sending them down the pathway created by our smooth, joyful tones that resonated perfectly with the healthy tissues – at least, no physical reason. I looked up to see disappointment on my friends' faces.

'There are some injuries that aren't ours to heal,' I reminded them. 'Let's move on.'

We moved our attention to the tissues of the right hip, all the way down to the right foot. All of them followed our intention to heal and realign completely, except for those which should stabilise the stifle joint. As with the tissues surrounding the pelvis, they healed to our satisfaction, but then they wouldn't follow our intention to align and tension in a way that would ensure the efficient and healthy functioning of the joint. We moved on to the strained tissues of the left leg, which were swiftly dealt with, and then we all stood up.

'She's still going to be lame,' said Marvel. 'Her pelvis is twisted and her right stifle won't allow her to extend her right hind properly.'

'Well, at least she's not in pain anymore,' said Vickery.

I nodded. 'We've done all we can physically for her, so we just need to leave her to her own devices for a bit while we figure out where to go from here.'

'Agreed. I'm starving,' said Aleks. 'Are we still on for my training session after dinner, Am? I've nearly got the timing right between asking for Nexus to step under more and catching her before she loses balance, but I still struggle at times without eyes on the ground.'

'I think we all need a night off tonight, Aleks,' said Sonja.

'But I'm not tired, all I've been doing all day is sitting, watching Flame,' said Aleks.

'Great. There's woodland a mile in that direction,' Marvel pointed, 'where you'll find a whole load of firewood that needs gathering. We're all going to rest by the campfire.' His tone left no room for argument as he glared at Aleks and then stomped off.

Rowena looked at Marvel with as much surprise as I did – he was the most even-tempered of all of us and it was rare for him to speak to anyone without warmth and humour. Our failure to completely heal Flame bothered him, I realised, and without meaning to be, I was Aware of his fear that someday there would be something in Broad's body that he wouldn't be able to heal. He was terrified at the thought of life without his horse; he wanted to believe that his life would always be as good as it was now. I'd known for some time that it was his fear of change that prevented him from pushing himself and Broad to achieve perfect balance, and I pondered for the hundredth time on how strong an emotion was fear, that it could so easily stand in the way of knowledge and progress.

Yet without it there would be no knowledge of love, Infinity told me.

?????? But everything is love, I argued.

That is the truth of reality. But love cannot be acknowledged if there is nothing with which to compare it. Only once fear has been experienced can love be recognised.

So, fear is a good thing?

It is neither good nor bad. It has its role. We have visited this subject before.

Yes, I know, I just hadn't considered fear from that viewpoint before.

Infinity wandered off to graze. I noticed that all of the other horses did too, except for Serene, who kept watch over a sleeping Flame – but that was all she did. She awarded Flame the security of being able to sleep soundly, knowing that a member of the herd kept watch, but neither she, nor any of the other horses, any longer felt the need to support Flame with their energy. My heart lifted.

'I'm glad she's not in pain anymore,' Holly said as she came to stand beside me. 'At least we could do that much for her.'

'It's a start,' I agreed. 'Come on, let's go and sort dinner and try to cheer Marvel up.'

'I think Rowena's one step ahead of us there,' Holly said, nodding to where Rowena sat next to Marvel on the ground by the campfire, rubbing his back and almost touching her head to his as she murmured to him.

I grinned. 'It looks as though Sonja's taken pity on Aleks and gone with him to fetch firewood, so we'll take our time fetching more water from the stream, then, shall we?'

When I woke the following morning, Flame was nowhere to be seen. My heart skipped a beat and then I came to properly, and was Aware that she now grazed with the other horses. She was weak, stiff and moved awkwardly due to the unresolved issues in her hind end, but she was relieved to be pain free and she was grazing hungrily. Now that she was no longer experiencing the agony that had dulled her senses, however, she was on a constant high alert for danger, and I felt the fear that wouldn't allow her to trust that she was safe, even though all of the other horses grazed peacefully around her.

All of my friends slept on, so I pulled on my boots as quietly as I could and tiptoed away through the mist that hugged the ground, towards my sense of Infinity and Flame. I radiated my light ahead of me, allowing it to settle around Flame before she saw me. Even so, as I squeezed through some bushes and appeared suddenly, she flinched violently, spun away from me and then sped off at a canter. I noted with satisfaction that she was fully engaging her hindquarters underneath her whilst moving at speed. That meant that the limited ability of her right hind leg to stretch forward was less of a problem. As her flare of panic began to subside and she dropped to a trot, however, she engaged her hindquarters less and her lameness became more obvious. When she dropped to a walk and circled back to rejoin the rest of the horses – who had grazed on peacefully throughout – she moved very awkwardly indeed. Her right hip dropped lower than her left and the right hind leg stayed too far behind her before halting halfway through its forward stride and slapping down onto the ground. I could almost see her attacker wrenching her leg back and to the side with every stride that she took.

It's okay, Flame, it's only me, I thought to her, aware that she wouldn't send thoughts in return, but knowing that she would understand the meaning of mine to her.

You state the obvious. Bonded horses become accustomed to the human need to do this. She will find it strange, Infinity informed me.

Hmmm, I see what you mean. I need to check her wounds though, Fin, do I ask her if she's okay for me to approach her, or do I just do it?

She would find your question distracting and unnecessary. Infinity returned her attention to her grazing.

Flame was also grazing now, although she was still on high alert. I radiated light once again but this time, I allowed it to settle over the whole herd, of which Flame was now a part. I felt her register that I saw her in this way and I felt her relax a little.

I began to walk towards Flame, still radiating light, with the intention only of checking her wounds. She raised her head to watch my approach and her eyes flicked to the other horses and then back to me. I approached her from the side, my body angled away from her, and then held my hand out for her to sniff. She raised her head and snorted, then slowly lowered her nose to sniff my hand. I loved her and she knew it. I stroked the side of her nose and then her cheek, with the back of my hand. I moved closer and rubbed her neck and then worked my way along her body to her rump, where I stood up on tiptoes to see her wounds. Flame flinched violently and side-stepped away from me. I loved her and love was all. I moved closer and stood on tiptoes again. She flinched but remained where she was. I felt her trembling under my fingers as I checked that the wounds were dry and healing, and I felt her stare as my fingers moved down her right hind to check the wounds there. She lifted her leg as if to kick – but I trusted her. I trusted her completely and I loved her. I had nothing to fear from her and she had nothing to fear from me. I knew it and so, then, did she. She lowered her leg again.

'How is she?' Marvel's voice called softly through the dawn.

Flame jumped violently, all four of her feet leaving the ground. Her front legs gave way as she came back down and she went down on her knees. I strengthened my flow of light towards her as she regained her feet, and rubbed her neck gently.

'Her wounds are healing well, thanks,' I replied, 'and she's going to be just fine.'

NINE

Friends
_____

*O*ver breakfast, my friends and I discussed how we should proceed now that Flame was up and moving about. I told of my knowledge that she wanted to remain as part of our herd, and we all agreed to stay put for a while longer to give her more time to recover from her healing. I voiced my hope that she would be interested in working with me on the ground in the same way that Infinity had when she was recovering from her injuries the previous year.

'Do you think you can heal her more before we move on?' Aleks asked me.

'I don't know. For now, I just want to help her to get used to how her body can move in its present condition and try to highlight to her where there is wrongness, so that maybe she'll concentrate her efforts on trying to move those areas differently. If she does that, then in time, maybe the memories and fear held in those areas will be stimulated and ready for release, and then we can help her to heal further.'

'But we won't be able to travel with a lame horse tagging along,' said Aleks. 'We've only encountered a single Kindred so far, but we're following your sense of the Kindred Elder, so there's a good chance that at some point, we're going to be bumping into a whole load more of them. What if our light isn't enough to keep them at bay? What if they hunt our horses and we have to make a run for it? Flame will slow us down, she could get us all killed.'

I was Aware of Nexus attempting to reach Aleks to counsel him but his rising panic was all of which his mind could be aware and he was blocking his horse out. Immediately, I radiated light in his direction. Rowena, who had opened her mouth to retort, closed it and her light joined mine, as did Sonja's, Holly's and then – once he'd finished wrestling with his irritation – Marvel's.

Nexus waited patiently as our light battered at Aleks's barrier of fear. He looked around at each of us in turn, open-mouthed. 'Aren't any of you going to answer me?' His voice was edged with hysteria. 'We're putting ourselves in danger every single day just by being out here on our own with a semi-tame Kindred on the loose, and now we're going to willingly endanger ourselves and OUR HORSES further by having a lame horse, who's already shown she can't escape a Kindred attack, slow us down? We've helped her as much as we can, now we need to leave her and give ourselves and our horses the best chance of surviving this ordeal.'

I felt my friends' light flows wane as they fought to overcome their anger at Aleks, and I increased my own flow to full strength to compensate. I knew what it was like to be so frightened that I blocked out my horse and I knew how hard Aleks battled every single day he was with us, to cope with what he considered to be the danger and hardships of our mission. I also knew that he would need to be pushed a lot further before he would be in a position to really address the issue that was blocking him from achieving perfect balance – his need for the comfort of feeling fully in control of his physical circumstances – and in the meantime, he needed us.

'None of us are perfect,' I said quietly. 'That's why we need friends to step in and help.'

Almost immediately, my friends' light flows strengthened again and combined with my own. Aleks's fear barrier shattered around him and as our light infused him and he felt the depth of our love, tears filled his eyes. Nexus was in his mind instantly, reassuring him and helping him to understand.

I grinned at Rowena, Holly, Sonja and then Marvel – who winked at me – as we released our light.

'I'm s-s-sorry,' said Aleks. 'I don't know what came over me. Of course Flame needs to stay with us, she needs us. I'll... I'll try to do better.'

Holly and Sonja shuffled closer to Aleks and each put an arm around his shoulders. Marvel stood up and walked around the campfire, slapping Aleks's shoulder companionably with a huge hand as he passed him. 'That's all you can do, mate,' he said and bent to pick up Broad's grooming brushes. 'It's all any of us can do.'

Aleks left with Nexus for Jonustown after breakfast, to get more supplies and to let Vickery know that we'd be staying put for another week or so. Marvel, Sonja and their horses went to fetch more firewood, and Rowena and Holly agreed to come and watch me try to work with Flame; Holly was an experienced Healer and Rowena's observations and suggestions had been invaluable when I was trying to work out how to help Infinity to achieve greater balance, so I wanted their eyes watching how Flame moved. I hoped that between us, we could decide on how I should work with her from the ground in order to be of the most help to her. They would also be my backup in case I became too absorbed in my Awareness of Flame to fully appreciate what was going on with her physically.

Preparing for failure merely attracts failure, Infinity told me and I sighed, knowing that she was right, but wanting the support from my friends anyway.

I squeezed through the bushes to where the remaining four horses of our herd grazed, to find Infinity watching for my arrival. Flame, on high alert as ever, was standing next to her, head and tail held high, ears pricked and nostrils flaring. She spun around and trotted off, her tail held high.

'Wow, if she wasn't lame, she'd be spectacular,' said Rowena. 'Those long legs of hers just eat up the ground.'

'Wait until you see her in canter, she could challenge Gas in terms of speed,' I said as I walked over to where Infinity waited for me. Dew dripped from her white whiskers as she chewed a mouthful of spring grass and I noted that she'd put on a little weight in the last couple of days. Good, there was clearly more nutritional value in the grass now, which would help Flame.

I gave Infinity's withers a good scratch, something she always loved, and then concentrated on grooming her thoroughly, whilst sorting through everything of which I was Aware. I knew that Oak had rested well during the night and wanted Rowena to ride him shortly. I also knew that Serene had overstretched herself yesterday when Holly rode her; they had achieved a higher level of balance than ever before and in their excitement, had carried on past the point where their bodies were tired and they should have stopped. Serene was happy, but she would need a rest from being ridden today. I sensed Broad and Bright grazing some distance away while Marvel and Sonja collected firewood. They were revelling in having found a herb that they hadn't eaten for some time. I was Aware that Aleks still felt badly about his earlier behaviour, but that he was finding his way through it with Nexus's help. I could feel the joy of the swallows swooping over our heads as they arrived at their mating territory after an arduous migration from the south. I sensed a deer making a hasty retreat from our location, having caught our scent. And I knew that Fitt wasn't far away.

I carried on grooming Infinity as I absorbed the information, and then focused on finding a solution to the situation rather than on allowing any emotion to attach to it, which would alert Flame. At the moment, Fitt was just another essence in All That Is, as far as Flame was concerned; she was too far away to have scented our horses, so she wouldn't be trying to overcome her instinct to hunt, something of which Flame would have been instantly Aware. Infinity, Oak and Serene recognised Fitt's essence and grazed on without concern. I needed to find a way to prevent Fitt coming any closer for now, I realised, keeping my thoughts calm and unhurried. Food must be sent, but I couldn't ride Infinity because if she and I both left, Flame would likely follow. I couldn't ask Rowena or Holly to take the food, as their minds would reveal Fitt's identity to Flame, something of which I was successfully avoiding thinking about. I felt a glimmer of approval from Infinity.

I reached out to Oak briefly and then said to Rowena, 'Ro, Oak's happy to help me with something I need to do, so is it okay with you if I take him for a ride? Infinity needs to stay here with Flame.'

Rowena paused from grooming Oak. 'Er, sure. Everything okay?'

'Yep, I'll fill you in later, we won't be long,' I said, reaching for Oak's saddle and bridle from the log on which they rested and handing the bridle to Rowena.

'Thanks,' I said as Rowena legged me up onto Oak's saddle a few minutes later. I reached down and squeezed her arm, and made sure she looked up into my eyes with her own dark ones before I said, 'You're the only one I could have asked this of, apart from Justin. Thank you.'

Rowena nodded thoughtfully. 'Oak wants to go with you and presumably I'll find out what this is all about at some point, but for now, take care of each other, and try not to slide around in my saddle too much okay? It's way too big for you.'

I laughed. 'I'll try. We won't be long.'

As Oak trotted towards the camp, I glanced over my shoulder to see Flame staring after us, her eyes bulging in their sockets as she assessed the new development. Then she glanced at Infinity grazing peacefully alongside Serene, and dropped her nose back down to snatch at the grass.

Oak waited patiently by the campfire as I filled my saddlebags with most of our remaining food, knowing that Aleks would soon be returning with more. I was Aware that Fitt was heading in our direction purposefully but unhurriedly; her attention was taken up mostly with a search for a herb with small purple flowers. Mennawort, I realised, used for its anti-inflammatory properties. She must have hurt herself somehow. I took my attention away from her so as not to alert Flame to her identity and I grabbed some mennawort roots from my store and shoved them into my pocket. I attached my saddlebags to Oak's saddle and then climbed onto an enormous boulder so that I could remount easily; Oak was a long way up compared with Infinity.

I gathered up Oak's reins and asked him to move forward with a squeeze of my legs against his sides. I experimented until I found a rein contact with which he was comfortable; a very light contact, just enough for him to feel the connection between my hands and his mouth. As soon as he was happy that I could support him with my rein contact if needed, he lifted at the withers, arched his neck and stepped under himself further without need of assistance from me. Rowena had been doing a good job of helping him to arrange himself so that he could carry his weight and hers more easily. There was so much more of which he was capable though. I could feel how easy it would be for him to make the final adjustments necessary to achieve perfect balance and I wondered if I should help him to do it. I knew what to do, but should it be me who helped him or should I leave Rowena to do it with him when she was able? I observed that my personality was running away with me and took a deep breath to centre myself. Awareness of Oak, his body, his soul. Awareness of what he needed. Awareness of what I could do. Nothing was right, nothing was wrong, it just was. I closed my thighs around Oak slightly and his ears flickered back towards me with interest.

I nudged him with my heels and tentatively, he stepped underneath himself further. I nudged again and was rewarded by him increasing his commitment and stepping underneath himself even further. The power generated from his hind legs was transmitted up and over his back, enabling him to lift his withers higher. I nudged him again and felt his slight uncertainty. I held complete confidence that he would be able to do what I was asking and I felt him trust me and power through with his hind legs. His withers lifted even higher and I felt his joy followed by another wave of uncertainty as his balance began to shift forward. Immediately I closed my thighs around him more and pulled back slightly whilst keeping the core of my body stable and strong. I knew absolutely and definitely that there was no way he would lose his balance – he was strong, he was capable and he had my support. I felt the moment that he knew it too. Keeping his front end lifted, he sat his weight and mine back over his hind legs and as they flexed beneath us, easily taking the load, everything slotted into place for him. He was a big, heavy horse and yet as he walked forward, he was as light as a feather.

As Oak moved into a trot, I was Aware both of Rowena's delight and her devastation at what Oak had achieved without her. She questioned her friendship with me and then questioned the lack of commitment she had shown to her horse that had resulted in him needing me to help him find the balance for which she should have had the nerve to push. I noticed her emotions but focused on staying present. I noted that Oak was unsure of his newfound balance now that he was in trot. He backed off a little, not committing enough with his hind legs, and lost some lift as a result. I nudged him with confident intent until his hind legs once more powered through beneath me and then I closed my thighs around him slightly, so that he knew they were ready to catch him, to pull him back over his hind legs if he found himself overbalancing forwards due to the extra power his hind legs were generating. He didn't need me. His body remembered the arrangement it had achieved in walk and found it again without difficulty.

As Oak trotted slowly, powerfully, majestically amongst the trees, his body found itself no longer capable of hosting negative emotions and memories, and those that had long been trapped within him began to stir. Oak released many of them effortlessly, his newfound lightness and happiness rendering him incapable of noticing them as they dissipated into the ether, despite the fact that they had been significant enough for his soul to have brought through past lives and into the present. Some memories, however, caused him to jolt in his pace as they came to the surface for release. I was there for him instantly, steadying and supporting his body with my own until the memory had passed and he was in charge of himself once more.

Oak side-stepped and bellowed as a memory surfaced of him being taken from a family who loved him dearly, and given to a life of starvation, pulling cannons through mud while the ground exploded all around him. He died in terror and agony, with the sounds of men and horses shrieking in his ears.

He bucked as he remembered being spurred into a pack of wolves so that his trusted rider could leap to the safety of an overhanging rock whilst he was torn to pieces.

Then, he tossed his head violently and reared as a memory surfaced that held significance for him above all of the others. He was taken from his mother too soon. While he endured the misery of grieving for her, children threw stones at him, causing wounds which were left untreated. Men came and tied his legs together and then tied his head to his legs.

They put a harness on him and tightened it, causing him to panic at the discomfort and lack of opportunity to escape. They only took it off once he stopped struggling. After weeks of the same treatment, he realised that there was no point in struggling. The men harnessed him to a wagon, which terrified him. They whipped him until he lurched forward, pulling the wagon behind him and then they laughed as they hauled on the wire in his mouth until he stopped, frothing and bleeding. They whipped him again until he pulled the wagon forward, then they hauled on his torn mouth to steer him in circles, laughing all the while. Days turned into weeks, and weeks into months. He was always hungry, weak, sore and bleeding. And then one day, as he hauled the wagon down a track, someone stepped out in front of him. He was hauled to a stop and stood dully while a female voice argued angrily with his tormentors. He heard the chink of coins and then the next thing he knew, gentle hands were freeing him from the harness. A rope was tied around his neck whilst the bloody wire in his mouth was eased out, and then the rope was tied loosely around his nose.

'It's alright now, beautiful boy, you're coming home with me and nobody's ever going to hurt you again,' said the female voice. Rowena's voice was huskier than in her current lifetime, but even if I hadn't recognised her from my own sense of her, I would have known her from how Oak thought of her.

She never asked anything of him in that lifetime; his body was too damaged from the harm done to him by his abusers. She looked after him and loved him dearly, and he learnt to trust her and to be happy. He recognised a soul with whom he would incarnate again, at a time when she would need another to love her and keep her safe. He would do for her as she had done for him and together they would do much for others.

I was Aware that Rowena now wept. I felt her understand the agreement that her soul had made with Oak's to reincarnate together again. I witnessed her guilt that she hadn't been willing to push herself past the fear that blocked her from being able to give everything of herself to Oak when she rode him – her fear that in giving her complete attention to being in the moment, able to respond instantly with whatever support he needed, she would give up her ability to hide the aspects of herself that she didn't want anyone to see – resulting in it being another who helped him to achieve that for which he had been yearning.

I sent a wave of love to my friend, understanding how she felt but not allowing myself to become involved in emotions that were hers to feel. I felt Infinity's approval and grinned just as I became Aware of Oak's intention to slow to a walk. I closed my thighs and pulled back a fraction, just enough to show him that he needed to keep his forequarter lifted and sitting on his hindquarters as he slowed his pace. He barely needed me.

I marvelled at how easily he was adjusting to his new balance, and not just physically; when Fitt dropped to the ground a little way in front of us, Oak held himself aside from the instinctive fear that horses feel in the presence of a predator and sent his calm, warm energy towards her, just as Infinity had done during our previous two encounters with Fitt. I immediately radiated my light and allowed it to settle around the three of us as Oak and I approached her.

It was the first time I had seen Fitt up close and I noted that she was quite a bit smaller than the Kindred who had nearly killed Infinity the year before. Her human-like face was covered in fine, downy brown hair, the pupils of her green eyes were slitted like a cat's and the fangs that jutted out from under her top lip almost seemed to clamp her mouth closed. The wiry fur through which her tough, leathery skin was visible, was dark brown and her powerfully muscled body stooped. The talons that protruded from her fingers and thumbs were menacing, and quickly I pushed away memories of Infinity's and Flame's injuries before they could take hold.

I was Aware that just as Oak had chosen to move away from his instinctive fear of a predator in order to send her his love and reassurance, Fitt had chosen to step aside from her instinct to see him as prey. She had been Aware of our approach and had experienced Oak's achievement alongside us. She was fascinated by what she had witnessed and she was intrigued by Oak now as well as by Infinity, both because of how they behaved towards her and because of her Awareness of them as beings far surpassing her expectation.

I felt Fitt's uncertainty at a decision she had made, but her resolve to stick to it nevertheless – she wanted to be friends. My heart leapt.

You're hungry. I've brought you more food, I told her.

'Thank you,' she said. 'In my hunger, I ate the fruit of a plant new to me and now my stomach is irritated.' Her voice rasped in her throat as if she were having to strain to get each word out.

'That's why you need the mennawort. Here, I brought you some roots. We normally grind them down and then make a tea with them, sweetened with...'

'...honey,' Fitt finished for me and the tops of her mouth turned up into what I took to be as much of a grin as her fangs would allow. 'So do we, but it's a long time since I've had anything that sweet; I'm nearly as bad at gathering as I am at hunting, in fact it's a wonder I'm still alive.' She reached for the roots and then retracted her hand suddenly. 'Your skin is so fragile and my talons are sharp. I don't want to hurt you.' I felt an overwhelming sense of shame from her.

It was a shame that was hers by inheritance. My heart went out to her as I became Aware of her revulsion at her own body, a revulsion absorbed by her ancestors from the humans of The Old whenever they had looked at their creations – their genetically modified humans, their necessary abominations created for the enforcing of law and order – a revulsion that had been passed subconsciously from generation to generation.

'You won't hurt me. Here, take them from me,' I said, holding my hand out to her.

Fitt looked at me uncertainly.

I wasn't revolted by her. I admired her courage in attempting to survive by herself and in trusting a human to help her. I appreciated her sensitivity and consideration towards the horses. I trusted her and I knew that she wouldn't hurt me. I felt her take stock of my thoughts and knew that they reached her in a way that I never could have with spoken words. She reached out and tentatively closed her talons around the roots in my hand.

'Thank you,' she said, her gratitude for more than just the mennawort.

'You're welcome. I hope it eases your stomach enough for you to be able to eat. I'd have invited you back to our camp to eat with us, only a new horse has joined our herd and she has a lot of fear to overcome before she'll be able to cope with anyone new.'

Fitt chewed on the mennawort roots. They were very bitter without honey to sweeten them, but she showed no sign of discomfort. 'You call her Flame,' she said, 'and she is recovering from being hunted by one of my kind.' Her eyes widened. 'She killed him, but not before he injured her terribly. He will have regretted that. We need to eat but we abhor suffering. My fear of causing suffering prevents me from committing to the hunt, that's what my father always tells me. He hoped I might get past it when I...' Fitt blinked and shook her head. 'I speak too much.'

'No, you don't, not at all, you can tell me anything. I want to learn about you and about your kind, and I'll be happy to answer any questions you have about me and mine. Please, carry on?'

Fitt shook her head. 'I'm not permitted to.'

I was Aware of the import of her words as well as of their spoken meaning. Fitt's decision to trust and befriend me was hers alone. The Kindred Elder had commended her for making her decision but the Kindred race had enough fear and mistrust of humans that Fitt had been forbidden from sharing any information with me that wasn't hers alone.

'I understand,' I said. 'Your Elder knows I'm Aware, though. She knows that if I wanted to, I could know anything about you that I choose to, just as you can with me?'

'She knows.'

'But she also knows that I wouldn't pry for information that you don't want to share. I wouldn't do that to you or to anyone else.'

'She hopes that is the case. We all do.' She closed her mouth suddenly and looked skyward.

I grinned. 'We'll change the subject before you say anything else you're not supposed to. Here, I'll show you the food I've brought for you, it should keep you going for a while.'

Several hours later, Oak and I made our way back to camp, leaving Fitt – who assured me that she was happy for me to call her that, since knowing her real name would tell me much about her kind that they didn't yet trust me to know – eating contentedly, the mennawort having eased her stomach.

Oak was keen to experiment with his body and after a brief spell in walk and trot, he surged forward into a powerful canter. I was amazed at how he adjusted to the change in gait and speed so easily, with only a slight amount of resistance needed from me in my seat and back, to help him maintain his balance.

Do not underestimate how valuable your own balance, strength and confidence are to him, Infinity's thoughts wove their way into my mind. *He will not find it so easy with a less accomplished rider.*

I remembered that it had been some time before Infinity had found it as easy to balance as Oak was, as she'd had to contend with me being inconsistent in my own balance. *Will Rowena find it more difficult to ride him now that he'll be striving for more?* I asked her.

That will depend on her choices.

Oak's canter ate up the distance back to camp and it seemed no time at all before we arrived back there. Oak was tired and sweaty, but his eyes shone and he radiated joy and power. A red-eyed Rowena flung her arms around his neck as I slid to the ground. I unsaddled him as she sobbed into his mane and then I gently disentangled her from his reins and took his bridle off. Oak moved off in the direction of the stream and Rowena walked beside him, her hand on his shoulder.

Marvel said, 'Flaming lanterns, Am, what's going on? Sonja and I get back to find that you've taken Oak off with little explanation, and Rowena's hysterical, then sinks into a weeping melancholy that's far more frightening than her temper. None of the horses will tell us what's going on but their lack of concern indicates it's nothing too serious, so we go to make some lunch only to find that most of our food is gone. When you and Oak finally return, he looks amazing, Rowena starts crying again and Holly, Sonja and I are as much in the dark as ever. Did I leave anything out, or does that just about cover it?' he asked Holly and Sonja.

Holly raised her hands and let them fall, and Sonja shrugged.

I nudged Justin's mind and once I knew that his attention was with me, I told my friends everything that had happened.

As they listened, all three of my friends' jaws dropped in horror at the thought of someone helping their horses to achieve that which they had so far failed to help them to achieve.

I would have done the same thing in your place, Am, but I admire your courage – didn't Rowena put one on you last time you offered unasked for help with Oak? Justin's teasing was accompanied by a sense of support for me.

You know full well she did since you were the one who scraped me off of the floor, but as everything happens as it should, it'll be interesting to see what happens now, I replied.

You think more and more like Infinity every day.

I'm just trying to keep myself centred, the same as you, Jus, but as with everything else, I have to try harder than you do.

That's just because you challenge yourself more than I do. I'm living in comfort, teaching students who think I'm wonderful, and I have Quinta and Feryl for support. You're camping out whilst befriending one Kindred and allowing another free access to your mind, as well as helping an injured, terrified horse to heal, challenging those with you to the point that they probably hate you, and if that weren't enough, you have to coach Aleks.

I sent love and gratitude to Justin as I wished for the millionth time that he were with me.

I'm just wondering whose horse I can run away with and help to achieve perfect balance in the hope that it might jolt their shocked and horrified Bond-Partner into finding their own, and then I can come after you, he thought to me.

Maybe the situation will present itself. Uh-oh, looks like Marvel is about to speak, and judging by the look on his face, you'll probably be able to hear him from where you are.

But Marvel simply said, 'How could you, Am?' and then turned to follow Rowena and Oak.

'Serene assures me that at some point, your behaviour will make sense, Amarilla,' said Holly, 'but until then, I think I need to be somewhere else.' She picked up Serene's grooming brushes and walked off towards the horses' grazing area.

Sonja stood where she was. I was Aware that her empathy with

Rowena warred with her delight at the prospect of a division between Rowena and me, one that might allow her to take Rowena's place as the person in the group closest to me. 'Why did you do it, Am?' she asked me.

'Why are you so upset that I did?' I said.

Sonja flushed. 'Because it wasn't your place? Because Rowena wanted to be the one to help Oak to achieve perfect balance? Because you've robbed her of the opportunity?'

'But what about what Oak wanted?' I said softly.

Sonja looked at me in confusion. 'Are you saying he asked you to help him? He wanted you to help him, rather than Rowena?' I felt her stab of fear that Bright might make the same choice.

'Do you think he achieved what he did against his will?' I said. 'He didn't ask me. He had no need to, any more than my hand needs asking to scratch my head.'

'But your hand and your head are both parts of you... oh.' Sonja looked searchingly into my eyes. 'It's about being one with everything, isn't it? Is that what it's like, being Aware? You just know what someone else wants and you respond to it without needing to be asked? Without conscious thought?'

'At times, yes. I'm learning that too much thought allows my personality to get in the way of my soul. Not enough thought, and I just drift around on the tides of consciousness, which isn't helpful either. It's a balance and I think I'm slowly getting better at finding it.'

'And that's a good thing? Even though you're upsetting people?'

'Why did you ask to come with us on this trip, Sonja, honestly?' I asked her.

'Because I believe that trying to befriend the Kindred is the right thing to do and because I wanted to travel with you, so I could carry on learning from you. Bright and I didn't want to interrupt our progress by changing instructors.'

'Honestly,' I repeated. I was Aware that Bright monitored our conversation. Sonja picked up a stick and threw it into the fire, causing sparks to shoot up into the air. She paced over to one of the seating logs and sat down. I lowered myself to sit on another log and waited. She got up and began to stalk away from the camp, before returning and sitting down beside me.

'I wanted to come with you because you're the hub of everything. Oh, I know Justin and Quinta have achieved everything you have, but they wouldn't have got that far without you. You're important and... and...'

'Say it, Sonja. You have to say it,' I said.

Sonja put her face into her hands for a long time. Bright was with her in her mind, lending support by his gentle presence but giving her the space to sort through her feelings. Finally, she said, 'You're important and I want to be with you so that I'll be important too. I hate that you speak to Justin in your mind. I hate that you and Rowena have been through so much together that you're as close as you are. I want to be the friend closest to you, so that when people look at me, they will see someone who is worthy of notice. There, I said it.'

'What people?'

'Huh?'

'Whose opinion is it that bothers you, as to whether or not you're worthy of notice?'

'Well, um there's... well, there's... um...' Sonja frowned. 'There's...'

'Only one of us in the room, actually,' I finished for her. 'We're all one. You've convinced yourself that you need others to look at you as if you have worth when in fact those others are you. It's your opinion of yourself, your lack of self-worth, that holds you back. You don't push yourself and Bright the little bit further that you need to in order to reach perfect balance, because you don't believe that you're good enough and you're terrified that all you'll do is prove it to yourself. You think you'll prove that you have no worth other than what you can persuade others to award you, even though those others are, in fact, you.'

Sonja stared into my eyes as if trying to find the lie in my words. Bright reminded her of the times that she had visited the subject with him and her expression softened as she put my words together with his counsel and realised that the answer to her torment was always the same.

'I understand what you're saying, but it doesn't change how I feel,' she said. 'I still feel a draw to be around you, to feel good about myself by being your friend and part of everything that's happening. Bright says it's impossible for me to be unworthy, because I'm part of All That Is. But I'm here, in my own head, as always. It isn't as lonely as it used to be now that I have Bright, but I still just feel like... little, insignificant me.'

'So, you need to take a risk. You need to get your saddle and bridle, go and tack up your beautiful boy, and you need to push yourself. You need to put your fears to one side and focus on Bright, only on him and what his body needs from yours, so that you can respond in every millisecond exactly as he needs you to, as you're very well capable of doing by now. You need to move past your belief that you're not good enough, that you have no worth and you need to ride Bright to a place where you will know all you need to know for yourself. Come on, it's time.'

'I can't,' Sonja said, her voice tight with fear. I looked at her and felt with her Bright's calm confidence that this was the right time and that she would find her courage. She breathed out deeply. 'But I have to. Will you come with me? Will you help?' Sonja said standing up, trembling.

'Fin and I will be with you and Bright every step of the way.'

Holly was still grooming Serene when Sonja and I arrived at the horses' grazing area. Flame and Infinity were grazing side by side, and I was pleased to see that Flame merely raised her head, still chewing, to watch my approach. She flinched when I flung my saddle onto Infinity's back, but then she reached out to sniff it gingerly before snorting and walking away.

Infinity's eagerness for what was about to come matched my own and as soon as I was on board, she cantered powerfully over to where Sonja was saddling Bright with trembling hands. There was a thunder of hooves and Flame skidded to a halt behind us. I held the intention in my mind that Infinity and I would work alongside Bright and Sonja within the confines of the grazing area. I felt Flame's anxiety subside and she dropped her head down to graze.

'Ready?' I asked Sonja, who had just mounted Bright.

She nodded. 'I think so.'

'You have to know so. Tell me when you know you're ready,' I said firmly.

Sonja breathed deeply for a while as she and Bright shared thoughts. Then she said, 'I'm ready. I'm going to do this. With your help, Bright and I are going to do this.'

'Right then, we'll move forward into walk. I'm going to push you whenever I can feel you backing off. Okay?'

'Okay.'

Sonja squeezed Bright's sides with her lower legs, and as he easily lifted his forequarter, she closed her thighs slightly, ready to pull back if she felt him overbalancing forwards. Then she nudged with her heels to ask him to step under more with his hind legs, which he did willingly. He was slightly crooked, so Sonja pushed against him with her right leg, supporting him with her left rein as he straightened through his body. I felt her hesitate. Bright's balance was a lot better, but it was a level of balance they had reached hundreds of times before and they both felt comfortable there.

'Ask more, Sonja,' I said as Infinity, bridleless, stepped alongside Bright. The difference in the amount of lift she was achieving compared with that of Bright was obvious, as was the level of engagement of her hindquarters as we powered past them both.

I felt a new determination welling up in Sonja, so Infinity and I circled away to give her and Bright more space. Within minutes, they had achieved a higher level of balance, exceeding their previous best.

Infinity and I moved alongside them again. 'Ask even more, Sonja,' I said, 'and keep asking until Bright is matching Infinity. We'll keep circling away and then coming alongside you and each time, Bright needs to be more lifted and more engaged than the last time. Sit into your pelvis a little more, check your shoulders are down and back, and keep your chest lifted. As he generates more power, he'll need to feel that you're completely stable so that he has confidence you can support him if he starts to feel unstable. As his balance improves, he'll feel vulnerable because his body will be arranged in a way that's unfamiliar to him. You need to have absolute concentration on what's happening to him so that you can step in and support him where he needs it. Absolute concentration, okay?'

I was pleased that Sonja was unwilling to break her focus by speaking and merely nodded. As Infinity and I circled away again, I felt Flame's interest in what was happening with Bright. She had moved to stand near Serene, and both horses and Holly stood watching.

By the time Infinity and I rejoined Bright and Sonja, they were nearly there but Sonja's worry that she wasn't good enough had crept its way through her concentration and was beginning to take hold. Tears ran down her face. Bright was slightly crooked again and he was hesitating about stepping underneath himself with his hind legs as much as he needed to.

'Sonja, focus on Bright. You saw him as a blinding white light when he revealed his essence to you, back when you bonded. You saw All That Is in him because that's who he is and because you have the potential to remember that it's also who you are. Focus and reach for it. Come on, push yourself, push Bright and you'll remember who you are. Push on, Sonja, that's it.'

All of a sudden, Bright was straight, lifted and his stride and power matched Infinity's. A look of wonder stole across Sonja's tear-streaked face.

'Trot?' I said and Bright stepped up into a majestic trot alongside Infinity. 'Keep your focus now, Sonja, whatever happens, keep your focus. Be there for him as he's always been for you,' I said and then Infinity and I peeled away from them.

Just as Infinity and I reached Flame's side, the weight of Bright's past came to the surface for release and he let out a roar.

TEN

Vortex
***

nfinity and I took ourselves away from camp for the afternoon, with Flame in tow. I knew that my friends could do with some time to process the events of the morning without me around, and having had to abandon my plan to try to work with Flame that morning, I decided that going for a gentle wander was an acceptable alternative; the extra movement would help her to get used to how her body felt after all the healing she had undergone.

Flame followed Infinity and me as we explored. She stopped occasionally to snatch at grass, tree leaves or herbs before thundering up behind us in a panic to catch up. Several times, Infinity turned her head back to Flame, her ears flat back and her nostrils wrinkled, warning her that she was too close to Infinity's hindquarters. On one such occasion, Infinity bucked and threatened to kick out. Flame grunted and flung herself to one side and Infinity squealed to drive her point home. I had to smile – Infinity may regard human social conventions as an irrelevance but she would not tolerate any breaches of the equine code of conduct.

When we came across a grassy glade, I dismounted and removed Infinity's saddle, then sat down to lean against a huge tree root whilst Infinity and Flame grazed. Flame was comforted by the warmth of the sun's rays, and reassured by Infinity's and my confirmation of her own feeling that there was nothing nearby that need disturb us. I was pleased to note that her constant state of high alertness decreased slightly. She gradually grazed further away from Infinity and nearer and nearer to where I was sitting. She snuffled around my boots, sniffed her way up to my knee where my hands rested, then nuzzled my fingers briefly before dropping her head back down to graze. My heart melted. As I watched her slowly graze her way around the glade, there was a definite sense of rightness about her being with Infinity and me.

I spent the next hour or so revelling in the feeling of peace that comes from watching horses graze. Then I dozed for a while, lulled by the sound of their munching and by the warmth of the sun on my face. When I opened my eyes, Infinity grazed at my feet while Flame attempted to doze nearby. I took in every detail of the two mares. As the sunlight bounced off of Infinity's shiny white fur, seeming to create a white nimbus around her that was almost too dazzling to look at, she radiated strength, intelligence, confidence and love. There was no mistaking that she was a being of immense power. Flame, on the other hand, was underweight and her coat was still dull and staring. Although I was Aware of her warmth, courage and determination, her character was dampened by the fear that seeped noxiously through her body from where it was concentrated in her pelvis and stifle. It weakened her in both body and mind. Her eyes would close for a few minutes and then open suddenly as her whole body jerked, ready to flee from whatever foe was sure to have sneaked closer.

I radiated a small amount of light and allowed it to settle around Flame, with the intention of increasing it if she wanted me to. I felt Flame's immediate acceptance of my energy. I steadily increased the flow of light to her and she allowed it to permeate throughout her being. I noticed, but gave no attention to, the fear that shrank away from my light, recoiling back to its places of refuge in the pelvis and stifle. I concentrated instead on the peace that replaced it and on Flame's courage and resolution to complete the task that she had undertaken when incarnating into her beautiful, chestnut body. She would do it and Infinity and I, and all of our friends, would help her. Flame sank into a peaceful doze. I kept my flow of light steady, ensuring that the nutrition she had taken into her body was available to be used in building it back up, rather than being directed by her fear towards maintaining her ever-ready flight response.

As the light began to fade, the mares and I left the glade. I became Aware of Aleks struggling to drag a litter which he'd loaded almost as heavily as Nexus's, whilst trying to make camp before nightfall. He could have had a comfortable bed for the night and returned to camp tomorrow, and he could have brought a smaller load, but I could feel his need to make amends for his behaviour regarding Flame. The mares and I intercepted him and Nexus, and Infinity took Aleks's load after I managed to persuade him that punishing himself wasn't necessary. I filled him in on the events of the day.

Aleks whistled. 'At least I'm no longer the most unpopular person in the group,' he said with a grin.

'I think you'll find yourself the most popular member of the group, once we get back to camp with this lot,' I replied.

'If I'd known you were going to give so much food to Fitt, I'd have brought more,' Aleks said. 'Well done, by the way, for making friends with her and everything, that must have taken real guts.'

'No, not at all. She's not dangerous, none of them are. They're just trying to survive.'

'By eating horses and attacking humans in the process.'

'By hunting their prey, just as any other predator does, including us,' I said. 'And don't forget that the Kindred are also Aware. Fitt's intrigued by our horses, she knows they're important to what we're trying to do and they're in no danger from her, so please stop worrying about Nexus's safety.'

'I'm sorry. I panic because I know I wouldn't be able to live with myself if anything happened to Nexus as a result of me knowingly taking her into danger. I want to help with this mission, we both do, but I can't seem to find a way to be calm about it.'

'If Sonja's got anything to do with it, you soon will, she's going to be after you to follow in her and Bright's footsteps after what they achieved today, so I'd get a good night's sleep tonight, if I were you,' I said with a grin.

Aleks chuckled. 'And what about you? What will you do about Rowena?'

'I'll just give her space to sort through her feelings and make her choices in her own time. We're almost there, I can smell the campfire. Are you ready for a hero's welcome?'

We arrived at camp to find everyone sitting around the campfire, sipping tea.

'Aleks,' Sonja cried and flung her arms around him. 'I've never been so pleased to see anyone, we thought we were going to go to bed hungry tonight. Oh, Am, there you are, we were worried about you. Aleks, has she told you about Bright and me? You have to try harder, and I'm going to make sure you do. Bright and I have more work to do until we're established in our new balance, but I know what to do and I know what you have to do, too, so as soon as I've ridden in the morning, I'll help you, that is unless you'd rather carry on working with Amarilla? I guess that would make sense...'

'Errr, Sonja, that's great and I'm really happy for you and everything, but we need to unload the litters and get dinner organised,' Aleks said, disentangling himself from her, 'and Amarilla and I need to see to our horses.'

'It's fine, Aleks, I'll take all three down to the stream for water and a rub down. You're needed here to unload the litters and Sonja has so much to tell you while you do it,' I said with a wink.

'Thanks a lot, wicked girl,' he whispered as he gave Nexus a rub on her neck before she left with me.

'I'll come and help you with the horses, Am,' Rowena said quietly out of the darkness, 'and we'll expect dinner to be cooked and waiting for us when we get back,' she said to the others in her normal, commanding tone.

Infinity and I led the way down the narrow path to the stream, walking between huge boulders that looked as if they'd been stacked either side on purpose, rather than pushed there by the force of frozen water, years past. Flame was close on Infinity's heels and Nexus and Rowena brought up the rear.

I was Aware of Flame's weariness. Soon, she would be able to rest in the safety of the herd. Her herd, where they would each take a turn at watch, while the others rested in peace. And if any danger arose, we would all protect her. She would be safe. I felt Flame recoil from my thoughts. I heard her footfalls, uneven due to her lameness, cease and as I turned to her in the moonlight, she looked away from me.

You should not pledge that which you are not certain of being able to provide, Infinity rebuked me.

I understood and was confused at the same time; my thoughts and feelings had been genuine, yet somehow, I had managed to lie to Flame.

Humans require reassurance to such an extent that they are reassured by reassurance itself. Bonded horses accept this but Flame merely knows that you offer something to her of which you cannot be sure and her trust in you is shaken, Infinity told me.

I get it. My intention of protecting Flame is genuine, but I can't possibly know that I'll be able to keep her safe. I suppose we humans lie to each other quite often in the name of well-intentioned reassurance.

Being untruthful is neither good nor bad. It is merely unhelpful when the recipient of your attempted reassurance knows the truth and is confused by your attempt to subvert it.

Okay, I understand, I'll watch myself more carefully.

I pictured the herd grazing peacefully through the night, taking turns at watch – something I could be sure of. I felt Flame's acceptance of the truth and she began to walk behind Infinity and me again. I wondered how many other times I'd offered well-intentioned advice or reassurance which if I'd thought about it, I would have known to be untrue.

When we reached the stream, the horses spread out along its length and drank thirstily. I began rubbing Infinity down where her saddle had been and saw Rowena doing the same for Nexus. When the horses had drunk their fill, they began to graze along the banks of the stream.

I finished rubbing Infinity down and moved towards Flame. I radiated a small amount of light to settle gently around her as I approached and then stroked her shoulder gently with the back of my hand, working up to her face. She didn't flinch or try to move away, but she stood rigidly, concentrating on my touch whilst deciding how she felt about it.

'I'm just going to rub you all over with my hands, just as I've done for Fin. You're a beautiful girl, you're putting on a bit of weight and your coat will shine soon. It'll gleam if you'll let me groom you with brushes, but I'm just using my hands for now, that's my brave, beautiful girl.' I spoke quietly as my hands worked their way around her eyes and ears, back down her neck to her torso and then on to her hindquarters.

I tuned into her body as I worked and anywhere that I could feel that her muscles were tight, I hummed, my voice resonating with the tired muscles and creating a pathway down which I sent my intention for the muscles to relax. All of them responded, apart from those around the pelvis and stifle. Flame breathed in deeply and then let out a long, relaxed sigh.

'It all comes so naturally to you now, doesn't it,' said Rowena.

'What does?' I asked, stepping back from Flame.

'Being you. You used to be so unsure of yourself, so eager to please, so apologetic at the slightest hint of discomfort from someone else, and now, you're just you. When you talk, it's impossible not to listen because your words ring with truth. You know what everyone needs without them asking, without them knowing they need it half the time, and you give it to them, not because you're a people-pleaser like you were, but because it's just what you do. Your light isn't just your light, it's you. It's not even as if you just performed tissue-singing just then, you were just being you. Everything is just an extension of you as well as being a part of you.'

'You're Aware. Thunder and lightning Ro, you're Aware.' I launched myself at her and she hugged me back, laughing.

'I thought you'd know straight away but you've been distracted, having Flame with you, so I got to spring it on you. It was worth everything I've been through today, just for that.'

Her recent experiences came to the forefront of her thoughts and I witnessed them instantly. I saw her accompany Oak down to the stream after he had returned to camp with me. She was furious with me; it was she who was bonded to Oak, she with whom he had chosen to share his life, not me, and it was her role to help him achieve perfect balance whilst she found hers alongside him. I had taken the opportunity to do that away from her. Oak offered her no counsel. Rowena could feel his elation as if it were her own and soon found her anger at me warring with her delight that her horse could balance his body with such perfection that he could experience the full power of who he was with no lingering memories or fears to hold him back. She saw the choice in front of her – whether to feel love for her horse, or anger at me. She remembered that she and Oak had agreed to incarnate together again so that he could provide a sanctuary for her as she had once done for him. Love flooded through her body until there was no room for any other emotion.

She revelled in his achievement with him, but realised that every time she rode him now, she would compromise him. For her to be able to ride Oak in the way that I had, she knew that she needed to sit into her pelvis more and lift her chest to a higher degree than her fears and insecurities had so far allowed her to; she had never before lifted her chest enough for her to be completely stable, because if she did, all of the hurt and rejection she carried there would come to the fore. She would have to feel it all over again and she would have to admit that the part of her life from whence it came had existed and was part of who she was. To acknowledge it might even change who she was now – she might not feel as confident and capable if she allowed the unloved, unwanted little girl she had been to again be part of her. Her fear of that happening prevented her from sitting deeply enough into her pelvis to be grounded and strong.

But now, she was overwhelmed by her love for her horse, a love that had existed in their previous life together, had existed all the while they were discarnate and existed now that they were incarnate together in this lifetime. It would always exist, she knew that now, and she could feel its power.

Marvel reached Oak and Rowena at the stream just in time to give Rowena a leg up on to Oak's bare back. Oak was tired but he knew that Rowena wouldn't need to ride him for long.

She didn't. She no longer cared about who she was in the eyes of anyone else; it didn't matter. Nothing mattered other than the love she shared with her horse. In the absence of any fear, of anything other than love, she made the adjustments to her body's position that allowed her to be the rider he needed her to be. She heard Marvel's cheering as she and her horse blurred into one being. Oak cleared the last remaining shreds of negative emotion from within his body as Rowena cleared all of hers. She knew of her oneness with All That Is. She was Aware.

'You wonderful, wonderful person, I'm so happy for you, you have no idea,' I said.

'Actually, I think you'll find that I do,' Rowena replied and we both laughed.

'Does Justin know yet?' I asked.

'Not that I know of. It's so overwhelming, being Aware of everything, that I haven't even tried to extend myself past all the things that are already bombarding my mind,' Rowena replied.

I grinned. 'Do you remember when you met me at The Gathering after I first bonded with Infinity, you told me that the first few months of being bonded were like being blindfolded and spun around until I wouldn't know which way was up and which was down?'

'Yup, and I have a feeling I know where you're heading.'

'This is as if you've been looking at the world through two narrow slits your whole life and all of a sudden, you can see to the sides, behind you, beneath you, above you and further into the distance than you thought possible. It's hard to stay rooted in the physical world sometimes and then at other times, you'll curse yourself for letting your personality take over so that you forget about everything you can be Aware of – but, Ro, you've done it. You've achieved perfect balance and so have Oak, Sonja and Bright, all in the same day. I can hardly believe it.'

'I told you, the Amarilla vortex is gathering strength,' Rowena said. 'I'm just glad I was strong enough to stay within it this time, instead of being spat out like I was the last time I found things tricky.'

'Not half as glad as I am. As Justin so helpfully reminded me, the last time you got "spat out", you punched me in the face and it was days before I could eat properly,' I said with a grin.

'On that note, I think it's time to see the horses back to the rest of the herd and then go to eat the dinner which I'm completely confident will be cooked to perfection by the time we get back to camp,' said Rowena, linking her arm through mine. 'Seriously though, I'm glad you find it easy being you now. Oak and I would never have got there if you'd still been the under-confident, insipid people-pleaser that you were.'

'And I'm glad that your ability to be you has been completely unaffected by the events of today. I'd miss the teasing, brutal truth-telling and downright insults if anything about you ever changed,' I replied.

As we laughed together, I was Aware of Rowena as She Who Is Oak. She had become the unlimited reservoir of love and strength that she saw in her horse when they first bonded. Together, she and Oak had achieved the first part of the agreement their souls had made. Now it was time for them to achieve the second.

'You realise that I fully intend to have a rest from teaching now that you can take over, don't you?' I told Rowena. 'I'll have more time to work with Flame, I'll be able to chat with Justin instead of just barging into his mind when something important is happening, oh and I'll also have more time and energy to spend battering at my sister's mind in case she ever lets me in.'

'Can I help with that now? If there are two of us trying to get through to her, will it speed things up?'

'No, it's not signal strength that's the problem. I can feel how hard Katonia's been working at imagining she can hear me in her mind, but she's very distracted now.'

'Because of Jack and the work they're doing together?'

'Partly, but mostly because she's in the early stages of pregnancy.'

'She's pregnant? Jack's going to be a father? We're going to have a baby Horse-Bonded? Well I'm not surprised she's distracted, she must be ecstatic.'

'She is. She's a jumbled mass of hormones and emotions and on top of that, she and Jack hardly have a moment to themselves – word has got around about their new multiskilling centre and they're flat out with people requesting their help. When they're not working, my mother's round there fussing and clucking.'

Rowena chuckled. 'I can imagine. There's nothing I can do to help there, then, but on the teaching front, how about I take Marvel and Holly and Sonja takes Aleks?'

'That would work, and Sonja did offer to help Aleks. Nicely dodged, my friend. Any ideas on how you're going to push Marvel and Holly past the issues that are blocking their progression, now that you're Aware of what they are?'

'Marvel's afraid of change and Holly uses her restless spirit reputation as a cover for a fear of commitment, which is actually down to a lack of confidence in her own judgment. I could take the raging bull approach as you did with Sonja, but I was thinking of a more measured approach.'

'So, you don't know,' I chuckled.

'No. And we've forgotten Vickery.'

'Focus on her essence, Ro.'

We walked on in silence. I was Aware of Rowena feeling around for Vickery, trying to find her in the myriad of essences of All That Is. 'Just think of an experience you and she have shared until you get a sense of her, then you'll feel her easily,' I suggested.

Almost immediately, Rowena was Aware of Vickery. 'Ohhhhh,' she said. 'She wants to ride Verve better so that he can carry her weight without harm to himself, but that's as far as it goes for her. She's been frustrated in previous lifetimes by allowing fear to stand in the way of her making a positive contribution, so Verve agreed to incarnate with her in this lifetime, to help her to break the pattern. She nearly fell into her old pattern by wanting to rid the world of the Kindred and trying to mobilise a team to hunt them down, but she's back on track now. She's found the courage to come with us on our mission, to help us. She's so close to becoming She Who Is Verve. This... almost... doesn't seem right.'

'Knowing things about other people when they can't know stuff about you? It's uncomfortable to begin with. As you get more used to it, you'll find that you only easily pick up what is at the forefront of someone's mind. For knowledge of anything else, you consciously have to delve deeper and that's something that won't feel right for you to do without the person's permission. Don't worry, it all seems very overwhelming to begin with, but you'll learn to trust yourself.'

'I'm counting on your help.'

'Stay in the middle of the vortex with me and it's there whenever you need it,' I giggled.

'You know, Am, there are some things you just shouldn't joke about,' Rowena said.

ELEVEN

Momentum

*A*s we lounged around the campfire the following morning, I noticed a very definite shift in the dynamic of our group. Sonja, who had usually seemed to find a way to sit next to me, sat on the log across the fire from me, chatting animatedly with Aleks, who was much more cheerful than normal. Rowena had a faraway look on her face which occasionally changed to one of wonder, confusion or joy, and Marvel and Holly both looked uncomfortable. They radiated uncertainty and anxiety, which I could feel their Bond-Partners attempting to alleviate. I felt Justin's presence in my mind, very quietly at first and then strengthening once he knew I'd noticed him.

That's an improvement, subtlety suits you, I told him.

I've been working on it with Quinta, he replied. *She complained that my thoughts were even more deafening than my teaching voice, so I've been trying to tone myself down. It's not something I've ever had to worry about with Gas as a Bond-Partner – his mind is everywhere at once and anything less than a mental yell to him just mingles in with everything else.*

I grinned. *I'll remember to thank Quinta, she's done us all a favour.*

All? Justin read my thoughts. *Flaming lanterns, Rowena and Sonja?*

In the same day? Oh, I see, good for Ro. And good for you for pushing Sonja like that.

She's determined now to pull Aleks along in her wake.

Well that'll make your life easier, especially now you need to start work with Flame. You'll start groundwork with her today? Justin asked.

Yes. She's determined to get better, but she's going to have to face the worst of her fears on her way to achieving soundness and then she's going to have to face them all over again in order to do what she's here to do. She's a brave mare and she's going to need to be.

Justin searched through my thoughts and I could almost hear him whistle to himself as he found what I knew about Flame. *We've all had to face our demons, but Flame's courage in going forward with this despite everything that's happened to her – well that's something else,* he observed.

It is. But she has Infinity, me and the rest of the group to support her. Everything happens as it should.

It does, Justin agreed. *That's why I'm going to give Rowena a little taste of her own medicine before I go down to breakfast. ROWENA, WAKE UP AND STOP DAYDREAMING.*

Rowena jumped so violently that she left the log on which she was sitting and then landed back down on it with a hard bump. Her look of astonishment turned into a scowl as I burst into laughter. I was Aware of her admonishing Justin, claiming that he could have given her a heart attack and demanding that he be more considerate in his communications from that point forward. She could feel his affection for her though, as well as his delight at her achievement and she couldn't stay angry at him for long. Soon, she was sharing thoughts with him excitedly about everything she was discovering. Marvel and Holly's confusion turned to understanding as they saw Rowena mouthing the words she was thinking to Justin. I felt Marvel making a decision.

It wasn't necessary to be Aware to feel the nervous excitement in the air as we all made our way to the horses' grazing area, which had now evolved into also being our riding paddock. Sonja was confident that she would be in a position to help Aleks and Nexus. Rowena was looking forward to riding Oak and seeing what they could do together now that they were both rested after the previous day. Once she had ridden, she would be teaching Marvel and Holly. And I was looking forward to beginning to work with Flame.

I remembered Infinity's advice from the previous day about failure being more likely if I prepared for it by asking for help which I didn't really need and I resolved to work with Flame on my own.

I felt Flame anticipating our arrival. She knew of my intention and she was keen to work with me. She was fascinated by what she had witnessed when Infinity and I helped Sonja and Bright the previous day, and her opinion of what might be possible with her own body had shifted as a result. That was something I hadn't picked up on until now and I paused in my thoughts to consider it. The way forward was suddenly clear.

My body will act as a template for hers, agreed Infinity.

When we reached the grazing area, all of our horses were waiting, ears pricked, keen for the session to begin. Flame stood next to Infinity and I was pleased to see that even at the sight of all six of us arriving together, she merely watched as we squeezed between the bushes and then separated to go to our own horses.

Flame registered my intention to groom her with brushes for the first time, and watched as I groomed Infinity first. I felt Flame ready herself when it was her turn and I held out the brush I would be using first, for her to sniff. She snorted and stepped back. I didn't follow her. Allowing me to groom her would be good for her well-being and would help her to feel more comfortable with me but I wouldn't inflict it on her. She lifted her head up high and peered at me and the brush down the length of her nose, making me laugh. She stepped back beside me and sniffed the brush thoroughly. I rubbed the wooden back of the brush against her shoulder. She was unable to stop herself from flinching, but she stayed where she was. The brush had stiff bristles, so when I turned it over and the bristles were against her coat, I used it in very light strokes. I worked from her shoulder, up her neck and then back down over the rest of her body, only increasing the pressure of my strokes where there was mud that needed to be worked loose. Flame coped well, even dropping her head down to graze for a few minutes at a time.

I moved on to a brush with softer bristles. She liked the feel of this one. She closed her eyes as I brushed her face and I felt her enjoyment as I worked the brush down her neck and over the rest of her body, lifting loose hair and dust from her coat. She was less enamoured by the mane and tail brush and it took a while for her to feel comfortable lifting her feet for me to pick the mud and stones out, but less than an hour later, I'd completed her first groom. She was ribby and her orange coat was dull and too thick for the time of year, but she looked clean and cared for.

Ready, Fin?

Infinity was by my side in an instant. *I will walk around you until Flame absorbs what she needs from me. Remember that I cannot move forward if your body blocks mine regardless of distance.*

I grinned. *How could I possibly forget?*

Infinity and I moved away from Flame and then Infinity put herself on a large circle with me as its centre. Her hind legs carried her weight and provided the power to propel her up and forward, her neck was arched and her front feet barely seemed to touch the ground. Her blue eyes sparkled with vitality and concentration as I felt her paying close attention to each and every part of her body in turn, from her hind feet all the way up to her ears, so that Flame's attention would be drawn to their arrangement. Flame was completely engrossed in the feel of a body in perfect balance both as a whole and as the composition of all its elements.

I turned slightly away from Infinity, drawing her onto a smaller circle. Her body made the necessary adjustments to keep itself balancing perfectly, and then made more as I turned to face her and walked towards her, my body level with her shoulder, so that she moved out onto a bigger circle. Flame followed all of the adjustments Infinity made with complete concentration.

Infinity moved up to a trot and as always, my breath caught in my throat. I didn't think I'd ever get over how beautiful she was. Her movement was effortlessly graceful, accentuated by her mane lifting and falling gently against her neck and by her silvery tail flowing out behind her with a gentle wave undulating along its length. She changed the size of her circle several times in response to changes I made in my body positioning and Flame was with her in every step.

Infinity moved up into canter and now it was just for enjoyment. Infinity, Flame and I rode together in Infinity's body, revelling in its grace and its power. Infinity slowed to a halt and then sat down further onto her hindquarters, lifting her forequarters into the air and striking out playfully with her front legs. We were Infinity! The three of us were one and there was nothing that we couldn't do. I laughed out loud, bringing myself back to my own body with a snap.

Infinity moved away from us and dropped her head down to graze. I turned my full attention towards Flame. She followed my intention for her to walk a large circle around me, with her lame right hind leg towards me so that I could easily see it. As she turned her forequarters onto the circle, her hindquarters swung to the outside, seemingly of their own volition. She lost her balance and her legs had to move faster to keep her upright. I held fast to my sense of how Infinity had organised her body, so that Flame had a constant reference point to which she could return. Once she managed to slow herself back down, she checked in with me and then tried again. This time as she turned onto a circle, she softened her back and moved her rib cage to the outside so that her body had a right bend through it and her hindquarters could follow her forequarters. She was stiff, but she could do it. My heart leapt.

Flame registered my delight briefly and then I felt her desire to push further. I turned away from her very slightly, bringing her onto a smaller circle. She began to lose her balance again but then allowed her rib cage to swing further to the outside, creating more of a bend through her body. She made it; she was able to maintain a smaller circle, despite the wrongness in her hindquarters. Her right hind slapped to the ground prematurely, short of its full stride, but her control of her body meant that while travelling to the right, she could balance. Time to up the challenge.

Flame followed my suggestion to change direction, turning away from me and then back on herself so that she now travelled to the left. I could see the problems her body was having but I kept the template of Infinity's body firmly at the forefront of my mind, together with the confidence that Flame would be able to emulate it someday – she just needed to make one small change at a time until she got there.

Flame was managing to walk a left circle by leaning in on her left shoulder to compensate for the twist in her pelvis and the fact that her right hind couldn't travel as far around the outside as it needed to. No. Compensating for her lameness was avoiding the issue. For Flame to get better, she would need to draw on the well of courage that I could feel inside her and meet her difficulties head on. I turned my body to the left a little more, indicating that Flame should turn with me onto a smaller circle. She followed my suggestion and her legs moved faster as she tried to keep her balance using her current body arrangement. I held in my mind not only a sense of Infinity's body walking on a left bend, but how she had felt in her body whilst doing it. Her absolute balance. Her power. Her ability to cope with anything. Flame was drawn into remembering her experience of Infinity's body alongside me. She slowed her walk down until she was only just moving and then tentatively swung her rib cage out to the right, pulling her weight off her left shoulder and back over onto her damaged right hind. She walked at snail's pace as she tried to reorganise herself according to the template I was holding for her of Infinity's body walking a smooth left bend. She managed it, making one adjustment at a time. Once she was there, the wrongness of her pelvis and stifle alignment were overwhelmingly obvious to her. Her pelvis wouldn't turn enough for the bend to be easily maintained and her right stifle stopped her right hind from coming through enough for her to be able to move at more than the slowest of walks.

Immediately, I moved level with Flame's nose, blocking her movement so that she halted. I radiated a strong flow of light towards her as I walked up to her and rubbed her gently on her neck. Her mind was a whirl. It leapt back and forth between her sense of how Infinity's body had moved on a left bend, and how her own body had felt. She felt again the parts of her body that had adjusted easily to her attempts to copy Infinity's template and then she settled on the parts that had held her body back from being able to arrange itself like Infinity's. I felt the stab of fear that shot through her as she realised where in her body she would have to make changes and I saw her mind flash back to how those parts of her body had come to be compromised in the first place. Instantly, Infinity's warm, nurturing energy wove its way through the light I was sending to Flame. We were Infinity and there was nothing we couldn't do. Flame absorbed our energy and our thoughts fleetingly as she continued to process her experience. She was still deep in contemplation hours later when my friends and I left the grazing area to get some lunch.

The mood around the campfire at lunchtime was jubilant. Rowena and Oak had made an impressive sight as they experimented with what their bodies could do together now. They had blurred into one another, making it impossible for onlookers to see them as anything other than one being as they moved up and down the paces, performing increasingly difficult manoeuvres. They had thoroughly enjoyed the appreciation and applause that they had received as a result. Sonja and Bright had spent some time galloping around the edge of the paddock with pure joy at their newfound balance and power. Their elation was infectious and we had all laughed and cheered as we witnessed another partnership blurring together into one being.

Rowena and Sonja had then proceeded to teach their pupils. We'd all laughed in sympathy with Marvel when Rowena told him that whilst I may have been content to let him progress at his own rate, he wouldn't be afforded that luxury by her. He made great strides forward in his riding in that session. While he allowed himself to appear hen-pecked, he and all of us who were Aware knew that he had already made a decision over breakfast that morning, not to let his fear of change stand in his way any longer as he saw the woman he loved evolving away from him. Holly, too, had allowed herself to be pushed further than normal, as had Aleks. Whilst sitting on a boulder watching them all, I had felt a momentum building within our group.

As I sat in silence, toasting a slice of bread over the fire and enjoying listening to my friends teasing one another whilst reliving the events of the morning, I realised that it had been a while since I had seen Bond-Partners blur together in their oneness in the way that I had seen happen twice in the past few hours. I missed Justin and Gas for the thousandth time and then with a pang, I missed Adam. I missed his easy company, his warm wisdom and his gentle humour. He would have loved being with us on a day like today.

Instantly, he and Peace were with me. Tears of happiness filled my eyes as I felt again their warm pride in our group and at what we were achieving together. They knew of my fledgling friendship with Fitt, of my tentative contact with the Kindred Elder and of whom I knew her to be, and of Flame. Where I empathised with Flame and the two Kindred over the difficulties that they were having to find the courage to face, Adam saw only the perfection in the roles that they would play in shaping the future. I sent him a wave of love in gratitude for helping me to see things from a different perspective. It was something he had always been able to do and it was yet another thing I missed about him.

'Am? Adam?' Rowena stared at me. 'And Peace. That must be Peace. He feels just as I imagined him to be.' She smiled as she felt everything that Adam wanted her to know.

Sonja stopped talking to Holly and a rapt expression settled on her face as she sensed Adam and his exchange with Rowena. All of a sudden, she shook herself out of it and looked embarrassed.

I moved to sit by her side. 'Sonja, it's okay,' I told her quietly. 'You can't help but pick up things from other people now that you're Aware. You still have to respect other people's privacy, but the lines are softer than before. You'll get used to trusting your judgment, don't worry.'

Sonja nodded. 'Thanks, Am. Once the initial elation wears off, this oneness stuff's, well it's all a bit...'

'Overwhelming?' I chuckled. 'You want to think yourself lucky that you weren't Aware before Justin learnt to be subtle. A few weeks back and your sense of being invaded and overwhelmed would have reached heights far higher than it will now.'

Everyone laughed, but I was Aware of Marvel trying to overcome his jealousy at Rowena's silent conversation with Adam; of Aleks feeling left out of my conversation with Sonja and wanting to be a part of it all, but wondering at the same time if he would cope with the new level of discomfort that would come with being newly Aware; and of Holly feeling resentful that she too was feeling left out, but not trusting herself to commit to progressing in the way that Sonja and Rowena had. She didn't trust that what she had seen in her horse when they bonded – a calm sea of peace and serenity – was truly what she had the potential to be. To commit to something of which she wasn't sure was to risk failure and disappointment. Better to hang about on the fringes and wait to see if things became clearer before committing herself completely.

Marvel would make the changes necessary to achieve perfect balance quickly now with Rowena's help. Aleks was still a long way off, and putting even more blocks in his own way. Holly, though, I could help, now that I had gleaned knowledge of the last, deepest, most protected layer of her block.

I felt the Kindred Elder's touch on my mind. I registered briefly that Rowena had managed to find Justin and Quinta, bringing them both into contact with Adam and Sonja. Good. While they were distracted, the Elder could read what she wanted to from my mind without any of my friends becoming Aware of her. I didn't think she was ready for their curiosity.

She lingered longer than she normally did. She could feel that our group was altering and she allowed me to be Aware of her eagerness to know what it was that was changing. As she sifted through my experiences, I felt Adam's attention touch my mind and hers ever so delicately. She recoiled away from us both, but then was back an instant later. She was intrigued by a discarnate essence that had obviously very recently incarnated as a human, yet was interminably intertwined with one that had recently incarnated as a horse. I felt her realisation that this was the mechanism by which we were evolving. All of her observations fell into place as she realised that we were moving past the point where we would ever see ourselves as separate beings whose primary concern was their own safety and comfort. The horses were helping us to see who we really were whilst we were incarnate, so that we could never see ourselves as being anything else.

Adam stayed as quiet and still as I did. The Kindred Elder realised that there were more of us who had become one with our horses now, more of us who were Aware, more of us who could help other Horse-Bonded to reach the same state, more of us to ensure that humanity strode forward past the point where they could ever return to the ways of

The Old. Her mind shuddered violently at the depths to which humanity had once sunk and doubt crept in to stifle the hope which had been slowly unfolding within her. What if it were a feature of humanity that we would always be capable of returning to being ruled by fear and insecurity, no matter how far we evolved? Her mind hardened. She wouldn't allow herself to be convinced that positive change could be permanent. Not yet. And then she was gone.

I took heart from Adam as he held to his view of the perfection of the Elder's role in shaping the future, then he and Peace retreated from my mind.

Sonja and Rowena were laughing at each other mouthing and muttering the words they were thinking to Justin and Quinta. Marvel, Holly and Aleks all sat in silence looking forlorn. I hugged myself inside and it was all I could do not to grin.

No, grinning would be considered unsympathetic and possibly mildly sadistic, agreed Justin.

If only they knew that it's always the most uncomfortable just before it gets amazing. I'd tell them if I thought they'd believe me, but they won't.

No, they won't believe it any more than we would have done, Am, and it'll only make Aleks even more sorry for himself. He's not nearly as uncomfortable as he's going to need to be for him to decide that change is preferable.

I nodded. *Agreed. It's going to be a long afternoon with the three of them, but I'm looking forward to tomorrow.*

Justin quickly picked up on what I was planning. *That will be interesting. You won't be letting Holly know what she's in for?*

No, tomorrow will be soon enough.

TWELVE

Centre

Flame was looking better, I decided as I caught my first glimpse of her in the morning sunshine. I had spent most of the previous afternoon infusing her with light as she grazed, ensuring that the fear within her was limited to its sanctuaries in the pelvis and stifle and not free to pervade her body. The grass she had eaten had therefore nourished her and not only were her ribs slightly less visible, but I thought I could see a slight gleam in the few patches of her coat that weren't caked in mud. My inward sigh at the amount of grooming I had ahead of me was quickly muted by my delight in realising that Flame had felt strong enough to roll repeatedly and with gusto in order to get herself into such a state.

I wasn't long grooming Infinity and then I set about finding Flame underneath her casing of mud. I was forced to be vigorous with my stiff-bristled brush, and soon clouds of mud and hair were flying loose and being carried away on the sharp spring breeze. Flame stopped grazing and bent around to wiggle her top lip on my back as I scrubbed away on her back. My heart leapt as I felt her acceptance of me as a grooming partner. I considered being a bit less forceful with my brush strokes, lest Flame opted to match my ferocity and groom me with her teeth instead of just her lip. Immediately, Flame's attentions became more gentle. She would make allowances for my feeble human skin. I grinned, thinking about how her view mirrored Fitt's, although Fitt had been more polite about it.

Flame recoiled from me as she registered my connection with the young Kindred. I almost cursed myself, but then I breathed deeply and regained my centre. Fitt was my friend. She was kin to the one who had hurt Flame but she was my friend nevertheless. Infinity and Oak had both been close to her and neither had been in any danger. She knew of Flame and she wouldn't come close enough for Flame to be uncomfortable. There was nothing to fear. I held my thoughts with absolute knowledge and confidence, Aware that Flame's courage to stay near me hovered at breaking point. I had no doubts. None whatsoever. Fitt was a Kindred but she was a friend and a brave one, who was stepping away from the conventions of her kind in her decisions to accept help from us and to see our horses as the teachers of truth that they were.

Flame snorted. Fear coursed through her as she stood tense and ready for flight. I calmly moved out of her way and went to stand at Infinity's side, draping an arm over her neck as she grazed. I was very carefully unconcerned by both Flame's fears and her readiness to leave us. She could flee if she wanted to and we wouldn't try to stop her. She would always move awkwardly but she could move without pain now and she would probably find a herd at some point, so she needn't be alone. Or she could stay. She could face her fears with Infinity's and my help. She was brave and strong. She could fully heal and she could fulfil the destiny that she had chosen for herself, but she would have to choose to stay with us in the centre of the vortex, where her fears would be magnified the most, where she would be challenged the most and where she would be the most uncomfortable. It was her choice.

Flame spun away from Infinity and me and took off as fast as she could. The other horses all watched her intently as she galloped around the outside of the grazing area but none made to join her. Rowena and Sonja looked over at me and I felt them grasp what had happened. Rowena nodded to herself and returned her attention to watching Flame, but Sonja's attention lingered with me longer, picking up all of what I knew about Flame. I nodded to her as her mouth dropped open with respect for what Flame intended to do if she could push her fear aside long enough to connect with the deep well of courage inside of her.

Now that Flame was moving at speed, her fear was subsiding, giving her the space to consider her choice. She could carry on going now that her body could move again, she could find a normal herd of horses to live with, maybe even find her old herd again. A feeling of safety washed over her briefly but it was tainted with the knowledge that safety wasn't real or even necessary. Or, she could stay with her new herd. A herd unlike any other. A herd that had change swirling around it in a way that was both disturbing and attractive at the same time. A herd that would enfold her and take her along with it, ensuring that she not only met but fulfilled her destiny.

There was no decision to make. Flame slowed to a canter and my friends cheered their appreciation as her long legs ate up the ground, her lameness hardly apparent as she engaged her hindquarters fully underneath herself. She slowed further to an ungraceful, wobbly halt in front of Infinity and me. I was stunned by the change in her countenance. Her warmth shone out in all directions, along with her confidence in herself as a force to be reckoned with. She had chosen courage and determination over fear and she was ready to do what she must.

Infinity whickered and reached forward to sniff noses with Flame. I laughed with delight and rubbed Flame's neck as Rowena and Sonja came running over.

'Flame, you're amazing,' said Rowena, reaching to rub Flame's neck, knowing that her touch would now be welcomed.

'She is,' agreed Sonja. 'Flame, you're a brave girl.' She turned to explain to Holly, Marvel and Aleks what had just transpired.

So, it's not just humans who have to find their centre, horses do too, sometimes, I observed to Infinity.

Horses are born with their personality and soul in balance. Any shift in focus is normally only a temporary deviation. Flame suffered trauma and pain over a sufficiently prolonged period that she became stuck more in her personality's worries and fears. Now that she has regained her centre she will find it easier to free herself of the other patterns which are unhelpful to her.

That's definitely how it feels when I'm centred, it's as if I'm harder to dislodge in any direction from my place of being.

I felt Infinity's assent. *Flame would not have rediscovered her centre today had you not remained in yours.*

But couldn't you have helped her? You and the other horses?

Everything happens as it should.

Of course it does.

Infinity, Flame and I worked together in the same way that we had done the previous day, with Infinity giving Flame and me a firm sense of her body's arrangement to use as a template, before moving to the side and giving Flame the space to work around me. Flame followed my intention for her to work to the right – her easier side – first again, concentrating deeply on organising her body the way she had done the day before. Once she had walked circles of varying sizes without losing the bend through her body and her muscles were thoroughly warmed up, she obliged me by turning to walk a circle to her left. Immediately, she slowed right down as her right hind slapped to the ground too early in its stride to allow her to bend to the left easily. I held firm to my sense of how Infinity's body moved and to my complete confidence that Flame would be able to begin to make small changes towards being able to move her body in the same way. Flame identified where her pelvis would need to begin to shift its alignment. Fear threatened to swamp her. I felt her hesitate in her decision to reorganise her body and I almost sent light to her. No. If I helped her, I would be shielding her from what she must face. Finding the courage to begin working through her fear was something that she must do for herself. I waited, confident that her courage would prevail.

Flame looked across and snaked her head at me, her ears flat back. She was desperately uncomfortable both physically and emotionally, and she wanted me to do something. I held firm to my sense of Infinity walking powerfully on a left bend, clear of any negative emotion, graceful, strong, capable. Flame could do what she needed to do. I knew she could. Flame looked across at me again and I felt the Kindred hanging on to her leg with her. The fear in her eyes almost shook me. Almost. I took a deep breath and remained centred.

And then Flame was with me. The second that she chose to believe in me more than in the fear that gripped her, she was able to step aside from some of it, leaving nowhere for it to be. As it dissipated into the ether, Flame tried to move her pelvis differently. Immediately, I hummed a low tone that resonated with the muscles and connective tissues in that area and then sent my intention down the pathway of sound to them, encouraging them to allow the movement that Flame was attempting. Now that Flame had released some of the fear that had been holding them in place, they were able to follow my intention and they shifted slightly. All of a sudden, Flame was able to turn her pelvis more to the left. Her jubilation sang out in my Awareness. The change she had made was small, but it was the beginning of her conscious return to health.

Flame walked circles to the left and right for a little while longer, fascinated with the change she had made in her body and how it affected both how she could move and how she felt. I was Aware of a hunger growing within her for more change. I smiled. My brave, beautiful, chestnut mare was indeed a force to be reckoned with.

I looked across to where my friends had been either grooming or riding their horses, to find that they had all stopped to watch. Rowena and Sonja were glassy-eyed, and Marvel, Holly and Aleks were looking from them to Flame, Infinity and me.

'Earth calling Rowena and Sonja,' I giggled. 'They're just a bit overwhelmed with everything they've just felt from Flame,' I explained to Marvel, Holly and Aleks. 'They'll be back with us in a minute.'

'Wow, Amarilla, just... wow,' Sonja said.

'She's a special mare, isn't she,' I agreed.

'You're a trio of special mares,' said Rowena, 'you, Flame and Infinity, and you're changing so fast. As Sonja said, wow. Marvel, the sooner you get on with it, the sooner you'll know what we're talking about. Hurry up and get Broad saddled, we have work to do.'

'Sonja, are you okay to help Aleks again today?' I asked her. 'Great. Holly, Infinity and I would love it if you and Serene would work with us?'

Holly looked at Rowena, who grinned and said, 'Fine with me, Marvel that means you have me all to yourself. You may want to take extra sustenance on board before we start, because after everything I've just witnessed, you're going to be experiencing a whole new kind of instruction from me.'

'When you say new, do you mean gentler, kinder, or... oh, okay, I'll just wait and find out. On my way to saddle Broad now,' Marvel said as Rowena stood pointing firmly to where Broad grazed some distance away, a look of determination on her face.

'When you say you and Infinity, are you going to ride around with me and Serene like you did when you helped Sonja?' said Holly.

'No, Infinity would like you to ride her,' I said.

'What? No, I couldn't possibly, what if I...'

'What?'

'Well, what if I can't ride her?' Holly said. 'I mean, I won't be able to ride her as well as you do, what if I stop her being able to move in perfect balance?'

'What if you do?'

'I'll be letting her down.'

'Decide not to let her down, then. You know that Infinity knows how to carry herself. She's happy to show you what that feels like, and then you'll be clearer about what it is you're aiming for with Serene.'

'I can't get on her.'

'Why?'

'Because I'm scared of what might happen.'

'What do you think might happen?'

'I'm going to ride Serene.' Holly turned and walked away from me. I ran to walk at her side.

'Holly, do you and Serene want to achieve perfect balance?' I asked her.

'Of course we do. That's why I'm going to ride her now.'

'Do you know, deep down in your heart, that you're going to push her and yourself enough for you both to be able to achieve it?'

Holly stopped in her tracks and glared at me. Tears filled her eyes as she whispered, 'No.'

'Then it's not Infinity you have to worry about letting down. You've done brilliantly to get to the stage you have with Serene and you're both so close. Tell me what it is that you're so scared of.'

'You're Aware, you must already know,' she accused me.

'It's your block. If you want to clear it, you have to admit that it's there.'

'Okay, fine. I'm frightened to commit to anything in case I fail. Serene tugged me when I was in the middle of my bone-singing apprenticeship and I couldn't have been happier. My Master was just about to get me finding the right tones on my own without his voice to copy and I was terrified I wouldn't be able to do it, so when Serene tugged me, I was off like a pebble from a sling-shot and I didn't look back. I practised finding and adjusting tones by myself, while Serene and I were on our way to The Gathering after we bonded, so that by the time we got there I was happy to resume my apprenticeship with the resident Master because I already knew I could do it.

'Riding Serene, trying to help her to balance better, is the only thing in my life that I've ever stuck to, because it isn't just about me. I know how important it is to her to do this so I've carried on, even coming on this mission with you because Serene wants us to be with you. But as time goes on and she and I progress, I get more and more terrified that I won't be good enough to make the final adjustments she needs me to, so I hold back. I know what I saw in Serene when we bonded, and I know that should mean that I have the potential to be what I saw, to be Aware like you and the others, but there's a part of me that doesn't believe it.' Holly's words tumbled out of her like water from an upturned barrel. She was breathless by the time she had finished but her purging had left a tiny hole in her idea of herself, an opening where a new idea, a new experience could take hold.

'You need to be clear that you can absolutely be what you saw in Serene when you and she bonded. Infinity can give you that clarity, if you'll ride her. Please, Holly, let Infinity and me help you?'

I felt Holly's attention go to Serene, who had been very quiet in Holly's mind during our conversation. Serene was loving as ever and hopeful, but nothing more. It was Holly's decision.

'Can we go off on our own? Where nobody can see us?'

'No, sorry.'

Holly rubbed her face vigorously with both hands. 'You'll help me? You'll make sure I don't fail?'

'Yes and no.'

Infinity wandered over and nuzzled Holly's shoulder. Holly turned to rub Infinity's face, which Infinity allowed briefly before stepping back and fixing Holly with her blue eyes. Then she walked over to where her saddle rested against a boulder and fixed her stare on Holly once more. I waited.

'Shall I saddle her, or will you?' Holly said.

'I'll do it while you decide how many holes we're going to need to let my stirrups down by to accommodate your impossibly long legs,' I said with a grin, and Holly laughed nervously.

Once Infinity was saddled, I put her bridle on. 'Fin doesn't need this anymore, but she's happy to wear it so that everything will be the same as when you ride Serene,' I explained. 'Okay, up you get.'

Holly's hands were shaking as she took Infinity's reins from me and then mounted. Serene appeared by my side. I felt her confidence that everything was proceeding as it should.

As Holly settled on Infinity's back, I felt Infinity bristle slightly. Holly was heavier than I, and her weight was distributed unevenly, with more to the right than the left. Her legs felt strange as they were so much longer than mine and hanging in a slightly different place.

I moved my attention to Holly's body and felt Serene there. She wrapped her energy around mine and drew me in. Holly took a sharp intake of breath. 'Am, how are you doing that? I can feel you.'

'Err, that was unexpected, but Serene's decided to help. Are you okay with this or shall I remove myself?' I said.

'No, stay, it feels better having you there, I can feel your confidence in me and suddenly I don't feel so scared.' Holly sent a huge wave of love to her horse for her help.

'Okay, well, before you ask Infinity to move, you need to stop collapsing your left hip because your weight's going over to the right. Sit like this.' Within her mind, I gave Holly a sense of how it felt to sit straight and I felt her body shift in response. 'That's better.'

'Flaming lanterns, I have no idea how this is happening but it's incredible. And I can feel that Infinity likes what I've done, through you. Okay, what else?'

'Ask Infinity to walk on and then ride as well as you can. Pay attention to what you feel from Infinity's body as well as what you feel from me. I'm not going to talk too much, so just feel and then do. Okay?'

Holly nodded and then tentatively closed her legs around Infinity's sides. I gave her a sense of being more definite, more confident and once she managed to replicate it, Infinity lifted her forequarter. Holly's first reaction was shock at the amount of lift Infinity achieved. Serene steadied Holly while I gave her a sense of what her body needed to do next. Holly responded quickly and a grin broke across her face as she felt what Infinity's body could do beneath her. But she wasn't quite there. Infinity couldn't sit back over her hindquarters properly because Holly's weight was a fraction too far forward. She needed to lift her head, against its tendency to always be looking slightly downward. As I gave her a sense of the final step she would need to take, I felt resistance from her. Looking down was her way of protecting herself from committing to anything. If she looked down, she could avoid what was in front of her, she could internalise herself with her fears. I knew that there was one thing that would make her look up.

Serene picked up on my thought and left my side. She trotted to a place in front of Infinity and whinnied. Holly lifted her head to look over Infinity's ears at her horse and immediately, I gave her a sense of always looking forward, looking to her horse, whom she had named for the person that she had the potential to be, the person she WOULD be.

Serene whinnied again as she walked along in front of Infinity and I felt Holly's love for her. She lifted her chin determinedly and set her head back, allowing her chest to lift and her shoulders to drop down and back. She was stable and strong and just where Infinity needed her to be. Infinity moved with ultimate grace and power into a trot and then a canter, with Serene now alongside her. Then, all of a sudden, Infinity collected herself into a halt. Holly dismounted, flung her arms around Infinity's neck and hugged her, then reached for Serene's saddle and bridle.

Within minutes, she was on Serene's back, focused, determined and confident. She knew exactly the corrections she needed to make to both her and her horse's bodies and she committed to making them. Within minutes, Holly and Serene blurred together into one being and my friends and I all cheered.

Over an hour later, a dripping Serene and an equally sweaty Broad finally came to a halt where the rest of us waited for them and their riders. Seeing Holly and Serene achieve perfect balance had been the final push that Marvel had needed for him and Broad to find their own. Marvel was a very capable rider and as soon as the last of his resistance to change had melted away, he had simply followed the confident instructions that Rowena gave him and become one with his horse.

It had sounded as if the horses were being murdered at times whilst Serene and Broad cleared the negativity from their past, with Broad's bellows being interspersed by shrieks from Serene. Their riders had stayed with them, keeping their own balance while their horses heaved and bucked beneath them, and helping Broad and Serene to regain their balance every time they lost it. Holly's and Marvel's insecurities were released without notice, and I knew that now they were Aware, they would wonder how they could ever have allowed them to stand in the way of the bliss of being at one with their horses and with All That Is.

Rowena rushed to embrace Marvel as he dismounted. 'I'm so proud of you,' she said.

'Proud enough to fetch the firewood in my place this afternoon?' Marvel hugged her back tiredly. 'Thanks, Ro. We couldn't have done it without you.'

'You mean you wouldn't have. You could have done it any time you wanted.'

I grinned. Interesting times were ahead now that Marvel and Rowena were both Aware.

As if reading my mind, Aleks said quietly, 'They were bad enough when they could only communicate by talking. They're going to be a nightmare now that they'll be doing it with their minds as well, we'll never get any sense out of either of them.'

'It's going to be very quiet for a while. Remember how I behaved before I began to get my Awareness into balance with the rest of my life? Well, we're going to have four of them all being vacant at the same time. I think we might be relying on each other and Vickery for conversation,' I said, smiling as I watched Sonja hugging Holly in congratulation.

'Thunder and lightning, I hadn't thought of that,' said Aleks, 'but you've got better really quickly recently, could the same happen with them?'

'Hmmmm, possibly. It was hard for Justin and me as we were the first to be Aware and we had to make sense of something that was previously unknown. Gas and Infinity gave us lots of time to get accustomed to our new Awareness before beginning to help us to balance it with our physical lives a bit more, and it was really only being on this mission that gave me the impetus to sort myself out.'

'Then I'm confident that being on this mission will also mean that these four will come back to their senses soon,' Aleks said cheerfully.

He was less confident once he and I were the sole conversationalists at lunchtime. Marvel had a faraway expression on his face as he muttered the words of his conversation with Justin, guffawing every now and then as I hadn't heard him do since he was last with his friend. Rowena gazed at him proudly, every now and then rolling her eyes at the humour he was sharing with Justin. Holly and Sonja were in conversation with Quinta, Sonja mouthing the words that formed in her mind and Holly whispering those that she both sent and received.

'This is eerie. I can't think of another word for it,' Aleks said.

'Well, you know the saying, if you can't beat them...' I teased.

'I feel further away from that than ever. Sonja's being great helping me and I'm doing my best, but I'm still finding this whole situation too much.'

'Could you help me then? We need to keep them all spending at least some time with us here in the physical world. They'll fight it at times, but we need them. They don't have the luxury of time like Justin and I did.'

'No problem. When do I start?'

'How about now?'

'Just remember, this was your idea,' Aleks said getting to his feet with a mischievous grin on his face. He picked up the water bucket and upended it over Marvel's head.

Marvel came to in a flash. 'ALEKS!' he roared, jerking the other three out of their reveries.

'It was Amarilla's idea,' Aleks said between breaths as Marvel chased him round the campfire holding his full water beaker aloft.

We all laughed as Marvel got close enough to empty his beaker over Aleks, and then laughed even harder as a dripping Aleks again tried to protest his innocence.

Hooves thumped through the scrub nearby. 'Vickery,' Rowena and Holly said at the same time.

Vickery rounded some bushes and came into sight alongside Verve, who was dragging a litter of supplies. 'Hi, guys,' she said, 'wha've I missed?'

THIRTEEN

Horses

Flame put on weight and condition steadily. As she continued to work with Infinity and me, she gradually released her fear, each time allowing me to help her pelvis to realign better. I was hopeful that soon, we could begin making the necessary changes in her stifle.

When we packed up camp and resumed our journey, Flame walked next to Infinity and me with a sense of purpose that wasn't even shaken by the discomfort she felt when I checked in with my sense of the Kindred Elder to make sure that we were still heading in the right direction.

The Elder returned my interest. She gently searched my mind for my most recent experiences and I was Aware of her refusal to allow herself to commit to feeling one way or another about the fact that most of our group were now Aware. Flame, however, gave her pause for thought. I felt her shock when she picked up the destiny that Flame had chosen for herself. She sifted carefully through all that I knew of Flame, all that we had experienced together and all that Flame was prepared to face in order to fulfil her destiny. A glimmer of hope flared within her and unlike the other times, when I had felt her extinguish any hope or faith that things could change, this time she allowed it to remain flickering deep inside of her. She made sure I knew, however, that her trust in humanity remained uncertain.

I was Aware that Flame's discomfort at the Kindred Elder's touch on my mind was now being quenched by her determination to forge onwards towards its source. The Elder and I were united in admiring Flame's courage before her touch on my mind receded.

'That was a fine line you just walked, Amarilla,' said Marvel from behind me. 'She's like a butterfly who'll take wing with the slightest breeze, isn't she?'

I nodded. 'Understandably, she's finding it hard to trust that humanity is capable of truly, fundamentally changing.'

'It isn't as if we can hand on heart be sure of that ourselves,' said Rowena, 'but that doesn't mean that the Kindred shouldn't allow us to try. The horses have invested themselves in us for generations to get us to this point, as the Kindred well know. Their faith in us should count for something.'

'I think it might be the faith that we and the horses have in the Kindred that will make the difference,' I replied thoughtfully.

'And Flame will be at the centre of that,' said Sonja, leaning across from Bright's back to rub Flame's back. 'I'll hold back and explain to Aleks and Vickery what just happened, they're looking disgruntled again.'

The days that followed fell into a routine. We would all rise at dawn and Marvel and Vickery would go off hunting while the rest of us groomed the horses, made breakfast and then packed up camp. Marvel and Vickery would eat what we had prepared for them on their return, while we prepared and packed whatever game they had brought back – usually rabbits and birds with the occasional deer. We would travel for most of the day, whatever the weather, and then stop somewhere between mid-afternoon and evening, whenever we came across suitable grazing for the horses. There, we would leave the horses to rest while we had dinner and then I would work with Flame while the others took it in turns to coach

Aleks with Nexus and occasionally Vickery with Verve, when Vickery requested it.

Fitt visited us every now and then, venturing only as close as she felt that Flame could cope with before waiting for one or more of us to go and meet her. I was Aware that Fitt focused on her respect for our horses whenever she was near, so as to make it clear that she represented no threat, and Flame was adjusting well to her presence as a result.

Fitt was good company. She carefully avoided giving us any information about her kind, but she seemed to set great store by her ability to listen to everything we told her about ourselves and the villages of The New and then to give us her opinions about every aspect of what she learnt. She would furrow her brow as she considered every detail that we gave her and then she would look earnestly into our eyes as she told us of her views with regard to each of them. Those of us who were Aware could feel how important this process was to her; it was as if she defined herself by her ability to decide for herself how she felt, and we could all feel her confidence growing in herself as we listened to and valued her opinons.

She decided that our communities were organised well, although our tendency to elect village Elders, rather than instinctively know who they were, was lacking. She knew of the Skills and largely approved of their use, but was astonished that we had only recently realised that they were basically all the same, and that anyone with a throat construction that allowed the creation of the range of sounds necessary could perform any of them. She disapproved of weather-singing, since creating the desired weather in one location would have ramifications for those in surrounding areas. She was surprised by the need for many of our Trades – Tailors, Heralds, Chandlers, Bakers and Carpenters were, in her view, superfluous – but she wanted to know everything we could tell her about the work of our Farmers, Charcoal Burners and Potters.

She had known that humans of The New allowed themselves to be guided by horses but her first encounter with Infinity and me had stunned her. As a result of everything that she had witnessed and felt from us and the rest of our group since then, she had developed a rapidly growing fascination with our horses. Sometimes she was slow to guard her

thoughts before giving away that of all the horses, it was Flame who took
her interest the most. On one such occasion, I felt the tiniest of tendrils
reach out from Fitt to Flame. The tendril was tentative but knew its way.
As soon as I was Aware of it, Fitt pulled it back into herself so fast that I
almost thought I'd imagined it. I pushed the episode immediately to one
side and spoke of something else. It wasn't until I was on my own with
Infinity that I allowed myself to mull over what exactly it was that I'd
sensed. I smiled as understanding dawned.

Everything happens as it should, Infinity echoed my thoughts.

*It took me a while to believe you when you first told me that. It used
to only make sense when used in combination with hindsight, but now
those words seem to come to me constantly,* I told her.

*It is a difficult concept to understand whilst believing that the dream
is real. Now that you are able to observe the dream whilst living within it
you are able to appreciate the simplicity of reality. There is no right and
no wrong. No good and no bad. We are all parts of All That Is. We are All
That Is. We always have been and we always will be. When we incarnate
we choose to be part of a system that strives towards balance as a
mechanism for remembering who we really are. When something is out of
balance it will seek to right itself. Everything happens as it should.*

Suddenly, nothing seemed as complicated as it had.

Marvel came back triumphant from meeting Fitt one day. He had
taken a spare bow and arrow set with him from our supplies and had
offered to teach Fitt to use them to hunt, as she seemed to struggle so
much with bringing down prey bodily. Apparently, she had leapt at his
offer, enthused by the idea of being able to be sure of killing prey
outright with no suffering involved. She had been an avid student and
was immensely grateful to Marvel for teaching her and for leaving the
bow and arrows with her as a gift. She assured him earnestly that she
would practise her archery until she could be sure of hitting her mark
every time and only then would she use her new skill to hunt for herself.

The only one who avoided going to meet Fitt was Aleks. I tried to
convince him of how Fitt felt about the horses, so that he might feel it
was safe for him to take Nexus to go to meet her, but he refused even to
consider going. 'Any encounters with Kindred will be too soon for me,

so there's no way on earth I'll go seeking one intentionally,' he replied on one occasion. He had found a certain level of comfort in our daily routine and he had no intention of disrupting it, but each and every time any of us went to meet Fitt, we invited him along anyway.

We came across villages from time to time, occasionally because they lay in our path but usually because those of us who were Aware would sense the presence of human thought processes concentrated in an area, and we would divert from our path to find them.

The first few times we came across villages, Infinity and I and Rowena and Oak camped a short distance away with Flame. She experienced the visits to the villages through the other horses and by the fourth village we came across, she was happy to join in, so we were all able to enjoy the warm hospitality provided by the villagers – grazing for the horses and soft beds, baths and meals for ourselves.

While it was usually tempting to stay for longer, we always moved on after a couple of nights after helping as many people as possible; we passed on our horses' counsel when it was requested and although Vickery took on the largest share, all of us except Aleks helped as many people to multiskill as we could. When it came time to leave, we advised anyone still wanting help to multiskill to travel to Jack and Katonia's centre in Rockwood. Aleks's job was to gather and pack the supplies that were always freely offered by the villagers in return for our help, and for the most part, we ate well as we travelled, with Marvel's and Vickery's hunting efforts supplementing what we and the horses could carry.

Infinity and I, with Flame alongside us, still led our group as we travelled, although as time went on, any of the others who were Aware could have taken over. All four of them were familiar with the Kindred Elder's essence and they knew in which direction we needed to travel, but we had reached an unspoken agreement that since it was my mind she chose to touch from time to time, I would continue to lead the group towards her, if only to keep everything as constant and unthreatening to her as we could.

Between us, we developed mental exercises to do to keep us focused in the physical world, such as finding something within view that began with each letter of the alphabet in sequence, or counting the number of strides our horses took in a straight line. We would take it in turns to do the exercises while being prompted by the others to explain exactly on what the bird of prey in the nearest tree was focused, how old the crooked tree was, whether the bee that buzzed along in front of us was returning to or departing from its hive, in which direction was the nearest village, what colour underpants Justin was wearing that day – getting that information from him while performing the mental exercises at the same time had proven the most difficult test to date – or any other detail that required use of our Awareness.

We pushed each other relentlessly to remain centred, however difficult the combination of tasks given to us by our fellows, and as a result, each of us was getting better and better at it. I became able to hold non-verbal conversations with no outward signs, as did Rowena and Sonja. Marvel only muttered when communicating with Justin, and Sonja only whispered occasionally, when she was tired.

We travelled steadily north-east as spring turned into summer. Occasionally, we would sense the essence of a Kindred nearby but as soon as we were sensed in return, the Kindred would very definitely turn his or her attention away from us. We knew Fitt's essence well enough to sense her imprint on the phenomenon and we were confused. All of us except for Aleks would have welcomed meeting more of the Kindred, yet Fitt appeared to be of the opinion that it would be unwise. We sensed her unease but she kept any further thoughts on the matter closely guarded and refused to discuss it or even to acknowledge that it was happening when any of us asked her, so we agreed between ourselves to let it be.

The further we travelled, the fewer and further between were the villages. As the pattern became apparent, we took on more and more food supplies at each village, to see us to the next. Our horses carried their extra saddlebags without complaint but we monitored them closely during the day and stopped for the night as soon as any of them began to show signs of weariness.

Flame let it be known that she was prepared to take a share of the supplies that we humans deemed so important, but none of us were happy for her to do that until she was completely sound. She was coming on in leaps and bounds; her pelvis was now correctly aligned and she had begun to face the fear that she held in her stifle joint as she and I slowly corrected its arrangement. Every time she made the smallest change, I relived with her the terror that she had felt when the Kindred had wrenched her leg out to the side so violently and so horribly. I had to concentrate hard to step aside from the fear and the pain that Flame's memories tried to convince her were still so real and so justified, so that I could heal her as she changed.

Aleks became more and more agitated as we travelled. The thought that at some point we may cease to come across any villages altogether became larger and more frightening in his mind, until it threatened to take him over completely. Nothing that any of us, including Nexus, did or said could shake his terror that he might die of thirst or hunger, leaving Nexus at the mercy of the Kindred or the large wild cats of which Marvel and Vickery were now catching regular glimpses as they hunted.

Vickery complained numerous times to the rest of us about our refusals to batter at Aleks's fear with our light until we got through to him as we had done before. We were Aware, however, that uncomfortable as Aleks was, we wouldn't be helping him by shielding him from his insecurity any longer. We would look out for him as he suffered and we would support him as best we could, but now it was up to him to find his way to achieve the potential he had seen for himself when he bonded with Nexus.

Aleks looked awful. He was losing weight and neglecting his personal hygiene, convinced that there was no point in looking after himself when he would likely die soon. Nexus didn't look much better. She too was thinner than she had been, despite the lush grazing that had been plentiful on our journey so far, and her coat had lost its shine. She was putting everything she had into her attempts to reach her Bond-Partner, but his fear was blocking her out.

When the forests and scrubland through which we had travelled for the majority of our journey gave way to massive expanses of grassy plains, we hoped that Aleks might be able to let go of the portion of his fear that was associated with the Kindred, since in the absence of the woodland which was their preferred habitat, we were unlikely to meet any. Sadly, he was almost beyond rational thought by that point and merely convinced himself that we and the horses were even more likely to be attacked by the wild cats that surely roamed in huge hunting groups in the absence of any Kindred to keep their numbers down.

None of us thought it wise to mention that there was at least one Kindred in the vicinity; Fitt was absenting herself from convention yet again by leaving the trees in which she had so far managed to stay as she tailed us and in which she could move comfortably and easily, and was following us on foot. She still kept at a distance that ensured Flame's comfort, and so wasn't close enough to be spotted by Aleks. I was concerned for her, as her body had been engineered to scale buildings, meaning that climbing trees and swinging through branches were as natural to her as walking on the ground was not. I was Aware that she was constantly stiff and sore but aside from leaving her herbal preparations along with the small amounts of food that we left to supplement her rapidly improving hunting, there wasn't much we could do to help; she was sufficiently far behind that asking the horses to take any of us back to her each night to offer healing would have left them too tired to carry us and all of our supplies the following day.

I was glad of the distance Fitt was keeping when I and my friends sensed wild horses. We had struck up camp by a small stand of trees that offered both shade and firewood, and we were waiting for our campfire to burn hot enough to cook the brace of rabbits that Vickery had hunted as we travelled that day. Our horses were dozing in the shade as we moved about in our well-practised routines – Marvel attending to the fire, Vickery and Rowena preparing the food, and Holly, Sonja and I gathering firewood, arranging bedding ready for later and securing waterproof sheeting over our bags and the horses' saddles and bridles.

Aleks's job had been to fetch water until fairly recently, but now even that was too much for him to cope with as he fought his constant battle for sanity. He knelt by the fire, appearing to watch Marvel as he fanned the flames with a large sheet of bark, but actually caught up with the images that flashed through his mind of himself and Nexus dying in all manner of horrific circumstances. He rocked back and forth on his heels, his dark, curly hair damp against his head and neck and his eyes almost insignificant in the middle of the black shadows that surrounded them.

He was suffering badly, we all knew that, and the temptation to send him the light that would break through the barrier of fear that prevented him from hearing his horse was almost overwhelming at times, but we knew that if we did that for him, we would merely be delaying the process rather than halting it for him.

As I held a waterproof sheet down so that Sonja could tap a peg into the ground at its corner, I was Aware of a group of essences all touching my mind at the same time, initially dismissing me as not being of concern and moving on, but then returning to me. Not just to me, I realised, but to me, my friends and our horses. Sonja looked over at Bright at the same time that I looked to Infinity. All of our horses were now alert and looking off to the west. Then, all of them except for Flame relaxed again and went back to their dozing. Flame focused on the essences briefly before joining the rest of our herd at peace.

'Horses.' Rowena's voice carried across the campsite.

'But not like ours,' I murmured, fascinated.

Aleks jumped and looked around himself frantically. 'Horses? Where? I don't see any horses,' he said. 'Where are they? We have to warn them of the danger they're in.' He got to his feet and squinted as he tried to see into the distance.

Marvel put a hand on his shoulder. 'Aleks, sit down,' he said kindly. 'They're not close, they were just checking to see if they could sense any predators in the area before stopping to graze, and they found us instead. Neither they, nor we, are in any danger.'

Aleks lifted his hands up into the air and stamped his foot as he flung them down by his sides again. 'YES, WE ARE. THIS MISSION HAS MOVED FROM DANGEROUS TO COMPLETELY HOPELESS, WHY AM I THE ONLY ONE WHO CAN SEE THAT?'

'Because you're the only one who has stopped listening to his horse and is currently having a meltdown,' said Rowena. 'I've been in the exact same position you're in, Aleks, and I know how scary it is, as I've already told you numerous times, but I know you can't really hear me. Your fear has blocked Nexus out of your mind and has made you irrational. The only way you can begin to feel better is to look around you, take comfort from the fact that none of us are concerned for either our or our horse's safety, and relax enough to let Nexus back into your mind.'

'Relax? Relax?' Aleks laughed a horrible, manic laugh. 'I'll relax when you all come to your senses, turn around and lead me and Nexus home.' His voice changed to a whine. 'Please? Rowena? Amarilla? Please, take us home?'

Rowena went to stand in front of Aleks. She put her hands on his shoulders and looked into his eyes. 'Aleks, we're trying to take you home, you just can't find a way to believe it. Sit down here by the fire. We'll be cooking dinner soon and I want you to eat well, so that Nexus will have one less thing to worry about. Will you do that for me? For her?'

Aleks glanced at each of us frantically and then his shoulders slumped and a look of hopelessness stole over his face. He allowed Rowena to sit him down and then he sat staring listlessly into the fire. Rowena jerked her head at Marvel, indicating for him to follow her over to where the rest of us stood.

'He's getting even worse,' she said to us, 'and, Vic, before you suggest it for the millionth time, no, giving him our light won't help him, not in the long run. All that will happen is that he'll allow Nexus to help him stay calm for a while, then his discomfort at travelling, camping, not knowing for sure when we'll find water and food supplies next, not knowing what we'll face with the Kindred and these wild cats we're coming across, all of it will weigh him down again until he ends up exactly where he is now. We all know that things have to reach a level of discomfort that's unbearable before we tend to try and do something about it, well this is Aleks having reached that level of discomfort. The problem we've got is that Nexus is getting weaker.'

Holly nodded. 'She's putting everything of herself into trying to reach Aleks. She's not going to be able to carry him for much longer and he's going to be in an even worse state if he has to walk. It's not going to be long before we'll have to stop travelling altogether so that she can conserve what little strength she'll have to keep herself alive.'

'It shames me that we're allowing Nexus to come to this,' said Vickery.

Instantly, Nexus was with all of us who were Aware.

'Vic, Nexus is adamant that we allow Aleks the freedom to address his own issues in his own time,' Holly said.

'Even if it kills her? Aleks is so obsessed with keeping her safe that his fear is killing both of them,' Vickery said. 'You all seem to forget that I've been in his position and I know how he feels. The light knows where I'd be now if you guys hadn't sent your light to me until I could see things more clearly. Are you really willing to see him and Nexus die, rather than give them the same help?'

'The difference in this case, is that Aleks needs to be in the position he's in, in order to achieve the potential he saw for himself. Nexus knows that and is a willing participant in this whole process,' I said. 'It's not easy for any of us to witness this and it's a lot harder for you, because you only have the evidence of what you're seeing to go on, but please, Vic, trust us when we tell you that helping Aleks in the way you want to won't be helping him, or Nexus.'

Vickery glared at each of us in turn and then looked to the skies and sighed. 'I do trust you all,' she said, 'and Verve confirms all you've said, but I can't find a way to be comfortable with it.'

Marvel drew her into a warm hug. 'You wouldn't be the friend we all love if you could,' he said.

Vickery hugged him back slightly awkwardly and then withdrew from him. 'Anyway, what's all this about horses?' she said.

'Well, they're wise and they're kind and they're everything to us, you know, with us being Horse-Bonded and all,' Marvel said, laughing.

The tension broke and Vickery laughed along with him. She punched him playfully and said, 'I mean the horses you sensed before Aleks went off again, as you very well know.'

Holly took pity on her. 'There's a herd somewhere not too far from here. They've sensed us and we appear to have taken their interest.'

'Are they anything to do with Flame?' Vickery asked.

'No, they aren't her original herd and they haven't had contact with it either, she's checked,' I said.

'So why the interest in us? Wild horses usually stay clear of humans,' Vickery said.

'They know what we've helped some of our horses to do,' I said,
Aware of the horses' continued interest in us all. I returned it. As I had
already noted, they weren't like our horses. I remembered back to when
Infinity and I had first bonded and she told me that bonding with a
human changed the essence of a horse. I could see what she meant;
whereas I could easily sense our horses' personalities, the wild horses'
minds were far less easy to distinguish as being separate from one
another. If I concentrated, I could make them out individually, but only
just. But something was changing. As I tried to separate the horses'
essences from one another in my mind, they slowly began to relate to
themselves more as individuals.

The observed is always affected by the observer, Infinity advised me.

I recoiled from the horses' minds as I understood.

*You do no harm. They require your help and they will need to adjust
in order to be able to receive it,* Infinity reassured me.

I looked at my friends, all of whom except Vickery and Aleks – who
was still staring into the fire – were nodding thoughtfully.

'Errr, guys? You're going to need to fill me in on whatever it is that
you're all sensing, I'm in the dark here,' said Vickery.

'The horses want our help to achieve perfect balance and release
everything that they will then have no further need of, just like our horses
have,' said Sonja. She rubbed her hands together and looked around at
the rest of us with a mischievous glint in her eye. 'Life in the vortex is
just about to get even more interesting.'

FOURTEEN

Collective

I leant back against a tree trunk and watched our horses grazing in the moonlight. I was wrapped in my blanket against the cool night air, upon which wafted smoke from our gently crackling campfire. I could hear Marvel's muffled snores and the sound of horses' teeth grinding the rough grass, but beyond the limits of our herd, all was still and quiet. I'd given up trying to sleep. I'd gone through my usual pre-sleep routine – catching up with Justin, trying to reach Katonia and then a final check in with Infinity and Flame to make sure they were content – but the sleep that usually came easily to me had stayed just out of reach. Eventually, I'd admitted defeat.

I was relieved to see Nexus eating hungrily. With Aleks asleep, she could rest from her vigil over his mind and look to her own needs. I sent a gentle flow of light towards her, which she accepted gratefully. I increased its strength. I greatly admired the level of support she was giving her Bond-Partner but I was saddened by what it was costing her. I'd seen other horses suffer in the same way in the past, although I noted that she didn't see herself as suffering, in fact she placed no judgment on her situation at all. She and Aleks had agreed to incarnate together with the aim of working to overcome a pattern which he had carried with him through lifetime after lifetime – that of needing to control his external circumstances in the belief that it would make him feel safe and happy. He had incarnated over and over in The Old, a culture that had only reinforced his belief. This was his first time incarnating in The New and, determined to clear the pattern which had plagued him, his soul had made an agreement with another, who would incarnate as a horse in order to try to help him. Nexus knew that she had ensured Aleks's best chance of success by keeping him with our group and she was focused on seeing her agreement through with him. That was all. I increased my flow of light to her to full strength, all the time ready to decrease or withdraw it if she found it too much. She didn't.

Infinity's nurturing energy joined mine, quickly followed by the loving warmth that was Flame. Oak added his gentle strength, which was followed by the quiet assurance of Serene, Verve's positivity, Bright's optimism and the patient understanding that was Broad. Together, we loved Nexus into the night.

I jerked upright, wondering if I had dozed off and dreamt that a wild horse's mind touched mine. I looked around me in the moonlight and saw that Nexus slept soundly nearby, Infinity and Serene grazed, Flame lay at my feet, resting but awake, and Broad, Verve and Oak stood over Nexus. All of us still directed our love to Nexus, all was just as it had been seconds before. Except that a wild horse now observed us through my mind. As the rest of the wild herd gradually added their interest, I noticed that they were far more easily distinguishable from one another than the last time I had been Aware of them; the change that I had set in motion when I had tried to separate them had continued to influence their idea of themselves.

I was Aware that the support our horses gave to Nexus was familiar to the wild horses and they barely noticed it. They were focused on what it was that had caught their attention as they ceased grazing to rest – the light that I was sending to Nexus. This was a new phenomenon to them and had drawn their essences to me like wasps to a ripe strawberry.

I noticed a purity about the wild horses' essences due to their lack of exposure to humans but they lacked the lightness that Infinity, Oak, Bright, Broad and Serene possessed since achieving perfect balance and clearing everything that had previously weighed them down.

It was as if a score of arrows hit the same target simultaneously as the whole of the wild herd's attention focused on my thoughts about what our horses had achieved. I felt their hunger to do the same. I thought about the sunrise and I pictured myself and my friends leaving our camp with our horses and riding to meet the wild horses. We would help them.

I was being gently shaken by my arm. 'Am,' said Rowena. 'Am, come on, breakfast is ready.'

I rubbed my eyes and then opened them blearily. I sat up and winced at the ache in my back. 'Take my hand,' Rowena said and pulled me to my feet. 'Nexus looks a lot better this morning, well done, we should have thought of doing that for her before.'

I looked over to where Nexus grazed in the early morning sunlight and was relieved to see that she did, indeed, look better. Her body looked fuller and her coat had recovered some of its shine. 'Aleks?' I said.

'Same as normal. He's eating without too much argument this morning though, Marvel's seeing to him,' she replied.

'We need to leave our stuff here and ride out to meet the wild horses this morning,' I said. 'It won't wait, witness for yourself.'

Rowena scanned my mind, nodded and said, 'Good job we've a hearty breakfast waiting for us, isn't it.'

An hour later, we were on our way to find the wild herd. I let Fitt know what we were about and that we would be returning to camp, so not to follow on, and she was happy to stay where she was for the day. She had been having a lot of success hunting with her bow and arrows and had been eating well, so a day spent resting would do her good, I pointed out to her. She agreed but I was Aware of her desire to track down one of the wild cats we had described seeing and that had so far managed to avoid her; I suspected that she would rest far less than her body needed.

Aleks insisted on coming with us, even though Vickery had selflessly volunteered to stay in camp with him. We would all have preferred for Nexus to have the chance to rest for the day, but Aleks had reacted with terror at the suggestion of being left behind, convinced that Nexus would be too vulnerable to predators with only one other horse and two people to protect her, so along with us they came.

Flame took up her usual place alongside Infinity and me. I pondered on how the wild horses felt so different from how she had felt when I had first been Aware of her, even though she had at that point been wild. She had been an easily identifiable entity in her own right, since her injuries, terror and sudden separation from her herd had thrust her into a very acute awareness of herself as an individual. Having now encountered the collective consciousness of a wild herd, I appreciated even more fully the trauma that Flame had endured by having been separated from her own herd so brutally on top of having been attacked. And I also realised just how much our bonded horses had given up of their natural way of being, in order to be all that they were to us.

It was a choice we made gladly. We have benefitted much in return, Infinity told me.

You may have done, you and the others who have achieved perfect balance with our help, but what about all of the horses who have gone before you? And all of those who are here now, whose Bond-Partners will never push themselves far enough to help their horses achieve what you have?

That which benefits one of us benefits us all. That which benefits more of us benefits us all to a greater extent. It is impossible to be otherwise. You know this.

Of course, because we are all one. Ohhhhhhhh! You don't just mean in the greater sense, do you? You mean in the sense that the horses know that they're all one. Why didn't I realise that before? When one of you achieves perfect balance, the rest of you are all moved a little bit closer to it by association. When more of you achieve it, the rest are moved closer still and if lots of you achieve it, the other horses can't help but be pulled along in your wake since they're not separate from you. And that goes for all of you, those incarnate now and those who have incarnated in the past, because you're all one!

The same is true for humans. As more of you evolve the rest cannot help but advance. The collective consciousness operates at the level of the species as well as at the level of the whole.

So, we can't fail. As long as we keep doing what we're doing, helping horses and humans to achieve perfect balance, we'll eventually reach a point where the remaining members of both species just find it automatically as a result of being one with the rest of us who've already found it.

For horses that is true. We already know for what we must strive in order to evolve and we have no barriers to doing so. The number of us required to achieve it before the rest do so by association is therefore relatively low. For humans it is more difficult since the majority have no knowledge of the truth of reality. They do not know what it is that they are missing and so they do not strive towards it. It will take a great many of you becoming Aware before the rest begin to feel that there is more that they should know and a great many more before they are moved to begin to look for it. That is why your kind require more help than we alone can offer.

The Kindred.

When humans allow themselves to be influenced by the Kindred their evolution will be certain.

It was as if a thousand lanterns all burst into flame simultaneously within my mind and I couldn't contain my excitement. Justin was with me instantly. He grasped the implications of everything Infinity had helped me to understand and I felt him make a decision.

Justin, they still need you there, I protested weakly.

I'm coming, he replied. *The wild horses aren't encumbered by bonds with humans and they already have a sense of what they need to do from our horses, so they'll be quick to make the changes needed and that will help all of the others, including those here at The Gathering. I can make a far greater contribution by helping you to help all of the other wild herds that will be heading your way than I can here, not to mention the fact that coming will restore my sanity.*

I sighed. *Quinta won't like it.*

She'll understand as soon as she knows what we now know. She has both Noble and Spider advising her now and she's changing fast, Am, check in with her and you'll see. She's adjusted to being Aware as fast as lightning strikes and now we know why – the collective consciousness. You and I have prepared the way for those who follow to find everything easier. I. Am. Coming.

You're so far behind us now though, Jus.

You won't be moving far for a while. And I have Gas.

I ran out of arguments that I didn't even really want to make. *Take care, then, we have Fitt looking out for us and our numbers seem to be deterring the wild cats, but you'll be alone.*

Really? You, of all people, are actually going to try to persuade me, of all people, that I'll be alone?

I chuckled. *Okay, I give in. But I'll be keeping a watch on you as you travel. If you go via Rockwood, let my family know how we're doing?*

There's a straight path to you, Am, and it goes nowhere near Rockwood. They'll know you're okay through Candour and to tell them the rest of it, you'll just have to keep trying to reach your sister.

Fat chance. She's one big jumble of hormones and emotions that I can't find a way through and she can't concentrate long enough to find a way to let me. Never mind, everything is as it should be.

Absolutely, Justin agreed. *I'm leaving in a few hours.*

'Well, I'm glad that's sorted. I for one will be mightily pleased when he gets here,' Marvel said, riding up beside me.

'So, you're not going to even try to pretend that you didn't just eavesdrop on a private conversation?' said Rowena.

'It was hardly private. Am, did you know that when you get excited about something, you broadcast it so loudly that it's almost like being shouted at by Rowena?' Marvel said.

I laughed. 'Sorry. So you picked up everything?'

'Yes.' Marvel turned around to look at the others and then confirmed, 'We all did, except for Vic and Aleks, obviously, and Holly's just filling them in now, although I'm not sure Aleks is even listening.'

Bright cantered up next to us. 'This is all very exciting, isn't it?' Sonja said with flushed cheeks.

'And it's about to get even more so,' I said as Infinity whinnied shrilly.

A dust cloud appeared on the horizon and before long, we could hear the thunder of many hooves pounding the plains. Gradually, a dark, moving mass became visible and as it got closer, I could make out the horses who galloped towards us. The mare who led the way was black. The horses of her herd were a mixture of browns, blacks and greys with one chestnut among them that I could see.

I was Aware of their excitement, their anticipation and their common purpose as they veered off to one side of us, slowing to a canter and then a trot. I felt the intense scrutiny of both the lead mare and the stallion who brought up the rear. They had sensed us from afar, but they had never seen humans before and the sight of humans mounted upon other horses was enough to give them pause to double check that there was nothing that could endanger their herd.

Our horses all whinnied to the wild herd and many of those who now trotted a wide circle around us responded in kind. There were mares, some with young foals alongside them and a few of them pregnant, and there were fillies and colts, but the stallion who still scrutinized us was the only mature male in the herd. As my Awareness wove its way gently through the herd, I gleaned an understanding of its dynamic.

This was a family group. The lead mare was trusted by the others to find grazing and water and to decide when it was time to move on. The stallion kept the herd together by pushing them from behind as they followed the lead mare. He kept other stallions away from his mares and offspring as well as resolving disputes between his herd members. The youngsters of the herd were all his offspring. Two of the colts and a filly were reaching maturity and the time was approaching when he would drive them off to join other herds, rather than risk either of the colts challenging him for his position, or risk inbreeding with the filly. He was open to fillies from other herds joining his family but he would tolerate no mature males. Except ours. He was Aware that Oak, Broad, Bright and Verve showed no interest in the mares of their own herd, let alone in those of his, in fact they showed little interest in much that was normal for a male horse; they were content to be part of a herd whose composition could change at any time and over which they had no say, and their instincts to breed were muted and ignored. They had no reason to challenge one another let alone to fight. They had sacrificed what it was to be a male horse in order to be with their Bond-Partners.

I looked around at my friends as I felt their anguish. Rowena, Marvel and Sonja felt keenly how much their horses had given up of themselves. I nudged their minds and reminded them of everything we had just learnt from Infinity; our horses had made sacrifices but they had also benefitted from their bonds with us and now their fellow horses would benefit as a result. We needed to concentrate on the situation in front of us. All three nodded and I felt Holly send her love to them all.

The wild horses came to a heaving, snorting halt off to one side of our herd. The stallion placed himself between them and us but there was no hint of aggression from him, only curiosity.

I had an idea and Infinity immediately agreed, followed by the rest of our group who were Aware. Marvel explained what was happening to Aleks and Vickery as they all moved away from the wild herd, leaving me and Infinity on our own. Infinity turned away from the herd and began to walk a circle. There was scuffling and snorting and the odd squeal of protest as the wild herd fanned out to watch us. I resisted the temptation to turn and watch them. Whilst I was turned away from them – the least threatening, physically, that I could be – I broadcast the suggestion that they feel not only what Infinity did with her body, but how she allowed me to influence her body with my own. In sharing her experience of being ridden with her, they would be prepared to accept a rider, they would know that going against their instinct and allowing a potential predator on their backs was safe and they would understand the physical signals that they would be given when they were ridden.

Infinity walked, trotted and cantered, responding instantly to signals when I gave them to her. The wild herd shifted around as they watched and felt what we did, unsure of being around such strangeness but unable to tear themselves away. Holly and Serene joined us. There was more shuffling around and jostling for position in the wild herd as they took in the additional horse and rider. One by one, Sonja and Bright, Rowena and Oak, and then Marvel and Broad joined us, keeping Serene and Infinity between them and the herd in order to help the stallion to remain relaxed in the presence of our stallions. Once we felt that the mature horses of the herd understood what they would need to do, we separated and came to a halt. We unharnessed our horses, who left us to go and wait with the rest of our group.

All five of us were available to help any of the horses who wished it. The choice was up to them.

The lead mare of the wild herd edged past the stallion. She would go first. She was strong, decisive and accustomed to being in charge. She needed help from someone who was experienced and confident enough that the mare wouldn't feel the need to take charge, whilst being sensitive enough to her high ranking within the herd that the mare need not give up who she was in order to take instruction. She was so like Infinity that it was no surprise when she chose me.

She circled around me and approached from the side, every now and then stopping to sniff my scent from the air and moving her head to adjust her view of me before coming closer. I held the back of my hand out for her to sniff, which she eventually did. I held firm to my intention to give her the help that she wanted from me. I felt her eagerness fast overtaking her wariness. She dropped her head down to sniff Infinity's saddle at my feet. She wouldn't be wearing that. She was not bonded. My heart tried to plummet but I caught it and centred myself. Despite my lack of prowess as a bareback rider to date, this would be the day that I would master it. Everything happens as it should. I hadn't been riding Infinity with her bridle on, so that was one less piece of harness to move to one side, as I knew the mare wouldn't have countenanced wearing that either.

The black mare let me know that she was ready for me to mount. I climbed onto a pile of boulders nearby and in my mind pictured putting a leg across the mare's back from there. The mare obligingly moved alongside. I felt Rowena's total confidence that I would be able to ride a wild horse without harness and I shot a quick grin at her. Marvel's confidence quickly made itself known, followed by Holly's and Sonja's. I was Aware of Vickery's shock at what I was about to do and also that Aleks's mental torment had abated slightly as he watched in disbelief.

Complete confidence. I knew that I was strong and capable. I knew that although carrying a rider would be a foreign sensation to the mare, she would feel as if I'd always been there. I put my leg across her back and lowered myself into a sitting position. The mare stiffened beneath me and then relaxed.

I rode her exactly as if she were Infinity. She remembered all of the signals she had felt me use when I rode my own mare and she responded to them only a fraction slower than Infinity did. I loved her fierce intelligence and her willingness to focus all of herself on what we were doing. I could feel how readily she would have questioned the instructions my body gave to hers had I been even a fraction less sure of myself, but as it was, her quick responses and eagerness to change ensured that we made rapid progress. Within the first hour, she was moving as well with my weight as she had without. After a further hour and a half, she was responding to my signals as quickly as Infinity would have and we were nearly there. She was now able to move straight, since I had corrected her tendency to hold her body on a slight right bend. She could lift from my lower leg and engage her hindquarters more and my thighs were burning from holding her back every time she was on the verge of losing her balance forwards with no bridle to support her. My back muscles were tired, but I knew we could do it. Just a little more engagement of her hindquarters and she would be there. I nudged her with absolute knowledge that this would be the final adjustment she would need to make. She was tired and sore from all the changes she had made but she responded instantly... and she was there. Each and every part of her body slotted into an alignment that allowed her to move with maximum power and grace. Her ecstasy rang out into the ether.

Her stallion whickered to her but she was too caught up in her achievement to notice. I nudged her to a trot and then to a canter, easily helping her to maintain her balance. I felt the negative memories within her begin to swirl around as their refuges in places of previous imbalance disappeared. I almost braced myself for what must come, but then relaxed. Everything happens as it should. The mare slowed gracefully to a halt. She needed me no longer. I slid off immediately and stepped back just as she began to scream.

They all lived it. They were one. The whole herd, including the foals, shed the lead mare's negative memories with her. They galloped and bucked and shied and spun and when they all came to a stop, the whole herd felt lighter.

The stallion stepped forward, his white neck arched and sweaty and his sides heaving. He also had no intention of wearing harness. He required a rider who, if they had incarnated as a horse, could have challenged him for his herd. He needed a rider with a strength of character he could respect but with a softness that would stop him short of wanting to fight. My friends and I all looked to Rowena even before he had taken his first step towards her. I made my confidence in her my primary thought and felt Sonja, Holly and Marvel do the same. I felt a wave of love for her as I felt her confidence in herself mirror ours.

Since his lead mare had opened the way and made it clear for the rest of her herd, the stallion was primed for the feel of Rowena's weight on his back and for what would follow. Rowena rode superbly. I could have cried with pride in my friend as I watched her sit the proud, powerful stallion with relaxed self-assurance, her timing perfect whether she was asking him to follow her instruction or whether she was responding to his need for her body to support his while he adjusted his balance. Both her concentration and his were absolute. They knew where they were headed and after only an hour or so, they arrived there. The stallion sat down on his hind legs and lifted his front legs in the air, striking out as he bellowed his newfound power. Rowena leant forward, clasping him with her arms and legs and grinning from ear to ear. Once he had allowed her to slide to the ground, he took off by himself, exploring all that his body could now do. His herd stood watching until his memories, bereft of anywhere to hide, came to the surface for release and then once again, the herd discharged the negative energy as one.

The two colts who were nearing maturity stepped away from the herd. They knew they would be leaving the herd soon as neither was strong enough to challenge the stallion. They would do this before they left. The one who would likely have the strength and presence to have his own herd one day approached Marvel and the one who would always be a follower, whether of a bachelor herd or of a herd whose stallion would tolerate the presence of an unthreatening male, approached Sonja. I could feel the ease with which both colts accepted their riders and their willingness to follow the path that their sire and lead mare had cleared before them. With the help of their riders, they followed the path with ease and in no time at all had reached their destination. As the herd released everything that had previously held the colts back from the total power that was now theirs, I could feel the collective consciousness of the herd changing. It was not only lighter, it held within it the impression of perfect balance.

The next to step forward was a tall brown mare with a brown and white filly foal at foot, who was near to weaning. We all knew she would approach Holly, and I began wondering if the horses had selected us in turn on purpose, before I remembered with a grin mirrored by Rowena as she wondered the same, that everything happens as it should.

What happened next was a beautiful sight to behold. Holly was as gentle and sympathetic as she was focused and determined, and it was as if the mare were just waiting for her signals before she leapt to respond, immediately and accurately, as did her foal who emulated every step beside her. The collective consciousness of the horses was made visible. When the mare achieved perfect balance, the foal absorbed the pattern for it from her mother. As she matured, her body would follow the pattern that had settled within it and she would never experience anything less than absolute strength and elegance.

The effect on all of us was profound, both those of us who were Aware and those who were not; Aleks's sobbing rang out across the plains despite Vickery's efforts to quieten him. I smiled with relief, Aware that the sight of the foal achieving what she had, had reached Aleks in a way that none of us had been able. He was deeply moved to the extent that Nexus was able to get through to him and explain exactly what it was that he had just witnessed.

Sonja, Holly, Marvel, Rowena and I spent the rest of the day riding our way through all of the herd who were mature and strong enough to carry a rider, each of them following the pathway made wider and clearer by those who had gone before them and achieving their objective increasingly quickly as a result. Those who weren't yet strong enough worked alongside their mothers, from young foals like the first one, to the older colts and fillies.

Aleks and Vickery brought us water and mouthfuls of food to eat in between rides, massaged our tired, aching muscles and kept up a constant stream of encouragement, Aleks almost manically so. Whenever a mare with a foal at foot was ridden, he watched from as close as possible, the delight on his face a joy to see after the dark terror that had been gripping him so relentlessly.

We were all exhausted by the time we had made our way through the whole herd. The wild horses were physically tired, but energised by what they had achieved. They cantered around us, joyfully, powerfully, gracefully and so light on their feet that the sound of their hooves on the ground belied their number. They were a magical sight to behold as the black mare lead them back in the direction from which they had come. They offered no gratitude and none was necessary. Everything happens as it should. I lowered myself down to the ground with a groan.

'I won't lie, what you lot just did was the most amazing thing I've ever seen and I'm in awe of you all,' said Vickery, 'but if any more of you sit down, I'll flick you with horse dung. Sonja, don't think I won't do it, stay on those two feet of yours. I know you're tired, but we need to get back to camp so Aleks and I can feed you all and that means we need to saddle the horses and get going. Marvel, there's a pile right here with your name on it unless you get moving right now. Aleks, saddle as many as you can and I'll do the same, and we'll get these weary heroes on board. Move this way, everyone, you too, Am.' She extended a hand and pulled me to my feet.

'Thanks, Vic, I can't remember ever having been this tired,' I said.

'I'm sorry I haven't got my act together enough to be in a position where I could have helped you all,' Vickery said.

'Well if you had, we'd be having to rely on Aleks to cajole us home now,' I said. 'We need you exactly as you are, Vic, you've been brilliant today.'

'Something happened to Aleks today, didn't it? He's calm and almost his old self,' Vickery said.

I nodded and explained what had happened, as we followed the others to where our horses grazed. 'It's a relief that Nexus has finally been able to reach him again.'

'That's not the only thing that Nexus has been able to do, by the look of it,' said Vickery.

We stopped in our tracks to watch Nexus sitting her weight onto her hind legs as they propelled her upwards and forward in an immensely powerful but totally controlled, elegant trot around an open-mouthed Aleks, who stood holding her saddle and bridle. She moved with an effortlessness that could only mean one thing.

'Aleks got her to a place where she was so close to achieving perfect balance before he had his breakdown, she had only the smallest of adjustments to make to achieve it, and the collective consciousness of the wild herd carried her along with it to make them. It's just as Infinity said it would be,' I said.

I made my tired legs run alongside Vickery to where my friends all embraced Aleks, who stood, still holding Nexus's harness, with tears making flesh-coloured tracks down his grimy face. 'She's done it,' he was saying over and over. 'She's done it.'

Marvel clapped a hand on his shoulder. 'She has. And now, mate, it's all up to you.'

FIFTEEN

Perfection

I was glad that Infinity only needed me to keep my own balance in order for her to maintain hers whilst she carried me over the flat, unchanging plains, as I had neither the energy nor strength to be able to offer her anything more. My exhaustion, however, and that of my friends who had ridden alongside me that day, was lifted by the happy chatter of Aleks and Vickery as we made our way back to camp.

Aleks was walking alongside Nexus, refusing to ride her lest he disrupt her body's newfound balance. He kept up an almost constant narrative about everything he had belatedly picked up from her; how she had been walking from one patch of grazing to another when she had felt herself lifted by the experiences of the wild herd nearby and how she had then suddenly felt herself wanting and able to move in a different way. She had proceeded to release the few negative memories lodged within her with so little problem that even Aleks had been unaware that she was doing it, caught up as he was in his delight at the antics of the foals. Aleks was proud of Nexus and delighted for her, but ashamed that he had neither helped her to achieve what she had so desperately sought, nor been there for her when she released the negative energy that she had been carrying. He was excited, though, as he felt his horse revelling in her achievement, and his excitement was infectious.

Vickery walked, trotted and cantered a very bouncy, happy Verve around us as he and she delighted in the improved way of going that he had found as a result of also being carried further along the path to perfection by the achievements of the wild horse herd. She compared notes with Aleks and every now and then stopped to ride next to the rest of us, thanking us over and over for what we had done that day. When she wondered out loud how many other horses would have made as much change as Nexus and Verve, it dawned on my tired mind to wonder the same thing.

Why wonder when you can know for yourself, or even just find out the easy way by asking? Justin's thoughts were for all of us. I heard Marvel chuckle.

Okay, wise one, what's happened? I asked Justin.

Quinta burst into my mind not ten minutes ago with the news that our top four students' horses all achieved perfect balance this afternoon, and their riders were so moved by what they felt from their horses that they threw all caution to the wind, blasted past whatever had been blocking them from getting there, and achieved it too. And that was just as a result of you lot helping one herd!

And there are more coming to find us, I knew all of a sudden as I sensed more horses turning their attention to our group.

My friends who were Aware of Justin's and my conversation looked around at me and then they and Justin read the information they needed from my mind.

Marvel related Justin's news to Aleks and Vickery, finishing with, 'And there are more herds heading our way. They know what happened today and they're on their way to find us.'

I hope I can get there in time to help with some of them. Justin's thoughts reverberated with his excitement. *Two weeks and I'll have caught up with you.*

Two weeks? There's no way you'll get here that quickly, we've been travelling for months, I argued.

And you've made detours to visit your family and all the villages you've stopped to help at along your way, you've delayed to spend time with Fitt, you camped for weeks in order to help Flame and unless a lot has changed since I last saw you all, there will have been even more time wasted chatting, eating and in Marvel's case, snoring.

'Oi!' Marvel said out loud.

Gas and I stop long enough for him to graze his fill while I grab a bite and have a snooze and then we're off, continued Justin, *and we're moving at Gas's pace, not the leisurely amble that you will have been enjoying. Two weeks, tops.*

'I'll give him leisurely amble,' grumbled Rowena as she rubbed her back. 'We wouldn't have been fit enough to do what we did today if that was all we'd been doing.'

We all felt Justin's satisfaction that his teasing had hit home, before Quinta came blasting excitedly into our minds with the same news that Justin had already told us. When she demanded to know what we'd all been up to in order for the phenomenon at The Gathering to have occurred, we were grateful that we could merely leave her to find the answers she needed from us, rather than having to find the energy to relate it all.

We arrived back at camp to find that the fire, which we had left banked and smouldering, had gone out. Marvel groaned and set about relighting it whilst Rowena saw to Broad alongside Oak. Vickery tended to Verve and then set about preparing dinner, and Aleks quickly unharnessed Nexus and then helped the rest of us to see to our own horses. As he rubbed Infinity down, I leant against her tiredly, and stroked her neck. She turned and nuzzled my hand, enfolding me in her energy as she had done so many times before. We were Infinity. We were happy and proud of what we had done today.

We remembered back to the out-of-body experience we had shared the previous year and we remembered the satisfaction we had felt at having accomplished what we had set out to do in this lifetime. And now, we were doing more, all the while becoming so closely interwoven that it was impossible to imagine ever being able to separate out which bits of our essence were me and which were her, in order to be able to incarnate into future bodies and lives.

That situation will not arise. This will be the last time we will enter the dream, Infinity informed me.

That makes sense. How do you know that when I don't?

I told you once that time in a linear form is a fabrication of the human mind. Events are perceived to be occurring one after the other when in truth they occur simultaneously. Everything has happened and yet is all still to come. Accept that this is the case and you will know both the past and the future.

It was like trying to stop sand from falling through my fingers. I could grasp grains of what Infinity had told me for a second at a time and almost, my mind understood before my humanity reordered my thoughts of time back into a linear format and I had to begin again.

For now merely accept the truth. Your mind is sufficiently open that as it settles within you your perception will begin to change without struggle, Infinity advised me and I instantly accepted her counsel.

As I lay down to sleep that night, sure that I would find it without issue after the exertions of the day, I checked in with Infinity and then with Flame. Infinity was grazing peacefully, much the same as when I had left her. Flame, however, was not. In my weariness, I hadn't taken account of the fact that she'd been withdrawn ever since our experiences with the wild herd and was now even more so. She was frustrated. The collective consciousness of the horses called for her to make the last small change to her stifle joint that would bring her to soundness and allow her to follow the pathway that was now clear before her. She wanted to be carried along with the achievements of all of the other horses, but there was still a small piece of fear within her of which she couldn't find a way to let go.

As her frustration grew, I tried to think of a way I could help her. She knew exactly how her stifle joint should move and exactly how her fear was stopping her from being able to move it so. That much, Infinity and I had been able to help her with, but now I was at a loss.

The softest, most gentle tendril of love and hope touched Flame and then instantly withdrew. Fitt! The thread that I had seen stretched between her and Flame, so thin, so tenuous that I wouldn't have noticed it had I not caught Fitt sending a tendril of interest along it to Flame weeks before, became more definite.

We must observe only, Infinity advised me and instantly, I withdrew to the very edge of Flame's mind and made myself small and silent.

Flame knew instantly who had touched her and fear stabbed through her. It was all I could do not to send light to her or go to her in person to reassure her that she was in no danger, but I knew that Infinity was right. This was up to Flame. I waited for Fitt to extend herself towards Flame again, but she did not.

Despite the fear that wanted to swamp her, Flame remained centred, paying attention to her soul and observing the knowledge that had been within her for so long. She pondered for a while and then she made her decision. She followed the thread that had always been there, linking her to Fitt but unnoticed until Fitt had recognised it and given it significance. Fitt was waiting for her and as soon as their minds touched in mutual recognition, the thread burst into life and solidified, reaffirming an agreement made long ago by the souls of my warm-hearted mare and my Kindred friend; they would help each other to balance aspects of themselves in this incarnation and propel forward the evolution of three species in the process.

I felt Fitt's excitement as she welcomed the touch of Flame's mind on her own and then I reeled as a whole world of information was transferred between the two of them in no more than a second. I realised how far ahead of me Fitt was in the use of her Awareness, that she could touch minds with another – even one of a different species – and relate so completely and so immediately that the level of communication I had just witnessed was possible.

Flame's fear didn't subside, in fact I felt her terror as the weight of her destiny became immediate and real for her; Flame would accept a Kindred Bond-Partner.

I was in awe of the perfection of it all. Everything wanted to find balance. In having a Kindred on her back, Flame would revisit the situation that had caused her so much pain and terror, giving her the opportunity to feel everything she needed to feel in order to clear the last of her fear and be able to achieve soundness. And then Flame and Fitt would work together to achieve perfect balance. Flame would add her experience to the horses' collective consciousness and Fitt would be the first Kindred Horse-Bonded, her position cemented by what she had achieved with her horse, and the first solid link between the Kindred and human races.

I sent a huge wave of love to my brave, beautiful Flame. She would be Fitt's Bond-Partner, but she would always hold a very special place in my heart.

I will look after her as you have. I will ensure that her destiny is fulfilled and my own along with it. My friend, I thank you for listening to your soul and befriending me. Thanks to you and all you have brought with you, the way in front of me is clear. Fitt's words arrived in my mind so gently that it was as if they had always been there, just waiting for me to notice them. I smiled as I realised that according to the non-linear nature of time, they always had been.

I sent my love to Fitt by way of reply even as I felt Flame gather her strength and resolve and leave our group to go to her. I bit my lip as a tear rolled down my cheek. Flame would follow the thread that linked her to Fitt and then she would face her worst nightmare. She would triumph though, I knew she would. She was brave, strong and determined and Fitt was on her side. They would find their way forward together and then, when they were ready, they would find us again.

The Kindred Elder placed her touch on my mind, ever so carefully so as not to alert Fitt. I felt her keenness to keep abreast of the situation with Fitt and Flame through her contact with me and – for reasons that she kept from me – without Fitt knowing that she was being monitored. Was this the beginning of trust between the Elder and me? I wondered to myself, careful not to make it a question to her. To my surprise, she allowed me to know that it may be a small beginning.

I drifted off into a restless sleep and dreamt that I limped across the plains in the moonlight. I had left behind the security of my herd and I was feeling scared and vulnerable. I followed the thread that bound me and pulled me towards my worst fear and my biggest hope. I walked for hours, alert to every sound and scent that snagged on my senses, and quietly watchful in my Awareness for predators. Several times, I ran from sounds that I couldn't immediately place, only to discover that my concerns were groundless. When hunger bade me stop to graze in the moonlight, I snatched at the course grasses, unable to relax as I continued to scan my surroundings with all of my senses. My agreement with the one I sought pulled at me through the thread that linked us, adding to my discomfort. When I scented water, I diverted from my path in order to find it and the pulling at my mind intensified, only relenting once I was once more travelling towards its source.

I caught the scent of wild cat only moments before I felt his stare. He was sleepy; I had woken him with the sound of my hoofbeats in the still night. He decided he was hungry enough to wake up completely. I was hunted. My lame hind leg guaranteed that my transition into a wild, flat-out gallop was ungainly and lacking in power, but my panic drove my hooves to pound the ground ferociously as I sought to escape. I heard the wild cat break his cover and launch after me and all thoughts fled my mind as my senses focused purely on my predator and my flight. I felt him getting closer at an impossible rate and then I heard the soft thumping of his feet just behind me. I could feel his hunger and his delight for the kill that he knew he would make. Even as I waited to feel the weight of him landing on my back, terror wouldn't let me give in but drove me on. I drew level with a large outcrop of rock as a shadow launched itself towards me.

I sat bolt upright, screaming. I got to my feet and tried to kick myself out of my bedding as Holly reached me and grabbed hold of my arms. 'Amarilla, are you awake? You are. What's the matter? Oh, thunder and lightning, Flame!'

'I need to get to her, need to help...'

Knowing that it must be too late, knowing what they would surely discover, I felt the others who were able reach out to Flame.

'Well, that won't have helped her hind leg, she's overstretched herself,' said Marvel.

Flame flooded my mind once more and she was galloping. She couldn't still be here, surely? She couldn't have escaped the wild cat? Yet she was definitely still galloping. She was exhausted and she was slowing, but she was alive. I searched her mind and watched again as the shadow launched itself into the air, but instead of being brought down, Flame had galloped on to the sound of yowling from the wild cat, first in anger and disbelief and then with pain. Abruptly, the yowls had ended.

'FITT!' I yelled out with relief. 'It was Fitt whose shadow I saw, she saved Flame, oh thank the light.'

I bent double, put my hands on my knees and tried to slow my breathing, to calm down. Infinity's love wound its way through me, helping instantly.

I was Aware of Fitt extending love and a warm welcome to Flame along the thread they shared, even as she held the wild cat down whilst his soul fled his body.

Flame came to a standstill in the moonlight, running with sweat, her sides heaving. She looked back towards where she knew Fitt to be. She didn't see her as Fitt. She saw her as kin to the one who had tried to kill her. She saw her as the soul with whom she had, eons ago, made an agreement. She saw her as the first flower to bloom in a meadow full of thistles. She saw her as the one who would both challenge and complete her. She saw her as her Bond-Partner.

Flame broke into her ungainly trot and then into a tired canter. When she neared Fitt, she slowed to a walk and then a halt. She dropped her head to graze as Fitt butchered the wild cat.

'That was almost as dramatic as when you were tugged by Infinity,' said Rowena, yawning. 'In fact, I'd even go so far as to say that Fitt has outdone you, Am. Saving your Bond-Partner from being savaged by a wild animal has to beat running yourself to exhaustion and collapsing in a heap like you did.'

I managed a grin. 'Sorry for waking you all,' I said and felt my bottom lip begin to quiver. 'And I'm sorry, but I need to cry. Flame's brave but she's so scared. She's been through so much and she still has so much to do and on top of it all, she had to go through being hunted again. I feel so far away from her, so helpless. I know I shouldn't feel like this but I'm just so...'

'Human,' said Rowena, wrapping her arms around me, 'and when you actually allow yourself to get a good night's sleep, you'll be able to see things as they really are again and you'll be fine. Fitt saving Flame from the wild cat has meant that their bonding has been given a headstart as well as giving Fitt some decent meals and giving the other wild cats pause to consider whether hunting horses is worth the risk of being taken down themselves. As a very good friend of mine is fond of saying, everything happens as it should. Back to bed now, Am, actually on second thoughts, wait a second. Holly, can you sort Am's bedding out? She's been tying it in knots. That's better, come on now, Am, into bed and I don't want to hear anything from you until morning. Let go of everything you think you are responsible for and just sleep.'

I was lowered into my bedding and as Infinity once more enfolded me in her nurturing energy, sleep found me.

I was wet, I realised as I woke the next morning. I rubbed my eyes open and sat up to see that the camp was deserted, apart from Aleks, who was sitting across the fire from me. He grinned.

'I told them you'd want to be woken, that you wouldn't appreciate waking up sopping wet, but I was shouted down,' he said. 'Actually, when I say shouted down, I mean frowned at, gesticulated at and told in stern, hushed tones to lower my voice so as not to wake you.'

'Rowena managed to speak in hushed tones?' I said, trying to separate myself from my wet, tangled bedding.

'Nope, Rowena did the frowning and gesticulating. It was Marvel who threatened me with banishment if I woke you.'

'Banishment? Aleks you know we'd never cast you out,'

'Of course I know that and Marvel knows I know, he was just trying to shut me up so you could sleep.'

'Where are they all now?'

'Far enough away for their weather-singing not to disturb you. They're worried about you,' said Aleks.

'They're weather-singing? For this amount of drizzle? It's hardly worth it,' I said.

'They're not trying to get rid of it, they're trying to amplify it,' said Aleks. 'Sonja's been concerned about the lack of rain the plains have been experiencing this year and now that she has a good amount of cloud to work with, she's intent on squeezing as much moisture out of them as possible. She's been a Weather-Singer for too long to be able to ignore a situation that could do with help. The pregnant mares and those who are suckling foals will benefit hugely if the grass greens up.'

'And the others are adding to their experience of weather-singing by helping her. You weren't tempted to join them?' I asked.

Aleks shook his head. 'No. I'll learn to multiskill at some point, but for now I need to focus on Nexus and me.'

I nodded. 'You're so close to finding your way, Aleks, especially now that Nexus has found hers, and when you do, everything will be so much easier for you.'

'In my saner moments, I know that, but I can't seem to keep my thoughts together for long enough to process what's been happening, what it means for Nexus and me and how I can make use of it. When we were with the wild herd yesterday, when I saw the foals moving as one with their mothers, not copying them but moving as if one consciousness operated through both of them simultaneously, it was as if the sun came out from behind the clouds and everything was clear to me. And now I can't remember what it was that was clear to me. When Nexus showed me how she made the final adjustments to get to where she has, I was ecstatic. It was so easy for her and I knew, just for a split second, that it would be easy for me, and now I can't remember how I could possibly have thought it would be.'

I finally managed to extricate myself from the wet tangle of my bedding. I went over to Aleks and knelt down in front of him. 'What happened with the foals and with Nexus touched you so deeply that your fear was pushed to one side and you were able to hear your soul. Now you're allowing your fear to seep back in and it's cutting you off from what you know. If you allow it to build, it will cut you off from Nexus again too. You have to try to hold your fear to one side. Please try, Aleks?'

He shook his head, sadly. 'I don't think I can. The others told me what happened to Flame last night and I almost passed out at the thought of it. We're surrounded by danger and it could take Nexus and me at any time.'

'But Flame is still alive. It's true that in choosing to leave us to go and face her fear, she had yet another trauma, but it helped her to be where she needs to be, doing what she needs to do.'

'I don't have her courage,' said Aleks. 'I could never make the choices that she's made.'

'You've already made one of them. Flame has pushed herself out of her comfort zone in order to fulfil her destiny and that's exactly the choice you made when you decided to travel with us. You've already done the hard part, Aleks, you've pushed yourself away from what's easy and into what's hard. All you need to do now is to choose different thoughts. You can dwell on your fears, on your need for comfort and absence of worry or you can focus on Nexus, her love for you, what she's achieved, what you can achieve with her if you'll let yourself, and then you'll realise that comfort and security are beliefs and nothing more.'

Aleks opened his eyes and looked into my own. 'It's not that easy,' he said.

'It can be if you choose it to be.'

Aleks looked away. I stood up. 'I'm going to get changed into dry clothes. Could you help me to string the waterproof sheets up in the trees, so we have somewhere to shelter when the real rain comes?' I asked.

Aleks nodded. I sighed inwardly, knowing that I couldn't spare him from what was to come, but knowing that I'd tried. I shook my head and blinked. For a second, I'd known what was in his future, as if it had already happened. I tried to remember what it was that I'd glimpsed, but my mind was blank.

When you attempt to grasp the future you merely reinforce it as a linear concept and render it invisible, Infinity informed me. *Allow yourself to merely know what you know without awarding it much attention.*

I shouldn't pay attention to the future when I get glimpses of it?

No more than to the present else it will serve only to act as a distraction from what we do.

I couldn't help feeling a little frustrated; being able to know the future was intriguing.

You demonstrate the danger. Merely knowing that seeing the future is now possible for you is providing enough of a distraction from the present that you fail to notice those who would have your help, I was told.

Who? Oh. As soon as I asked the question, I was Aware of the closest of the herds of wild horses moving steadily in our direction, following the sense of us that they had picked up from the horses we had helped the previous day. I was also Aware that Rowena, Marvel, Holly and Sonja knew of the situation even as they and Vickery sang the drizzle into rain that was steadily becoming heavier, as did Justin, who urged Gas on as he cantered through pastureland.

As Aleks and I hurriedly strung up waterproof sheets to make a shelter for all of us, my mind flickered towards Flame and Fitt and I knew that Flame grazed while Fitt slept curled up on the ground nearby. We all had roles to play in the here and now. I understood Infinity's counsel.

All you need do is trust yourself, she told me. *If you need to know something then you will know it.*

I know there's heavy rain coming and I'm hungry, I thought to myself as much as to Infinity and was unsurprised when she returned her attention to her grazing.

SIXTEEN

Courage

*O*nce the rain started, it seemed as though it would never stop. Aleks and I had managed to hang up our waterproof sheets before it really came down and with the new camp fire that Marvel got going at the edge of our shelter, we were able to cook and make tea, so for the first time in ages, all of us were content just to rest and relax – except for Aleks who either sat and moaned, paced back and forth, or dashed out to check on Nexus, despite reassurance from all of us and Nexus that there were no wild cats in the vicinity.

I appreciated the opportunity to be able to closely monitor how Flame and Fitt were doing. Flame was finding Fitt's company very difficult. She could cope with being near her if Fitt were occupied with something, her attention taken elsewhere, but if Fitt glanced in Flame's direction or moved, Flame would flinch and jump away. Fitt knew that Flame thought of her as her Bond-Partner and that she was comfortable with Fitt's touch on her mind, but she also knew the distress that her physical appearance caused her horse. She learnt to stay a minimum distance from Flame, moving slowly and ensuring that she was always turned slightly away from her, so as to be as physically unthreatening as she could be. She sent a constant, gentle wave of love to Flame, reassuring her and providing a constant reminder that she was indeed the soul whom Flame could sense and recognise with her Awareness, even as her physical senses tried to persuade her that one with Fitt's appearance was a danger.

During the second day of rain, we all grew restless. Those of us who were Aware could sense the next wild horse herd drawing closer and we let them know of our intention to help them, just as we had helped the last herd. We itched to go to meet them. And we all needed a break from Aleks.

When I awoke on the morning of the third day of rain and it was still teeming down, I knew we couldn't shelter any longer. Aleks was already up and had gone to check Nexus yet again, which meant that, yet again, he would return soaking wet and Sonja and Rowena would berate him for what must have been the hundredth time for trailing mud and water into our shelter.

The wild horses were close now; only a short ride away, I judged, and they were waiting for us, eager for our help whilst wary of the unknown.

Our horses were also restless. The warm rain didn't bother them at all and as they sensed the anticipation of the wild horses, they were keen to play their part. I had an idea.

'Wakey wakey, everyone, rise and shine and prepare for a soaking,' I said.

Marvel pulled his blanket over his head and Vickery buried her face in the cloak that she was using as a pillow. Holly opened her eyes, yawned and sat up. She looked out at the rain. 'Go out in this? Have you gone mad?' she asked.

'Yes, definitely, and no I don't think so,' I replied. 'The wild horses are waiting for us and we're all going stir crazy, so I think we should just go out, get wet and get on with it.'

'But we won't be able to dry our clothes, we'll have piles of sopping wet gear in here with us,' said Holly, rubbing her eyes. 'It's bad enough having Aleks's cloak strung up and dripping every time he comes back, but if all of our stuff gets wet too, it'll be unbearable.'

'You all should have thought of that before you summoned up a monsoon,' said Aleks, appearing out of the grey gloom.

'ALEKS!' Rowena, Holly and Sonja all shouted in unison as Aleks took off his cloak and shook it at the edge of the shelter, spraying them all with water.

'We can just take our clothes off and leave them here,' I said.

'What? Ride naked?' Marvel sat up very suddenly and squinted at me, his hazel eyes incredulous.

'I suppose you could ride naked if you want to, I was thinking more of just wearing small clothes. It's warm, we don't need to wear much anyway and the less we wear, the less wet gear we'll have,' I replied. 'Unless, of course, you're shy?'

'Good plan, I'm in,' said Rowena.

'Me too,' said Vickery. 'If you need me?'

'We do, thanks,' I said without hesitation.

The others all looked at one another.

'Looks like it's just going to be the three of us, then, that's a whoooooole lot of horses for me and Am to ride, if this herd's anywhere near the size of the last one,' said Rowena. 'Who's going to gather the last few scraps of food we have and make us a hearty breakfast before we go?'

'But you'll be riding bareback,' protested Marvel, 'and those horses will be wet, you'll have wet horse hair, well... everywhere.'

'Who are you, my mother?' Rowena said. 'It's not as if we don't have enough water for a wash down afterwards, is it?'

That's settled then, Ro and Am will take on the wild horse herd by themselves with Vic providing massage and support, and Marvel's a chicken. Rowena and I grinned as Justin's thoughts rang out to all who were Aware of him and I quickly related what he'd said to Vickery, who laughed.

'He's not a chicken, he's, well he's just decent,' said Aleks.

'Marvel's a chicken and Aleks is a prude. Anyone want to add anything?' Rowena said. 'No? Good, because there are some things that you all clearly need reminding of. Our horses have given up their natural way of life to be with us, to teach us, and they've helped us to be more than we ever knew was possible. Flame is, at this moment, coming to terms with having a predator as her Bond-Partner in order to ensure that everything the horses have done doesn't go to waste, and you lot are whining about riding bareback in your smalls, when there is a whole herd of horses waiting out there for our help? You should be ashamed of yourselves. Look, this is how easy it is to put your instincts to one side for the sake of something bigger than you.' She stripped until she stood only in her small clothes.

Sonja nodded. 'Good speech, Ro, sorry you had to make it. I'm in.'

Holly said, 'Me too. Consider me suitably ashamed.'

'I'm coming, but my stuff's already wet so I may as well just keep it on,' said Aleks and Rowena rolled her eyes.

'I was always coming, I was just waiting for Ro to get angry enough to have one of her rants, it's been a while,' said Marvel.

Nice attempt at recovery, mate, Justin's thought carried his amusement.

'Attempt is right,' said Rowena. 'Let it be noted that Marvel was the last to agree to come.'

'Noted,' I said with a grin.

'Noted for what purpose?' Marvel asked.

'Until Rowena decides to use it against you. Even I can see that,' said Aleks, without humour.

As the others rose and began shaking out and rolling up bedding, still teasing Marvel, I went to Aleks's side and said, quietly, 'There are foals in the wild herd. If you watch them working with their mothers as you did before, you'll be at your best and then you might feel able to ride Nexus. Good luck, Aleks.'

His eyes brightened in his gaunt face and for a fraction of a second, I saw the person he had the potential to be looking out at me... and then he was gone again. But he was in there, I reminded myself.

I had often felt that my youth and inexperience in comparison with the rest of the Horse-Bonded were very obvious. On the morning that my friends and I rode out bareback in the rain in our undergarments, however, I realised that they were far less so. I looked about me with amusement and bewilderment as my friends shrieked and giggled at themselves and each other. I smiled to myself as I realised that I was beginning to take a lot of the same views as Infinity – in a lot of ways, humans were slightly ridiculous.

'I don't know why you can't just sing the rain away, seeing as it was you who sang it into existence in the first place,' moaned Aleks to no one in particular as he trudged along by Nexus's side.

'We merely encouraged a weather pattern that was already there, Aleks, as we've explained to you on countless occasions,' said Sonja. 'Now we leave nature to itself. Look on the bright side, the rain will keep the wild cats under shelter, so you can relax on that count.'

'And then when the rain stops, they'll be twice as hungry. Marvellous,' Aleks retorted.

'Look,' said Holly, 'there they are.'

There was a stand of trees in the distance, below which the wild horses must have been sheltering. Now, they were visible as they hurtled towards us through the rain, splashing through the standing water and flinging wet mud in their wake. A dapple-grey mare led the way with another grey mare just behind her. Their family followed, a similar mixture of mares, foals and youngsters as the group we had met before, and this time a huge blue roan stallion brought up the rear. Our horses whinnied to them as they circled us at a distance, gradually drawing closer and finally coming to a sliding, splashing halt nearby.

The lead mare and stallion eyed us curiously as Rowena, Sonja, Marvel and Vickery moved their horses away, so that the mares of our group stood between them and the wild stallion, making it as easy as possible for him to accept their presence near his own mares. We were all scrutinized and then accepted as readily as we had been by the previous stallion.

'I think we should stick to the same plan as last time, with a mare showing them the way,' Holly said, blinking furiously to keep the rain out of her eyes. 'Am, do you and Infinity want to do the honours again, or shall Serene and I do it this time?'

'You and Serene go ahead,' I said.

Holly said, 'Okay, join in whenever you like.'

I nodded and all of us except Holly and Serene moved further away from the wild herd. When Serene obliged Holly by walking a circle, there was splashing and snorting with the odd squeal as the wild horses shifted their positions whilst keeping an eye on their lead mare in case she deemed it necessary for them all to leave. She and the wild stallion merely stood watching, however, and gradually, the other herd members followed their example.

Serene walked, trotted and cantered, responding instantly to signals Holly gave her to help her keep her balance in the extremely difficult conditions; there was standing water of varying depths and where the ground was visible, it was saturated and slippery. However, Serene and Holly blurred together as one powerful, graceful, beautiful entity that seemed almost to glide over the treacherous terrain rather than to negotiate it.

Once I felt the wild horses beginning to absorb the information that they needed from Serene and Holly, Infinity and I joined them to give the pattern strength. I revelled in the feeling of oneness with my horse and in the rapt attention I could feel from the wild horses. They were with Infinity and Serene at every step, feeling how their bodies were aligned so that such power could be generated by their hindquarters and transferred all the way up to the tips of their ears, feeling the lightness about them that was far more than just physical, feeling the way their bodies moved in effortless harmony with ours. As they began to understand what they would need to accept in order to have our help and what changes they would need to make, I felt them put what they were learning into a context that already existed for them – the template for perfect balance that had already begun to establish within the horses' collective consciousness. As Bright, Broad and Oak and their riders joined us and all five horses moved as one, the template was clarified and magnified for the wild horses. I knew, with absolute certainty, that today's work would be easy.

I lost count of how many horses I rode that day, but with each one, it was the same. I was accepted as a welcome inevitability, listened and responded to without question until no more help was required, and then left standing in the rain, watching as my latest mount revelled in the feeling of a newly empowered body whilst clearing the negative memories and emotions – the weight – of the past.

At one point, as Vickery massaged my back muscles, ensuring that I stayed soft and supple for my next mount, I thought I could make out a blob in the distance that might have been Aleks riding Nexus. My Awareness told me that my water-filled vision saw true. Having seen foal after foal work alongside their mothers, Aleks had become clear and calm enough to know what he needed to do. He was struggling, I could feel it, but as a strawberry roan mare came to stand by my side, I knew I couldn't help him. Not now. I reminded myself that everything happens as it should and accepted a leg up from Vickery onto the mare, whose eagerness to follow the path that she had felt others of her herd travelling was all-consuming. Aleks slipped from my mind.

By the time we had ridden all of the horses mature enough to carry a rider, we were hot, wet and tired, but very, very happy. This herd was comprised of many more horses than the previous one, yet they had needed far less help from us and we had worked our way through them in half the time. When the herd finally galloped off, carrying their joy and lightness with them, we knew that we had made another big stride towards repaying all that the horses had done for us.

We stood in the rain for a while, allowing it to wash the horse hair from us as it continued to lash down, and then we wandered tiredly over to the shallow mound where our horses had managed to find grass that was available as more than just tips poking above water level. It was then that we realised that Nexus and Aleks were missing. I remembered having seen them working together and when I felt for him, I knew where he was.

'He's having a hard time, I'll go to him,' I said.

The others all assessed the situation and nodded, apart from Vickery, who said, 'When isn't he? And now you've got to go and find him when you should be getting back to camp and getting some warm clothes on those tired muscles of yours. I'll go and get him, Am, if you point me in the right direction.'

I shook my head. 'Thanks, but I've got this. He's not far away, we'll be back to camp by the time you've brewed tea.'

Infinity and I found Nexus browsing the lower leaves of a huge tree, as she sheltered beneath it. Aleks leant against the tree trunk, his head tilted upwards and his eyes closed. He radiated despair and his sadness was allowing his fear to steadily rise again. I jumped from Infinity's back and went to him.

'Aleks?' I said.

'Just leave me alone, Amarilla,' he replied.

'No way. Come on, come back to camp with me.'

'No. It's all hopeless.'

'So, you didn't quite get there. Big deal. You're so close, we've all told you that a thousand times and now that you're trying again, you'll be there in no time.'

'I am close. There were brief moments riding Nexus today when I knew that. But what stands between me being able to let go of myself enough to just be in the moment with Nexus, the way you all can with your horses, is too big for me to overcome. I thought that the frame of mind I found myself in from watching the foals would be enough for me to overcome it, but it wasn't. And if that wasn't enough, then nothing ever will be.'

The future that I'd glimpsed and forgotten the last time Aleks and I had spoken flashed through my mind once more and this time I didn't try to hold on to it. I allowed it to settle within me until I knew it. I felt Infinity's approval even as I reeled from knowing what Aleks would face. What we would all face. I tried in vain to think how to provide reassurance for Aleks whilst something that was just about as far from being reassuring as possible was at the forefront of my mind. He looked desperately into my eyes, which I felt widen as a flash of pure unadulterated terror shot through me. And it wasn't mine.

'Flame,' I gasped.

Aleks stood up straight and took a hold on both of my arms as I stood, rooted to the spot in horror. 'What's happened? Is she alright? Thunder and lightning, it's that Kindred isn't it? I knew we shouldn't trust her, I told you all. What's she done to Flame?' he demanded.

Your centre. Remember it and you will be there, Infinity reminded me gently.

Instantly, I was. *Thanks, Fin.* I saw everything for what it was. I saw its perfection. I had an idea, of which Infinity instantly approved.

'Amarilla?' Aleks's fear was rising further and soon he would block Nexus out again. I felt Infinity extend her energy to Nexus, just as she would if Nexus were ill or injured and needed support.

'Aleks, check in with Nexus. With our horses linked as strongly as they are at the moment, there's a direct link between your mind and mine because of our bonds with them. There. Can you feel me?'

Aleks's face slowly relaxed as a look of wonderment stole over it. 'Yes... I can!'

'Good, because I'm going to watch what's happening with Flame, and you're coming with me. It will help you to witness this, but you can only witness, Aleks, okay? You can't get in the way. Aleks?'

He nodded, his mouth opening and closing with words that he couldn't form.

I turned my attention back to Flame. As her terror washed over me once more, Aleks took a step back, horrified. I took his arm. 'This is Flame's fear, not yours. Do you understand? I'm not asking you to face your fears, Aleks, just to witness Flame facing hers. You can feel what I know. You are in no danger and neither is Flame, you can feel that's true. ALEKS!'

Aleks jumped. 'Yes, I... yes. I understand. Sorry.'

'I'm going to scan Flame's mind to pick up what's been happening. Remember, Aleks, just witness.'

Flame had been Aware of everything the wild horses had accomplished and she had felt the template for perfect balance strengthening within the horses' collective consciousness as a result of them all achieving it. As the pathway towards her objective became ever clearer to her, the draw to follow it had become stronger than her fear of what she must face... and she had invited Fitt to sit upon her back.

Fitt was sending Flame her love and reassurance as her horse sidled up to the outcropping of rock upon which she waited. Flame trembled throughout her body and sweat glistened on her coat. Her nostrils flared and her ears flicked back and forth. There was no mistaking the level of her discomfort but as her courage and determination combined with the draw of the collective, she stepped very definitely into place for her rider to mount. Fitt waited a little longer, giving Flame the opportunity to move away if her courage failed. It didn't.

I was Aware of Fitt's care as she gently stroked Flame's neck with the back of her hand, ensuring that her talons were curled safely away. She stroked Flame's back and then her sides, loving her all the while. Then she leant forward, over Flame's back. Flame shuddered but stood her ground. Fitt swung her leg over Flame's back and sat up. Flame's front legs gave way in her terror and she went down on her knees. Fitt was almost thrown, but she never stopped sending all of her love to her horse as she used all of her balance and strength to stay on board. Flame struggled back to her feet and stood with her legs splayed, sweat dripping from her. Fitt stroked her neck again and I could feel her admiration for Flame, her pride in her horse's courage. They stood so for what seemed like days, but was probably no more than an hour. I was glad that the rainstorm my friends had sung up hadn't extended as far as where Flame and Fitt were, as Flame would surely have been chilled to the bone by the time she announced to Fitt that she would move.

I felt Fitt's delight as she encouraged Flame to do whatever she felt she could. As she took hold of a small chunk of Flame's mane, I nudged Fitt's mind as gently as I could with my offer of help. She accepted immediately and welcomed me into her body with her. I almost recoiled, but managed to switch my focus to assessing what Fitt could do with her – as it felt to me – maimed body in order to prevent it from being a burden to her horse. The toughness of Fitt's skin prevented her from being very flexible. Her posture was hunched, which meant that keeping her weight off of Flame's forequarter would be difficult and supporting her horse would be even more so. Fitt's legs were short and immensely muscular, meaning that they couldn't easily wrap around Flame's sides to help her to lift.

Fitt's body followed my suggestion to adjust her upper body angle so that she was leaning back more, and less of a burden to Flame's forequarters. I was pleased to feel that sitting deeply into her pelvis was something that came naturally to Fitt, giving her a stable anchoring point. She dropped her legs around Flame's sides as long as they could extend, and squeezed gently. Flame leapt forward and shuddered again, before walking on. Fitt's body came along with me as I turned it to the right, bringing Flame to walk on a circle – a way of working that was familiar to her and would hopefully give her some confidence. It did. She walked forward more surely. Once I had shown Fitt how to ask Flame to turn in both directions, adjust circle size and stop, I withdrew from her, leaving her in no doubt as to the importance of keeping her weight away from Flame's front end. Then I watched again.

Fitt focused intently on practising what I had shown her and Flame was steadily drawn into focusing with a matching intensity, on responding to what Fitt's body asked of her. I felt something begin to shift. Flame's stifle was changing! The fear that had been trapped there was oozing out of it and, bereft of any notice from either Fitt or Flame, dissipating into the ether. Flame suddenly noticed that her right leg could move more freely, yet still not as much as her left one. She would need help from a Tissue-Singer, I realised. The fear that had blocked the connective tissues from realigning healthily was gone, but they had forgotten where that healthy alignment was – and I was too far away to sing them the intention necessary for them to find it.

He Who Is Peace needed no sound, Infinity reminded me.

My heart leapt in my chest. Justin and I had once watched Adam grow plants to three times their size in little more than a minute and when Justin questioned him about it, he told us that he had used tree-singing to grow them. I'd observed that he hadn't actually sung, to which he'd replied that he had sung, just not out loud. I smiled as I realised that I'd drawn Adam and Peace to me with my thoughts of them. I absorbed the information I needed from Adam and relished his amusement that finally, I knew what he'd done. He knew of my love and gratitude as he and Peace drifted away.

I let Flame know that I could heal her stifle if she wanted me to. I felt her eagerness for me to begin and focused my Awareness on the connective tissues in her stifle joint. I felt where they were too tight and where more tightening was needed. I tuned into the tissues just as I had done so many times with plants when assessing their usefulness as cures in herbalism. I was the tissues. I allowed my energy to resonate with them instead of using sound to do it. The healing was immediate; since I was resonating with them myself, I merely had to think of the alterations they needed to make and it was done. I shook my head in wonder and withdrew from Flame.

She was sound. Sound, ecstatic... and tired. Fitt slid immediately from her back. She went to Flame's head and held out her hand, tentatively. Flame sniffed it and then proceeded to sniff up a delighted Fitt's arm to her shoulder, before blowing into her ear. She embraced every detail of Fitt's personality in her Awareness as she sniffed all the way down to Fitt's feet, occasionally pausing to draw in a deeper breath as she took in Fitt's physicality. Finally, she knew Fitt's body and personality as well as she knew her soul. I felt something slide into place between them – their bond.

I had closed my eyes in order to concentrate on Flame's healing and as I opened them, I noticed how tired I was. An ashen-faced Aleks stood in front of me, oblivious of the large drops of rain that penetrated the leafy canopy above where he stood and splattered the top of his head.

'Aleks, are you alright?'

Aleks shook his head. 'No, I don't think I am.'

'Flame has been wanting to get past the fear that's been holding her back, but like you, she couldn't find a way to do it. Not until she felt the call of something that was bigger, more important to her than her fear. And you've seen, she's done it. You can too.'

Aleks went even paler. 'I know her fear was great. I felt it. But, Am, mine is greater. It shouldn't be, I know that, but it is.'

'Flame's fear was based on something that actually happened to her. Yours is based on something that you worry might happen to you and there is the difference – fear of the actual has a limit but fear of the imagined can only be limited only by your imagination, which is limitless. But fear is fear. Great or small, it can be eclipsed by love.' As the words left my mouth, I felt as if Infinity were speaking through me.

We are speaking through us. We are Infinity. I smiled.

'My fear can't,' said Aleks. 'That's what I've learnt today. If seeing what those foals achieved, almost feeling it, can't eclipse my fear, what can?'

'Your worst nightmare,' I told him. 'When it presents itself, you'll know what to do, just as Flame did. Her fear became secondary to her destiny when the time was right and so will yours.'

'My worst nightmare? I'm going to have to live my worst nightmare? How do you know that?' Aleks squeaked.

'You'll only have to live it if you choose to. Your other choice will be to make it something other than your worst nightmare and then it will transform into something else, something wonderful, just as it has for Flame. Don't panic, Aleks, just think over everything you've experienced today, let it settle and know that you have a way forward out of this. You know my mind, now. You know I wouldn't lie to you.'

Aleks nodded slowly. Nexus appeared at his side and rested her chin gently on his shoulder.

'Come on, we need to get back to camp,' I said. 'Give me a leg up?'

We made our way back to camp with Aleks splashing miserably through the water next to Nexus. At least the rain seemed to be getting lighter.

Way to go, Am, that's another outstanding day's work under your belt if you were wearing one, or indeed any clothes, but you're tired. Justin's thoughts were like balm to my soul.

I am. And so are you. You need to rest for longer at a time.

I rest long enough. It's not just me who wants to reach you all, Gas does too and you know what he's like, if I don't keep up with him, he's just as likely to go on without me.

I chuckled. *Well, at last we know Adam's secret, wicked old man keeping it from us.*

I felt Justin's affection for Adam match mine. *He kept it from us until we were ready for it. I miss him. But at the moment, I'm more concerned about you,* he told me.

I'm fine, we're nearly at camp and the rain's easing. Remind me to run for the hills next time Sonja's concerned about there being a drought.

Rest easy, Am.

The rain was almost drizzle when the camp finally came into sight. Rowena rushed out to meet me with a blanket, which she wrapped around my shoulders after dragging me down from Infinity. 'Well done,

Am, we all felt what happened with Flame,' she said. Then she lowered her voice and added, 'It was a risk allowing Aleks with you. I haven't delved deeper to find out why you did it, but I assume there was method in your madness?'

I nodded and said quietly, 'We're heading towards a situation that will be a challenge for all of us. Nothing the rest of us can't handle, but Aleks wouldn't have stood a chance. He stands one now, small though it is.'

'For you to call something a challenge, I'm thinking it's probably something that everyone else would call a catastrophe, but we're all learning to expect the unexpected these days,' said Rowena. 'Talking of which, tissue-singing without the singing? We're just getting people used to the idea of multiskilling and now we've found a new way to befuddle them? More interesting times ahead then.'

I nodded. Lots more interesting times ahead.

SEVENTEEN

Obstruction

*T*he rain continued to ease during the evening and by the time we settled down to sleep, a breeze was chasing the last of the clouds away. Large water drops, dislodged from the leaves above us, made loud splatting noises on our waterproof sheeting, causing us to jump and rest less easily than when the rain had been coming down in a steady rhythm.

I thought to begin with that it was one such disturbance that roused me just as dawn was breaking, but as I came to properly, I felt the Kindred Elder's presence at the edge of my mind. Once she knew that I was Aware of her, she explored my mind for recent events. Her interest lingered on everything that had occurred between Fitt and Flame and then flared when she learnt that I had performed healing without the need to produce sound. She was unable to hide the importance of this to her kind. I felt her take a firm hold of her mind to prevent herself revealing anything else. I kept very still and quiet, hoping I reassured her that I wouldn't wonder about her revelation. I felt her relax and then she was gone, leaving a very definite sense of purpose behind her.

I was wide awake now. I slipped out of my bedding and stoked the fire, adding more firewood before putting the kettle over it to boil.

'You just refuse to rest, don't you?' Vickery whispered as she lowered herself to sit beside me.

I chuckled. 'It's not that I refuse, so much as I don't seem to be getting much opportunity at the moment; if it's not one thing that grabs my attention, it's another.'

'What about the others? Can't they take some of the load off of you?' said Vickery.

'They can and they do, but I guess the fact that it was my intention that started all of this means that I attract a lot of what happens. It was the Kindred Elder this morning; she wanted to catch up on everything to do with Fitt and Flame and then she picked up on the fact that healing can happen without singing. It seems to be something that will be really important to the Kindred,' I replied.

'And not just to them. I can't believe you did it, Am. Is it something I can learn to do, or is it something that can only be done if you're Aware?'

'To do it from a distance as I did yesterday, you'd need to be Aware, but you'll be able to heal that way when the patient is in front of you right away, that's what Adam did when Justin and I saw him grow plants using silent tree-singing.'

Vickery sighed. 'If the patient's in front of me, then I might as well just sing. To be able to heal from a distance though, that would be amazing. I'm limiting myself, aren't I? Not being Aware?'

'There's a lot that would be easier for you if you were Aware, definitely.'

'Like being able to cope with whatever catastrophe is coming our way next? Sorry, I was coming back from the waste hole yesterday as you got back with Aleks and I heard you telling Rowena.'

I paused to choose my words. 'Vic, you're close to achieving the potential you saw for yourself when you bonded to Verve, you know you are; you throw yourself into everything we do, no matter how weird or challenging. The situation that we'll be walking into will give you the chance to measure yourself and hence give you the final proof that you're She Who Is Verve. You're more than capable of stepping up to the challenge whether you're Aware or not, but at the same time, Adam surpassed the potential he saw for himself when he bonded with Peace and so can you. You don't have to limit yourself if you don't want to.'

Vickery nodded thoughtfully. 'Verve's close to achieving perfect balance now after what you all did with the wild horses yesterday, I can feel him being drawn along the path towards it. He'd love it if I found it alongside him, I know he would. I'll think on what you've said, Am.'

I nodded. 'It's exciting isn't it, what's happening with the horses?'

Exciting and deafening, Justin broke in. *Quinta's just been using me as target practice for all of the students who are newly Aware – they all homed in on me at the same time to tell me what happened yesterday and my mind jangled so much I nearly passed out. Fair warning, she's planning on moving them on to you guys next.*

Jangled? Is that even a word? I asked and just about had time to tell Vickery of Justin's and my exchange when I realised that "jangled" was a perfect word to describe the assault Justin had just experienced; a cacophony of excited thoughts burst into my mind, seemingly oblivious of the fact that I couldn't possibly make even one of them out from the others.

'Aaaaaaaaah!' Rowena shouted and sat up in her bedding, holding her head.

Aleks sat bolt upright. 'What's happening? Is this it? Is this my worst nightmare?'

'No, Aleks, it's mine. What seems like a hundred people are all shouting in my head at the same time,' moaned Holly.

'FOR THE LOVE OF WINTER, GET LOST!' Marvel shouted, also holding his head, and all went quiet.

'What on earth was Quinta thinking, letting them all do that at the same time?' Sonja said to nobody in particular.

Justin's thoughts were for us all. *I don't think she's got enough time to be thinking much at all at the moment – seven more horses and their Bond-Partners achieved perfect balance at The Gathering yesterday. The rest of the horses are all focused on what they can feel happening in the collective consciousness and what they know they'll be able to achieve now, and their Bond-Partners are hopping around with excitement and demanding extra coaching from Quinta, Feryl and any of the others who are now in a position to teach. It seems that The Gathering is a very happy place to be at the moment, but Quinta's got her work cut out keeping those who are newly Aware grounded enough to be of help to her – we all know how hard that is in the beginning.*

We could show her and them the exercises we developed to help us to be centred, and then they can all help each other as we did, I thought to Justin, and my friends nodded around me.

I explained to Vickery and Aleks the help that Quinta would need from us that day and Vickery immediately said that she would go hunting and Aleks would haul water and gather firewood, while the rest of us helped those at The Gathering.

Marvel said, 'We've got no meat left at all, so I'll hunt with Vic, but I'll still help you all at the same time.'

'You all heard the man,' said Rowena, 'he can multi-task. We'll remember that the next time we set up camp and there are more jobs to do than just lighting the camp fire.'

'You just don't learn, do you, Marvel?' Aleks said. 'Never give her ammunition. Never.'

We all laughed.

It transpired that Marvel wasn't the only one required to multi-task that day; in addition to asking Quinta's students questions, via thought, whilst she gave them exercises to do that kept them focused on their physical surroundings – and finding that the technique helped them to improve their ability to be more centred every bit as quickly as it had us – I was repeatedly asked by Fitt to help her as she worked with Flame.

Don't you think you've ridden enough for today? I asked her when she stopped being able to ignore her fatigue and soreness.

Flame doesn't think so, you can feel her determination as well as I, Fitt replied. *She knows exactly what she is aiming for and she is determined that we get there together. I will not let her down. Ride through me again? I know I sit into my pelvis enough and I can use my legs well enough for the little support that Flame needs from me, but I still cannot seem to find the adjustment I need to keep my upper body stable.*

I sighed. Everything was happening so fast now. Whereas Justin and I had had over a year to come around to the idea of being centred, the latest Horse-Bonded to become Aware would achieve it within days or weeks. And where most of us had had months to build the strength and confidence to deal with whatever issues had held us back from achieving perfect balance, Fitt had beaten a path to her stumbling block on only her second day of riding. But then, she was Flame's Bond-Partner. They had already achieved the impossible just by bonding and working together as they now were, and they were matched in determination and courage. It was just as well.

I can feel the problem, I told her. *If you sit up so that you feel you are straight, your weight is too far forward because of your hunched posture and you're unbalancing Flame. If you lean back as I showed you yesterday, Flame can lift more but you're not stable and so you can't support either her or yourself. Normally, I would be asking you to lift and open your chest, but there is something very strong there which will resist you doing it.*

The Kindred are all built like this. We were bred with ape genes, Fitt replied.

That has always been the excuse so far. I almost shocked myself with my response, knowing that it was pure Infinity. We were Infinity. My horse responded from within me with a subtle wave of love, just enough to keep Fitt's shock from reverberating through my being.

Flame came to a halt beneath Fitt, sensing that her Bond-Partner reeled from my thoughts. She reassured Fitt that all would be well whilst letting her know that I spoke the truth.

All of a sudden, the Kindred Elder slammed herself in between Fitt and me. I jumped violently and banged my head on the tree trunk against which I had been leaning. Infinity's nurturing energy wove its way throughout my being, helping me to recover from being separated from Fitt's mind in such an abrupt manner. I couldn't find her. Normally, I only had to think of Fitt and our minds would touch. Now, all I could feel was the Kindred Elder's fury.

We begin to open wounds that will resist being opened, observed Infinity, who had wandered over to stand next to where I sat. She rested her muzzle on the top of my head and I stroked her front leg thoughtfully.

I reached for Flame and found that I was blocked from her as well. For a moment, I felt fury at the Elder's intrusion. Then I felt Infinity's approval as I regained my centre. I had a sense of an old, well-established pattern beginning to shift in the ether and I knew that Fitt and Flame were at the heart of it every bit as much as Infinity and I were ensuring that it would happen. I felt a bit sorry for the Kindred Elder; she had to know that putting herself between We Who Are Infinity and Flame and Fitt was like trying to hold back the wind with a paper plate.

Nevertheless she must do what she thinks best to protect her kind. She will not risk the wound opening that festers within them unless she is certain that it can be healed, observed Infinity.

I saw the perfection in everything once more. Events were converging on a single point in time and space and it was time for us all to make our way there. *We need to move on,* Infinity and I agreed.

We ate well that evening thanks to the hunting and gathering skills of Vickery and Marvel. Not content to leave his achievements for the day at providing us with food as well as fulfilling his promise to help us all with Quinta's students, Marvel then proceeded to attempt a new Skill he had discovered within his Awareness: fire-singing. Since most of the wood that Aleks had gathered that day was damp from all of the rain, Marvel wanted to encourage our fire to roar with heat, thus drying out the wood laid out to dry around it.

He stared intently into the fire and was soon producing a smooth hum with which he experimented until he found the exact tone he wanted. I felt him send his intention along the pathway of sound that linked him to the fire, and the fire began to draw more air. Just as if invisible bellows were at work, the fire began to burn more strongly, and we all clapped and cheered as it then began to roar. We then collapsed with laughter as Rowena only just pulled Marvel back away from it in time to prevent his eyebrows singeing.

When all of the excitement had died down, I suggested to my friends that we needed to continue our journey.

'But what about Justin and Gas?' Aleks said. 'From what you've told me, they're busting their guts trying to catch up with us. We can't just move on without them?'

'And what about Fitt and Flame?' said Vickery. 'Do we wait for them to come with us?'

I looked around at the rest of my friends as they picked up from me what had happened between me, Fitt and the Kindred Elder. Eyebrows were raised, brief discussions were had with Bond-Partners and then one by one, they all nodded.

'The Kindred Elder is preventing contact between any of us and Fitt and Flame at the moment, so they'll have to decide for themselves what to do for the best. Justin and Gas are moving much quicker than we will be, especially as we'll be stopping to help the wild horse herds that are making their way to meet us, so they'll still catch us up. Everything will happen when the time is right,' I said, staring at Vickery.

Vickery's eyes widened. She looked down into her lap for a few minutes while she discussed what I had meant with Verve, and then she looked up and nodded.

We all looked at Aleks. He raked a dirty, thin hand through his now lank, black hair. His pale blue eyes peered out from the dark shadows that surrounded them, flicking from one of us to the other. He communicated with Nexus by the weakest of mental whispers, most of their bond once more cloaked in his fear, but at her whole-hearted agreement that it was time to move on, he gave a stiff flick of his head into a nod.

He was managing to hang on to his sanity by a thread as a result of flickering his thoughts between the sight of the foals working with their mothers, the way Nexus had moved the last time he'd ridden her, and the courage he had felt within Flame as she chose to transform her worst nightmare into her biggest opportunity. He was hanging on by a thread, but he was hanging on.

Just hang on a little longer, Aleks, I thought to him, knowing he couldn't hear me. But Nexus could. I felt her pass on my thought to her Bond-Partner and his eyes immediately flicked to meet mine. I grinned at him and mouthed, 'Just a little longer.'

He clenched his fists and closed his eyes tightly. Then he took a deep breath and opened his eyes. He nodded, more strongly this time.

Blessedly, I slept soundly that night and was the last to wake the following morning. When I did, I felt Justin waiting for me.

You needed that, he told me.

And you need at least that, plus a whole load more. You're still pushing yourself too hard, Jus.

Gas and I refuse to acknowledge any such concept, he replied cheerfully, *especially now that you're on your way again. We'll be there, Am, when it counts. I promise you.*

It all counts and you're always there.

Justin paused, taken aback. *Was that you or Fin? I can't tell your thoughts apart from hers anymore.*

You're not the only one. Several times, now, I've opened my mouth and words that I could never have strung together without Infinity have come out.

It's to be expected for all of us, I guess, Justin observed. *We're one with our horses and their insights are becoming as much a part of us as they are of them. Seriously though, we'll be there.*

'When you two have finished chatting, there's breakfast to be eaten and then camp to be cleared, Am?' Rowena called across the campfire.

Being Aware hasn't made you any less bossy, has it, Ro? Justin directed his thought to all of us.

Amidst the sniggering that followed, Marvel said, 'It's made her worse, and her respect for private conversations has taken a nosedive as well, but we wouldn't have her any other way.'

'Speak for yourself,' grumbled Aleks as he draped bedding over nearby saplings to air.

Rowena scolded Justin for not resting more, until he finally gave in and promised to rest for the whole of the following night instead of just a small part of it. I agreed with Marvel. We wouldn't have Rowena any other way.

Rowena caught my thought about her and winked at me as she moved on to giving Holly and Sonja their chores for packing up camp. I watched all of my friends about their tasks for a few moments before finally rising, and I felt a huge amount of fondness for all of them. They and their horses had all come with Infinity and me for different reasons, and yet those reasons had all ended up being the same. We were all on a path towards helping the Kindred, thereby eliciting change. As a group, we made that aim more defined and we gave it strength. As a group, we had power. In the weeks to come, we would need it.

EIGHTEEN

Weight

*W*hen we finally got going, it was mid-morning and the sun's rays were gaining strength. A mist was rising from the plains in front of us as the water began to evaporate from where it had been deposited so ferociously, and the air felt warm and damp around us.

Infinity and I took our place at the front of the group and for a moment, I missed Flame not being at our side. Then I remembered all that she was achieving with Fitt and all I could feel was pride and love for her.

She comes, Infinity informed me. As I reached forward to stroke the white neck that gleamed in the summer sunshine, I felt what Infinity could feel and I laughed out loud.

'What gives?' Vickery asked from just behind me.

'The Kindred Elder may have managed to block us from Flame and Fitt, but she can't block Flame from Infinity. They're coming to join us.'

'Oh, no,' moaned Aleks. 'No, no, no. I can't have Fitt near Nexus, this is too much.'

'Even though she's one of the Horse-Bonded? One of us? Even though Flame is happy to be ridden by her?' Sonja asked him.

'They won't catch us up for a day, maybe two if Fitt needs to hunt,'

Marvel said, 'so you'll have plenty of time to get used to the idea, Aleks.'

'Remember what you felt from Flame when she bonded with Fitt. She knows Fitt inside out and she knows that Fitt poses no danger to any of us,' I tried to reassure Aleks.

Aleks shook his head miserably as he walked alongside his horse, and Nexus moved closer to him and nuzzled his arm. I left her to counsel him and returned my attention to what I could feel of Flame, through Infinity.

Flame's determination had reached new heights as she walked along with Fitt on her back. She wanted to go faster, indeed they had tried that already for a short time, but having felt the damage that her weight did to Flame by pushing her down onto her forequarter as it had, Fitt had insisted that they go no faster than a walk until they found us and she had received the help she needed to balance her upper body. My heart leapt and I considered waiting for them. No. I knew that we needed to move on and I trusted that everything else would fall into place as it needed to.

I was following my sense of the Kindred Elder, knowing at the same time that several more wild horse herds were converging on us, but my attention was mainly on the joy I felt at just being at one with my horse. When we came across a raised area of land that was drier than the rest of the plains upon which we splashed, the urge took us to run with the breeze, outpacing it as easily as we did our friends. Infinity may not have been the tallest of horses, but she was all power. I gloried in her strength as her hind legs reached underneath us, pushing hard into the ground and propelling us ever forward with breathtaking speed.

All of a sudden, Justin and Gas were with us. Not physically, but as they, too, powered on as fast as Gas's long legs could carry them, the four of us were one. We revelled in the feeling of our hooves pummelling the soft earth, in the feeling of freedom, of lightness, of oneness. Then Adam and Peace were with us! We drew them into our bodies with us and felt their exhilaration as they shared our physical experience. Sonja and Bright joined our being, followed by Marvel and Broad, then Holly and Serene and finally Rowena and Oak. We were horse. We were human. We were one.

We pulled up just before the ground began to shimmer with water again. Adam and Peace drifted away, leaving behind a subtle imprint of their love on all of us. I looked around at my friends.

'There are no words,' said Marvel simply.

Vickery looked around at us in confusion, but the rest of us knew exactly what he meant. As we waited for Aleks – who was still refusing to ride – and Nexus to catch up, nobody spoke. I was Aware of Vickery's realisation that we had all shared something from which she had excluded herself by not being Aware. I felt a decision beginning to take hold in her mind.

When Aleks finally caught up with us, he was more disgruntled than ever, but nothing could dampen any of our spirits. Justin and Gas were as elated as we were and I was relieved to feel how much energy our shared experience had given them. When we stopped to make camp that evening, I was Aware that, true to his word, Justin stopped and made his own small camp. He ate a full meal and then lay down to sleep as Gas grazed alongside him. I felt Rowena checking in on him too, and grinned at her gratefully.

The next morning, we woke to the sounds of whinnying and galloping hooves, and realised that the wild horse herd that had been closest when we made camp the previous night, was upon us. We felt the horses' anticipation and enthusiasm for what they would achieve with our help, and we all leapt out of bed. Even Aleks looked slightly energised by what he was feeling from Nexus as the wild herd called to our horses.

I stood up and looked over the top of the bushes in whose lee we camped, to where the wild herd galloped a huge circle around our horses. Every now and then, one of our horses would go for a trot or a canter, tail held out behind, neck arched and ears pricked as their powerful strides carried them around the rest of our herd. Then they would come to a graceful halt, snorting and blowing, as the next horse took a turn.

We dressed hurriedly and then, at Vickery's insistence, each downed a bowl of the previous night's soup, before going to join our horses. As soon as we reached them, the wild herd circled closer and then came to a snorting, wild-eyed halt.

The lead mare, a tall, skewbald horse, was in foal. Even as I began to wonder whether she would be strong enough to be ridden, I felt her absolute certainty that she was. She was horse. She could feel the pathway to lightness in front of her and she would tread it. She would go first as was expected and she would be ridden now.

I looked over at Holly, who had just mounted Serene in order to begin the demonstration that we had given to the previous two herds. She turned to look at me at the same time, as we realised the same thing – no demonstration was needed. The pattern for perfect balance was now strong enough within the collective consciousness that these horses already knew what they needed to do and they required only a small amount of help to do it.

The lead mare approached Holly as she dismounted from Serene as we all knew she would; so far, all of the mares who were pregnant or with foals had chosen Holly with whom to work, feeling most comfortable with her gentle, unassuming nature. Marvel gave Holly a careful leg up onto the skewbald mare's back.

Holly was everything the mare needed her to be. She sat lightly and beautifully and in complete control of her body. She was careful where she used her legs, but the mare was never without support or direction when she needed it.

The mare responded easily to all of Holly's signals as if she had been ridden a thousand times before. She felt a profound satisfaction as her rider guided her along the pathway that beckoned to her and when, less than half an hour later, she reached its destination, she halted gracefully. Her foal began to move within her and I was Aware of subtle adjustments already being made within his still-forming body as his mother's perfect balance took a hold on him, priming him for a life of being able to live his full power.

Once Holly had slid carefully to the ground, the mare sat all of her and her foal's weight on her hindquarters, and struck the air with both forelegs. She whinnied shrilly as everything that had burdened her from her past began to leave her – joined by everything that was also clearing from her foal.

I put both of my hands to my mouth as Rowena gasped beside me.

'By the wind of autumn,' breathed Sonja.

Holly sobbed unashamedly and Marvel put an arm around her shoulder, unable to stop his own tears from flowing.

'Her foal will be born into a body that will never know anything but perfect balance,' I whispered to Aleks and Vickery. 'He's able to clear his negative energy now, while she's clearing hers.'

'Ohhhhhhhh,' breathed Vickery.

Aleks looked at me with tear-filled eyes, unable to speak.

I felt a presence at my shoulder and turned to see that a dark bay mare stood waiting for me. 'Please could one of you give me a leg up?' I said to my friends.

We were finished by lunchtime. Each of us who had ridden had been astounded by how little help the horses had needed from us. A tiny adjustment in straightness, a little extra lift, some resistance to excess forward movement until weight distribution had been adjusted correctly, and usually a small amount of help to find the final coordination of body parts, and then it had been on to the next horse.

'Is it just me, or did it feel strange riding wild horses whilst fully clothed?' Marvel said as we watched the herd gallop joyfully off into the distance.

'It's you,' said Sonja.

'Just you,' said Holly.

'I wouldn't know,' said Aleks.

'I'm with Marvel,' said Rowena. 'There was something very liberating about riding in my underwear. What about you, Am? Am?'

I had turned to watch Vickery riding Verve in the distance.

Holly gasped and clapped her hands together. 'Fantastic! She and Verve are nearly there, she just needs to stop holding back.'

'She doesn't know she's holding back though, she thinks she's giving it everything,' said Sonja.

All of us who were Aware had the same realisation at the same time.

'We'll go and make lunch. She'll be tired once she's finished,' said Rowena.

'But won't any of you go and help her?' Aleks said. 'Surely one of you could easily help her if she's nearly there?'

'Just like we've easily helped you?' Rowena said.

Aleks looked around at us, his confusion plain.

Sonja took pity on him. 'It's great that Vic's decided to try to achieve perfect balance with Verve but she's going to need to fulfil the potential she saw for herself when she bonded to Verve before she can achieve it; she's nearly there, but she needs to realise for herself that she still has a slight tendency to hold herself back, and correct it. Once she does that, she'll become She Who Is Verve. The rest will be easy.'

'But why can't you help her to realise that she's holding back?' Aleks said.

'Vickery is a headstrong person. She won't agree that she's holding back and arguing with us will only make her more determined that she's right,' explained Sonja.

'It'll be easier for her to learn what she needs to know by being in a situation that makes it obvious to her,' I said, 'and on this trip, we're not short of situations.'

Aleks looked at me sharply and then mouthed the words, 'My worst nightmare,' to himself. 'Why have you told me this about Vickery?' he asked, suddenly. 'Do you all talk about me this way?'

'Because it will be helpful for you to know, and yes of course,' said Marvel. 'Don't fret it, Aleks.'

'Don't fret it? If I could manage not to fret it, I wouldn't need to be here,' Aleks said as he and Marvel walked back towards our camp.

'We're not short of situations?' Rowena said to me with a grin. 'I take it you're referring to the "challenge" that's waiting for us on the horizon?'

I felt her restrain herself from searching my mind for the information that I hadn't chosen to share with her, or with any of my friends except Justin. I grinned as I replied, 'There are no flies on you. Thanks for trusting me. I haven't told you more about it because we'll all know what to do when the time comes, so it's better to just let it happen than to be distracted by it now.'

Rowena nodded. 'And you know about it in advance how, exactly? From the Kindred Elder?'

'Nope, from knowing that time is non-linear,' I said.

'And what, in the name of summer, is that supposed to mean?' Rowena demanded.

'I'll let Oak help you with that, good luck with it,' I said, laughing.

We were just clearing up after lunch when Fitt rode Flame into camp. The sight of a Kindred riding a horse was enough by itself to give us pause, but the way Fitt sat, leaning backwards whilst gripping with her legs, made it an even more peculiar sight.

Aleks dropped his head into his hands.

'It won't mean she's not there just because you can't see her,' Sonja whispered to him as we all got up to greet our friends. 'Come on, it's time for you to meet the newest member of the Horse-Bonded.'

Flame was tired, yet looked magnificent. Her white socks and blaze stood out in dazzling contrast to her deep orange coat, which gleamed in the sun. Her ears were pricked with interest and her eyes sparkled. She radiated the truth of herself; she was strong, intelligent, determined and... whole. She had cleared that which had broken her, and now she, along with her Bond-Partner, had work to do.

Fitt was exhausted and as she dropped to the ground from Flame's back, her legs gave way. Powerful as they were, she had pushed them beyond their endurance in using them to cling to Flame to prevent overbalancing backwards as she leant back in her efforts to keep her weight off of Flame's forequarter. I felt her determination not to compromise her horse any more than she could avoid whilst she was learning to ride, and my heart went out to her. I remembered only too well when I'd had the same concerns whilst learning to ride Infinity.

I crouched down beside her and hugged her. 'You need food and rest, and then we'll help you,' I told her. 'Welcome to our group, Fitt.'

She leant against me slightly and I had to brace my legs against the ground to prevent being pushed over by her weight. 'I do need rest, but I won't get it until I understand what you meant when you said that I'm using my breeding as an excuse for my posture,' she said in her strained, husky voice.

'You really should rest first,' I said, but she shook her head furiously. I sighed. 'Okay, but it will be easiest if I show you, and your Elder is still between us.'

Fitt frowned thoughtfully. 'She thinks she does what is best and she is my Elder, but I left my family to find out if I could make my own decisions and I have discovered that I can. I decided to trust you and as a result, I have found Flame. Someone has to take a risk, or we'll never move forward. I will defy my Elder,' she said simply but definitely. And then I could feel her in my mind.

How did you do that? How did you remove the block? I asked her.

It was no block, it was a suggestion of one that you believed and that I chose to respect, Fitt replied. *Now, I choose to ignore it and so it is rendered ineffective.*

The Elder's fury hit both of us. I felt Fitt reel from her Elder's disapproval and for a moment, I felt doubt. Would I be putting everything at risk by defying the Elder and attempting to help Fitt?

Your centre... Infinity's thought was so subtle that only one who shared her being as did I would notice it. It was enough. I regained my centre and knew the Elder's anger for what it really was – fear, pure and simple. She was learned and wise but at that moment, her actions were being ruled by her fear that Fitt and I would open a wound that we couldn't heal, leaving the Kindred in a worse situation than that in which they found themselves presently. But I also knew that as soon as Fitt and I had met, a wheel had been set in motion and as time went on and our friendship progressed, it was getting less and less likely that it could be halted.

'Fitt, I can show you something that will help you to understand why you have the posture that you do, if you're ready?' I said out loud so that my friends would all know what we were about.

I felt Fitt steel herself and step aside from her Elder's anger. 'I am ready,' she said.

I took Fitt back with me to when I was experiencing pain in my chest. At first, I had thought I had indigestion, but when I realised that my pain was emanating from my heart, I could find no physical cause for it and neither could Adam or Thuma, an experienced Tissue-Singer. Thuma told me that my heart was being prohibited from working at full capacity due to being weighed down by the huge amount of emotional pain that I was carrying. Only by addressing the issue that caused my emotional pain could I clear it and allow my heart to function without restriction.

Fitt mulled over what she had witnessed. *You think I am hunched because I carry emotional pain that weighs down on me? But what about the rest of my kind?* she asked me.

Is there something that weighs down on you all? That has always weighed down on you all?

Not that I can think of.

Infinity and I thought as one. *Then do not think. Be Aware.*

Fitt knew immediately to what we referred; the collective consciousness of the Kindred. It was the sum total of all of their thoughts, all of their experiences, all of their history. It held all of the answers to all of the questions. As a human, I wouldn't have dreamt of searching it without being invited by the Kindred Elder, but Fitt was under no such restriction. It was a part of her as much as she was a part of it and she immersed herself in it. She hadn't paused for food or water and I could feel how desperately her body needed both, but her mind needed information more.

We piled our bedding behind her and guided her to lean back and rest, which she did without argument or even notice. Sometimes, she shut her eyes tightly, other times she opened them and stared at nothing or flicked them between sights that we couldn't see. A few times, she shed tears, which slid over one downy hair after another as they streaked her face.

Flame stayed by Fitt's side throughout, sending gentle waves of love and support to her Bond-Partner as she searched for the knowledge that she needed. I sat on the ground by Fitt's feet and Infinity grazed close by.

When I ate my dinner, Fitt's flat nose twitched and she licked her lips to clear the saliva that moistened them and ran down her fangs, but other than that, she didn't move a muscle. She had gone somewhere and she would not return until she knew all that she needed to know.

Just as the sun was setting, her eyes flashed as she saw through them again, and she gasped and sat up. She looked all around her in apparent confusion and disbelief, and I was Aware of her desperately trying to fit in what she had learnt with what she had known before. Flame immediately flooded her with love and understanding.

'Fitt, breathe,' I said quietly. 'Slowly and deeply. Like this... that's a bit better.'

'She knows,' Fitt wheezed.

That made sense. 'Okay, the Elder knows and presumably she thought that you wouldn't cope with knowing. Was she right?' I said.

Fitt shook her head. 'No. Yes. No, well I knew some of it anyway, without realising I knew, but all of it... I can see why she won't let herself trust you.'

'Has it stopped you from trusting me?' I asked her.

'No, but I'm glad I trusted you before I learnt all of this.'

'And you can feel how it affects you?' I said.

Fitt nodded. 'I can feel the weight that presses down on my shoulders now. It's always been there, so I never thought about it, never even noticed it, but now I want it gone. I want to be able to stand up straight, to sit up straight on Flame, to open and lift my chest so that I can be stable for her. For us both.'

'Do you know how to clear whatever it is that weighs on you?'

'Flame does,' said Fitt. 'She thinks I need to find a way to forgive you.'

NINETEEN

Forgiveness

*M*e? Forgive me?' I said, aghast. 'Oh I see, you mean us humans.'

'Am?' Aleks called from where he and the rest of our group sat around the campfire.

There was a lot of shushing and whispering as my friends sought to prevent him from interrupting further.

'I will be the first of the Kindred to forgive your kind,' said Fitt. 'I will set a trail for the rest of the Kindred to follow within our collective consciousness, and when they do, it will set them free.

'And can you find a way to forgive what it is that you must forgive?' I asked.

'Flame is already helping me to understand what forgiveness is, in truth. Ahh, I see the error that most of us make.'

I was Aware that Flame and Fitt communicated in the way that they had when their minds first touched – huge amounts of information were being transferred back and forth in mere seconds. Fitt was totally consumed by what she was learning. I left them to it, rising stiffly from where I had held my vigil, and stretching before joining my friends at the campfire.

'How are they doing that?' Sonja asked. 'It's incredible, it's as if their minds are communicating at the speed of light.'

'I think the fact that Fitt's always been Aware means that her mind can accept more than ours,' I said. 'Our horses learnt to communicate with us in ways our minds could cope with but Flame hasn't needed to do that with Fitt, she just turns her attention to something and Fitt immediately knows it.'

'And she's learning about forgiveness,' Sonja said thoughtfully.

Aleks said, 'Well, we can tell her what that is.'

'I think it's far more likely that we're about to learn it isn't what we thought it was,' said Marvel. 'Brace yourself, Aleks, Fitt's coming over.'

As Fitt stepped out of the twilight and into the glowing light of our campfire, all of us gasped. Fitt was standing straighter! I leapt to my feet and stood in front of her. She was definitely taller than she had been before.

'Fitt, you're already less hunched, you're doing it,' I said.

She nodded. 'I am learning forgiveness. I can show you its energy, if you would like to learn?'

I looked around at my friends. All of them were nodding except Aleks, who sat in the foetal position, his forehead resting on his knees. His arms were wrapped tightly around his legs as he rocked from side to side.

'Aleks?' I said.

He shook his head from side to side, without looking up. 'I can't do it,' he said. 'This is it, isn't it? This is my worst nightmare happening for real. I can't cope, I can't do this.'

I looked apologetically at Fitt, who merely smiled back at me and then sat down. *I will wait,* she told me.

As Sonja handed Fitt a full bowl of rabbit stew, I went to sit next to Aleks. 'Aleks, this isn't your worst nightmare, in fact, it's not even close,' I said, gently.

Aleks jerked his head up. 'WHAT?'

'Where's Nexus?' I said.

'She's grazing over there.'

'She's content?'

He raked his fingers through his hair. 'Yes.'

'So then all this is, is a group of friends sitting together around a campfire. You're close enough to Fitt to pick up information about her, just like you all did the first few times we met her, before anyone except me was Aware. Let yourself know her, Aleks.'

I felt Nexus add her support to my suggestion and Aleks flicked his eyes to Fitt and then quickly away again. We all sat in silence. Aleks breathed his fear in and out in short, sharp pants, which gradually became softer. We waited. Eventually, he said, in a cracked voice, 'Fitt, I know you mean no harm. I'm sorry for... the way I am.'

'I forgive you.'

Fitt spoke three words that had always held a certain meaning for me – an entirely different one from that which she gave them. Rather than using them to tell of her choice to put aside a wrong done to her, she used them to dismiss the idea that any wrong had existed. She had grasped, in full, the meaning of the concept that everything happens as it should.

'Forgiveness means knowing that there is nothing to forgive,' I whispered.

'It is so. I will need to apply my new understanding to every aspect of the resentment and shame that is carried within the collective consciousness of the Kindred, in order to clear it from my own shoulders and set an example for the rest of my kind. When I have done it, I will stand tall,' rasped Fitt.

'Is there anything I can do to help you?' I asked her.

'Everything your ancestors did that led to the Kindred carrying the emotional weight that disfigures them will be remembered by me and forgiven. Some of it will not be easy to forgive, but it must be so and I would have you by my side as I do it,' Fitt said.

I was Aware that she didn't just mean physically. She wanted me to relive her memories with her as she forgave everything that weighed her down. I could see the sense; I would be the focal point for her forgiveness. If she could forgive the actions of humans while a human rode her memories with her, then she could be sure that her forgiveness was complete and absolute. There was one glaring obstacle, though.

'Your Elder will be furious, Fitt,' I said. 'I've been careful not to overstep the boundary that she's needed in place in order to be in contact with me and this won't just be overstepping it, it will be smashing it to smithereens.'

'She is already furious, but where her anger is fuelled by fear for our kind, my request to you is fuelled by love for them,' Fitt replied. 'I would be the catalyst to my kind that you have been to yours in bringing about change. You could not have done all that you have without Infinity and your friends. I cannot do all that I must without Flame and my friends. You are my friend and I am asking for your help.'

Loathe as I was to alienate the Elder, my choice was clear. 'I'll be by your side as you forgive,' I said. 'When do you want to begin?'

Fitt lowered her empty bowl to the ground. 'It cannot wait and I doubt that either you or I would be able to sleep even if it could. Are you happy to start now?'

'I am,' I said.

Immediately, Rowena leapt to her feet and I heard her organising the others to bring blankets for us as Fitt's mind gently entwined itself through mine and then drew it into the collective consciousness of the Kindred.

There were incubators. Hundreds of them, each containing a small, hairy baby with fangs, tiny talons and eyes with slitted pupils. The babies were strangely quiet as they lay staring at the ceiling, blinking only occasionally. Thick needles pierced their leathery skin, attaching them to tubes containing various coloured fluids. One of the babies had streaks of dried blood down his hairy face.

Two humans with clipboards entered the nursery. They selected a baby and then took her into a brightly-lit room with a metal table upon which were various metal implements. She gave a husky whimper as a mask was placed over her face, until her eyes closed. I wanted to look away as her scalp was sliced open and her skull was punctured with well-practised precision, but my mind witnessed whatever Fitt chose to witness. Wires were inserted into the various holes in her skull and then joined into a small rectangle of metal that I recognised from descriptions of The Old as a computer chip. The baby began to stir and the humans turned on a machine that could only have been a computer, and began pressing buttons on it. The baby either screamed, cried or calmed as different buttons were pressed in turn. When the humans were satisfied that all was working as it should, the chip was embedded in her skull and then the skin was stapled together over the top of it. The baby made strained wailing noises as she kicked her feet and clenched her fists. She was in pain and the humans didn't care. They merely lifted her from the table, wiped the worst of the blood away and then returned her to her incubator.

I wanted to scream. *Your centre...* Infinity reminded me and I found it just before I felt the energy of Fitt's forgiveness. Flame was with her, giving her the strength she needed to remember that we are all parts of the same whole and we are all merely dreaming a dream. Those who had incarnated as humans of The Old had made a mistake. They thought they were all separate beings, needing to compete with and control one another and as a result, they were fearful and unstable. They lost the ability to empathise or even love and they could not see that they were heading for their own destruction.

I thought of Aleks, whose soul had incarnated over and over in The Old and was now battling so desperately to clear his need to be in control of his external circumstances. Everything found its way back into balance, eventually, regardless of what occurred and who did what to whom. Blame, anger and guilt merely stood in the way of that balance being found.

Together, Fitt and I understood that we were seeing various parts of the same whole coming together and playing the parts in the dream from which each would learn and that would propel each towards finding balance. Together, we forgave.

We saw the babies grow without love or any form of nourishment other than that which entered their veins from the tubes to which they were attached, night and day. Any attempt to touch the tubes left them screaming as their computer chips registered a deviation from acceptable behaviour and stimulated nerves that would create pain.

As they grew, we saw them moved from incubators to cots, which they were only allowed to leave in order to use the bathroom or to attend their lessons. They were forbidden to communicate with one another except during language lessons and they learnt quickly to obey the rules in order to avoid the instantaneous pain that would result from any infraction.

As they matured, they were transferred to stark, grey holding cells, from which they were taken from time to time to walk the streets in small groups with human handlers. Due to their animal heritage, they were Aware. They could feel the mental instability that permeated the cities and they fought hard to keep their behaviour calm, controlled and within the parameters of the computer programs that controlled them. Children were allowed and often encouraged to taunt them and throw stones, in order to instil into them the fact that they were different and also in the hope of encouraging controlled anger and ruthlessness in the young Kindred, known then as Enforcers. If no abuse from children was forthcoming then the handlers themselves would dispense it. The Enforcers knew that however much humiliation and pain they experienced, it was nothing compared to the pain they would endure as a result of their chips if they were to retaliate, so they were forced to tolerate all abuse without complaint or reaction. They felt fury, shame, resentment and a continual, soul-sapping sadness.

As the Enforcers became powerful adults, capable of scaling buildings, ripping humans to shreds with their fangs and talons and being almost impossible to harm due to their power, speed and exceedingly tough skin, they underwent training to be members of the ultimate police force. Infraction of rules by any human resulted in their elimination by the Enforcers, who followed orders issued by the computers that controlled them without delay in order to avoid the pain that would otherwise result. There was no place for any moral judgment of their own; they were bred and raised purely to obey and to do despicable things to humans who broke the law. Some of them came to relish inflicting abuse on humans in return for all that they had suffered, despite the agony of being Aware of the suffering of their victims. A few of them learnt to remove themselves from what they were forced to do, to go elsewhere within their minds as their bodies carried out their instructions, in order to protect themselves from the horror. Many more merely withered away inside.

When the people of The Old destroyed themselves, their computers were destroyed with them. All of the Enforcers who were above ground when the explosions occurred, died alongside the humans. Those who were off-duty and in their holding cells many floors below ground were surprised by the sudden opening of their cell doors as the lights went out. They stayed where they were, too frightened of the pain that would result from them stepping outside their cells unbidden. After a while, when no humans appeared, a few dared to venture out into the corridor. No pain. After some hours of waiting to see what would happen next, over a hundred Enforcers tentatively climbed the stairs up towards ground level. The higher they went, the more rubble they had to shift in order to continue their journey, but their powerful limbs made little of the work. When they finally reached what had been the second-to-top floor, they found themselves standing in fresh air with warm rain falling gently about them. Of the humans and computers who had controlled them, there was no evidence. Once they had climbed to the top of the crater in which they had found themselves, and looked all around at the levelled city, a previously unthinkable idea began to hit them. They were free.

They had no idea what they should do; bred and trained only to obey, they were left adrift. Some merely sat down where they were and looked aimlessly about themselves. Others didn't even manage that, but just stood, shamed by their hopes that someone would come and tell them what to do. A few let out savage roars and took off with the intention of extracting revenge on any surviving humans they could find.

Eventually, hunger drove the Enforcers back down to the lower levels. They found store rooms full of their tinned, processed food and returned to their cells out of habit, to eat. It was then that they became Aware of the panic and confusion of the younglings. Some of the Enforcers ignored what they could feel, intent only on feeding themselves. The rest descended the stairs to the lower levels, forced to remember as they did so the conditions in which they, themselves had been raised. They found the dormitories first. The younglings cowered in their cots amidst the stench of urine and excrement. The Enforcers had to lift each youngling, kicking and screaming, from his or her cot in order to prove that they would suffer no pain as a result of leaving without the permission of a human. There was little communication, merely action based on need. Some of the Enforcers led the younglings up to the food stores while the rest descended to the nurseries.

The Enforcers entered cautiously, expecting at least here to encounter humans, but as with the rest of what was left of "Freak's Paradise", as the building was known, there were none to be found. They had abandoned their charges in the last throes of their desperate, mad war. Most of the babies were screaming strange, husky screams. When the computers had been destroyed, their calm-inducing signals to the infants' intracranial chips had ceased, as had instructions to the machines that controlled supply of nutrients, water and growth hormones via the tubes to which each baby was attached. As a result, the babies were hungry, thirsty and very frightened by the range of emotions their bodies were now allowed to experience.

The Enforcers stood grouped at the door end of the nursery, overwhelmed by the noise and unsure what to do. Eventually, one of the females stepped forward. Something – a feeling that she did not recognise – pulled her towards the nearest baby. She reached out a hand and touched the baby's arm. His wailing stopped for a few seconds and then began again. The strange sensation that had drawn her to him began to spread within her. It was like a comforting warmth that calmed her and made her want the baby to feel it too. She picked him up and he screamed even louder as she gently removed the tubes from him. She held him close and felt his heart beating against her own. The baby quieted and whatever the foreign feeling was, it flooded her. Tears flowed silently down her face and for the first time in her life, she smiled.

The other Enforcers were Aware of her feelings and some of them made choking sounds as the unfamiliar emotion took them over too. One by one, they moved to the incubators and lifted the babies out, releasing them from the tubes and holding them close. A few of the babies were dead, their tiny brains unable to cope with the sudden influx of sensation once the chips that had held them trancelike failed. Another emotion stole over the Enforcers who found the dead infants, similar to the first but tinged with sadness and a sense of something lost. That emotion was felt in combination with anger when the Enforcers discovered halls at even deeper levels below ground that housed hundreds of liquid-filled tanks, each of which was linked by tubes to multiple tanks of different coloured fluids similar to those that had nourished the infants on the floors above, and each of which now contained a dead foetus.

We saw the Enforcers leave the city, taking the younglings and babies with them. We saw their struggles to make decisions for themselves every step of the way. For some, it became too hard, and they simply sat down and gave up the will to live. Those who struggled on did it for the love they had found for the babies and younglings, but the effort took its toll on them and they died young. The younglings fared slightly better, but it wasn't until the infants matured that the Kindred, as they had chosen to call themselves, began to flourish. The first to have been raised with love and kindness, they found it easier to listen to their Awareness, to know themselves and to be happy. Easier, yet still not easy. The intention with which the Kindred were created – to obey without question, no matter how terrible the order – still left its imprint upon them and making decisions according to what they could feel inside of themselves, rather than following rules, was something they had to practise over and over. Much, I suddenly realised, as their descendants still did in the present day.

Fitt and I forgave it all. Flame and Infinity were with us every step of the way, providing a calm, reassuring strength and confidence that we would see it all for what it was and that we would let it go.

I opened my eyes. The campfire was banked and glowing in the soft predawn twilight. I was propped up against saddlebags and covered with blankets, as was Fitt. Rowena slept curled up almost on top of me, as if she'd nodded off whilst keeping guard. Everyone else slept too, except Fitt, who sat up and reached across for my hand. *Thank you, my friend.* Her thought was laced with affection.

She sat straight! I leant over and hugged her for all that I was worth. I was so proud of her. It had been hard enough for me to forgive all that I had seen, and for her it could have been impossible, but she had taken all of Flame's counsel and made it a part of herself. She knew the truth of who she was, of who we all were and, even whilst incarnate as one whose kind had suffered so much, she had remembered that however real her life seemed, she and we were all really just parts of the same whole, dreaming the same dream.

Do you think the rest of your kind will be able to forgive us as readily as you have? I asked her.

Fitt sighed. *It will not be so easy for them. They do not have Flame, nor the benefit of human friends and they are not yet confident that my trust in you is well placed. The Elders are all suspicious of what you and your friends do, due to the very memories they have inherited from our ancestors that they must forgive. The fact that you and I have defied my Elder has angered her to the point where listening to her Awareness will prove difficult and the others will take her lead.*

The future I had seen flashed into and back out of my mind so quickly that I barely had time to notice it, but notice it I did, and so did Fitt. Her eyes widened and she drew breath sharply, before realising that it was information I hadn't shared with my friends. Instantly, she hid what she had picked up from me deep within her mind, in case any of them woke up.

Thanks, Fitt, that's for another day, I told her. *There's something far more pressing that you need to focus on right now.*

We could both feel Flame's impatience. Fitt smiled and stood up. She had always had to look down to me but now that she was no longer hunched, she towered above me. I noted that it was a good job that Flame was also tall. I followed Fitt as she made her way to where her horse waited for her. She vaulted straight on to Flame's back and then the two of them set about making their final adjustments. As the first rays of sun broke over the horizon, Fitt and Flame became everything that they could be.

Flame's long legs didn't appear to be moving with any speed, yet she swept effortlessly across the plains, her rhythm of movement barely disrupted at all as she cleared the few issues that no longer had a place within her. I felt her release her sadness and grief at the loss of her herd when she was attacked. I felt various disappointments from former lives leave her. And then I felt joy burst from They Who Are Flame as they moved back and forth through the paces, their delight ever increasing as they realised that there was nothing that they couldn't do now that they were one.

The Kindred Elder observed them briefly with a mixture of awe dampened by fury and then she was gone.

I felt warm breath on my neck and without thinking, reached up to stroke the pink muzzle that I knew would be there. *They are amazing,* I observed to my horse as we watched our friends.

They have achieved much, she agreed. *They are ready for what approaches.*

I nodded. There would have been a time when I would have hoped that the rest of us were too. Now, I knew that the fact that it was going to happen meant that there could be no doubt.

TWENTY

Enough

There were celebrations and hilarity from all except for Vickery and Aleks as we breakfasted. Vickery tried to be as happy for Fitt and Flame as the rest of us were, but I could feel her envy that Fitt had achieved so quickly that for which she herself now strived. Aleks managed to smile and congratulate Fitt, but he still struggled with her presence. It was a relief for him when after breakfast, Fitt remained in camp with Flame while the rest of us rode out to meet the next wild horse herd that was nearing our location. The wild horses knew that Fitt was with us and they seemed to have accepted her bond with Flame after some examination of the two of them, but we all agreed that her physical presence might be too much of a distraction for them to be able to settle and work with us as easily as their predecessors had done. And after everything Fitt had put herself through in recent days, she needed rest and she was to be sure that she got some, she was told firmly by Rowena as we were leaving.

The wild horse herd was the largest that we had met yet. As they milled around us, we could feel their openness to working with us, their eagerness for the help that they knew we could give us. Like the previous herd, they would need no demonstration from our horses. All of us slid to the ground and the second that Infinity had moved far enough away from me for another horse's approach not to be considered impolite, the lead mare, a stocky grey, was at my side.

I smiled as she snuffled my outstretched hand and as soon as Aleks legged me up onto her back, we were away. She had a cumbersome body, but she knew in advance how I would suggest she arrange it and how I would support her, and she responded to me instantly. In no time at all, I was dismounting and she was off, leaping into the air in huge fly bucks as she cantered around the other horses waiting their turn for our help. I felt her release the last of what she needed to just as the next mare sidled up to me.

It was Aleks who once more gave me a leg up. As I settled into position on my new mount's back, I noticed briefly that Vickery rode Verve some distance away, before I was required to give all of my attention to the feisty black mare who fidgeted beneath me. She had lived many times and had waited a long time for this – she would wait no longer. She leapt forward into a fast walk, too fast to be balanced on her own let alone carrying my weight. Instantly, I closed my thighs and pulled back. I was almost getting used to the fact that horses who had never been ridden before could respond to a signal as if they had felt it a thousand times, but I still felt a thrill when the mare slowed her pace and then lifted as my calves closed around her sides. Like water released from a dam, she burst along the pathway that was so clear in her mind, and barely stopped long enough for me to dismount before sitting down onto her haunches and striking out with her front legs as the painful memories that had burdened her for so long began to dissipate into the ether.

She was a long time in releasing all that she no longer needed to be part of her. I was Aware that a colt waited for my attention, but I felt that I owed it to the black mare to witness all that she had experienced at the hands of humans, all that was so painful as to have affected her for so long. When she had finally finished, I felt her joy and her lightness as she floated around at a magnificent trot. She dripped with sweat and her sides heaved, yet she was energised and vital. I smiled my happiness for her and then switched my attention to the colt.

Only a few hours later, my friends and I stood watching the heels of the wild horses disappear into the distance. Those of us who had ridden were feeling the now familiar satisfaction of a job well done.

'The pattern is so strong within their collective consciousness now,' said Marvel. 'It won't be much longer before the horses don't need our help at all, they'll all just find themselves in perfect balance as a consequence of being a horse.'

Aleks sighed. 'I wish it were that easy for me.'

'Thanks for your help this morning, Aleks,' said Rowena. 'We couldn't have done it without you.'

'There would have been two of us legging you up if any one of you would just tell Vickery that what she's attempting is futile,' Aleks said, gazing over to where Vickery still worked with Verve.

'It isn't futile,' said Sonja. 'What Vickery is doing now is all part of her journey, just the same as it is for you and the same as it was for each of us. She needs to realise that what she's doing isn't enough, in order to be open to giving more of herself.'

Soon, Infinity echoed my thought. I mounted her and then stood in my stirrups and beckoned Vickery and Verve to come with us. 'We need to get back to camp, pack up and move on,' I said.

I feel it too, the time is very near, Fitt's thought whispered in my mind.

When we arrived back at camp, we could see Fitt riding Flame a short distance away. Each magnified the best of the other so that together, they were a strong, confident, elegant being who radiated warmth and power. I wasn't the only one to marvel at how much they had changed from when we had first met each of them, and to appreciate afresh what they had achieved. Rowena whistled in admiration and Sonja began to clap. Within seconds, all of us were cheering and clapping, even Aleks, and Fitt's face broke into a shy grin that wasn't made any less soft by the fangs that clamped down upon her chin.

When we left the spot in which we had camped, Flame once more walked beside Infinity. There was a sense of rightness about her being there again, that warmed my heart. Fitt picked up on it and looked across at me with another of her grins. There was even more strength about our group now, I noticed, and my thoughts turned to the two who would complete us.

I could feel that they flew across a grassy hillside whilst warm summer rain lashed down upon them. Gas was fitter than he'd ever been and he delighted in the feeling of being able to use the full extent of his balance and strength as he blasted his way onwards, causing sheep to scatter before him. I smiled, remembering how often people had been forced to jump aside when Gas was on one of his missions. For once, I couldn't bring myself to caution Justin to slow him down, conserve energy and look after them both. Once they were with us, our group would be able to realise the full potential of its power.

Once we had eaten that evening, Fitt announced that she had decided to share the Kindred's history – everything that she and I had forgiven – with any of our group who would like to know it. It would help them to understand what we would all face much better, I realised and Fitt flicked her eyes to meet mine briefly in agreement. I remembered then, that Justin already knew.

If I had not wanted your mate to know, I would have made that clear. Do not be concerned, Fitt informed me and then winked, as she had seen Marvel do.

My m... oh, er, well that's okay then, I mean I realise now that I should have checked with you first, I'm sorry, I flushed scarlet whilst trying very hard not to.

Rowena's chortle was interrupted by Holly. 'Yes please,' she said to Fitt. 'We wouldn't have pried, but I think we're all dying to know.'

'I'm not sure I want...' Aleks began.

'Aleks, you do, please believe me,' I said. 'I'm sure Infinity and Nexus will link your mind to mine as we did before. Vic, Verve can help you link to one of the others if their horses will allow it.'

'Bright will help,' Sonja said, and Vickery nodded her thanks.

As soon as Aleks joined me in my mind and Vickery joined Sonja in hers, Fitt brought to the forefront of her mind all of the memories that she and I had explored the previous evening. She had just begun to guide us through them when the Kindred Elder desperately slammed herself between us all and Fitt. Fitt wouldn't allow it. She dismissed every suggestion made to all of our minds that a block existed, until eventually, the Elder gave up. I felt her shock at Fitt's continued and escalating defiance and then I had to hold on to Aleks's mind with everything I had, as the Elder flung her rage at us all. Aleks's mind almost shattered under the impact of the Elder's wrath at a group of humans invading the Kindred's privacy, gaining knowledge of their weaknesses, gaining power over them as their ancestors had sworn would never happen again. Infinity and Nexus surrounded and infused Aleks with their energy, soothing and protecting him as he recovered from the shock of the mental onslaught to which we had all been subjected.

I managed to remain centred, as did Fitt, Rowena and Sonja. Marvel and Holly were knocked slightly off balance before recovering quickly, and Vickery was held together by Sonja, Bright and Verve. Fitt demonstrated to us how to take our attention away from the Elder and refuse her influence, which one by one, we all managed to do.

'I can't do this, I'm not strong enough,' wheezed Aleks.

Nexus spoke to his mind as it rested within mine. *You will be helped greatly by what the Kindred will share. Your friends and I will assist you in finding the strength that you believe you lack. The time is fast approaching when you will need it.* She increased the support she was sending to her Bond-Partner and Aleks breathed deeply several times, shaking his head. At last, looking wretched, he nodded.

Fitt focused on the memories of the Kindred once more and we witnessed them alongside her. When we saw the younglings being abused by their handlers, Aleks drew breath and held it so that for a second, I thought he'd died of shock.

'That's m-m-me,' he managed to gasp. 'I w-was th-there. I d-did th-th-those th-things.'

I felt his recognition of himself in a former incarnation and as I focused more closely on the handler who had taken his attention, as I looked into eyes that were full of fear, I saw that it was, indeed, Aleks.

'Thunder and lightning,' breathed Holly.

We all felt Aleks's horror and then the strength of his remorse. Nexus wrapped herself around him, loving him as he couldn't love himself.

Aleks, you have to forgive yourself, Fitt spoke to him within my mind.

Your fear helped to create the very beings of whom you are now so afraid. The only way to step out of the circle in which you find yourself is to see it for what it is and then forgive it. Clear it. Let it go.

'But I was a m-monster,' gulped Aleks.

You were afraid. You're still afraid and the only way to stop feeling that way is to love. Love yourself as your horse loves you, as your friends love you. As I love you.

'But how can you love me when you know what I did?' Aleks challenged her.

Because I forgive you, Fitt told him, patiently. *Now forgive yourself. Know that what you did, while unhelpful, was part of your journey towards balance. You spent a few lifetimes learning what takes you further away from it and now you are learning to move closer towards it. That is all you have done and we have all done the same on our own journeys. Forgive everything that I will show you. It is the only way.*

I felt the moment that Aleks believed her. I felt him forgive himself and instantly, he was stronger. Nestled in my mind as he was, he felt approval not only from his horse, but from all of us. We loved him and we were happy for him. We wanted him to move past his fears as much as he did. He was a part of our group. He was our friend.

Aleks felt calmer than he could remember. Then he looked over at Fitt and we all felt his confusion. Habit made him want to still be fearful and mistrustful of her, yet he found that he wasn't feeling either of those emotions. Something else was beginning to blossom within him, something which was foreign and which he resisted whilst he tried to work out what it meant. But it was there.

Fitt continued sharing memories into the night, finishing just before dawn, as she had when sharing them with me the previous night. Everyone sat in silence for a long while.

'Thank you, Fitt,' Holly said finally, and the others all echoed her thanks.

'I understand the Elder's reaction last night now,' said Aleks, yawning. 'No wonder she's scared to trust us.'

'Patience and compassion arise from understanding,' I murmured, remembering counsel that Infinity had once given me. I looked up to see Rowena looking at me with a raised eyebrow as she remembered too. I grinned at her. 'And very lucky that is too. If Fin hadn't helped me to understand you better, I'd never have had the patience or the compassion to forgive you after you punched me in the face whilst making out it was my fault.'

Rowena came to sit next to me and drew me into a hug. She sighed. 'That all seems so long ago now, doesn't it,' she said, tiredly.

'Yep,' I nodded against her shoulder.

'And it's all been leading up to what we're moving towards now,' she said.

'Uh huh.' I could feel my eyes closing and sleep trying to wrestle me from my thoughts.

'Best get some rest then.'

I dreamt of Justin and Gas moving as one alongside a river made orange by the rise of the sun. They were pleased that our group was forced to stay put for the day in order to catch up on sleep, and relieved that we would be further delayed once we left camp, by another herd of horses who were moving in our direction. They Who Are Gas weren't far away now and the closer they got, the more energy and strength they found. It wasn't all theirs, I realised; our horses supported them. They wouldn't allow Gas's body to be tired or strained. He and Justin would increase the strength and purpose of our group. They were necessary.

We all slept into the afternoon. I woke to the sound of Marvel cursing that the fire had gone out. One by one, we all roused, stretched and began to move about, performing camp chores in sleepy silence.

I checked in with Infinity, who was grazing only a short distance away but was out of sight behind some trees. She was enjoying the feeling of the hot summer sun on her back but she was irritated by the flies that buzzed around her eyes. I didn't know whether the thought to move into the trees for respite from them originated from me or from her, but she acted on it and was soon snoozing nose to nose with Oak and Flame in the shade.

Infinity knew what was to come as well as I did and neither of us knew what the outcome would be. It didn't matter really, not in truth. Our souls were entwined and that would always be so, wherever we were and whatever happened. We were still dreaming the dream but it was no longer necessary for either of us to. We would do what we had resolved to do and we would do our best for those to whom it would matter, but it was impossible for us to be affected by the outcome either way. We were Infinity.

I felt Flame and Fitt pick up on my musings. Fitt looked over at me and nodded slowly, smiling her shy smile as she allowed me to know of her own musings in return. She had been Aware from the moment she was born. Whilst always having been encouraged to use her Awareness to have empathy and understanding of those around her, to communicate easily and to sense the location of both food and danger, the fear and mistrust that ran deeply within the Kindred had prevented her from using it to its full extent. Her bond with Flame had changed everything. Together, they had healed their hurts and found the balance for which their souls had searched for so long. Fitt had been left with an Awareness that was unfettered; she had a whole new way of experiencing the world and understanding All That Is. And she and her horse were one. Always. I returned Fitt's smile and then we both went about our chores.

We were all still subdued as we ate dinner that evening, absorbed in our own thoughts or those shared with our horses. Aleks was deep in conversation with Nexus about all manner of things and after dinner, he announced that he was going off to ride his horse. He returned just as the rest of us were getting ready for bed, looking pleased with himself and I could feel a definite shift occurring within him. None of us spoke, but Sonja hugged him before getting into her bedding, and Marvel clapped him on the back as Aleks crouched down beside him to help bank the fire.

Fitt and I were both up at dawn, well rested and itching to get going. We fetched water from the watering hole and then set about cooking breakfast, in the hope that the smell of roasting meat would rouse the others. Our plan worked and our friends were soon up and dressed, Marvel and Vickery leaving to go hunting whilst the others aired bedding and packed up camp.

The sun was higher in the sky than I would have liked by the time we got going, but I was happy to be on our way. The sky was a cloudless, vivid blue, only punctuated by the odd flock of small birds or pairs of larger ones that circled, cawing to one another as they hunted. A warm breeze carried the smell of the summer plains – an earthy scent laced with a hint of wild flowers – and kept us comfortable under the hot sun as we once again followed our sense of the Kindred Elder.

I was careful not to allow my thoughts to dwell upon her once I had a sense of her, but even in the fraction of a second that my mind touched upon hers, I knew of her continued rage. She was angry, fearful and irrational and had lost all sense of much else. As I began to wonder how she could forget all that she knew of me, both from our past together and from the frequent searching of my mind that I had allowed her since my mission began, I understood.

The Kindred had kept themselves away from humans as much as possible since the collapse of The Old, and their Elders had used what they knew of us to keep them safe. As soon as we met and befriended Fitt, everything had begun to spiral out of the Kindred Elder's control. I had done everything I could to help the Elder to trust me, but my continued advance towards her had exerted a steadily increasing pressure, only made more intense by my strengthening friendship with Fitt and then our recent decision to defy the Elder. The fear that resided within the collective consciousness of the Kindred was fuelling the Elder's own fear that she had made a mistake in ever touching my mind, in giving any encouragement for my mission to find her to try to right the situation between humans and the Kindred. She doubted herself and therefore she doubted me. She was terrified that she would be the downfall of the Kindred by allowing her past life with me to tempt her into trusting me and my fellow humans in this life.

All I could feel for her was love and compassion, but she couldn't feel it. As happened so often, fear was blocking out everything else.

But not for much longer. Infinity and I were resolute as we framed the thought together.

Not for much longer, Justin and Gas agreed.

Not for much longer, echoed Fitt and Flame.

'What isn't for much longer?' Marvel enquired, politely refraining from searching my thoughts.

'How things have always been,' I replied. 'Enough is enough.'

TWENTY-ONE

Love

*W*e could see woodland far off in the distance as the wild horse herd approached us at a gallop and then swept around us in a huge circle. By now, most of the sitting water had evaporated from the plains, leaving a slippery, squelching mud that flicked up from the horses' hooves, hitting those of their herd who galloped behind them. Despite the difficult footing, the herd slowed to a graceful halt and stood in an arc, regarding us. They were curious about us in so far as they had never seen humans before and had caught only glimpses of Kindred as they fled from them, but beyond that, they took us in their stride. They all knew of the horse who had a Kindred as her Bond-Partner, they knew what they had achieved together and they accepted the partnership without question. They also knew of what our group was capable and what we had so far accomplished with the other wild herds. And they were very close to achieving the same already, by themselves.

As the wild horses sensed my friends and I realising that we were seeing a wild herd only a breath away from being in perfect balance within themselves and with one another, they flowed back into movement. They were breathtaking to watch as they, including the foals, changed between the paces in unison in a graceful swirl of bodies, manes and tails.

I felt Infinity move beneath me and smiled as we and our friends joined the wild horses' dance. We felt them absorb the last remaining details they required from our horses and we lived all of the memories and emotions that they released, alongside them. And then they were gone.

'YESSSSSSSSSSSS, THE HORSES HAVE DONE IT!' Marvel shouted with joy. 'ENOUGH OF THEM HAVE ACHIEVED PERFECT BALANCE THAT IT'S THE WAY THEY ALL ARE NOW. THEY DON'T NEED US ANYMORE.' His voice broke. 'After everything the horses have done for us, we've finally been able to do something for them in return.'

I slithered to the ground and wrapped my arms around Infinity's neck. Her elation was mine as we felt all of the horses rejoice. After all of the lifetimes each of them had lived in service to humankind, we had finally returned to them what we owed. Everything found balance, eventually.

The euphoria we all felt gave us new momentum as we carried on, laughing and singing, towards the woodland that loomed on the horizon. Vickery joined Aleks in walking beside Verve and Nexus, like him now unwilling to ride her horse for any length of time until she could ride without compromising the effortless balance in which he now moved. They chatted happily as they walked, sharing Vickery's delight at Verve's achievement.

As we entered the forest, a sense of foreboding stole across us all. All of us who were Aware knew that we were now heavily monitored from afar. Infinity and I took our places at the front of the group once more and when Flame appeared alongside Infinity, I smiled my welcome to Fitt. The warmth and determination of They Who Are Flame was unwavering as ever as they stepped around trees and undergrowth, always returning to our side.

I glanced behind us and saw that Marvel and Rowena rode two abreast in the same fashion as Fitt and I, ushering Aleks along in front of them with Nexus.

'I don't like this... at... all,' said Aleks.

'You don't have to like it, mate, you just have to knuckle down and get on with it, as always,' said Marvel firmly.

Rowena mouthed, 'Flight risk,' at me and grinned.

I couldn't help but grin back at her and pitied Aleks if he so much as tried to turn tail.

The birds sang and chirped in the trees, leaves rustled soothingly in the breeze and the forest floor was dappled with enough light that we could see easily whilst enjoying a break from the heat of the sun. As a result, all of us except Aleks were able to enjoy our ride through the forest during the next few days, despite the knowledge that we were edging ever closer to those who may not welcome us. Often, the horses were restricted to walking due to the density of the woodland, but sometimes we could canter, weaving through the trees, laughing as we narrowly avoided colliding with one another. Nighttime was difficult though, as our horses were forced to wander some distance from where we camped in order to graze sufficiently, and Aleks had to be continually reassured that no Kindred other than Fitt were in the vicinity.

The forest was thinning and we were climbing higher, I realised one morning. Feeling chilly, I pulled my jumper out from my saddlebag and donned it. A few of my friends had done the same, I saw from a glance behind to where Aleks and Sonja were being teased by the others. We rode on for a few more hours and were just about to stop for lunch, when as one, the birds stopped their chattering and without more than a flutter, were gone. All of us who were Aware felt three Kindred converging on us from behind. They were herding us forward and blocking off our retreat, we all realised.

We'll need to give light to Aleks and to Vic if she needs it, I thought to myself and turned to see my friends nodding their agreement.

We reached the top of the slope that we had been ascending and found ourselves in a roughly level clearing. I was Aware of more Kindred rapidly approaching from all directions and the Kindred behind us were now close enough to stare. They were two males and a female, all younglings, all hungry and all fuelled with a desire to prove themselves.

To whom? I wondered.

To her. She will regret this, Fitt told me sadly.

'This is bad, this is really bad,' Aleks said breathlessly from behind me. 'We need to get out of here.'

Panic was erupting from him and I could feel the excitement of the younglings as they became Aware of it. Light burst from all of our group, directed towards Aleks. Fitt and I then diverted our flows of light towards the three Kindred who were moving ever closer to us.

Infinity halted beneath me and we turned around to face the rest of our group. 'Aleks, this is what you've been waiting for,' I said, desperate to say all I had to before my concentration was taken up by everything that was to come. 'The Kindred you can feel behind us are only the advance party. Lots more are coming and you and Nexus have no way of escape. You can give in to your fear and hinder what the rest of us need to do, or you can choose love. You know why the Kindred feel as they do towards us, you understand why they haven't been able to let themselves trust us. We have this one chance to prove to them that we have changed. All of us must demonstrate to them that we will never choose fear over love. If even one of us still shows that tendency, they will never trust us. We all need to send them our light. All of us, and no matter what they do. At the moment, your friends are sending light to you that is needed by the Kindred. Join us, Aleks, please, choose to love the Kindred. Send them your light so that we can all send them all of ours. Vic, you need to do the same and just when you think you're giving all you've got, you'll need to give more.'

A loud thump came from behind me and Infinity spun around. A Kindred youngling had dropped from a tree at the far edge of the clearing. I could feel Aleks's terror escalate.

'Love, Aleks,' Rowena said gently. 'Choose love.'

'Aleks, we need you. Please, choose love,' said Holly.

Thump. Another Kindred dropped to the ground.

'Aleks, they are like me, just like me,' rasped Fitt, 'and they need your help. You're strong. You can do this. Please, choose love.'

I could feel Aleks trying desperately to get a hold of himself.

'That's it, Aleks, you're doing it, now find your light and give it to them. They need you. We need you. That's it, well done, Aleks, strengthen your light as much as you can now and keep sending it,' said Sonja.

Thump. Thump. Thump. Kindred were dropping from the trees all around us. Aleks's light winked out.

'Aleks, we owe it to our friends to do this,' said Vickery. 'We owe it to our horses and we owe it to the Kindred. You forgave yourself for what you did in your past life, now you need to help us heal the wounds that you helped to create.'

Aleks's light flickered back and strengthened. He directed it towards the nearest Kindred.

'Good man,' said Marvel. 'Now keep it up. Whatever happens, keep it up.'

More and more Kindred younglings landed on the ground around us, all hungry and all intent on killing. Their fangs dripped with saliva as they regarded us, waiting for... something.

We all strengthened our light flows and directed them all around us, bathing the younglings in our love and assurance. Our horses infused the atmosphere with their calm love of ages. None of us were afraid. We all chose love. The younglings began to look about themselves in confusion.

You don't need to let her use you this way, Fitt told them. *She has chosen you for this because she is too frightened to approach us herself. She is angry and afraid and she would let you all taint yourselves by killing those who offer you love and the chance for our kind to have a better life. We never eat bonded horses and we never kill humans if we want to live with ourselves. You're hungry. Go and hunt and let the Elder face what she tries to avoid.*

'Don't move,' rasped a Kindred voice, full of authority. The younglings at the far edge of the clearing parted and the Kindred Elder moved into view. She was huge, hunched and her brown pelt was flecked with white. Her fangs were yellow with age but her green eyes flashed and glittered with the strength of her fear and her fury.

The thread that had tied us since we had incarnated together as mother and daughter flared into life. When she hit me full force with all that she felt, her emotions floored me, literally.

'KEEP SENDING YOUR LIGHT,' shouted Rowena. 'I'VE GOT

HER. ALEKS, CONCENTRATE. CHOOSE LOVE, REMEMBER
WHO YOU WANT TO BE.'

Dazed, I realised that I was sitting on the ground. Infinity snuffled my
ear. *Remain centred,* was all she offered before redirecting all of her
energy back to the Kindred.

'Am, why on earth didn't you let us know who she is to you? We
could have talked this through, prepared for this,' Rowena whispered in
my ear. 'Can you stand?'

I nodded. 'I think so. Thanks, I'm okay. I can handle this.'

Rowena heaved me to my feet until I leant on Infinity and then she
remounted Oak, her light at full strength and directed fully at the Kindred
Elder.

Still feeling the full strength of the Elder's emotions as she continued
to fling them at me, I remembered who I was. I was Infinity. My light
burned within me like a raging bonfire. I hurled it towards the Elder,
determined to love her and determined that my love would break through
to her, that she would remember who I had been to her and what we had
agreed to do in this lifetime. But I hadn't reckoned on the strength of the
collective. The Elder's fear and anger were not just her own, they were
the sum total of all of the Kindred who had lived before her. She hurled it
all down the thread that linked us, with full force, her determination to
hurt me equal to mine to love her. She floored me again.

Your centre... Infinity reminded me again. It was all that she could do.
I had to do this by myself, otherwise the Kindred wouldn't believe that
humans could truly change, could truly choose love of their own volition.

I could feel the Kindred younglings' drive to kill being fuelled by the
behaviour of their Elder. My friends – including Vickery and Aleks – and
our horses were giving everything that they had in order to hold them at
bay. My love for them all gave me new strength and my light burned
within me once more. I sent it back, full strength, towards the Elder.

I loved her. I remembered the agreement that she and I had made to
work together to help two races to find peace, even if she refused to. We
had known we could work together. From the moment she had given
birth to me, she knew me inside out. She knew how to quieten me when I
was sore or afraid. She knew when to step back and let me learn for

myself. She knew when to step in and deal with a situation beyond my ability to handle. She knew when to hug me and when to leave me alone. As I matured and became adult, we found that we were kindred spirits. We loved the simple things in life – walking in the woods while autumn leaves crunched underfoot, sharing a pot of tea at the end of a busy day, reading in companionable silence – and we loved to discover new things, especially phenomena that were on the fringes of the norm, not recognised or accepted by the world at large. We loved horses – being with them, learning from them, even just the smell of them. We loved each other in the way that only a mother and daughter can. We were fierce friends and we were there for each other through the happy and the hard times.

When it was time for her to leave her body, we both knew that she wasn't really leaving me, we knew that a thread connected us and always would. That thread drew our souls together once it was time for me to leave the body that she had created, birthed and protected. We revelled in our reunion and we agreed that our time together in the dream was not over. Two souls who resonated as easily as ours could achieve much in another lifetime, and we would remember that when the time came.

The time had come. I loved her as the mother she had been to me and as the Elder she was now, still trying desperately to protect those for whom she was responsible, those whom she loved. I felt her falter. She remembered. Briefly, her love for me threaded its way through her fear and anger. But then the weight of her responsibility to the Kindred crushed her personal feelings and she pushed back at me once more. I refused to brace myself for the storm of emotion that would floor me for the third time. I wouldn't fight her. She could floor me as many times as she wanted to and I would just carry on loving her.

And then Justin's light joined mine. For a moment, I thought he was sending it to the Elder through me, but then there was a shuffling, a grunt and a loud thump on the forest floor and Justin and Gas appeared by my side.

'They're here.' Rowena's voice was incredulous.

'Gas only flipping well jumped those Kindred,' Vickery said.

'Better late than never, mate,' Marvel's voice couldn't hide his affection and his relief.

Justin's warm hand enveloped mine. 'Together, Am,' he said. His light burned ferociously as he directed it towards me. I funnelled it down the thread that joined me to the Elder, along with my own. My light held my love for the Elder. Justin's held his love for me. He showed the Elder the shy, self-doubting young girl he had met two years previously. He showed her my determination to do the best for my horse and all of the conventions I was prepared to go against in order to do it. He showed her how I had healed Infinity after she was attacked and how I had subsequently stood up for her attackers, insisting that we help them. He showed her the day that I had my out-of-body experience and the decision I had made to continue in the dream purely in order to help the Kindred. He showed her all that he knew of me, all that the one who had been her daughter had grown to be. She knew it all from her delvings into my mind, he knew she did, but she needed to remember it. For her own sake and for that of the Kindred, she needed to admit that I was all she had hoped I would be. She needed to remember me and she needed to remember herself.

Finally, our love reached her. The mother I had known and loved so dearly held out her arms to me, as she had so many times before. Justin let go of my hand and gently pushed me to go to her. I saw the confusion and disappointment on the faces of the younglings that I passed before I was embraced firmly but tenderly by the huge, brown Kindred Elder. It was as if we had never parted. Her embrace awoke memories from the life we had lived together, of feeling that nothing could hurt me, nothing could even come close as long as she held me tight.

I felt the presence of more Kindred who could only be Elders. Stepping reluctantly away from Mother Elder, as I realised I now thought of her, I saw that a grey-pelted Kindred stood behind her, along with five others. The younglings all sank into a crouch, their expressions avid as they felt the atmosphere within the clearing shift yet again. They awaited the order to kill.

My friends and I all included the Elders in our light flows.

'You would turn traitor, Elder Hobday?' rasped the grey Kindred.

'We adhere to the plan. Younglings, you are hungry. You may attack. Kill the humans, feed on their horses and take Lacejoy prisoner.'

'No,' Elder Hobday rasped. She put herself in front of me and pushed me backward until we both stood in front of my friends and our horses. 'Elder Frankson, this is no longer necessary. There is another way forward.'

She was ignored. The younglings began to advance. We all sent them as much light as we could possibly find within ourselves, even Aleks, but it wasn't enough. There was only one thing that possibly could be. I turned to my friends. Those who were Aware picked up on my intention before I had a chance to speak. Holly turned ashen, then ground her teeth together and nodded. Sonja put her arm around Bright's neck and gave a short nod, her green eyes flashing. Rowena and Marvel each put a hand on their horses' necks and an arm around one another.

It is the only way, agreed Fitt. *I will come with you all.*

'We need to leave,' I told Aleks and Vickery.

'Well, finally,' said Aleks, his voice shaking. 'We'll head for the ones Gas clonked when he jumped them. We can break through them easily and then hopefully the horses can outrun them.'

'We're not leaving the clearing, Aleks, we're leaving our bodies,' I said.

'We're... what?' Aleks said, his eyes flicking over my shoulder to where the younglings moved in slow, crouching steps towards us.

'The Kindred want us to fight them or run. They want us to prove to ourselves and to them that eventually, we will always act out of fear. Instead, we'll act out of love. If they want our bodies, they can have them. We'll leave them willingly and we'll continue to love the Kindred as we leave.'

'But...' Aleks said.

'No time for buts, Aleks,' said Justin. 'We're all leaving. The horses will help us to do it. Are you both coming with us?' He looked from Aleks to Vickery.

'I am,' said Vickery.

'But I... Adam,' Aleks said, his eyes widening.

Adam and Peace stood just to the side of us, silvery-white and almost transparent. Adam was smiling. The younglings stopped in their tracks as a profound peace stole across the clearing.

'He's giving us more time, but we don't have long,' I said. 'We need to leave before they attack. Aleks, will you come with us? If even one of us resists them, they will have the proof that they expect to find.'

Aleks looked desperately from me to Adam, who nodded encouragingly at him. I felt something break inside of Aleks and then something else very definitely strengthen. 'I'll do it,' he said. 'What do I have to do?'

'The horses will leave and take us with them. Concentrate on the part of your mind that you share with Nexus. Put all of yourself there and when she draws you into herself, go with her. Don't hold back anything of yourself, just go with her and she'll take you. Okay?'

Aleks nodded.

'Vic?'

'Already going,' Vickery said faintly.

'Everyone, please remember, keep sending your light to the Kindred as you leave. They can be in no doubt that we do this out of love,' I said.

'I will make sure that there is no misunderstanding,' rasped Elder Hobday. 'I am more sorry than I can say for my part in this.'

You have nothing to be sorry for. Everything finds a balance. Everything is as it should be, I thought to her. And then Infinity and I willingly, lovingly, left our bodies behind.

TWENTY-TWO

Sacrifice

*T*he vast greyness in which we floated was familiar and blissful. Since thought was all there was, our ecstatic celebrations at what Aleks and Vickery had achieved were all-consuming. In choosing to relinquish all control over what happened to his body and that of his horse, Aleks had broken the pattern that had blocked him from being all he could be. He had realised the potential he saw for himself when he bonded with Nexus and if he returned to his body, he would find himself in perfect balance with his horse the moment he sat on her back, as would Vickery. She had given everything of herself when it mattered most and if she were able to ride her horse again, she would feel the proof of that which she had achieved. It was as if all of the joy that any of us had ever felt were magnified a thousand-fold as we revelled in their success and then in our shared euphoria at having arrived where we were. Justin and I – the only ones who had been here before whilst still incarnate – were required to hold firm to our sense of who we were, and to our mission.

Remember what we do, we thought to our friends. *If the Kindred will not take the chance we offer them, if they kill our bodies, then we can celebrate our return to All That Is. But for now, we must concentrate.*

Our physical bodies had collapsed to the ground. Each of us was attached to our body by the thinnest of cords that yet pulsed with life, but could be retrieved into our energy bodies at any time, permanently severing us from the lives we had been living.

The younglings stopped in their tracks, suspicious to begin with that we attempted some sort of trick. Their Awareness told them that we were no longer within our bodies, yet their physical senses told them that our bodies were not quite devoid of life. We all continued to send them our light, bathing the clearing in a white haze.

They give their bodies freely to you all if you wish them, Mother Elder told the younglings and the other Elders. *If you truly want them dead, then they offer no argument.*

'They would rather die than fight?' One of the Elders scratched her head as she rasped her bewilderment to herself.

They will live in love or not at all, replied Mother Elder. *Allow yourselves to feel what it is that they are sending to us all. They have evolved and, with the exception of Lacejoy, we have not. We hold to the fear and shame of our ancestors when we should be embracing those who would help us to find a better way to live.*

'Lacejoy is a traitor,' growled one of the younglings.

Lacejoy has set an example for us all to follow, corrected Mother Elder. *When we send you younglings out on your year's Findself, the hope is that you will turn away from our inherited tendency to find it easier to obey than to think for ourselves. Those of you who have had friends fail to return from their Findself will know, whether you admit it to yourselves or not, that they either failed to find a way to think for themselves and therefore perished, or were only able to make decisions by giving up all that we are. Those too will have perished eventually. Lacejoy has achieved all that she has by making her choices based purely on what she saw and felt in each moment. She has not only achieved Findself, she has trusted it at every step of her journey and has made her decisions according to its influence. She has accepted help and friendship from these humans. She has become one with a horse whose courage matches her own and she has allowed her horse to influence her. As a result, she is healed of what ails us all and she now walks tall.*

Mother Elder allowed thoughts of Lacejoy's process of forgiveness to permeate throughout the Elders and younglings.

'That's... not... possible,' rasped a smaller, completely white Elder. 'How did she find the strength?'

Feel it from her as she sends her love to you now. Feel the trust she has in her horse and the strength that trust gives her. And she's had the support of her human friends. Those who now lie at our feet alongside her.

'One of them was your daughter,' the grey-pelted Elder rasped accusingly.

She still is in the ways that matter, replied Mother Elder. *And now she is willing, happy even, to give up her life for us all, as are they all. Here is your test, younglings, for if you pass it, none of you will need to go on your Findself, in fact no other youngling will need to go, ever again. You are all hungry. Will you take the bodies offered to you and keep our race as it is – afraid, struggling? Or will you emulate the strength and courage that Lacejoy has demonstrated and call our friends back to their bodies, humans and horses both, and accept the help that they would give us?*

One of the other Elders opened his mouth to speak and another began to send thoughts to the younglings, but both stopped in surprise as Mother Elder streamed a flow of light towards them. If I'd been in my body, I would have jumped for joy. As it was, I directed my own flow to her alone for a few seconds, giving her as much of my love as I could.

'We could kill the horses and leave the humans and Lacejoy unharmed,' one youngling rasped, looking around at his companions for their reactions.

That is a decision you could make, Evansson, Mother Elder agreed, *and I ask you all to forgive me that in my fear, I encouraged you to make it only a short time ago. But I would remind you that it is not our way to hunt horses who have chosen to bond with humans. We have been Aware of the many times that humans have wanted to rise up against us, to hunt us down and remove us from existence. Always, they have refrained as a result of counsel given by the Horse-Bonded, at the urging of their horses. These horses have given their lives to their humans to ensure that they do not return to the ways of The Old and they are to be respected, not seen as prey by our kind. Those younglings who choose to hunt bonded horses during their Findself are those whose only way of making decisions is to entirely forget who we are and it is the beginning of their end.*

The younglings looked around at one another and from one Elder to the next. The Elders remained silent both in voice and mind, fascinated now by what Mother Elder was attempting.

As the younglings pondered and my friends and I continued to send them our light, I allowed my attention to rest with Infinity. She observed the scene with vague interest. It mattered not at all to her whether she and I returned to our bodies or not, just as it hadn't the last time she and I had left them. I wondered what I'd do if the younglings decided to kill her body but call me back to mine. As my thought became all of ours, my friends and I pondered it together. It didn't matter, not in truth, we all knew that. We were all one regardless of who was in a physical body and who wasn't. But would we humans want to live the lives we had grown used to living, without our Bond-Partners? Maybe the Kindred would use it as the ultimate test for us, to see if we would still choose to love them if they killed our horses. We felt our horses' pride in us as we realised that we would still choose love. Even in the face of the toughest question, we hadn't forgotten everything that they had taught us, everything that they had helped us to know. Whatever happened, we would return to our bodies if the Kindred called us, and we would give them all the love and help that they needed.

The younglings and the Elders all felt our decision. Within seconds, the first youngling accepted our love. He allowed himself to know all of us. He asked for our help. Within a single instant, Lacejoy transferred all the memories she had drawn from the collective consciousness to him along with her forgiveness of them. He absorbed everything and welcomed it as part of him, and then stood up tall. What had taken us all night to go through with her had taken the youngling less time than a single breath.

We see how they do that now, my friends and I thought as one. *If they call us back to our bodies, we will remember.*

Lacejoy's jubilation that her fellow Kindred had joined her in standing tall became everything to all of us, to the extent that one by one, our horses had to intervene to separate us back out from one another.

The youngling sent us his love. It called to us, beckoning us back to the bodies that lay in front of him. Bodies that may not be viable if the other younglings succumbed to their bloodlust, he realised. He redirected his love towards his brethren and to a one, they started and then gasped as they turned to him and saw that, no longer hunched, he towered over them.

They scrutinized him in their Awareness and one by one, realised the decision that he had made and its consequence. Immediately, a female youngling followed his example. She allowed us to show her all that she needed to know. A few breaths later, she stood almost as tall as her brother. She sent us her love and gratitude and then turned all of her energy towards the other younglings, another three of whom soon followed in her footsteps.

One by one, the younglings chose to heal. Their experiences accumulated in the collective consciousness of the Kindred, making it increasingly easier for their brethren to make the same choice. Soon, only five remained who were yet intent on killing. The five were younglings who would, if they'd had a chance to go on their Findself, have foregone all that the Kindred were and it would have killed them. The only way they would have been able to leave behind their tendency to obey rather than decide would have been to leave behind everything of their upbringing, leaving them lost, unstable and violent. Like those who had made similar choices before them, they would have felt unable to return to their communities at the end of their Findself, knowing that the way of life they had chosen for themselves would not be accepted. They would have been content with their solitary lives, for a time. But then a sense of emptiness would have stolen over them and taken root. They wouldn't have felt much like hunting anymore, or indeed like doing anything. They would have been relieved when the time came to leave their bodies, and then disappointed with themselves once they returned to the oneness and realised that they could have been so much more, had they made different choices.

They could make those choices this time around, Lacejoy infused them with her confidence. All of their brethren bombarded them with light, also confident that the five could make the choice to join them and to stand tall. The five became Aware that not only were my friends and I willing to leave our bodies for them, but that their kin were willing to let them kill us, rather than force them to obey. The love they felt for their brethren in that instant was all it took. They turned away from our bodies and allowed their kin to crowd around them, congratulating them on their decision. We felt them embrace who they were with help from their friends, and, finally, embrace us. When the five of them stood tall, all of the younglings focused on the humans and horses who yet supported them, and called for us to return.

Adam and Peace peeled themselves away from the rest of us, pleased to have played their part. Aleks held to them briefly to ensure they knew of his gratitude and then they were suddenly somewhere distant. My friends and I let them go, knowing that they had done what they could to make it easier for us to return to our bodies. As one, we were hesitant. Much as we could be Aware of one another's thoughts and feelings when in our bodies, here, we felt everything as one. We rejoiced as one. We pondered as one. We decided as one. It wasn't possible to be any other way and we felt the bliss of it as one. We should return. We would return. And yet, we lingered.

Infinity made her presence known as a purposefully discreet entity as she wove herself around me and directed me to the cord that connected me to my body. It pulsed very faintly now. It was time. I imagined following the cord back to my body and instantly, I was there.

My throat was dry and my breathing shallow. My eyes felt crusty as I opened them to see that a fire burned nearby. I breathed in deeply a few times and felt my breathing reset itself to a healthier depth and rhythm. I sat up, coughing, thirsty and ravenous. Infinity was a short distance away, sitting up and then heaving herself to her feet and taking a long draught of water from a bucket that had been placed close by. She had lost weight.

'Your horse yet looks after you. Any longer and return would have been impossible. Drink this.' Mother Elder held a wooden beaker of water in front of me.

'But we weren't gone that long, the younglings called us back after only an hour or so, surely?'

'They called you back and you were coming, but then you didn't. That was three weeks ago. A lot has happened while we've been waiting for you to return.'

'Three weeks...' My voice was almost as raspy as Mother Elder's and I had a bout of coughing, during which I remembered that time passed differently in the greyness. 'I'm so sorry. We took our attention away from here for what seemed like only a few minutes. I need to stand up.'

'You are weak. Let me support you.' Mother Elder put a hand under each of my elbows and easily drew me to my feet, steadying me on my trembling legs once I was standing.

As I turned to thank her, I saw that she stood tall. 'You've done it,' I said. 'How many of the others?'

'All of them.'

'ALL OF THEM?' I was unable to prevent my shock and delight from making me shout, and subsequently set myself off on another bout of coughing.

All of them. Forgive me, I will use mindspeak, as my voice has become more and more difficult to use comfortably in recent years. The Elders followed the younglings' example and forgave our past. They returned to their communities to share their experience and as more and more of the Kindred chose to forgive, it became easier for more to do the same. And now we all know the details of our history and we have all forgiven all of it. We all stand tall, thanks to you, your horses and Lacejoy. She is still a youngling in age but she has unanimously been raised to Elder in her absence. And now, I see that she too has returned. I am much relieved.

I saw Fitt sitting up next to where Flame was lurching to her feet. She was immediately offered water by another Kindred. The rest of our friends were either sitting or being helped to their feet at other campfires dotted throughout the clearing.

We knew you would want to be with your horses if you ever woke up and we didn't like to move them, so we have kept you all safe and warm out here. Your human bodies don't retain heat as well as your horses' bodies though, so we had to move the humans close to the fires, Mother Elder told me apologetically.

Thank you. As I conveyed my appreciation to Mother Elder for the Kindreds' thoughtfulness, I felt her embrace the touch of my mind upon hers. She wanted me to know everything about her and about the Kindred. Her eyes widened slightly in the firelight as she sensed that, as a result of being completely at one with Lacejoy in the greyness, my mind could now accept how the Kindred transferred so much information so quickly. It had merely been a case of stepping aside from the need to have thoughts in a linear form, allowing even the concept of linearity to melt into nothing, just as when accepting the non-linear nature of time. Mother Elder transferred everything to me and within seconds, I knew.

I knew that in a conscious attempt to honour the only members of The Old who had resisted the regime – a criminal underground of women who had called themselves the Kindred – the present Kindred named both their species after them, and themselves down the female line. The Kindred of The Old had helped those who would become the founding fathers of The New to escape, incited protests whenever new controlling measures were introduced, including the creation of the Enforcers, and had tried to befriend Enforcers whenever they came across them. And in return, the Enforcers had been compelled by their controllers to kill the only humans who had seen them for who they really were and tried to help.

Mother Elder's family originated with a female who had taken the surname of a woman called Hob, so she was Hobday, and her cousin was Hobson. Her mother was Hobtidy and her aunt was Hoblove but her father was Dayknow, since all of his mother's line were Days.

I knew that Mother Elder had no mate and no children. I also knew that the Kindred were neither very fecund nor as long-lived as humans, so their communities remained small. Younglings were treasured and yet were encouraged to go on their Findself, even with the knowledge that some would never return; the Kindred knew that it was essential to the survival of their species that their inbred instinct to look to others for instruction rather than to think for themselves, was constantly, vigilantly, overcome. Until now. Now that they had forgiven their past and cleared all holds it had had over them, their understanding of everything they could sense within their Awareness was finally unencumbered. They were free.

I was vaguely Aware that Mother Elder was lowering me back to the ground and covering me with a blanket, but she did not try to disturb me as I sifted through all that I now knew.

I knew that the Kindred lived in discreet communities, which travelled between homesteads in different seasons and different years, to allow plants and prey to recover and support their hunter-gatherer way of living. They moved up close to the mountains – just below which we were now – in the hotter months, since their tough skin prevented efficient heat loss. As the weather got colder, they moved to homesteads further south, nearer to human villages. They were always careful to avoid humans, both their villages and anywhere they were likely to travel. Every now and then, younglings on their Findself would encounter humans and usually, little came of the encounter. Occasionally though, as when Infinity and I had been hunted, the youngling made a decision that involved relinquishing the morals and integrity of the Kindred, to his or her eventual cost. I searched my Awareness for the youngling who had left an imprint on my mind as a result of hunting Infinity and me, and found that she was indeed now a discarnate soul. I sent her my love and hope that in her next incarnation, she would fare better.

I realised fully how desperate the Kindred who attacked The Gathering must have been to kill not only bonded horses but, inadvertently, humans. My heart went out to those who had been involved as I found them in my Awareness and let them know that the sorrow they yet carried was groundless. Without their desperate attempt to feed their families as they starved in that unforgiving, relentless winter, none of us would be where we were now. Everything had happened as it should. I felt their gratitude for my thoughts and also for what had been achieved over the last few weeks. A warm feeling stole over me and Infinity and I enjoyed the feeling of a circle closing.

Infinity and the other horses grazed from the surrounding branches as they made their way to a patch of grass that they could smell in a nearby clearing. I almost felt bad for them that we had kept them from their bodies for so long – it was only due to their intervention that we had all made it back to our bodies at all – but then I found that I just didn't seem to have it in me. Everything was as it should be. Infinity's approval was mine and mine was hers. We didn't think thoughts to one another much anymore, I realised. There would be as little point as if I talked to myself. We were one. We returned to what we knew.

The Kindred had long been adept at healing with herbs. Being Aware, they had known of the Skills since the time that humans first remembered them, but until recently, they hadn't been able to perform them due to their limited vocal range. Their frustration at their inability to sing had disappeared in an instant once I had shared with Mother Elder my newfound ability to heal from a distance. She had instantly made the knowledge available to all and the Kindred were all now practising multiskilling in silence and wondering at the uses to which they could put their new Skills.

I decided that farming was an option for them now that tree-singing and earth-singing could provide the means to grow and harvest. Like Lacejoy, the Kindred tended to frown upon weather-singing as an indulgence of the few at the potential cost of many and whilst I could see their point, I felt that if we could persuade them to use it in moderation, as we did, their future farming efforts would be greatly aided. As would they be if the Kindred could tolerate going back to the vicinities of the cities of The Old – they could harvest metal in the same way as did our Pedlars, and then use metal-singing to make their own tools. There was so much we could teach them, so much with which we could help them.

I felt Mother Elder's amusement as my thoughts tried to run away with me, and I refocused on my information sifting.

I knew that the Kindred were Aware to varying degrees from birth, as a result of their animal heritage. Many younglings had no concept of being anything other than Aware of the thoughts and feelings of others, and mindspeak was so easy for them that they had to be strongly encouraged to use their voices at all. Others were born with a lesser ability to mindspeak and able to sense only the most pressing thoughts of those in their immediate vicinity. Often their abilities grew as they matured, but these Kindred tended to prefer to talk out loud, even as they aged and their voices grew more strained. Some Kindred were born with very little Awareness at all – throwbacks to their human heritage, I realised. These never developed the ability to mindspeak or to know what their peers instinctively knew about one another, without help from an Elder. My interest peaked as I realised that the Kindred had a way to open them up to their Awareness and then a surge of excitement shot through me as I realised that I knew how they did it.

If a Kindred youngling hadn't shown any signs of being Aware by the time they were five years old, the parents would request help from their Elder, knowing that the help would need to come from someone familiar, but not close to the youngling – someone who could be dispassionate about the outcome of the proceedings and so not apply any kind of mental pressure, yet someone from whom the youngling would not shy away. The Elder would reveal her essence to the youngling, in the same way that our horses had done for us when we bonded. The Kindreds' animal ability to resonate and connect with others, particularly with those of the same human descent as themselves, made them a potent force when it came to transferring a sense of themselves, as my friends and I had all discovered when we knew things about the Kindred we had met even before we were Aware. Once the youngling's mind accepted the Elder's essence, the Elder would lead it to experience Awareness of other essences and then the youngling couldn't help but awaken to their connection to All That Is. As with the Kindred whose Awareness had awakened naturally, some of those awakened by Elders found that their abilities strengthened as they matured and some found that they would always be secondary to the five physical senses, but all of the Kindred were Aware to some extent.

This was how the Kindred could help my fellow humans. Where the horses had managed to alter their thought patterns enough to reach some of us with their minds, the Kindred's thought patterns resonated easily with ours and so they would be able to reach everyone. They did it instinctively, it was a part of who they were. They could awaken humans to their oneness with All That Is in the same way that they did with some of their younglings, and once humans were Aware, they could never return to the ways of The Old. They would know the Kindred for who they were and they would welcome them to be part of our way of life. They would help them to live an easier life, one where they would never face starvation again.

We can reach your minds easily enough, but it will depend on how open an individual is to receiving our help, as to how far they are able to progress, Mother Elder pointed out. *Our younglings, even those with a greater human heritage than the rest, still have enough animal heritage that they are instantly open to the possibility of their oneness with All That Is. Humans are the most closed of all the animals. Your horses have had enormous patience to persevere with teaching those of you that they managed to reach.*

I nodded. *I know. It will take time. But will you come back to our villages with us and help us? There is so much that we can help the Kindred with in return. You can be Aware of the methods of farming from any of us, any time you wish, but experiencing the process alongside our Farmers will help you so much more. We have houses of stone that stay cool in the summer, so you wouldn't need to migrate to the mountains any more. You could establish villages of your own or integrate into ours. So much could be learnt by both races if we cooperate.*

There will be much fear to be overcome by your people. We will help wherever we can, but I do not foresee it being easy, Mother Elder told me.

My sister will help.

I felt Mother Elder read from my mind the role that Katonia would play. *You and she made this agreement long ago and she does not remember it,* she observed.

Not yet, but she will. Katonia will not let us down.

We will not know until the time is upon us, but I hope that you are right, Mother Elder replied.

Katonia was my sister. I didn't hope, I knew.

TWENTY-THREE

Group

My friends and I remained in the clearing for some days, recovering our strength. Our horses grazed bare the nearby grassy clearing and then followed some Kindred younglings to more grazing just beyond the edge of the woodland. None of us held the remotest concern for our horses' safety as they disappeared through the trees; the Kindred were treating them with the utmost reverence.

We spent our time cooking the food that was brought to us by the Kindred, resting and enjoying being part of the group that we had become. We all had our individual identities, but we now resonated so closely with one another as a result of our shared experience and purpose, that together, we were something more, as if everyone was magnified by everyone else. We were a profound strength.

Fitt politely but firmly resisted requests from her family to return to them and she insisted that we continue to call her Fitt, and not her given name of Lacejoy. We could feel her sense of belonging with us, and the name we had given her seemed to be part of that identity for her, so we happily agreed. She didn't hide her eagerness for us all to catch up with her astonishingly fast recovery, so that she and Flame could continue their mission alongside us. They were both revelling in everything they had achieved and were as determined as ever to push onwards.

Aleks was a different person. He had put to good use the water that the Kindred had hauled to us in deer bladders, and was now clean, shaven and wearing freshly washed clothes. Despite being as thin as the rest of us, he no longer looked gaunt and his eyes sparkled. We felt his frustration that neither he nor his horse were strong enough for him to ride her yet, but we were also astonished by how quickly he found his centre. It seemed that as soon as he was Aware, he was easily able to keep his concentration on the physical whilst exploring all of the sensory input to which his mind was now subject, and he was not in the least overwhelmed by it all as the rest of us had been. It seemed that, ironically, the intense focus on his physicality that had previously hindered him so much was now the attribute that helped him to both find and maintain his centre. I saw yet again the perfection that existed as everything found a balance.

Vickery was different too. The toughness that she had always presented as her exterior had softened into a sense of capable confidence. Her face, previously quite square, was now dominated not by angles but by relaxed, blue eyes and a smiling mouth. She had always had a restless energy about her, but that had changed to a more purposeful, dynamic energy, despite the weakness of her recovering body. She Is Verve, I thought to myself as I watched her exchanging banter with Marvel. I couldn't wait to see her ride her beautiful white stallion once they were both strong enough.

Sonja was as jolly and encouraging as always. She had never hidden her fondness for Aleks and now that he was free of himself and returning her interest, her blushes at our silent teasing frequently matched the red of her hair, despite her efforts to remain unaffected.

Holly was as serene as ever and recovering almost as quickly as Fitt. Her long, blond hair framed a face that was warm in its expression as her long legs stretched out towards the fire in front of her.

Rowena and Marvel leant affectionately into one another, more comfortable showing their feelings for one another now that our group had been so intimately one. Marvel looked thinner than the rest of us, though it was merely the size of his frame that accentuated his weight loss, but he had lost none of his handsomeness. His hazel eyes twinkled in the firelight as he looked down at Rowena, easily supporting her weight with his own as she leant against him. Rowena's smile back up at him was easy and shone from her dark eyes as much as from the curve of her lips. The pair radiated strength.

Justin and I were the quietest of the group. We had missed each other keenly and were glad of the comfort our physical bodies afforded one another, but neither of us could shake off a feeling of listlessness. The first time I found myself alone with my thoughts after my return to my body, I felt a sense of loneliness and grief, despite the sense of my soul being entwined with Infinity's and despite my Awareness of everyone around me; it wasn't the same as the all-encompassing oneness that we had all recently experienced, but a muted connection by comparison. Infinity immediately made herself more of our mind by way of comfort and reassurance and Justin, whose feelings mirrored my own, appeared out of the darkness and sat down behind me, his legs either side of mine. He drew me to lean back against him, hugging me tight as he murmured in my ear, 'It's harder, returning this time, isn't it?'

I nodded as I sighed and nestled back against his warmth. 'Much. I suppose it will pass. I'm glad you're here.'

His chest rumbled against my back as he said, 'Gas and I were always going to make it, however much Marvel jokes about our timely arrival.'

I chuckled. 'I never doubted you both.'

'Timely arrival? Is that what it's called when you leave your friends dangling from a cliff edge and then make an entrance no less dramatic than what was already unfolding, in order to save the day?' Marvel said.

'Those ears of yours haven't got any smaller since you left The Gathering, I see, Marv,' Justin retorted.

But we all knew that Marvel hadn't been listening with his ears; our thoughts were less of our own than they had been since our shared experience in the oneness. A collective laugh reverberated between us all, an echo of the intensity of feeling we had shared, but a comfort to us all.

Justin and I found that we preferred to speak to each other in our thoughts rather than to talk and we ate with far less fervour than our peers. When we slept, Gas and Infinity joined us in our dreams and the four of us were one as we flew over the hills. That was all we needed. That was all we wanted, really. Gas had been as impassive as Infinity about whether or not he returned to his body, and we wondered if our horses' lack of concern over their future was influencing how we felt now. Or, possibly, it was Fitt's enthusiasm and the rest of our friends' excitement at what was to come that merely accentuated our lack of feeling about it either way.

Infinity chose to enlighten Justin and me one morning as we were waking. *You are merely more conscious than you were of your lack of need to be here. But you chose to return. Whilst you are here you will better serve your friends by embracing your choice.*

'That's us told,' Justin whispered as he gently extricated his arm from underneath me, stretched and sat up.

'She's right as always,' I whispered back, sitting up beside him to see that our friends all slept still. 'We've been feeling sorry for ourselves.'

Justin nodded and I felt him make the same necessary changes to his mind that I did. He poked the banked fire with a stick and blew the sparks into flames. Adding more wood, he said, 'It's time to get this party started.' He stood up, threw his arms wide and hollered, 'LET THE DAY BEGIN!'

I laughed as Fitt and Marvel both sat bolt upright with a wild look in their eyes. Rowena groaned and pulled her blanket over her head, as did Holly.

Sonja giggled and leapt to her feet. 'Today's the day,' she said and nudged Aleks with her foot. 'Wake up, it's time to see you in action. And you, Vic, I know you're awake because I heard you yawn, come on, the mood has lifted and it's time to push on.'

'And it was us holding the mood down, sorry guys, we've been feeling a bit sorry for ourselves,' I said.

'We didn't really like to say,' Marvel said, chuckling.

'More likely Rowena told you not to,' said Justin with a grin.

'What if I did?' Rowena appeared suddenly from under her blanket. 'It's not like we can all keep anything from one another anymore and we knew you two were struggling a bit, understandably so. It was hard enough for us to return here, in fact without the horses, we never would have, and this is the second time that you and Amarilla have done it, Jus. We felt your weariness and if you needed a bit longer than the rest of us to readjust to being here, then it wasn't anyone's place to mention it.'

'Unless you had decided it was yours, and then it would have been fine,' Marvel said and then defended himself from her fingers as she tried to flick his ears. We all laughed.

Once we had quietened down, Justin said, 'Thank you.' He put his gratitude for our friends' understanding and support into his words with such intent that everyone immediately became serious.

'And thanks from me, too,' I said. 'Ever since Infinity and I bonded, I've blundered from one situation to the next and somehow along the way, I've managed to make some amazing friends. You've helped me, protected me and trusted me and now look where we all are – lying in the dirt, the light only knows where, no horses in sight and with no immediate plans to rectify the situation. I think we should all drink a toast to the futility of life.' I giggled and then couldn't stop. The toast was forgotten as my friends all joined in with me.

'Am, I'm going to repeat what I've said before... motivational speeches are Ro's domain. You just stick to leading us into one mess after another, that's yours,' said Marvel, still laughing.

'Okay then, I suggest that rather than waiting for the Kindred to bring our food for today, we go to ride our beautiful Bond-Partners and then make our way up to meet the Kindred,' I said.

'I second that,' said Sonja. 'Bright's up for it, and... I think that's a good example of no sooner said than done,' she added at Aleks's rapidly retreating back as he jogged towards where his horse waited for him.

If we had been Aware of our strength as a group whilst we lazed around the campfire, it became something that was impossible to miss once we were all astride our horses. As we rode bareback and bridleless and wherever our horses wanted to take us as they used the ground merely as a reference point rather than a medium to take their weight, it was impossible not to feel the magnitude of the positive force that we had all become – the air almost seemed to ripple with it.

Gas fell in beside Infinity and as they cantered a large circle, they, Justin and I became one powerful being as easily as breathing. When

Infinity and I peeled away from the other two, however, we weren't diminished. Infinity caught up with Flame and then slowed to match her collected trot. Fitt grinned down at me as the four of us shared pure delight at how easily we knew ourselves as parts of the same whole.

We passed Rowena and Oak, and Rowena and I revelled in our friendship as Oak and Infinity pirouetted in unison and then took off side by side at a gallop. As we circled and slowed, my breath caught in my throat at the sight of Justin riding Gas alongside Fitt and Flame. The two leggy chestnuts matched each other stride for stride as they extended in trot as one. The sun almost seemed to pick them out as it cancelled the dawn, intensifying the orange of their coats to the extent that they appeared on the verge of exploding into fire.

Vickery crossed in front of me, upon Verve. The stocky white stallion had always been a strong horse, but now he was powerful. He collected Serene and Holly as he passed them and the tall, delicately graceful, grey mare only accentuated his power as she glided effortlessly at his side.

An ecstatic shout from Aleks drew my gaze to where he and Sonja galloped Nexus and Bright. The grey and bay slowed to a canter in unison and then to a trot, as if they were joined by strings and operated by the same puppeteer. They barely appeared to touch the ground at all as they eased back up to a gallop, enjoying the delight of their riders as much as the proof of their balance and return to strength.

Oak slowed his pace to fall behind Infinity and join Marvel and Broad. As Infinity and I circled to watch them, I was struck for what must have been the hundredth time, by how two such large, heavy horses could defy their build to move with such poise and elegance.

Balance, Infinity and I thought together. *Everything searches for balance and everything finds it, eventually.*

I glanced down at the arched, silvery-white neck in front of me and love for my beautiful mare flooded through me. Her wavy mane rose and fell as she carried me at a slow, collected canter. Her ears were pricked forward, ever confident, and she was as strong and sure beneath me as I was on her back. I wondered how I could ever have felt down-hearted about returning to my body when it meant that I could share this very physical experience with my soul mate. I smiled. Infinity always rescued me from the pitfalls of my humanity in one way or another.

Justin's mind nudged mine, showing me a slim young woman astride a slender yet muscled piebald mare with blue eyes. They almost appeared not to be real as they moved as one in the early morning sunshine. They touched the ground briefly in between strides that were longer than should have been possible, light as the air that was barely required to part before them. They were surrounded by a white haze, barely discernible yet there for those capable of seeing it, a link to the ethereal with which they identified and had been unable to leave behind when returning to the physical.

I looked over at Justin and saw that he and Gas, too, were surrounded by the haze. I had to almost unfocus my eyes to see it, but it was there. I smiled gratefully at Justin.

Caught up in the elation of nine horses and riders in perfect balance weaving between one another in complete harmony, we all lost track of time. It wasn't until, as one, we all became Aware of the wonder of the Kindred, that we noticed them lining the trees alongside the pasture in which we rode. As one, we drew to a graceful halt, facing them.

We were Aware that the Kindred had been concerned for us when they took food and water to the clearing for us and found us gone. They had followed their sense of us and found us with our horses. They were unprepared for what they had then witnessed. They had broadcast it to their peers, more of whom had arrived to watch.

'You were like the starlings when they fly in waves, as if they are small parts of the same being,' rasped a black-pelted youngling.

'I could see all of you individually if I really concentrated, but otherwise you all melded into one another, sometimes just horse with rider, sometimes groups of you together. There were times when all of you were just one being and I couldn't pick out any of you, not even my own Lacejoy,' rasped an adult female with light brown fur and vivid green eyes that glistened with emotion. 'I'm sorry if we have intruded, but we are all honoured to have seen you and your horses demonstrating physically the beauty of which we are all Aware. I've never witnessed anything so moving. Lacejoy, there was a time when I was horrified by the decisions you were making but I couldn't be prouder to have been wrong.'

The Kindred all began to cheer their agreement. It was an odd noise, like a crowd of people who had almost lost their voices all trying to shout, but we felt their emotion and appreciation. We grinned and nodded our thanks. Fitt slid from Flame's back and embraced her mother, before returning to vault back onto her horse. We all followed the Kindred back through the trees, glad of the opportunity to walk the horses as they cooled down.

The Kindred led us past and then away from the clearing where we had camped, some of them walking tall and others choosing to leap spectacularly between the trees. I was awed by their power and speed. I was chuckling and waving at a cheeky youngling who was wiggling his tongue at me from the tree in which he had just landed, when Rowena gasped beside me. I followed her gaze to what appeared to be enormous wasp nests up in the trees. They were made from vines, I realised. Vines woven tightly and anchored in various spots along the branches to provide both shelter and flooring. Outside the vine shelters hung bladders of water and clumps of various fruits and vegetables.

Trees that were too far apart to be leapt between were linked by ropes made of twisted and plaited vines, one horizontally above the other, and there were Kindred almost running along the lower ropes, barely touching the upper ones that would aid their balance.

At the bases of trees that housed vine shelters there were fires, surrounded by large, flat stones. Meat and fish were hung to smoke above some of the fires and cooked meat and vegetables rested on the stones around others, keeping warm. Kindred moved around within the trees and on the ground, and some were beginning to peer out of their tree homes. There was a sense of lives being lived in harmony with nature that appealed to me greatly.

But nature can be cruel, Mother Elder observed as she appeared at my side, almost as tall on her feet as I was whilst mounted on Infinity.

I nodded, remembering only too well the harsh winter before last, when Kindred had been driven by hunger to attack bonded horses at The Gathering.

It is not just the winters, Mother Elder told me. *We dwell here every third summer, to allow plants and prey to recover their numbers in our absence. Whilst we are away, our homes rot and on our return, we must weave them anew. Some years, if the seasons have been harsh, food is scarce and no sooner than we have rebuilt our homes, we must move on in search of somewhere that will sustain us until it is cool enough for us to move back south, where the climate allows for an easier existence. Except for when it doesn't, as happened the winter before last, and then we must either watch while the weakest of us perish, or take desperate measures.*

I'm sorry you've been neglected for so long, I replied. *We need to have you all living with us as soon as possible.*

The idea is very tempting, but how will we live? Your houses of stone sound wonderful and they may well keep us cool in the heat of summer, but will we never venture outside between spring's end and autumn's beginning? And though our communities are small, in total we are too many for your people to accommodate in their homes, let alone in their minds, which I foresee being the biggest obstacle, as I know you do.

We'll work it out, I assured her. *Maybe we could tailor clothes that would keep you cool. Rowena's a Tailor and one of the best – she often comes up with solutions to problems that haven't even been thought of, so I'm sure she'll think of something. And we'll help you to build your own buildings from stone with smaller windows and thicker walls than ours, so that they stay even cooler. Maybe we could link them with stone corridors or underground tunnels so that you can move around when it's hot outside. As for your numbers, we'll take a small number of you back with us to begin with, until our people are used to the idea. Then, as the Kindred begin to help them, they will help in return and build homes for more of you. It's perfect. Our two races will help one another, and in the process, they'll integrate. Before we know it, the Kindred will be back where you all belong, with the rest of us.*

A warm weight rested on my leg and I looked down to see that Mother Elder had placed her hand there, her fingers outstretched so as not to score my leggings with her talons. Her gratitude and relief spilled into me. *Daughter of my heart, I'm sorry I didn't trust you from the beginning. I should have, and not just because of all we are to one another. When you think of what will be, it's as if everything swirls around you – as if just by thinking of something, you can make it so.*

I chuckled. *My friends call it my vortex and I'm afraid it looks as though I've managed to pull you into it.*

She laughed a hoarse laugh. *There is nowhere I'd rather be.*

When will the first of you be able to leave with us? I asked.

If you take only younglings, then as soon as you are ready. Their skin is not yet so thickened that the heat is a problem for them, as Lacejoy has demonstrated with her escapades. If you require adults to accompany you, then they cannot leave for at least a month, after the heat of summer has passed. Even then, they will have to take a longer route than that which you took in finding me, since they will have to restrict themselves to the cool of the forests. I know you intend to go to your own village first. They will not make it there until late autumn.

Late autumn it is, then, because I'm not leaving without you, I told her.

Whilst I am happy to make the journey to your village to try to help your people, I am not among the adults who would be suitable choices to go with you on your return. The skin of my throat is so thickened now that I rarely use my voice, so I would be of little help in the early stages of befriending your people, and I am old and slow. I would be of much hindrance to you all on the journey. It would be well into winter before we arrived at your village, were I to accompany you.

'I'm not leaving without you,' I said out loud and Mother Elder looked at me in surprise at the conviction of my words as much as at the sound of my voice. *We'll rest here another month,* I continued, *and while we're here, we'll teach your community all the uses for their newfound Skills, including how to build dwellings with rock-singing. That way, they'll be able to start building as soon as they decide where they would like to live, down south. We'll make sure that everyone who will be travelling with us, including you, is as healthy as they can possibly be and while we're about it, if you're willing, we'll see how we can use tissue-singing to ease your throats.*

'And they tell me I'm bossy,' Rowena said.

'You are, Ro,' said Aleks from behind us. 'Interminably. You are also, however, as Am pointed out, a very good Tailor. Any ideas on the cool clothes front?'

'As it happens, yes. There's a moss that's particularly good at holding water and I was thinking of drying it and weaving it into a fabric to make bottle sleeves, you know that you'd soak and then put around bottles to keep drinks cool. There may be something I could do with that, or I was also thinking of trying to produce a fabric with reflective qualities to make covers for babies' prams, you know to keep the sun off them, maybe I should make that a priority now...'

You see? My thoughts were aimed towards Mother Elder, although I realised now that I may just as well have been speaking out loud. *Whatever problems come up, we'll find a way around them.*

I will accept your help and I will travel with you to help your people in whichever way I can, Mother Elder thought to our group. *I am proud of you, daughter of my heart. Now, let me show you my home.*

We spent the day in Shady Mountain, as the Kindred referred to their settlement, whilst our horses grazed the trees around the perimeter. Between us, we visited all of the vine shelters. Some, like Mother Elder's, housed a single occupant. They were just large enough for a sleeping mattress made of the finer vines woven together to produce large sheets, which were then bound together around the edges and stuffed with moss. The shelters were usually anchored between the branches of a single large tree, but some of them reached across to a second tree for extra space and security.

Other shelters housed families, usually of two parents and a youngling but occasionally with the addition of an elderly relative. These were stretched between three or four trees and consisted of sleeping mattresses around the edge and a communal area in the middle. There were few possessions in evidence anywhere. When I voiced my observation to Mother Elder, she replied that the younglings were off playing in the trees as soon as they were old enough and the adults were always busy hunting, gathering, cooking or making the constant repairs needed to their vine shelters. They had no need for possessions that would only weigh them down as they travelled between settlements with the change of the seasons.

We received a warm welcome from the occupants of each and every shelter but we found them much quieter than humans. Their babies rarely cried for long, if at all, since their mothers were Aware of and addressed their needs immediately, and provided comfort and reassurance by weaving nurturing energy around them in the same way that Infinity had always done for me. Mindspeak and Awareness of the immediate thoughts of those around them negated the need for much talking out loud, and once of a certain age, adults found it too uncomfortable and too much of a strain anyway. Younglings came and went with ease and lack of instruction, since their parents could be Aware of their whereabouts at will and they could easily be recalled or instructed by mindspeak.

There was a calm, measured sense of purpose about the Kindred and a love and loyalty that extended far beyond immediate families. But there was also something missing. Humour, I realised. The Kindred had the ability to recognise humour and to laugh, I had seen that in both Fitt and Mother Elder, but they didn't seem to incorporate either as part of their daily life. I grinned as I realised that with us around, that was about to change.

'Horse dung in my bed, I'm sore,' Vickery said as she dropped to the ground beside me from the tree down which we had both just scrambled. 'I was born to ride horses, not shin up and down trees like a squirrel hiding acorns. What?' she added as I began to laugh.

Her laughter joined mine as she read my thoughts about her comment being so much at odds with the polite introversion we had witnessed all day. Then she came to the same realisation that I had; we were inflicting Marvel, Justin, Rowena and Aleks on a community that wasn't used to humour.

'Maybe we should keep them away while the Kindred get used to the rest of us, you know, break them in gently?' Vickery suggested.

'Now where would be the fun in that?' I said with a wink.

TWENTY-FOUR

Humour

*A*fter an evening meal around Mother Elder's fire, we returned to sleep for the night in the clearing in which we had spent our recovery. We had been invited by some of the Kindred to sleep in singles and pairs in their vine shelters, but we knew that our horses would want to return to the grassland that they had been grazing, for the night, and we wanted to be near them. As we shook out and reorganised bedding, we discussed our findings of the day.

Justin and Aleks had spent some time with a couple whose youngling hadn't returned from his Findself, and whom they knew to be dead. Mother Elder had observed him during his trial, as she did all of the younglings of her community – her attention tended to be less of a disturbance and less likely to incite homesickness than that of their parents – and after only a few months had passed back the sad news to his parents that he had perished due to his inability to be decisive.

He had already been underweight due to a failure to prioritise his needs, when he found himself too far north and without shelter as winter arrived. He then hadn't been able to decide whether to attempt the journey south, or start work on a shelter and hope that he could hunt enough in the harshness of a northern winter to keep himself alive. He had done neither and within days, the winter snows had seen him dead.

His parents had been near paralysed with grief and had blamed the human race for his death on top of everything else that had befallen the Kindred as a result of their creation and abandonment. In forgiving their past in recent weeks, however, in clearing all of the holds it had had over them, they were free to explore the full extent of their Awareness and had been able to find their son within it. He was so proud of them. His death had given them every reason to resist forgiving what humans had done to their race, yet they had chosen bravely and well. His parents would always miss his physical presence, but they were thrilled that the choice they had made meant that he was once more a part of their lives.

All of us, except Fitt, had been disturbed by the changes that occurred within the Kindred as they aged, due to their skin. We knew that the creators of the Enforcers had introduced genes from something with an exoskeleton to give them extremely tough skin, capable of repelling any weaponry that might be used against them. It had proven to be extremely effective, but had the unfortunate side effect of continuing to thicken both to the outside and inside as the individual aged, with the result that body heat regulation became more difficult, limb movement became more restricted, their voices failed and eventually, their internal organs were crushed. Older Enforcers had been given duties inside the carefully air-conditioned buildings of The Old during summer so that they didn't overheat, and had used the voices of the younglings they were training to give orders to the public when their own voices failed. Once they were in the throes of being killed by their own skin, they had been put down by lethal injection.

'The oldest of my community here in Shady Mountain is only a few years older than Elder Hobday, and she's around fifty,' Fitt told us. 'Natural death is a lengthy and painful process for us, so once our elderly reach the beginning of the end, they choose to stay north as winter approaches. That way they aren't a burden to their families and they find a quicker and less painful conclusion.'

'Unless we can use tissue-singing to help,' Holly said. 'All of us can multiskill now that Aleks has finally caught up. Sorry, Aleks, no offence...'

'None taken, I think,' said Aleks.

'...and the Kindred are discovering how they can use their Skills now that they know how to perform them silently, so between us, we'll find a way to stop the process, or at least heal it as it happens so it doesn't limit you all the way it does, Fitt.'

'If we can use bone-singing to break healed bones in order to re-heal them correctly, as we did for Flame, then I wonder if we can use tissue-singing to do something similar,' said Marvel thoughtfully.

'That's it!' Vickery said. 'We'll just break the skin down. It'll have to be done slowly, so that the body can eliminate the waste products easily, but as long as the Healer is pinpoint accurate and only affects the tissue she means to, it will work. The Kindred can heal themselves and their families, every day, every week, or whenever they want, to keep the newly forming skin from building up, and then who knows how long they'll be able to live.'

Fitt looked around at us all in the fading light. 'I think it will be too late for those who are already elderly and have much thickening,' she rasped sadly, 'but for the rest of us, it would be marvellous indeed.'

'We'll do what we can for those who are older,' I said. 'We can at least halt the process so that their skin doesn't kill them, and we can try to ease their throats. With cool housing and Rowena's tailoring, there will be no need for them to come north to die in the snow.'

'That would be a huge relief for us all,' said Fitt. 'I keep finding myself amazed by how much change can come about in such a short space of time.'

'Talking of which, Fitt, do you think your community will cope with what passes for humour in this little group of ours?' Vickery asked. 'You seem to go along with it okay, but do you think Shady Mountain is ready for our teasing, Marvel and Rowena's pretend arguments, and Aleks and Marvel chasing one another around the campfire with water or socks as weapons, while the rest of us make out that we think they're funny?'

She spluttered suddenly as a damp and particularly smelly sock slapped against her cheek and its toe flicked into her mouth. Then she screamed as a beaker of water was upturned over her head.

'Your mistake there, Vic, was to think that chasing around the campfire is a necessary element to the use of socks and water as weapons,' advised Aleks, still leaning towards her with his empty beaker in his hand. It was his turn to cough and splutter when the contents of Vickery's beaker were hurled into his face.

'And yours, Aleks, was to be sitting beside your victim,' said Marvel, waving the partner to the sock that he had hurled at Vickery.

'Teasing,' said Justin, 'is an affectionate kind of humour and I think the Kindred will be more than ready for it.' He removed Marvel's other sock from where it had just landed in his lap, and said, 'This, though? I'm not so sure. Fitt?'

Fitt was grinning as much as her fangs allowed whilst her shoulders shook with mirth. 'When we are younglings, we know of humour but we put it to one side during our Findself and never seem to take it back up again. It will be good for you to remind us all of what we have been in the habit of forgetting.'

'No soooooooner said than done.' Aleks picked Marvel's sock up from where Vickery had thrown it, and launched it at Fitt.

'I should warn you that a game we play when we are small is to take a friend on our backs and see who can climb the highest tree carrying double our weight,' rasped Fitt. 'You weigh less than I do, Aleks, and I'm three times as strong as I was then. Climbing to the top of those trees carrying you will not be a problem and neither will be coming back down on my own.'

We all looked up to where we could just see the dark leaves of the highest branches waving around in the moonlight and then we looked back at Fitt in wonder. She slapped her leg and emitted a sound like a cough that we realised was her laughing.

'I think they'll cope with us just fine, Vic,' Sonja said.

And so they did. We were careful to use our humour only on one another and not to direct it towards the Kindred during the first few weeks that we spent with them. After initial bemusement at our teasing of one another and the pranks that Marvel, Aleks and Justin insisted on playing on one another and the rest of us, the Kindred began to smile and laugh with us.

As we coached them in groups on the various uses to which their newfound Skills could be put, we increasingly found that younglings who weren't part of the groups that we were teaching began to gather to watch, eager to join in with us when we laughed and hopeful of witnessing behaviour that they could emulate.

After watching Justin demonstrate the harvesting of root vegetables using earth-singing by lifting a not inconsiderable amount of earth and depositing it on Marvel's foot, the younglings' response was to lift an even larger amount of earth, hold it hovering above the entrance to the settlement until Justin walked underneath it, and then let it drop on his head.

When Marvel demonstrated the use of tree-singing for the rapid growth of crops by singing a tree sapling to where Rowena sat in discussion with some older Kindred so that it tickled the back of her neck, he woke the following morning to find that the younglings had silently sung the branches from the trees above us down to form an almost impenetrable barrier around him as he slept.

And following Aleks's demonstrations of using fire-singing safely so that it wasn't used to create bigger fires than intended – which he demonstrated by bringing the banked fire near which Holly sat to full flame with a roar, making her jump and spill her drink down her front – he found that he was constantly jumping out of his skin as fires that were either banked or dying down exploded into flames when he walked near them.

'It's just so satisfying seeing you all on the receiving end of your own jokes,' Rowena said one evening as we relaxed around our own campfire in the clearing while our horses rested nearby.

'We should show the younglings how to be bossy next, and see how funny you think that is,' said Marvel.

'I'm looking forward to letting them loose on my brothers,' I said.

'It's just good to see them all laughing,' said Fitt. 'And it's not just the younglings now, my mother saw Harrisbud ignite a fire just as Aleks was about to step over it, and she laughed so much that she actually cried.'

'We just need to hear them all laughing now,' said Holly. 'It's time to use tissue-singing as it's never been used before, and get their voices back.'

We'd been mulling over how best to go about using tissue-singing to remove the thickened skin of the Kindred, and had decided that to begin with, we'd work together, as we'd done when we healed Flame. Holly would be the lead Healer and the rest of us would lend our strength whilst observing and making any suggestions should they occur to us. It would be a dangerous procedure the first few times, whilst we judged how much skin we could safely cause to break up and disperse without causing the body problems.

'We haven't decided how to go about asking for our first volunteer,' said Marvel.

'No need, it'll be me,' said Fitt. 'I'm the perfect choice. We're all closer than it's possible for anyone else to be and since I trust you all implicitly, I have absolutely no reservations. My body will follow your suggestions instantly, just as if you were healing yourselves. And while the horses will support you all and your volunteer while you attempt this anyway, one of those horses is mine. I will be able to make more use of her support than any other volunteer could.'

'Your skin thickening isn't enough to inhibit you much, but it is there,' said Holly thoughtfully. 'And if we worked on your throat, maybe we could help your voice to be a bit stronger.'

We all nodded. Fitt was right, she was the obvious choice. Flame appeared just behind where Fitt sat and nuzzled her shoulder. We felt her energy weave its way into Fitt's body, bolstering their sense of themselves as one immensely strong, determined being.

'Right now?' Rowena said.

Sonja chuckled. 'This is Fitt and Flame we're talking about. How could it be at any other time?'

As we felt our horses steady us all, Holly tuned into the tissues in Fitt's throat, taking us with her. We felt our way around and found that, due to the animal genes she carried, Fitt's throat structure differed markedly from our human throats. And that was okay. Her body had followed its genetic blueprint and it was content to be that way. Her voice would always be limited in its range, but she would always have a voice if we could take away the layers of skin that were already beginning to accumulate where there was no need for them to be.

Fitt's fascination almost distracted us, but Flame pulled her attention away slightly. The rest of the horses steadied us while we refocused. Holly took us to the uppermost layer of new internal skin. Being the newest layer, it had a different vibration from those underneath it and Holly immediately resonated with it with all of herself and with all of us. There was no need for singing out loud. We strengthened her intention for it to separate from the layers beneath and break apart, and we observed as the layer of skin, one cell thick, duly dispersed.

Holly pulled us back and we waited while the waste products of our healing dispersed. It worked! We were jubilant – as long as we didn't take off too much skin in one go and cause a build-up of waste, clearing the Kindred's throats would be easy. As would clearing the skin that was building up internally elsewhere in their bodies, we realised. The fact that the different layers of skin vibrated differently according to their age, meant that we could easily isolate them and disperse them as they formed, and the waste would be taken away with the fluid that bathed all cells, just like any other waste. And the Kindred would learn to perform the healing on themselves. Fitt had been correct that it would be too late to reverse all of the thickening that the older Kindred had undergone – once the skin layers were old and compacted, separating them would be impossible and they would end up being broken up in chunks too large for the body to deal with – but this healing would at least halt the process so that any Kindred alive now needn't die as a result of accumulating more skin.

We were Aware of Fitt's desire for more skin to be cleared from her throat and now she wanted to do it herself. Holly took her with us as we tuned into the next layer of skin to be removed. We resonated with it with all of ourselves and then all of us except Fitt and Holly withdrew. Fitt matched Holly's intention for the skin layer to disperse and then when it did, Holly withdrew, leaving Fitt to judge when to disperse the next layer. Flame was there with Fitt at every stage and we were intimately Aware of her pride in her Bond-Partner as Fitt systematically healed her own throat.

When she had taken her throat back to its blueprint for health, we all withdrew. Fitt, however, wasn't finished. She moved on to other areas of her body where she could feel that thickening had begun. Flame continued to stand over her, supporting her in her quest to be rid of that which, if left, would shorten her life.

'Should we help?' Aleks whispered.

'I don't think so,' said Holly. 'We might hold her back. None of us can match the determination that defines Fitt and Flame once they're on one of their missions, so they're probably best left to it.'

We all knew that she was right. My heart felt like it would burst with affection for the tall, chestnut mare who was so dear to me, and her Bond-Partner. Flame would support Fitt while she healed her body and then Fitt would transfer the knowledge of how to do it to the rest of the Kindred. She would show them what she had done to her own body and then they would use her knowledge and confidence to know what to do with their own.

Perfect, I thought.

I realised, vaguely, that there had been a time when I hadn't been able to see the perfection in everything. I couldn't seem to remember when that was. I frowned.

You are too far removed from the person you were to be able to identify with her memories. Many will be lost to you now that they are not needed, observed Infinity.

As we no longer need any of this, I mused.

No longer need. Chose, Infinity reminded me.

I snapped back to myself and saw that Justin was looking at me knowingly. He winked and grinned and I remembered that being in the physical world was okay.

'It's more than okay, it's wonderful,' said a voice that I didn't recognise. Fitt was grinning from ear to ear as she looked between us in the firelight, her fangs looking almost out of place as they never had before. Flame breathed in and out deeply and with a sense of satisfaction, then wandered off.

'Fitt, your voice is so much stronger,' Holly said. 'And a bit smoother, how does your throat feel?'

'A bit tender, but now I remember that it feels just like it used to when I was little,' said Fitt. 'I hadn't realised how much it had changed, it happened so gradually, but I can talk without straining and look how much more I can move my head. And I've removed the thickening from around my hips and knees, look how much longer I can stretch my legs.'

We all took it in turns to hug Fitt and congratulate her on her achievement.

'We'll be able to make a start first thing on the next volunteers,' said Aleks.

'They've already started on themselves, witness for yourselves,' Fitt said proudly. She showed us how she had brought Mother Elder in to witness what she was doing after we left her to it, and how Mother Elder was now excitedly broadcasting the intricacies of her achievements to the rest of the community at Shady Mountain, as well as to the Elders from all of the other Kindred communities. 'Nobody's going to be getting much sleep tonight.'

While I could sense the truth of her words from the Kindred communities, I could also sense that there were those who were more confident to press on with the healing than others.

'We'll help any who need it tomorrow,' Justin said, yawning as he lay down in his bedding, holding his arm out to one side for me to snuggle up next to him.

'We should offer it now,' said Fitt.

'We should sleep. You too, Fitt,' said Rowena. 'Even Flame knows it's time to stop and rest for a while, see, she's lain herself down over there with Infinity and Oak. Tomorrow will come soon enough.'

'The oracle has spoken,' came Marvel's muffled voice from under his blanket. 'Oooof!'

Sonja giggled and said to the mound that was Marvel, 'You can't have thought that your blanket was any kind of hiding place to tease Rowena from?'

'He barely thinks at all, Sonn,' said Rowena, 'that's why...'

I fell asleep to the sound of my friends' teasing. Justin and Gas were with Infinity and me as we wove our way up through the trees and then carried on up towards the mountains. We wove our way in between the peaks and then aimed ever upwards, towards the stars. We lost sight of them long before we reached them, finding ourselves instead floating in greyness.

We were thought without limit. We created ourselves anew in a thousand different ways, each version of ourselves merging flawlessly into the next the instant it occurred to us. We were colour, then we were grey. We were mist that hung motionless and then we were waves of energy, undulating through the infinite and then smoothing out to stream ever onwards. We curved around to one side and dispersed into a million droplets. Each one was us and we revelled in them colliding back together and merging to form an arrow that aimed itself at impossible speed at a massive circular target, becoming one with the target once it hit. We spread out as thinly as we could, forming a sheet, the corners of which gathered, enveloping the greyness within. We rejoiced as we furled ourselves into a ball, trapping the oneness within but knowing that it wasn't trapped for it was us. We hurled ourselves through the limitless. We were Infinity.

All the time that we gloried in our pure, unadulterated oneness, Infinity and Gas never let me or Justin forget ourselves. Our draw to visit home had taken us there, but we were merely visiting and we would be returning to the dream. Eventually, Adam and Peace joined us, understanding our presence there but pushing us gently as Infinity and Gas drew us away.

'They're so sweet,' whispered Sonja. 'Just look at them, we can't possibly wake them.'

'Trust me when I tell you that Justin will not appreciate you referring to him as sweet,' said Aleks.

'One of these days, you'll learn to whisper, Aleks, and the rest of us will think we've gone deaf,' whispered Rowena.

I felt Justin shaking with laughter as I lay sprawled across his chest. *Do we admit we're awake?* I tried to make my thoughts small enough that only Justin would notice them.

'Do you honestly think you can hide it from us, Am?' Rowena said.

Justin sighed and then his voice rumbled from beneath me. 'There are advantages to having friends who know your thoughts, and there are drawbacks. Right now, Rowena, you count as a drawback. Yes, Am, I think we admit that we're awake.'

'I call her the oracle and I get booted in the shins. Justin sleeps in, misses all his chores and then calls her a drawback and... nothing,' said Marvel.

'It's like we never fell asleep isn't it?' Justin grinned up at me as I sat up and smoothed my hair away from my face.

We both remembered where we'd been and I saw that the look in Justin's eyes mirrored my own homesickness. Infinity and Gas made their presence known in our minds, reminding us of who we were and why we were there, and then they backed it up with their physical presence. Gas leant down over Justin and nuzzled his forehead as Infinity's face appeared in front of me, her blue eyes holding mine. We knew where home was. It had always been there and would always be there. For now, we were where we were, and we had work to do.

'Thanks, Fin, I know,' I said, smiling gratefully to Holly as I accepted the bowl of stew she was holding in front of me.

Justin sat up and thanked Holly as he accepted his own bowl. 'Maybe we shouldn't do that again, not while we still have things to do here,' he said quietly. 'The horses can be there or here or both whenever they want and with no ill effect, but it's harder for us.'

'Maybe that's just because we have less practice? The horses are born that way but we aren't – maybe we just need to go back and forth more and then it will be easier for us to tear ourselves away?' I said.

Justin was thoughtful and for once, Infinity was quiet. She didn't know either. We were pushing what it was to be human beyond the boundaries that had previously existed. Who knew where we would end up?

'Still finding it hard being back here, huh?' Aleks said, crouching down with Justin and me as we ate. 'I wouldn't worry about it too much. Things happen the way they should and they always will, so I think you just have to trust the process.'

Justin and I looked at one another and then nodded in unison.

'Thanks, Aleks,' I said.

'Spot on. Thanks, mate,' Justin said.

'Any time,' Aleks replied. He fetched his brushes and went to groom Nexus.

'The counselled becomes the counsellor,' Justin murmured.

'Everything comes into balance,' I murmured in reply.

'And it's good that it has. You've achieved most of what you wanted to on this mission, you can relax a bit now,' Justin said.

'I still think you're the best at leading us into messes though, Am,' Marvel said.

'That's just because we haven't yet seen what you can do in that department, Marv,' said Justin. 'I'm willing to bet that, given the chance, you could be the destruction of us all that Am has so far avoided being.'

'Agreed,' said Vickery.

'Agreed,' said Rowena.

'Heartily agreed,' Aleks called over.

'Sorry, Marvel, I do have to agree to that,' said Holly.

Fitt laughed a hearty laugh. 'I agree,' she said.

'Then we're agreed that Am is still in charge of driving this little adventure of ours to its conclusion?' Sonja said.

At the smiling nods, including Marvel's, I said, 'Okay, well we have another couple of weeks here to allow everyone to heal their bodies as much as they can and so that the Kindred can decide who will be travelling with us in their advance party, and then I think we should leave for Rockwood. We'll arrive there in mid-winter, which will be perfect timing.'

'For what?' Rowena said.

'Why Rockwood?' Aleks asked.

I shared my thoughts with them all and saw understanding dawn.

'Katonia,' breathed Holly.

I nodded. 'We need to go to Rockwood, because that's where my sister is.'

TWENTY-FIVE

Rejoice

*W*e left Shady Mountain nearly three weeks later, joined by seven Kindred – eight if Fitt were included in the count, although none of us ever did; since she was Horse-Bonded, to us she was no more Kindred than the rest of us were human. We just were.

Mother Elder was, of course, with us, and so was Fitt's mother, Lacemore, who had been overjoyed to have been able to argue vociferously – as a result of her newly healed throat – for her inclusion in the group. She had successfully pointed out that as the mother of one of the Horse-Bonded, her acceptance by humans should be easier. She had also admitted to feeling pride in her daughter's achievements and to her wish to be able to observe first-hand this next instalment of Fitt's journey. Her arguments had succeeded in winning her mate's place on the journey alongside her and Fitt's father, the physically imposing, black-pelted Ashwell, was equally delighted to be accompanying us.

The first two younglings who had stood tall in the clearing – a rare brother and sister – had also requested to come with us and Mother Elder had instantly included them in our group. Harperlake and Harperleaf were very alike and only easily discernible from one another by Harperlake's greater height – as with all Kindred, their genders weren't physically obvious despite their lack of clothing, since their Enforcer ancestors had been bred with their genitalia hidden behind folds of toughened skin so as not to present a point of weakness – both having pelts of such a light brown as to almost be blond, and eyes of the darkest blue. Both were quiet, thoughtful characters to whom decision making had always been less troublesome than most Kindred found it to be; both would have thrived during their Findself experiences had they had a chance to undertake them.

The sixth addition to our group was Levitsson, a tawny-pelted Kindred who had been elevated to adult status on his return from his Findself, shortly before our arrival at Shady Mountain. He was young enough not to have chosen a mate but old enough to be leaving his parents' shelter. He had no responsibilities and was eager for the challenge of attempting to integrate into human society so that the rest of his community could follow. He had been one of the first to both understand and join in with the humour of our group and had an easy-going nature, so we were all very happy when Mother Elder chose him to accompany us.

The last of the seven was Foxstep, the oldest member of the Shady Mountain community. A few years older than Mother Elder, his skin thickening had been causing him considerable pain and discomfort in recent months and if it weren't for the healing with which Fitt had helped him over the past week, he would have chosen to remain in the north this winter. Whilst Fitt had reduced his skin thickening as much as she could, it still prevented him from straightening all of his joints, causing him to be a little stooped, but he stood tall along with the rest of the Kindred in the way that mattered. Though his black pelt was streaked with white and his fangs were dark yellow with age, he could use his voice once more and he could swing through the trees almost with the best of them. Mother Elder had felt that having another elderly Kindred accompany us as well as herself would be of benefit in convincing the humans that they were no threat.

The thought that age could make a Kindred look any less threatening to humans who were unaccustomed to the sight of them made us all chortle – including Mother Elder when she picked up on our thoughts – but we appreciated her sentiment and her care in making her selections.

We were also thankful for the rest of the community's thoughtfulness in either putting themselves forward as candidates to come with us or standing back in the knowledge that others would be better suited to the task than they.

We left the Shady Mountain community with regret at not taking them all with us and a deep hope that before long, we would be sending for them to join us at Rockwood and its surrounding villages. The community would make its way south to its winter settlement in the autumn as usual and would wait to hear from us, although Mother Elder would be keeping them, as well as the Elders of the other communities, informed of our progress.

The Kindred made far better time than we Horse-Bonded and our horses for the first few days. We would see them up into the trees first thing in the morning and watch them swinging and leaping off into the distance, marvelling at how fast they were – even Foxstep and Mother Elder – while we began our slow walk downhill over ground that was soft and more giving than to be easily negotiable for the horses whilst both descending and weaving between closely growing trees. The horses insisted that their difficulty was made no greater by carrying us on their backs, yet we all walked alongside them, preferring not to add our weight to that of our baggage. Fitt walked alongside Flame and none of us thought to question her decision to walk with her horse rather than to travel with ease and speed through the trees.

We would catch up with Mother Elder and Foxstep sometime during the afternoon as they rested from their exertions of the morning, then we would all continue together on foot until we came across the other five Kindred sometime in the early evening. They would already have a fire going and would have dinner hunted, gathered, cooked and waiting for us on the flat stones that they always managed to find to surround their fires.

It was a constant source of amazement to the humans of our group that the Kindred were so efficient at providing for themselves in the absence of any equipment – in fact they carried no baggage at all with the exception of Fitt, who was rarely without the bow and arrows that Marvel had once gifted to her, strapped to her back.

The first time that Fitt was Aware of our admiration for the Kindreds' survival abilities, she was quick to exclude herself from it, reminding us with a grin of how and why we had first befriended her. Flame was equally quick to remind Fitt of how she had brought down a wild cat in order to save her horse's life. Hunting well and with consideration for one's prey was a matter of self-trust and self-belief, Flame informed her Bond-Partner firmly, of which Fitt now had both in unlimited amounts, so it would no longer be a problem.

It was slightly strange to be party to a prey animal giving a predator hunting advice, but so had the lines blurred between us all, I realised. Kindred, human, horse, prey, predator – none of those descriptions had much of a place in who and what we now were to one another.

As the forest floor levelled out and the trees became more widely spaced, the going became easier. We could all feel the rise in temperature now that we had finished our descent, and I was glad for Foxstep and Mother Elder that we would remain under cover of the trees; the real heat of summer may have passed, but it was still warm enough to cause them problems during the daylight hours.

For the first few hours of the day, we and the Kindred above us leap-frogged each other, with them going away in front of us when we were forced to go slowly, then us overtaking them as we rode the horses with bursts of speed through the more open sections of the woodland. By mid-morning, Mother Elder and Foxstep were forced to the ground to walk, in order for their bodies not to overheat from exertion.

'At least we walk more comfortably now that we walk tall.' Mother Elder made light of the situation over dinner one day. 'However, I regret that we are slowing you all down.'

'When I first bonded with Infinity and we were making our way to The Gathering to learn from the other Horse-Bonded, we couldn't go very quickly, either,' I said. 'I couldn't ride her without causing her a problem...'

'Not to mention that you broke your arm the first time you tried,' interrupted Rowena with a wink.

'...so she had to walk at my pace when we were on the move, and she couldn't travel for as long each day as I would have done on my own because she needed to graze where she could.' I paused to stick my tongue out at Rowena. 'It seemed to take us forever to get anywhere, but during that time, we got to know one another, we bonded, so it was a good thing, really.'

Everyone nodded.

'It's hard to imagine that there was a time when you couldn't ride Infinity, seeing the two of you together now,' said Harperleaf shyly. 'I mean you're not even two anymore, are you?'

'Oh, believe me, there was a time when Amarilla couldn't sit on Infinity for longer than ten minutes without either collapsing in tears or being thrown off, usually in front of an audience,' said Rowena with a cheeky grin.

I nodded. 'Harsh, but true.'

'But a bit of a simplification of the situation,' said Justin, flooding his thoughts with the events that had followed my and Infinity's arrival at The Gathering.

None of it was news to Mother Elder, but the other Kindred explored his memories avidly.

'Rowena selects aspects of the truth to use in her teasing, which she uses as a mask for the depth of her affection,' Harperlake observed, thoughtfully, looking at Rowena as if she were a bug on his finger that he'd never seen before.

'That's not the only time she homes in on mere aspects of the truth,' said Marvel. 'You'll find that out sometime soon, when she decides that you've transgressed.'

'And you invite Rowena to tease you because you know that she finds it difficult to tell you of her affection as a result of losing her previous mate,' said Harperleaf. 'You reciprocate with the same kind of teasing because you know that she finds it easier to receive that form of affection from you than a more overt display.' Her eyes roved over Marvel as she spoke, drinking in all details of him physically as well as in her Awareness.

Rowena and Marvel looked at one another. Rowena shrugged and nodded, and Marvel held his hands out, palms upwards, in front of him.

'Rumbled,' Marvel said. 'I'm devastated.'

'No, you aren't. You're amused and delighted,' said Levitsson, staring at Marvel intensely.

'Welcome to the complexity of human behaviour,' said Sonja. 'We do this a lot, I'm afraid.'

'Use a behaviour to give the impression of feeling one way, to mask the fact that you're actually feeling something else? Isn't that a little counterproductive, not to mention time-consuming?' Foxstep asked.

'Yep,' Aleks said. 'And believe it or not, we're the least complicated examples of human beings, you know with us being Aware and everything. Just so you know, you won't meet many people in the villages who will take your observations of their behaviour as easily as Ro and Marv just did. If you point out the real meanings of what most people say, they'll be embarrassed and furious with you.'

'For trying to help them to know themselves?'

'Yes,' said Vickery. 'Humans lie to themselves continually and they won't thank you for pointing it out.'

'Except for us. We're more than happy for you to do it,' said Marvel.

'Because you know that in reality, it doesn't matter,' observed Levitsson.

'Exactly. But the humans you will meet don't yet know that this is just a dream that they have chosen to dream while they are remembering their oneness with All That Is. Until you've helped them to remember, you'll find that they accept you far more easily if you don't point out in public the things that they lie to themselves about – in fact it would be best not to do it at all,' said Justin.

'But you, however, will appreciate my observation that you and your mate are so at one with your horses and with one another that you allow the boundaries that define you to blur far more than your friends do,' Levitsson told Justin.

'Eloquently put,' said Justin.

'Is this us all bonding? Because I feel like we're bonding,' Aleks said.

'You use your previous history of trailing behind your friends to pretend that you still understand less than they do, when in fact you understand at least as much,' observed Levitsson with a fanged grin.

Aleks chuckled, nodding. 'I do. I absolutely do that.'

The following days and weeks followed the same routine. We moved at speed during the mornings and then when Mother Elder and Foxstep tired, we Horse-Bonded and our horses walked with them while the other five went on ahead, hunting and gathering as they went, so that by the time we caught up with them, they had made camp for the evening and a meal awaited us. We would talk into the night, as one big group or in smaller groups, getting to know one another more as we prepared for our arrival at Rockwood.

Infinity knew what I knew as I learnt it, just as I knew exactly what she was grazing, when she stopped to groom with one of the others or rest and where she was. We didn't just share minds anymore, we were the same mind, capable of just knowing what we knew without any of it burdening us or even interesting us, particularly. We had a job to do and we were doing it. When our bodies worked together as one as we travelled during the day, we didn't bother to compare it with a past that we couldn't remember. As Levitsson had observed, what little boundary there had been between us was becoming more and more hazy, as was that between us and Justin and Gas.

I was Aware of Mother Elder's concern about the matter on a number of occasions. She worried that Justin and I would become too disinterested to be of use to the mission that we had once felt so important to undertake. Whenever I felt her apprehension, I invited her to feel the purpose that hummed through all of us, that had originated with Gas and Infinity reminding Justin and me of our choice to be there, to help. It anchored us all to our mission, regardless of our inclination to completely be our oneness rather than just being Aware of it.

Humans and Kindred came to know each other well. We found Lacemore and Ashwell to be a devoted couple and extremely proud parents. They had worried when Fitt went off on her Findself. They had known that her lack of belief in her hunting ability could prove her downfall, despite all of the time that fierce, confident Ashwell had spent with her, helping her to improve her commitment to bringing down prey so that her fear of causing suffering could be laid to one side. Never had they envisaged that she would find such a unique solution to her problem as to accept help from humans, with the chain of consequences that had ultimately followed. They watched her every move with reverence and they adored Flame, who quickly became used to having three of them caring for her needs once we stopped for the evening.

Ashwell learnt to be quieter and more measured in his movements around Flame if he wanted her to remain near him. Lacemore learnt to be less concerned about the impact of her size and physical attributes on Flame and more definite with her strokes when she groomed her, so as to be more effective and less of an irritation. It wasn't lost on anyone that Flame's influence on Fitt's parents would help them to integrate more easily into human society, and Fitt couldn't have been prouder of the three of them.

Foxstep could be grumpy, but he was observant and wise and he had taken to heart Aleks's warning about being careful with the sensitivities of humans once we reached Rockwood. He took it upon himself to search our minds for the information needed to school Levitsson and the Harper siblings regularly on the matter, ensuring that they knew what would and wouldn't be helpful to say.

Harperlake and Harperleaf were always reserved but they were interested in everything that we could tell them or show them in our thoughts, and they quickly learnt whatever they wanted from us. To begin with, they were rarely apart, but as time went on, Harperleaf could often be found in quiet conversation with Holly or Sonja, whilst Harperlake observed and smiled at the banter that was always part of the conversation wherever Marvel, Aleks or Levitsson were.

Levitsson was hilarious. He flouted the human taboo of voicing the truth behind actions and words with precision timing, frequently leaving us in stitches. He always assured Foxstep that he was taking seriously his schooling as to what to say to "regular humans", as he called them, but he had such a mischievous glint in his eye whenever he used his humour on us that we all found it hard to believe he would be able to completely restrain his conversation to appropriate topics once in Rockwood.

Mother Elder became as dear to my heart as she was to my soul. She watched over us all unobtrusively but consistently, even when it was she who needed looking after. When the days cooled as they welcomed autumn, she and Foxstep could swing and leap through the trees well into the afternoon, but at a cost. When they dropped to walk on the forest floor, neither of them could hide their winces as their already tired and aching bodies received their final jolt of the day. We knew exactly the extent of Foxstep's discomfort as his grumpiness tended to be in direct proportion, but Mother Elder bore the tiredness, soreness and stiffness of her ageing body with silent determination. As we walked, she distracted herself by contacting the other Elders and updating them on progress regarding both our journey and what she and the other Kindred of our group were learning from us.

No information is wasted, she informed me, *one never knows when it may be useful.*

I saw her point, and soon found myself following her example. Quinta was delighted when I suggested a regular catch up with her so that she could pass on everything we were learning from our time with our Kindred friends to all at The Gathering; when the villagers began to accept the idea of Kindred integrating into their societies, the Horse-Bonded would be needed to help it happen on a large scale and the more they knew in advance of that time, the better.

Quinta was itching to leave The Gathering, but she was resigned to the fact that for now, she was needed there to organise the Horse-Bonded into working groups – groups of those who were newly Aware and overwhelmed by the sensory input that they were now receiving; groups of those whose horses had achieved perfect balance without them and wanted help to achieve the same; groups of those who were centred and could therefore help the other groups. Quinta's task seemed endless and complicated. I realised that it was just one of the many ripples spreading out from the vortex within which my friends and I had been swirling.

Change begets change, Infinity and I observed mildly. *And the greater the change, the stronger the force that is needed to set it into motion. We have been that force. And that must also change.*

I looked over at Fitt as she sat astride Flame, animatedly discussing the future of the Kindred and human races with Holly, Sonja and Aleks. Her passion and determination, fuelled by Flame's, was creating a new swirl of change. A swirl that was gaining momentum. A swirl that would be the centre of a new vortex – her vortex. I smiled wearily.

As the leaves blew from the branches, and raindrops reached us more easily and frequently, the days, and therefore our travelling time, became much shorter. We stuck to the trees as much as we could for ease of movement for the Kindred, but where a shortcut took us across pasture or scrubland, we took it. Almost the second we left the trees, our horses, glad to have the space in which to open up, took to leaping into a gallop, whilst I and my fellow Horse-Bonded whooped with unabandoned joy. It was always Flame and Gas who sped away from the rest of us, their long chestnut legs taking them at what to the rest of us seemed impossible speed, but Infinity was always next in line. Our hearts danced in time as we skimmed the ground, following the orange tails that streamed in front of us, beckoning us to find ever more speed.

By the time we were forced to slow down by the sight of more trees in front of us, our horses' sides would be heaving and we riders would all be breathless and sightless from the tears that had protected our eyes from the onslaught of the cold autumn air.

While we waited for our Kindred friends to catch up with us, we would unsaddle the horses so that they could roll and gambol around on their own, enjoying the novelty of plentiful grass and space. On one such occasion, as we perched on some boulders on the side of a hill in the autumn sunshine, a wild herd entered our Awareness. They were hidden by the hills, yet not far away. They knew who we were and they knew who were our travelling companions, yet they would approach us. Our own horses grazed, rolled and groomed one another without concern or even much notice, so we shrugged and awaited our first sight of both the wild horses and our Kindred friends.

It wasn't long before we felt the boulders beneath us vibrating with the pounding of nearby hooves. Our horses all looked up with pricked ears and Infinity whinnied shrilly. She was answered by the dark brown lead mare of the wild herd as she appeared over the brow of the hill. The herd slowed as one to a collected canter as they passed our horses, who, as one, fell in with them. They all moved off as one mass of brown, white, black, chestnut and dun, in their slow, perfectly balanced, rhythmic canter. They turned as one, slowed as one, sped up as one, sat on their haunches to release their front legs into the air as one, before powering elegantly back into canter, as one. There wasn't a sound in the autumn air other than the rhythmic beat of hooves on earth as they performed their beautiful, hypnotic dance.

I felt the strength of Lacemore's and Mother Elder's emotion and looked across the hillside to where the Kindred had appeared and were as entranced as the rest of us as we watched the horses rejoice. They had advanced as a species. They hadn't done it by avoiding or attempting to destroy those who had held them back, but by engaging with us, helping us and accepting our help in return. And now they demonstrated the joy of what they had achieved. Of what the Kindred and human races would achieve if we stayed our course.

We were all moved beyond words by what we were witnessing, by the message the horses were conveying in such a profound way.

Our horses peeled away from the wild herd and cantered back to where we sat, then dropped their heads down to graze as if nothing had happened. There was a split second when I questioned whether anything actually had. But then my eyes were drawn to the last few horses of the wild herd as they disappeared over the hilltop in front of us and I allowed the scene that we had just witnessed, with our eyes and our Awareness, to play over and over in my mind.

We were all still sitting in silence when the Kindred reached us. They took up places alongside us on our boulders and watched our horses graze. None of us spoke, indeed we felt to a one that we would break the spell of what we had just witnessed if we did. Our group of sixteen was the product of all of the horses' efforts since the beginning of The New. Their species had triumphed and now it was down to us to ensure that both of ours did the same.

We were quiet in the weeks that followed. The horses' dance had been so beautiful, so powerful, and their message so simple, that the thought of having any discussions about what we were aiming to achieve seemed an over-complication. We travelled doggedly on as the weather worsened, covering as many miles as we could each day and then hunkering down companionably in as much shelter as we could find by nightfall. Often, the horses would lie down behind us as we circled the campfire, sharing our warmth and shelter. The mornings that I woke curled up against Infinity always found me warm, well rested and less than eager to rise, and I know that the other Horse-Bonded had feelings that matched mine as they awoke next to their own Bond-Partners. But rise we did and onward we journeyed.

As we got closer to Rockwood, we began to come back to ourselves a bit more. There was more banter around the camp fire, more grumbling by Foxstep and more discussion about the welcome we were likely to receive. What we would do once there, however, none of us felt the need to discuss. As a group, we were who we were and we would know what to do.

It was as the snow arrived one evening that I heard my sister scream. My ears picked up no sound but my mind shuddered with her pain.

'Her baby is early, but he's coming,' Justin said and squeezed my hand. 'You're going to be an auntie.'

My grin turned into a grimace as another contraction held Katonia in its grasp. I was sorry not to be there with her, but I knew Jack would be all the comfort and source of healing she would need. She would have a few weeks to enjoy her baby before we arrived to shatter the peace.

TWENTY-SIX

Evolution

*T*he villagers of Rockwood were just beginning to leave their houses and go about their daily tasks when Infinity's, Serene's and Flame's hooves touched the first cobblestones. There were startled glances and voices questioning one another urgently and then the first screams rang out.

'THAT'S A WOEFUL! THERE'S A WOEFUL IN ROCKWOOD!' shouted a boy, pointing at Fitt.

'It's on a horse. Curse the clouds, it's on a horse. And there are more on foot. RUN!' screamed his mother.

More screaming followed as some people ran back into their houses, slamming and bolting their doors behind them, while others ran off down the street, shouting that the village was under attack.

'I don't know whether to be amused or insulted,' said Aleks from somewhere behind Fitt and me. 'There are just as many humans as Kindred in this group, yet we all appear to be invisible.'

Justin chuckled as he and Gas appeared beside Infinity and me. 'Shall we place bets over how long it takes for anyone to notice that not only are there humans here, but that the most visible two were born and have family here? I'm going to guess at ten minutes.'

Levitsson immediately went for twenty and Aleks for twenty-five.

'I'm going to have more faith in Amarilla's and Holly's kin and say five minutes,' said Marvel.

We waited. Fitt, Holly, Justin and I sat our horses in a line, with Lacemore and Ashwell standing at Flame's side and Mother Elder standing at mine. Vickery, Rowena and Marvel sat their horses just behind us along with Levitsson and Foxstep, and Aleks, Sonja and their horses waited at the back with Harperlake and Harperleaf.

There was an uneasy silence emanating from the houses at our end of the village but we could hear shouting and screaming spreading through the village in all directions away from us, as if it were being dispersed by the chill winter wind that buffeted past us.

Ten minutes passed before I saw two figures hurrying towards us against the wind. One of them was bent over the wailing bundle that she carried in her arms as she tried to shelter it from the snowflakes that had just begun to fall.

'KATONIA,' someone shouted from a window. 'GET IN HERE, YOU TOO JACK, THERE ARE WOEFUL DOWN THERE. KATONIA, DIDN'T YOU HEAR ME? AND FLAMING LANTERNS, YOU'VE GOT WILL WITH YOU, WHAT ARE YOU THINKING? GET IN HERE. KATONIA!'

'AMARILLA, INFINITY, OH, AND HOLLY AND SERENE ARE THERE, THEY'RE ALL THERE, CAN'T YOU SEE WHO IT IS, EVERYONE?' Katonia shouted at the closed doors and windows as she passed them. She waved frantically to me and then her waving faltered as she drank in the presence of Fitt astride Flame, then the rest of the Kindred.

People began to open doors and appear on their doorsteps to watch as my sister and her husband continued down the street towards us. We could have sent them all our light in order to ease their fears, but it would not be necessary. My sister was here.

'The Woeful must have done something to them, captured them and enslaved them in revenge for what was done to them in The Old. Jack don't go any closer, think of your wife and child,' a woman pleaded from the safety of her doorway.

'AND THEIR HORSES?' My sister continued to shout, ensuring that all in the vicinity could hear her whether their doors were barred or not. 'DO YOU THINK THEIR HORSES WOULD BE STANDING THERE SO CALMLY IF THOSE WOEFUL ARE TRULY A DANGER? DO YOU? REALLY? AFTER EVERYTHING THE HORSES HAVE DONE FOR US ALL? YOU REALLY THINK THEY WOULD ENDANGER THEMSELVES, THEIR BOND-PARTNERS AND US? YOU SHOULD BE ASHAMED OF YOURSELVES.'

Jack kept quiet but nodded at his wife's words as he looked about him at the villagers who were beginning to gather in the street some distance behind.

'KATONIAAAAAAAAAAAAAAAA!' A gut-wrenching scream wove its way down the street.

'Brace yourself, Justin, you're about to have your first glimpse of my mother,' I told him as she burst through the crowd of villagers and ran to Katonia, grabbing her arm and pulling her behind herself so that she shielded her daughter and grandchild from us. Her eyes widened as she took in Fitt, her parents and Mother Elder. Then she saw me. 'Amarilla, oh my goodness, my poor baby Amarilla...' she said and promptly fainted.

Jack caught her as she fell, just as my father and brothers appeared out of the sizeable crowd that was gathering in front of us. Con immediately took off his coat and put it beneath my mother's head as Jack laid her on the cobblestones, and my father put his coat over her to keep her warm.

'They have practised roles,' observed Levitsson from behind me.

I nodded and said, 'She does this a lot.'

'Amarilla? Is that really you? With these... these...' called out my father.

'Kindred. They're the Kindred, and they're our friends,' I called back. 'And, Dad, yes of course it's me. Holly's here too, and this is Justin, and this is Fitt, the newest of the Horse-Bonded.'

Whispering spread through the crowd as my father and brothers stared at me.

'Am, are you sure? Are you telling us the truth or are they making you say that?' Robbie said.

'THEY'RE MAKING AMARILLA SAY SHE'S THEIR FRIEND, THEY'RE TRYING TO TRICK US,' someone shouted from the middle of the crowd and the whispering turned to angry muttering.

As voices began to be raised everywhere, Katonia stepped a little closer to us, jiggling her baby in her arms to try to quieten his wailing.

'KATONIA, DON'T.'

'WHAT ARE YOU DOING?'

'JACK STOP HER,' came more cries.

Jack's eyes roved over all of the Kindred. As they broadcast their calm determination to help the villagers, their wish to integrate, he felt it. When his eyes rested on Fitt, he smiled. I felt him recognise her from our first encounter with her. He and Candour exchanged thoughts and Jack's smile broadened.

'None of us are in any danger,' he said loudly. 'Allow yourselves to trust what I know you can feel from the Kindred. They want our friendship, not our blood.'

'THAT'S NOT POSSIBLE,' shouted a voice. 'THEY'RE USING SOME SORT OT TRICKERY ON US ALL.'

Katonia spoke loudly but without shouting. 'Amarilla, maybe it would help to prove that you aren't a prisoner if you and Infinity come over to us? And Holly and Serene?'

We knew that would prove nothing while the rest of our friends were still among the Kindred, and further, would fuel the fear of the crowd if we even entertained the idea that our imprisonment was possible.

I smiled at my sister. 'Did I hear right that my nephew's name is Will?' I called out to her.

She looked at me, her face full of question and then finally looked down at her wailing baby. 'Yes, we called him Will, because he has such a strong one. He wouldn't stay inside me full term, he wouldn't even be born at a safe speed, he was in such a hurry to be here, and he's been acting his strength of character out on us ever since.'

'You have healed him where he needed it after he was birthed and you feed and love him yet he does not have everything he needs,' said Lacemore. Her voice was smoother and stronger than it had been, yet the rasp that persisted within it clearly distinguished it from the voices of humans.

Someone screamed and while part of the crowd stepped back, others surged forward.

Jack stood firm and raised a hand to those behind him. 'HOLD YOUR PLACES,' he bellowed and then turned back to Lacemore. 'What does he need?' he asked her as his son began to cry in earnest.

'I cannot tell you but I can show you,' Lacemore replied. 'We would have had many sleepless nights with my daughter had I not known how to nurture her, but as you see, she is healthy and strong and is now counted among the Horse-Bonded.' She looked up and smiled at Fitt proudly.

There was more muttering from the crowd.

Lacemore spoke again to Katonia. 'I know that your son has barely allowed you to rest since he was born. He cries out for what he needs and because he senses that you have the ability to give it to him, he will continue to cry until he gets it – as you say, his will is strong. If you'll trust me with your son, I can help you.' She slowly lifted her hands, her sharp talons outstretched at the end of her fingers, and held out her arms.

'No,' said my father.

'Kat, no,' Robbie said, moving to block her from us.

I watched my sister step out from behind Robbie. She looked up into my eyes. I smiled at her with all the love that my heart held for my sister. She was strong, beautiful and sensitive. I could feel her love for her baby and what that had awakened inside of her. She would know what was right for him, she would always know. My eyes spoke of my confidence in her. I knew that she would do what was right for her baby and I knew that she would remember our agreement. The two were one and the same thing.

Katonia's blue eyes widened and then mirrored my own in more than their colour. We remembered together.

'Jack, the Woeful – sorry, the Kindred – can help me to help Will and if I accept her help, it will help everyone else. I'm going to hand him to her,' she said.

Jack nodded slowly. 'You have my support.'

'Dad, Rob, don't stand in our way, this is important. You have to trust us. Trust us and Amarilla, okay?' Katonia said to them.

My family looked from Katonia to me frantically. Finally, my father nodded and took a step back, and my brothers followed suit.

Jack and Katonia walked towards us.

'STOP, HE'S ONLY A BABY,' shouted someone and the crowd began to surge forward once more.

Jack left Katonia's side and marched back to them with his hands up. 'HOLD,' he shouted. 'YOU ALL REFUSE TO LISTEN TO WHAT YOU CAN FEEL FROM THESE KINDRED, BUT YOU ALL KNOW AND LOVE CANDOUR. HE'S GIVEN YOU COUNSEL THROUGH ME WHENEVER YOU NEEDED IT AND HE TELLS ME, AS IF I NEEDED TO BE TOLD, AS IF ANY OF YOU NEEDED TO BE TOLD, THAT THE KINDRED ARE HERE TO HELP. WE HAVE A WEIRD SIGHT IN FRONT OF US ALL, THERE'S NO DOUBT ABOUT IT, BUT IF YOU CAN'T FIND IT IN YOURSELVES TO TRUST AMARILLA, HOLLY AND THE OTHER HORSE-BONDED WHO ARE HERE, IF YOU CAN'T EVEN TRUST ME AND MY WIFE, THEN TRUST CANDOUR.'

The crowd stopped short of him. There was much muttering and shaking of heads, and a few uncertain nods. Jack remained where he was but turned and winked at Katonia. She smiled back at him and then continued on her way to us. She put her baby in Lacemore's arms and tucked his blanket back around him where it had fallen open.

'There's a cold wind,' she explained to Lacemore in a shaky voice.

'I will keep him warm,' Lacemore told her, enfolding him in her arms and holding him close.

Immediately, I felt her weave her energy into a warm, nurturing net that surrounded Will and then gently closed around him. His screaming quietened. A cold blast of air hit us all from the side and caught the top of Will's head. Immediately the energy net closed more tightly there, soothing the chill away. He made not a murmur.

'How... how did you do that?' said Katonia, peering at her baby. 'Flaming lanterns, he's gone to sleep! He hardly does that at night, let alone during the day. How? How?' she repeated more urgently.

'I can show you, but first, I will need to help you to be Aware,' said Lacemore.

'Aware? Like Am is?'

'As all of us here are, Kat,' I told her. 'The Kindred have always been Aware and now, finally, this lot all are too.' I grinned cheekily at my friends.

'I object to the word "finally",' said Aleks.

'You object to everything, Aleks, put a sock in it,' said Rowena with a scowl at him and then a wink at Katonia, who smiled uncertainly.

I dismounted from Infinity and gave her neck a rub as I left her to go to my sister. 'I'm prouder of you than I can ever tell you,' I whispered to Katonia as we hugged one another fiercely. 'Now, can I hold my nephew while Lacemore helps you to be the first of the non-bonded to be Aware? You know that it has to be you, and Will has made sure that it will be.'

Katonia nodded and looked at Lacemore. 'Thank you, Lacemore, I would love your help,' she said.

I held my arms out to accept my sleeping nephew from Lacemore and then held him closely. He was exhausted. His soul had been determined to ensure that Katonia became the mother she had promised to be to him before they incarnated, and he had played his role to perfection. He had my sister's nose, I realised, and Jack's white-blond hair. He would be the first child to have a Horse-Bonded father and a mother who was Aware. He was here to help them fulfil the unique role that they were carving for themselves, before treading the difficult path he had chosen for himself. It was a good job that he was named for his strongest characteristic.

'We would normally do this for a youngling rather than an adult, and it would usually be done in privacy by an Elder,' Lacemore was explaining to Katonia, 'but in your case, you have the opportunity to help your friends and family by allowing them to bear witness as you come to your Awareness. And as you have already trusted me with your baby, I think you will find it easier if it is me who helps you to know yourself, rather than Elder Hobday, here, if you are willing?'

Katonia nodded. 'I'm willing. What do you need me to do?'

'You do not need to do anything other than observe what I will show you.'

Our group all felt the ease with which Lacemore resonated and then connected with Katonia. And then she revealed the whole of herself to my sister's mind – not just her uppermost thoughts and feelings that any human could pick up from a Kindred's natural tendency to broadcast, but everything about herself. Katonia's mind opened easily and she drank in all the information she was being given. She smiled the most beautiful smile at Lacemore. She knew her as the loving, devoted wife and mother that she was and she saw how Lacemore's priorities mirrored her own in a life that had been lived so differently. As Katonia absorbed all that made Lacemore who she was, Lacemore guided her blossoming Awareness towards Fitt.

Welcome, sister of my friend, Fitt spoke in Katonia's mind.

Katonia jumped on the spot and then laughed delightedly. Jack appeared by her side, having been enlightened by Candour as to what was transpiring.

'I can hear her, Jack, the Kindred Horse-Bonded. Her name is Fitt but her parents call her Lacejoy, and she's talking in my mind. Her horse is called Flame and she's just showing me how they came to find each other and bond... oh my goodness, there's so much to know and it's so much quicker when you can just know it instead of having to ask someone to describe it to you, this is wonderful.'

My father and Robbie supported my newly awakened mother as they and Con all moved closer so that they could hear what Katonia was saying. The rest of the crowd came with them.

'And this is Elder Hobday, she's very dear to Amarilla because...' Katonia looked horrified as she looked from me to Mother Elder and then to my own mother. She flushed red and looked at me desperately.

'Because she's been through a lot to help us,' I explained. *Nice one, Sis.*

Katonia's eyes widened as she heard me in her mind for the first time, and then she flung her arms around me, waking up her son. Lacemore drew back her energy net and Will began to wail again. I handed him back to Katonia.

'Lacemore will show you how to do what she did for yourself, now that you can,' I said. 'Feel what she does and let yourself copy her. Don't think about it, just know that you can do it.'

Within minutes, Katonia's energy net soothed and nurtured her son. 'I did it,' she said. 'Lacemore, thank you.' Katonia stood on her tiptoes and just about managed to reach Lacemore's chin with a kiss.

A gasp went up from the gathered crowd.

'I can't believe all of this,' Katonia said as she held her sleeping son close. 'I know these Kindred as if I've always known them. They're kind and caring and funny and... they're missing their friends and family. Only seven of them came as well as Fitt, because they didn't want to frighten us. They want to help us all in the way that Lacemore has just helped me.'

'How has she helped you, Kat? Help me to understand what's happening?' said my father whilst my mother looked from Katonia to me as if the world had just ended.

'I'm Aware, Dad. I know the Kindred as well as I know you. Better, actually, because I haven't looked into you as they've allowed me to do to them. I know that Candour is proud of Jack and me. He's missed the physical company of the other horses but his sacrifice has been worthwhile. I know that Amarilla and her friends travelled far to find the Kindred, and that they and their horses were willing to give up everything to win the Kindreds' trust. I know that I've lived other lives before this one, and that Amarilla has lived one of them with me. As has Jack, more than one, actually, and so has Will. I know that the trees have withdrawn into themselves but are ever watchful for the first sign of spring. I know that there is a bird of prey nearby who defends her kill from another. I feel as if I'm her, we're one and the same...'

I put my arm around my sister and spoke into her ear. 'Katonia, listen to me. You're becoming overwhelmed by everything you're Aware of. We'll help you with that over the coming days, but for now, you need to come back to yourself before you frighten everyone. Focus on Will and what he needs from you for now, okay?'

'Will,' Katonia whispered and snapped back to herself. 'I know that Will's bladder will be emptying very soon and I need to get back to change him before he becomes uncomfortable,' she announced to the crowd. 'Amarilla and Holly have brought the Kindred – they are Kindred, NOT Woeful – to Rockwood because they can help us and we can help them in return. I have trusted them with the life of my son and they have given me the greatest gift in return. I would ask that you all make every effort to make them feel welcome here.

'Lacemore, you and your family will stay with Jack, Will and me. We have a paddock behind our house for Flame, if she'll be okay there by herself? Oh, I know the answer, she would prefer to have Infinity with her – Am, you'd better come too.' Katonia turned to carve a path through the crowd, but continued to speak to us all over her shoulder. 'Justin, you can stay with my parents and they would love to have one of your Kindred friends as their guest too. Now who else has space? Ah, Uncle Jod, can you have Rowena, Marvel and another two of the Kindred? Harperlake and Harperleaf are quiet, you'll like them...'

As Katonia made her way home, still giving orders, Jack made his way among us, hugging his friends and shaking the hands of the Kindred.

'Flaming lanterns, Jack, just because you can bone-sing, doesn't mean you get to break my ribs, that's some hug,' said Vickery when it was her turn.

'You've no idea how much I've missed you sorry lot,' said Jack. 'Good to see you too, Justin, couldn't stay away from my wife's sister for long, then?'

Justin laughed. 'I almost stayed away for too long, as it happens,' he said and then turned to the Kindred. 'No offence,' he added.

'Lots taken,' said Levitsson with a newly mastered wink.

Jack frowned. 'I can see that there's more to your tale than Candour has seen fit to tell me,' he said, 'but I'm in awe of what you've done for him and for all of the horses. I was with you at times, through Candour, as you rode those wild horses to perfect balance, and when Candour achieved his as a result of your efforts, I cried like a baby.'

'And you haven't ridden him since,' said Marvel. 'We'll soon see about that.'

'I can't do it to him, I'll compromise him. No horse should ever have to suffer that again.'

'Then don't let him suffer it,' said Rowena. 'Achieve perfect balance with your horse and come to Awareness the hard way, the way we all did. You'll have to overcome whatever blocks you currently have in place in order to achieve it, as we all did, but in doing so, unlike those who will be Aware as a result of the Kindred's help, you'll have complete, unfettered Awareness because there will be nothing blocking you from knowing all there is to know. And then you'll be of even more help to everyone here; they won't all come to their Awareness as easily as Katonia did, or be able to use it to the same extent. We'll help you to get there,' said Rowena.

'I don't think I can, though. I've tried in the past, but I'm just not a good enough rider,' said Jack.

'You're surrounded by nine determined friends and yet you think you have a choice,' said Levitsson. 'You hold a position of respect in Rockwood. People come from all around for your help and you're very good at what you do. So good that you are no longer willing to attempt something at which you might fail.'

'There he goes again,' said Aleks with a grin. 'I knew he wouldn't be able to contain himself.'

'Levitsson,' growled Foxstep.

Jack looked at Levitsson with a scowl that softened into a thoughtful frown. Finally, he said, 'You have a point, my friend.'

'Oh, he has lots of them,' said Aleks.

Levitsson nodded gravely.

There was a cough behind us and we all turned to find my parents and brothers standing in a huddle.

'Am?' said my father.

I ran to him and flung my arms around his neck, and was then almost suffocated as he and my family all hugged and kissed me at once.

Finally, Robbie stepped away and held out his hand to Levitsson. 'I'm Robbie. I don't know how it's happening, but somehow, I know that you're easy-going but clever, and you like a joke, very like myself and Con. I would say, if I may, that I feel we're kindred spirits.'

We all groaned but Levitsson laughed as he shook my brother's hand. 'I agree, although I no longer live with my parents. There comes a time when humour must stand on its own and no longer be used as a diversion from taking responsibility.'

I like it, Levitsson's learning subtlety. Justin's thoughts carried his amusement, and I grinned.

My brothers stared at Levitsson in amused confusion while my father smiled and stepped forward to offer his own hand to Levitsson. 'I'm Frank, and this is my wife, Mailen. You would be very welcome to stay at our home,' he said.

I saw my mother's knees buckle slightly, but she rallied and focused her attention on Justin. She braced her shoulders and walked up to where he sat astride Gas. Immediately, Justin leapt to the ground, landing beside her. She looked him up and down appraisingly, and I saw Rowena trying not to laugh.

'So, you're the Justin we've heard all about,' my mother said, offering him her hand.

Justin shook it. 'I am, and I'm very pleased to meet you. This is Gas.'

My mother held her hand out and Gas sniffed it and then nuzzled her wrist, making her giggle. 'You're very welcome to stay in my home,' she said to Justin.

Justin glanced at me and his brown eyes twinkled as he smiled.

Epilogue

*R*ockwood is double the size it was before the Kindred of Shady Mountain came to live amongst us. It is a happy place. Those villagers whose minds have opened readily to their oneness with All That Is have cleared a path in our collective consciousness for the rest to follow, and they do, at an ever increasing rate.

The villagers are Aware to differing degrees. Some minds are so ready and open for change that they welcome their Awareness as an old friend, instantly comfortable with it and open to everything they feel with only minimal blocks – grief for a loved one, sadness at an opportunity missed, pressure to fulfil the expectations of their family – to knowing the full extent of what they can know. Others accept their connection to All That Is when shown it by the Kindred, yet fight the implications of it, too reluctant or too fearful to give up their idea of themselves as completely individual and unique. For them, their Awareness is something that is precious in that it gives them a sense of belonging and kinship with all beings, but yields little more. All who are Aware, however, have a newfound sense of happiness and relief that only increases the longer the Kindred are with us, Levitsson in particular.

Levitsson has developed a passion – against the advice we gave him and in defiance of Foxstep's protestations – for highlighting the things about which people lie to themselves. He has developed a manner of delivering his observations that is subtle and humorous and is proving very effective in helping people to move past their blocks and experience their Awareness more fully. With Levitsson's help, Jack has become almost as skilled, and Katonia, Harperlake and Harperleaf aren't far behind.

I always know when Fitt and Flame have reached a new village with Aleks and Nexus, Sonja and Bright at their side. I feel their focus and concentration as Aleks and Sonja confirm the message that the Heralds have taken ahead of them – that Fitt will help as many of them as she can to know the truth of themselves before she moves on to the next village, and that there are more Kindred willing to help those whose minds need longer exposure to a Kindred in order to become Aware, if they are willing to welcome them to live in their villages. Then I feel the human collective consciousness shifting further towards knowledge of oneness as Fitt begins her work.

Vickery, Holly, Marvel and Rowena are at The Gathering, organising our fellow Horse-Bonded to visit the villages that Fitt and Flame leave in their wake, where they will help the humans and Kindred to integrate. It's working. The Kindred race is flourishing every bit as much as the human race as the two live with and learn from each other. The Kindred are healthier and will live longer lives now that they can combat their build-up of skin and there are early signs that their fecundity is increasing. They delight in working alongside their human friends as they practise their newfound Skills or choose Trades in which to apprentice, and now that their time is no longer consumed by mere survival, they are revelling in learning and playing as many games as the village children will teach them, as well as discovering the joys of the arts and crafts.

When I visit Mother Elder and Foxstep in the thick-walled stone cottage that they have chosen to share, I find them happy. Often, Lacemore and Ashwell are with them, visiting whilst they babysit Will for my sister. Mother Elder delights in bouncing my blond-haired nephew on her knee while he hangs on to her pelt with his little fists, gurgling with laughter.

Will is always prone to smiling and laughter, except for when he's focusing on something he either does or specifically doesn't want to do, and then we all feel the strength of his character. There are times when the only way to distract him from his resolve is to place him on Candour's back. Immediately, his face will light up as he grabs handfuls of mane and bounces around, with Candour stepping aside frequently to stay underneath his tiny passenger. Often, Jack will leap up behind him and the three of them will take a tour of the village, to the smiles and waves of the villagers, human and Kindred.

My nephew will be much needed in times to come, and when I get glimpses of his future, I'm already proud. He has chosen his parents well, but I will ensure he knows that Infinity and I will always be there for him if he needs us.

Justin and I are settled in Rockwood for now. We have been requested to write for the Histories not only our own stories, but those of the Kindred, the other Horse-Bonded, and the newly Aware villagers – in fact anyone and everyone who has a story to tell in this time of change. It's a huge undertaking, but it awards us the chance to live a quieter life than in recent years. When we're not working, we love spending time with our friends and family. It is when we have time with our horses, away from Rockwood, however, that we are most at ease.

People smile and wave as we ride Infinity and Gas bareback and bridleless down the street. Gas is much taller than Infinity and yet somehow, without effort, they walk in step, her silvery-white legs matching his long, chestnut ones as they flick out in front and almost seem not to land and take weight before they are lifted once more. Once our hooves leave the cobblestones behind, we run. We run until we can no longer feel the earth beneath us – until we are home. We soar. In the oneness, we are everything we can think of being, with no restraints. When it is time for us to return to our lives within the dream, we do, feeling refreshed. We are happy and fulfilled. We are Infinity.

Books by Lynn Mann

It has been more than twenty years since the Kindred came to live in Rockwood. Most of the villagers have embraced the Kindred and all that they have to teach, but there are those who fear the Kindreds' influence, and so have drifted away to live as outcasts. The outcasts suffer, living as they do, but they refuse help, even from the Horse-Bonded.

Will is adamant that he can succeed where the Horse-Bonded have failed, and bring the outcasts home. But his forceful personality constantly gets in his way. He is the key to the future, but if he is to play his part, he must allow a herd of wild horses to show him how to be the person he needs to be. Only then will he fully understand the lengths to which Amarilla and Infinity have gone to ensure that he can fulfil his destiny and reunite the human race…

Acknowledgments

There are a number of people who have been instrumental in bringing this book into existence: Darren Mann gives me the space I need in order to write, as well as his support and insights – he's a husband in a million; I have a fantastic editing, copy editing and proofreading team, whose influences are woven into my books – Fern Sherry, Leonard Palmer, Rebecca Walters and Susan Wilkinson, I couldn't write without you; Jon Morris of MoPhoto has not only provided the fabulous shots of the horses for inclusion in the covers of both The Horses Know and The Horses Rejoice, but also has generously allowed the use of his photos for their promotion. A massive thank you to you all.

I also have to put my thanks out there to the animals who enrich my life and inspire me to write: Coxstone Infinity (Pie), who is behind it all; Lady of Flame (Eden) who was the inspiration for Flame; Braveheart and the late Marcus, Leiko and Mac, all of whom frequently dance around in my mind; Hector the cat who keeps my lap warm and distracts me in equal measures; and last but by no means least, my dogs, Dashel and Ivy, who are my constant companions.

Lastly, a massive thank you to my readers for the support you have given me by leaving reviews, commenting on and sharing facebook posts and contacting me directly – it's hugely appreciated.

**The subtitle of The Horses Know books is
'A Bond with a Horse Can Change Everything'.**

**In order to celebrate the release of The Horses Rejoice, Lynn asked
you to send in stories of how your bond with your horse has changed
things for you.
These are some of the beautiful stories that were received.**

STEPHANIE MILLER AND MILLIE

Millie is my horse of a lifetime. I have worked as a professional groom
and Millie has moved everywhere with me. I don't have many friends, so
Millie is the only one I want to see. She grooms me so I will groom her
back. If a stranger talks to me over the stable door, Millie stands over me,
protectively. When I hit rock bottom and was homeless, I cried next to
her while she lowered her head and cuddled into me. She is loving when
I struggle to find good in anything or anybody. Millie has the most big
beautiful eyes, when you look into them all you see is kindness,
contentment, trust and love. I feel I have learnt an awful lot, not just
about Millie or horses but about myself – how to love and care and to
open my eyes to situations. I hope we have many more years growing
together.

CHERYLYN GIBBS AND TUPPENCE

I was given Tuppence as a four-year-old pony when I was twelve. She
was beautiful but so temperamental and naughty – but I loved her even
though people told me to get rid of her. A year later, I lost my Dad
suddenly. I went up to the yard the next day and she was lying down in
the stable. I cried in her mane and slept in her legs and she didn't move
for an hour. Over the years she found the way home when I was lost,
protected me and chased a burglar and was always there for me. She
passed away with her head on my lap. We were there for each other from
the beginning to the very end. RIP my special girl.

DANIELLE HARTLEY AND LADDIE BOY

When I went to try Laddie Boy, I knew he was the one. I was so excited. The morning after arriving, he was crazy, running round the stable, rearing, kicking the door and his water bucket. The vet diagnosed him with ring worm, lung worm and dehydration. After getting him well enough to go in with other horses, he went straight in for a fight with the only gelding in the field. When he bit me on the back because he was scared of the broom, the vet deduced that he had been used as a stallion in Ireland and then been shipped by the dealer, hence all the problems. I moved to a yard where there were only mares. I rode him and he was crazy, rearing vertically up in the air, side dancing, the works. I persisted with him and took him to shows and did well. He would follow me round the yard, I taught him to bow on one leg, I rode him bareback and I would lie with him in the field. Four years later, I got pregnant so needed help with him but he wouldn't allow anyone else to ride him and would only be lunged if I stood nearby giving him voice commands. It was like I had saved him from this bad place that he was in and he didn't trust anyone but me. I had a lot of trouble with him but he was worth it and he thought I was too.

JESSICA DARNTON AND ABBI

When I first met Abbi, I knew she was something special. I could see it, not on the outside but on the inside. She may not have been the most well-trained, talented or beautiful pony in the world but to me, she was perfect. She gave me my confidence back so much that we ventured out to shows. She taught me so much over the years, while helping me to have fun on a horse again. Then Abbi took ill. Our vet tried everything, but I knew I had to do right by her and let her go. My heart shattered into a million pieces. Words can't explain what she meant to me. I'm a girl who loved her, how lucky am I! She made my life but I was only a chapter in hers. I thank Abbi for our time together. We had the time of our lives.

TRACY MARCH AND CHUTNEY

When I applied to Bransby Horse Rescue (www.bransbyhorses.co.uk) to rehome a horse, I was offered the chance to meet Chutney. The minute she looked up at me I knew she had been waiting for me. She was an angel as I took her out of the field, groomed, tacked up and rode her. I found out later that another lady had tried her before me and she had dragged her about and walked all over her. Once she came home she showed her true personality – she's bolshy, stubborn and always tries to have the last word, but I wouldn't change her for the world because she's also honest, trusting and melts my heart. It's the little things, like how she watches me if I walk away, the way she only hesitates for a second before doing what I ask. I've loved many horses but Chutney is my once in a lifetime horse and I can't imagine us not being together.

MEG HIGGINSON AND ELLA

I lost a special mare, Dolly, to colic. A family friend, David, who had found Dolly for me, sadly died soon afterward. One of the last things he said to my Mum was, "don't worry, I'll always be here for you, just look up." When looking for a new companion, I found Ella, a six-year-old mare who had already had ten owners. She was lovely natured but quite untrusting and very green to ride. Her passport had been lost so we had to apply for a new one. It took a few months to arrive and in this time, Ella was a nightmare. I was on the floor A LOT but something kept telling me to keep going. When Ella's passport arrived, we found that Ella's grand dam had belonged to David! We feel Ella was a gift to us. She will stay with me forever. We have such a bond now. She whickers every time she sees me, we enjoy competing and she's doing so well. She is my bit of treasure, my world, my best friend.

～

HAYLEY MARIE JONES AND ZARA (racing name: Ivebeenthinking)

I bought my beautiful ex-racehorse Zara from a racing yard and within days we were out riding. Within two months we went to our first in hand show and then did ridden showing and dressage, a first for us both which we now enjoy regularly. When Zara pined at the loss of her equine companion, she refused to eat unless I was there with her – we are each other's comfort. Around that time, I was made aware of Zara's behaviour while she was in racing. Zara had thrown nearly every jockey off, a side she has never shown me. Zara and I have a new life together built on the bond that we share which is truly beautiful and rare. We have put our trust in each other like neither of us have with anyone before.

RAE VICKERS AND MAY

My best friend May brought me out of a very dark place and gave me confidence I never knew I had. She knows me inside out and I know her. She always trusts me when she's unsure of something. I always trust her to look after me when I'm unsure too. May taught me to ride, the meaning of trust and what it meant to have a bond with another being without ever having a single conversation. May is so gentle with my son and has not got a single nasty bone in her body. I had a nasty riding accident (not on her) where I broke my leg in five places. She helped me gain my confidence and I'm back riding stronger than ever. I could never put into words the bond I share with this girl.

RACHEL STOCK AND HARRIET

I bought Harriet in her early years as an unwanted psycho type TB. For three months I couldn't click with her. I cried a lot. She taught me very quickly that you couldn't use force to train horses. She protected me when we were attacked out riding, she protected an old man when a gang of youths cornered him. She laid bolt still after getting herself tangled up in wire, waiting for me to save her. She was always steady when I was injured and bouncy when I was well. She would put her head on my shoulder when I was sad and on the day she died, she vocally told me her time was up. Every horse that came after her arrival has been ethically trained, no gadgets, no force, time and patience given. She changed the world for any horse who came my way.

MAGGIE MARSDEN AND DONKS

I was looking for my first horse a year ago as I had always wanted one from when I was young. I looked at many horses before I came across Donks. I fell in love with him straight away and bought him. He was very naughty when I got him, he wouldn't let anyone ride him and kept pushing and shoving. I worked with him every single day and now, because of the bond we have, he is a completely different horse. He doesn't like anyone else to ride him, only me. I have taught him to give cuddles and kisses for his treats. This horse is one in a million and I love him so much. I couldn't be without him – no Donks, no me, that's how I feel about him.

MICHELE SAVORY AND RISARIA

I lost Risaria four days before her thirtieth birthday. My Dad bought her for me when I was sixteen, and she was two. My Mum and Dad were divorcing and I was an only child. Risaria was my baby, we spent so much time together. I broke her in myself with no experience at all. We learnt together, in all ways. She never bit or kicked me. We would play and chase each other round the field. She would take mints from my mouth and enjoy a can of coke with me. I could be sat in her stable crying and she would come over and rest her head on my shoulder. We went through twenty-eight years of life with friends coming and going, on both sides. I am married with two girls that had the pleasure of knowing her. I miss her every day and always will.

LILY McKENZIE AND BRENAN, IVY AND SALLY

When I was eight, I was having friendship problems. My best friend at the time started to do and say horrible things, it made me so sad I wanted to leave the school, she made me feel miserable and lonely. Around that time I started riding, it made me feel excited and gave me something to focus on. I began riding lessons on a pony called Brenan. Riding him made me feel happy again, which I had not felt in a long time. Animals showed more affection to me at that time, I trusted and loved Brenan, and he loved me too. I now have Sally and Ivy, they are there for me always. Ivy didn't have a happy time in Ireland, just like I hadn't had the nicest of time at school, and with Sally and her trumpy bottom, life's never dull!

DONNA BATES, JOE AND SPLASH

Joe had been badly treated, so was very untrusting of humans. For this reason, although a talented horse, he had been passed from yard to yard as no one had the patience or understanding Joe required – until my partner of thirteen years, Richard, bought him. He built a strong partnership with Joe, whose confidence began to grow. One day while competing Joe in eventing, Richard felt faint, collapsed and very suddenly passed away. I was left completely devastated and Joe was left without the one person he had learnt to trust. I knew I owed it to Richard and Joe to work on being another person Joe could rely on. Working with Joe helped me so much with the loss of Richard as I knew he was missing him just as much as I was. That was seven years ago and Joe has grown to be the most affectionate and loyal horse anyone could ever wish for.

When I first saw Splash, I didn't think he was my sort of horse but as soon as I sat on him, I knew he was going to be special. Sixteen years later I still own him and we know each other inside out. When my life has been in turmoil, Splash has been my rock, always consistent no matter how I've been feeling. He is my horse of a lifetime. Splash and

Joe are the best of friends and I consider myself very lucky to have two such well-mannered, gentle horses.

SKYE COVERDALE AND MEG

Meg is my rescue pony. I first went to try her with no confidence. I felt like a total beginner. She's lively with a difficult past and I couldn't trot her in a circle without tensing up. Her faith in me was non-existent. That's how it remained for an entire year. We couldn't get a bridle on her for three months and picking up her feet was out of the question. My instructor was worried that Meg would cause me to lose my confidence completely, but I believed in her. For hours I would sit in her stable singing, reading and brushing her. An opportunity came up to take her to an agility session, desensitising her and allowing her to trust me. A year later we clicked – in an open field with acres of land to jump in, she trusted me fully for the first time and I trusted her.

TRACEY WHATLEY AND JACK

I got Jack as a four-year-old and he is now rising ten. During the time I have had him I have been diagnosed with fibromyalgia. When I'm feeling down he makes me smile. He takes polos from my mouth and is so gentle. He loves nothing better than having a butt or hind leg rub. If I try and walk away, he will either put his butt in my way or cross my path to make me stop. Tickle him anywhere and he's happy. When I ride him, he's forward and likes to shy at things but with my daughter, he's like a kitten and looks after her. I can't get off normally, I have to swing my leg over his neck and he lowers his head for me to do it. He is my horse of a lifetime and my reason for getting up and leaving the house daily. He is my everything.

REBECCA WALTERS AND RUBY

Eight years ago, she shone the brightest light in my dark. I knew it had to be her. Every day since, she has illuminated my world in more ways than I knew was possible. My teacher and my pupil. My competitor and my team mate. My strength and my weakness. Whilst leading her... she in fact leads me. Whilst tending her... she in fact tends me. It is honest, woven and written. It just "is"... my mare and me.

AUTHOR'S NOTE

Just as this book was in its final stages of production, Pie – the real Infinity – moved on from this world, aged twenty-two, following a sudden and very aggressive illness. It seemed only right that, at the eleventh hour, her story should be included:

LYNN MANN AND PIE

Pie was black and white in far more than just her colouring. She was crystal clear about what she wanted – and fully expected – from me as her rider and carer, and that made her the amazing teacher she was. I learnt so much from her in the eighteen years she was my partner that I couldn't contain it all, hence the creation of The Horses Know and The Horses Rejoice. Pie was fiercely intelligent, immensely strong, kind and loving. She was always looking to go out into the world and conquer and she pulled me along in her wake, making me more than I thought I could be. I knew she was "the one" from the minute I saw her and if I hadn't found her, I would have spent my whole life looking for her. Run free my beautiful girl.

Manufactured by Amazon.ca
Bolton, ON

30020935R00186